The House of Pr

Indrajit GARAI

The legal stuff

Published by Indrajit GARAI, April 2025

This is a work of fiction. All characters and events portrayed in this work are
results of the author's imagination alone. The names of certain places and
institutions may be real, but any eventual resemblances to actual persons
(living or dead), incidents, times, figures, and places are entirely accidental
and involuntary. San Taurino is a fictional city.

For Estelle and Mylène

Part I

1

Ignaçio slowed his spin. He didn't see Nuria in his troupe at the front.

Paloma lowered her voice from *alegría* to *intermedio*. Juan's guitar strums followed her descent. The easing spin reassembled the sloping roofs, the slanting walls, the shining doors and rebuilt the pagoda on the opera hall's background.

Paloma's voice descended further. Through the guitar's mellowing strokes, the cherry trees bloomed one by one on the hall's backdrop. The dancers' faces glowed against the meadow's lush green. Ignaçio scanned the rows. Nuria wasn't anywhere. The Japanese ballet corps sat still, solemn and silent, and watched him spin on the podium.

Except for one ballerina at the back; Naomi was rising from her seat.

Paloma's voice sank to *cante profundo*. Juan's strokes deepened and lengthened. The longing notes lingered in the oval hall's wings. Ignaçio sprawled his arms, checked his spin, and matched the *palo*'s tempo and mood. Naomi left her row and marched up the aisle toward the podium. Heads turned toward her; eyes followed her moves. Ignaçio slowed further and searched for Nuria. She didn't return to her place between Paloma and Juan.

Naomi reached the podium and climbed its stoop. Between the palo's lyrics, the guitar's strokes, and the *cajon*'s percussion, her leather ankle-boots clacked up the wooden stairs. Her kimono's edge brushed her flexing quadriceps. Ignaçio chose his stopping point, regarded his troupe, and arrested his spin.

He missed his target. He didn't face his troupe; he faced Naomi.

The palo halted. Murmur rose and revived the hall. Ignaçio

lowered his folded leg and placed its foot behind the other.

Naomi approached him. Her charcoal-black chignon pulled her brows and slanted her eyes. From her each temple, a single bang hung like a sickle and swung across her shining cheek. She stopped. Her chiseled jaws and cheekbones' crests framed her tanned face. Her pupils froze on his chest where his shirt's lapels split. A scarlet dot, shaped like an inverted teardrop, glared between her pulsating eyebrows and flickered from her throbbing veins.

Ignaçio drew his feet and squared his hips. Her forehead creased, her eyebrows twisted. Her gaze shifted to her ballet corps and then returned to his chest. The murmur stopped. The hum continued in his ears. She stepped forward, lifted her hand, and placed its palm on his chest. His skin flinched from the cold. Ignaçio steadied his breath, recovered his poise, and held his ground.

Her breath hastened. The gold threads glittered on her shimmering sleeves and shivered on her shaking shoulders. Her eyes widened. Their capillaries reddened, their rims glistened. Ignaçio lowered his gaze. Her neck moistened, its sinews stiffened. Below her neck's hollow, where her azure-blue silk parted, a diamond pendant, shaped like an ace, quivered above her breastbone's tip and glimmered from her skin's liquid glow.

Ignaçio stepped back; her palm stuck to his chest. Blood shot into his head and beat his eardrums. Her palm warmed, her fingers pulsed. He stepped backward; her hand crawled up his throat and slid on his cheek. His chest heaved, his stomach sank. His eyes burned, his ears roared. He recoiled farther; his back hit the wall. Bees swarmed into the hall, hummed across the podium, and blurred his vision.

His eyelids drooped. He tossed his head, caught his breath, and regained his calm. Her hand stopped crawling on his face. Her eyes

6

moved up and met his. She lifted his chin and touched its contour. He steadied his trembling legs; they buckled at the knees.

Under his feet, the podium caved in. The planks cracked and gave away. Her stern figure loomed above him; he sank before her. His hands flung toward her arms; she withdrew them and moved back. The platform split, the slot widened. He fell through the gap and slid into a narrowing hole. Above his head, the opening shut and killed the hall's light. His hands groped for a hold and scrambled to rise. The slide scourged his fingers and scraped their flesh.

The air thinned. The silence thickened. The growing dark garbed him and sank him deeper into the well.

Ignaçio lost his breath and cried out for help.

***

"Nacho!"

Ignaçio startled; his eyelids parted. Nuria leaned from his right and pored over his face. He slid up his backrest and sat up straight. Nuria pushed aside his bangs, rubbed his cheeks, neck, and shoulders, and then turned toward Paloma and Juan in the facing seats.

Juan's eyes lowered; Paloma's beamed a knowing smile.

She started a new song and clapped its beats. Juan crossed his legs, placed the guitar on his knee, and strummed to her rising palo. Nuria tapped her feet and snapped her fingers. The dawn's nascent rays pierced the panes and lit their compartment. Ignaçio rubbed his face and checked his watch. The train would reach San Taurino in fifty-five minutes. After four weeks abroad, his troupe members were impatient like him to return home and go on with their lives.

The passengers woke and applauded the troupe. Those who knew this *bulería* sang along, clapped, and snapped. Some tourists at the back raised their arms and demanded silence. More voices, hands,

7

and fingers joined the palo and drowned their demand. Waiters went up and down the aisle, serving breakfast. Ignaçio didn't feel like eating or drinking. He returned his tray to a passing waitress. The woman frowned. Ignaçio thanked her, turned his face toward the panoramic window, and peered into the vertiginous depth below.

The wild Atlantic's folds rolled to the sheer cliffs, pounded their feet, broke into a froth sheet, and covered the glistening sand. The returning waves clashed the approaching breakers, raised walls, and crushed the shore. A lone skimmer circled the whitecaps but didn't dare the reeling water barrels. The seamount defied the ocean's menace. Its rugged flanks welcomed the brightening dawn and resisted the threatening swells. The ocean submitted. Its raging walls collapsed. Water splashed the mount's foot. Glowing fog rose, wove wreaths, and crept up the rocks' gleaming slopes. They arched at the mount's crest and built a rising rainbow.

The train curved a bend and leaned over the abyss. Ignaçio raised his eyes.

Miles ahead, a mist veil lifted from the estuary. The double-decked bridge's silhouette emerged. The rising sun illuminated its piles and cross-beams. The bridge's trestle soaked the incandescence and reflected the light back to the sun. Wheels rattled the tracks below, buried the compartment's clamor, and shattered his nightmare's remnants. The roaring train hurled their stubborn fragments across the ocean, toward the hills towering over San Taurino.

Spring clouds joined and circled the hills. The blazing garlands burned the hills' flanks, sprayed their glow over the somber city, and woke its citizens to a promising dawn. The rays rolled and bathed the cathedral's steeple, flamed the arena's crest, and streaked the

8

hospice's portico in warm lights and cold shadows. The three stood behind the flared terrace, watched the port working below, and claimed their places among the city's monuments.

2

The overnight train clattered the bridge, entered San Taurino, and taxied at the station. Nuria switched on her cell phone: no message. By now, Mother should be at the arena. Father never called anyone, but he would come with their farm's van. The complaining tourists rushed to descend. Nuria let them pass, collected her luggage, and joined Paloma and Juan waiting on the platform. Ignaçio wasn't with them.

The international taurine fair had opened this week. Announcements in multiple languages boomed the station's vault. Trains came and left. The platforms burst with passengers. The halls bustled with porters and chauffeurs. Travelers hustled around the booths and hassled for information. Vapor left from their nervous mouths. Their anxious breath rose, condensed, and fogged the etched glasses on the roof and gables. The troupe waited; Ignaçio didn't come.

They gave up and wedged through the milling crowd. Nuria scanned for Ignaçio. Farther ahead, she found him peering into the station's aquarium. Inside, the sea turtles ignored the human rush and glided at their own speed. Chirps, chatters, squeaks, and tweets came from the indoor tropical garden. The migratory birds had returned from Africa and retrieved their nests. Some flew toward the station's exit while others brought back food for their nestlings. A gush brought the fragrance of jasmine, exhaust from cars, and moisture from the river. The wind shook the potters' creepers, rattled the palms' leaves, and swayed the burgeoning date clusters. Spring reigned, in full swing, the taurine city's fair.

Uncle Manu waited at the station's parking lot. He told Nuria her father couldn't leave an unusual event at their farm this morning; he didn't reveal what it was. She noticed her uncle's car instead of her parents' van. Paloma and Juan glanced at the small vehicle and tried to put Uncle Manu at ease.

"No problem," Uncle Manu said. "I'll make two trips."

"Don't worry, Manuel." Juan patted him on the shoulder. "We'll take the bus."

"If there's one."

"There'll be one."

"They cut more," Uncle Manu said. "And the routes too."

"Like it's new."

"You'll really wait for a bus?"

"No!" Juan laughed. "We'll just walk."

"With all these bags?"

"Hey, Manu." Paloma stepped forward and tapped him on the chest. "How many bags do you carry per week for your tourists?"

"I don't fly to Japan like you."

"You drive your coach at night."

"Tell you what." Uncle Manu surveyed the troupe's luggage. "There's enough room for everyone in this car. Let's leave all these bags at the station's locker and then I can—"

"Make yourself our slave too."

"Why do you say that?"

"You know why." Paloma flung her hand over the head. "We have arms and legs. We can carry our bags and walk. That'll be good for health after sitting so many hours. You take these two kids back to their farm and then give my kisses to Paula and Belen."

"They're at work now."

"Good," Paloma said. "Save my kisses till the evening."

11

Uncle Manu hugged Juan and kissed Paloma on both cheeks. The aged couple took their luggage from the pile, headed up the paved road, and dragged their suitcases behind. They passed the bus stop without looking at the information panel. Nuria watched them leave and then opened the hatchback's rear door. Ignaçio stepped forward, loaded his bags and hers, and held the passenger-side door open. Nuria got into the car and sat beside Uncle Manu.

The arena's acoustics broke the city's rhythm. Angel's voice rose above the din, greeted the citizens, and announced the taurine fair's program for the day. The resonance rebounded on the city's upper level, descended lower, and reflected from the station's façade. The twin bells peeled the hours from Iglesia Sacrata di Ser Vivo and drowned the city's early-morning clamor. Angel waited for the tolls to end and then resumed his announcement. The morning session's first bullfight would start in two hours.

A coach from Willem's fleet entered the parking lot. The station's porters ushered their clients toward the vehicle. Among them, Nuria recognized the group that traveled with her troupe and complained about their flamenco. These taurine tourists always lacked patience. Ignaçio shut the car's rear and sat in the backseat. They closed the doors and opened the windows. Uncle Manu let the limousines pass and then left the station's enclosure.

The hatchback lumbered up Avenida de Corrida. Vintage cars jammed the avenue and moved by jolts and jerks. Most bore license plates from abroad. Satin posters, glossing on all lampposts, featured the week's matadors and bulls. Municipal workers, wearing fluorescent jackets, moved the grills that would keep spectators off the running bulls' course. Most faces here belonged to tired tourists. They stood on trembling legs and choked the sidewalks. Their puffed eyes glittered for the morning's bull-run, about to begin.

A wad of papers flew in through the car's window. Nuria turned and saw the fliers' distributor reach another stalled car and repeat the process. He was one of those youths from her farmers' community that Willem employed during the taurine season and paid in cash. The ambitious boy, having deserted his parents' farm for Willem's job, ignored her stare.

The flying *cartels*, crafted on rag-paper and engraved in antic letters, stated in multiple languages the lampposts' information, embellished by three taurine artists' works: a Spanish painter, a South American poet, and a North American prose writer. Underneath, two curved swords pointed to Willem's corporate website. Nuria stooped, gathered the fliers, and stacked them aside. Before her taurine tour next week, she would take those back to Willem.

"There's a *mano-a-mano* next week," Ignaçio said.

"It's not on these cartels," Nuria said.

"Those fliers are for this week."

"How do you know then?"

"I just do."

"Who will be the matadors?"

"Esteban and Julio."

"How many bulls?"

"Six," Ignaçio said. "All from Rafaela's ranch."

"Wonderful!" Nuria turned toward him. "Thanks for the information."

"Don't bore me with your sarcasm."

"Nacho."

"Yes?"

"I thought we already settled this topic."

"What's wrong with knowing?"

"It shows."

"Shows what?"

"You tell me."

The old car labored up the avenue's steep slope. Asphalt gave into paving stones. From the thermal bath, vapor columns spiraled upward, spread over the marketplace, and shrouded its vendors. A mist curtain covered the basin's far end. Sulfurous smoke came blended with Cuban tobacco. Taurine veterans sat on the basin's border and placed their bets on the week's bullfights. Nuria recognized a few who used their social-security checks for betting.

Farther up, the car entered San Taurino's first settlement. The whitewashed mansions, boasting their terra-cotta roofs and flowering balconies, ignored the jagged columns and the rugged walls of an unborn school-cum-daycare center, abandoned in mid-construction. The thwarted center lamented the construction frenzy that swept Spain after the recession arrived from the Atlantic's far side and prolonged its spell. Now, the center's half-finished jungle gym served as a labyrinth for kids whose parents were still out of work.

Among the parents today, Nuria saw a co-worker of her sister's.

After the local government forced austerity measures, trimmed its budget, and froze its bloated payroll, this young colleague of Ines's never received any salary from the hospice, yet the woman seemed content in this city with her three kids at this skeletal gym. The car skirted the failed construction site's glare and lumbered toward the city's upper level.

They climbed by the fort's grills and reached the city's terrace from its western end. The paved sidewalk vaunted its easels and tripods. Painters from all ages and nations ignored the city's taurine

14

fair and pored over their canvases. This kilometer-long balcony, overlooking the city's port and its estuary, had served these painters for epochs; no downturns, no austerities could kill its perennial appeal. While edgy tourists, anxious for the day's first corrida, rushed toward the arena without glancing at these street-art jewels, their artists lost themselves into their work and nourished themselves with the city's monuments, gardens, and surroundings.

The car proceeded on the terrace toward the bridge. On Plaza de Toreros, anti-bullfighting groups raised their banners. At their front, Miguel lifted his: "Stop going to corrida." Willem stood on the city hall's staircase, held a megaphone in one hand, and lifted the other at his taurine clients. He recounted, in five languages, this city's history of two thousand years and its bullfighting tradition from Rome's epoch. Tension hung in the air and simmered the plaza's crowd. Among the police, national guards, and firefighters, Vincente stood like a statue at the center, crossing his arms over the chest and giving a stubborn back to Willem.

Willem's words stiffened Uncle Manu's jaw. He turned his face away from the square, shook his head, and pressed the gas pedal harder. Nuria understood her uncle's frustration. She, too, was exhausting her patience with the bullfighting industry. At the same time, in this harsh economic reality, Willem's taurine empire furnished bread and ham for the young and the old alike. In her extended family, everyone except for her father counted on bullfighting for employment. The state cut education's budget. Universities raised their fees. She couldn't pay for her law school if she didn't have her part-time job as Willem's tour operator. This bullfighting magnate was punctual and generous in paying his employees.

The church bell peeled nine times. Angel announced the bull run and stated the safety measures. The arena's acoustics echoed his words. They rebounded from the surrounding hills, from the monuments' façades, from the fort's battlement, sloping vineyards, olive fields, and orange orchards. The echoes clashed, fused, and raised a continuous commotion. The port opened the bull run. The uproar shook the terrace and stopped the pedestrians. Angel raised his voice and repeated his cautions.

The bell tolled again. The car left Avenida de Corrida and turned north for the double-decked bridge. The animal-rights activists had left its both entries free this morning. The vehicle entered the upper deck and crossed the Sangre de Toros River. Clatter rose from the lower deck's train tracks and shook the trestle bridge's structure.

"Jaime will return with Elena to San Taurino," Uncle Manu said.

"They sold their flat?" Nuria asked.

"Their bank kicked them out."

"What happened to their downpayment?"

"What do you think?" Uncle Manu glanced at her. "You study law, you should sue their bank."

"Where are they staying now?"

"With Elena's friends."

"What will Jaime do in San Taurino?"

"Help Jorge at his farm."

"Father accepts that?"

"The boy is good with his hands."

"And Elena?"

"She has applied for her transfer."

That was some development during her four weeks away from Spain. Nuria wondered why her brother's emails never mentioned these events. Jaime must be living in shame from losing their apartment. After a master's degree in mechanical engineering, no one finds it easy to work for a thousand euros a month, in a series of three-month contracts, then lose that job and stay unemployed for nine months. The couple had to ask their parents to help them pay their fifty-year mortgage's installments. They would have left their descendants to clear this mortgage for owning their apartment. She couldn't vilify their creditor: it borrowed its funds from the financial market. The bank had renegotiated their mortgage once. But after the state cut Elena's salary, as it did for all functionaries, the couple could no longer pay their reduced installments without going hungry. Fortunately, Jaime and Elena had no children yet.

Jaime wasn't the only *mileurista* in Spain who now stood ready to work for less than a thousand euros a month. He belonged to that generation from the roaring nineties that wanted to outdo their ancestors from Franco's epoch and then fell back to their parents' aegis under the recession's thickening spell.

The car left the bridge and sputtered up the hill. Below, on the river's far side, cheers met scare, songs joined music. Twelve disoriented bulls, lifted from their ranches' pastures and released on the city's cobblestones, left the port by Avenida de Corrida. Before the day's end, the arena's two sessions would shatter their illusions about applauding humans.

The region's shriveling olive, orange, and wine industries had grown its dependence on Willem's flourishing taurine business. Under Pedro's tutelage, since the regional legislature elected him president two years ago, the government executives had renewed their vigor for bullfights. The tradition of two sessions a day, removed at the last century's beginning, had been restored in this city. Now, each session filled its arena and killed six bulls. Each year, from spring to autumn, three thousand six hundred bulls faced torture and death in the city's ring, generated its citizens' lifeblood from tourists, and set model for the four hundred eighty thousand bulls that gave their lives to the fourteen billion taurine dollars around the globe.

Over the last decade and a half, since Willem came and settled in San Taurino, this city of six hundred fifty-seven thousand people, nested in the Pyrenean range's niche, had grown its renown as the paradise of bullfighting. The city's sublime beauty and sensuous surroundings didn't bring its taurine tourists and take their breath; they needed blood to quench their thirst. Willem didn't sell these tours cheap, yet his clients paid any price for blood.

And that blood didn't always come from the bulls.

The car reached the plateau then cruised on the cliff-side highway. Beyond the sheer cliffs' eroding crests, the roaring Atlantic shimmered from the breeze and scintillated under the sun. Saline mist wafted and dilated her nostrils. After a suffocating month in Japan's cramped cities and hotels, Nuria welcomed this draft that cleaned her lungs and revived her spirit.

She was born and raised in a farm that sat at this city's crown. She couldn't see herself leaving this place or living somewhere else. Flamenco furnished her the reckless abandon to escape the realities of studying and working in Spain but didn't promise her a decent living. Paloma and Juan, advancing in age, were limiting their performances. The troupe's revenues barely covered the couple's food, roof, and the flamenco bar. If this year she couldn't find a law job that earned her enough money, she would have to keep working for Willem.

The car turned right from the smooth asphalt and started its bumpy ride on the mud trail's ruts. Nuria glanced at the rearview mirror. Ignaçio was peering left and watching that spot on his farm. Aspens, oaks, birches, and beeches bloomed along his farm's fence. Apples and figs, cherries and chestnuts blossomed behind its wires. The red squirrels that had survived the cold and the chipmunks' invasion skipped up the trees' inviting trunks, skittered on their warming branches, and relished their burgeoning leaves, buds, and flowers. The succulent fruit's scents intoxicated the bees. Their growing buzz scared the nascent butterflies—fresh out of cocoons, fluttering from fear, glowing with hope. High above, in the trees' thickening canopy, tweeting nestlings sharpened their cries and sent their worried parents foraging for feed.

The car reached her parents' farm. Ignaçio got out and raised the cattle bar. The car passed under and waited for him; he didn't get back in. He walked along the farm's fence, entered the woods, and went toward his parents' farm. Uncle Manu hollered for him; Ignaçio didn't turn back. Nuria knew he wanted to see the spot where his parents' homestead stood sixteen years ago, until that notorious mudslide came and took it down with them while he was playing at her parents' farm. He was barely five when her parents took him in as their second son.

The passing years no longer assured whether he considered her family as his. He was returning more often to see his parents' farm, which was now his. Beside the stone pile that remained of his parents' ruined home, his favorite cottonwood tree bloomed every spring and sheltered the solitary heron that fished in the pond. The place revived his precious souvenirs.

Nuria nudged Uncle Manu. He understood her and rolled the car forward. She turned her head and searched for Santos. The dog didn't run out of her parents' homestead to greet them in the car. The cattle grazed on the fresh pasture with their offspring. The Pyrenean shepherd wasn't with them to restore order. Three years' herding had taught Santos when to leave his snow-white fur unsoiled by this farm's cattle. A loon and an eagle circled above the henhouse and angered Maria. The Brahma hen had no feathers left on her neck this spring. Enrico, her Gallic rooster, had discarded his gallantry this morning and left her to defend their progeny. The hen cackled and spread her wings. Her hatchling brood refused to come under.

Carlota's service vehicle, parked in a rush, blocked the driveway ahead. The van's doors stood ajar, but the vet wasn't anywhere nearby. A faint moan, punctuated by muffled groans, came from far. Uncle Manu cut the engine and ran toward the cowshed. Nuria checked the sheep's stall, peeked into the pig pen, and saw Magdalena purr on a lying heifer's back. The cries of pain didn't originate from this part of the farm.

The driveway's gravel crunched. Nuria turned and saw Ignaçio frown at the vet's van. A beseeching bleat jolted her. Ignaçio jumped from the driveway and dashed toward the farm's back. She ran after him. Behind the stable's closed door, Father despaired for Yolanda, and Carlota tried to reassure him about the cow. Ignaçio entered the stable and left its door open.

Nuria didn't go in; she stood at the door.

Ignaçio knelt beside Father. The two men held the oversized calf while Carlota sheared its umbilical cord from Yolanda. The cow lay on her side. Her amniotic liquid and hemorrhaging blood steeped the stable's soil. The moans didn't come from Yolanda; they came from Santos. The desolate dog took the bleeding birth as his failure, whimpered around the fallen cow, and sniffed her newborn calf.

20

Nuria caught Santos, hugged him, and patted his head. The dog sat on his haunches, raised his snout, and emitted a howl that pierced the stable.

Herman groaned outside. The German bull knew this newborn male hadn't come from him. Ignaçio lifted the black calf's muzzle and placed its mouth against Yolanda's bursting udder. The poor fellow hadn't been licked. Its inert lips couldn't draw the colostrum from its mother's nipples. The failed efforts bulged the calf's eyes. Their wet lids, fringed by long dark lashes, batted over their reddening corneas. Tear filled them up. Ignaçio lowered the calf's head, rose to his feet, and turned his face aside.

The calf withdrew its mouth from the udder, strived to raise its head, and bleated louder. Yolanda strained her neck and mooed to reassure her calf. The strain drained her. She rested her head on the ground, panted and heaved, and rolled her watering eye. This rebellious cow had once jumped the farm's barrier and copulated with a virile bull on the high pastures. Now, she lay powerless to guide her calf she had just dropped on this earth. Her mouth foamed. A brown-white froth oozed from her nostrils.

Carlota shook her head and opened her satchel. She took out a syringe and two vials.

"Charo!" Father sprang up. "Yolanda is my best cow."

"I know."

"I have no money to pay you."

"Stop," Carlota said. "Ignaçio volunteers at my clinic."

"Do we really have to—"

"Jorge, please."

"I trust your judgment."

"Then don't make my task more difficult."

21

"I'll leave."

"You stay here with your cow."

"I can't see you doing this to her."

Carlota reached up and touched Father's shoulder. He squeezed his lips and covered his face. The black calf cried at his mother. Every desperate bleat popped its glistening eyes from their orbits. Carlota ordered Ignaçio to take the despairing calf out. The calf understood her order, mourned louder, and refused to leave. Uncle Manu stepped in and helped Ignaçio carry the thrashing calf. Santos barked, bristled, and blocked their path. Nuria caught the resisting dog, soothed him with reassuring words, then led him out and closed the stable's door.

Santos retrieved his shepherd's instincts the moment she freed him. While Ignaçio rubbed the calf's coat, the protective dog growled at contemptuous Herman and kept the bull at a safe distance. The massage worked. The black calf sat up and bleated with a renewed vigor. Nuria observed the newborn male. She saw the impact its size had delivered to Yolanda's birth canal. From its father's imposing stature, they had expected this calf to be big, but not so large.

The newborn male already had its father's distinctive dewlap. The velvety folds shook under the bleating calf's neck. Nuria reached for the dewlap. The orphan lowered its mouth and sucked her fingers. She bit her lip. Ignaçio's massage had honed the calf's appetite. She closed her eyes and left her fingers in the hungry calf's mouth to stop its piercing bleats.

Crunching hooves approached from behind. Santos stopped growling. Nuria turned her head and saw Esperanza advancing in measured steps. This cow had given birth before they left for Japan. Her six-week old female offspring stood afar and watched her mother. Ignaçio stopped rubbing the newborn male. He rose to his feet, stepped aside, and asked Nuria and Uncle Manu to move. The orphaned calf saw the cow coming and bleated louder.

Esperanza went straight to the newborn male and sniffed its glistening coat.

The bleats stopped. The black calf lifted its muzzle and met hers. Their muzzles stayed locked for several seconds. Then Esperanza lifted her mouth and licked the calf's face, ears, and forehead. Herman bellowed. Santos kept the jealous bull at bay. The dog then turned his head and watched the exchanges growing between the cow and the calf. Esperanza's tongue swept the newborn male's neck, shoulders, and back. Each pass removed the placental sac's remnants and shined the calf's black coat brighter. The revived calf strived to rise to its feet. The cow lowered her mouth, licked the calf's legs, flanks, and abdomen, and encouraged its efforts with her reassuring calls and sniffs. The jealous bull gave up and walked away.

Carlota emerged from the stable. Father stayed at the door, his eyes lowered.

After a few awkward falls and shameful bleats, the persistent calf finally stood on his four legs, and drew applause from Ignaçio, Uncle Manu, and Carlota. Santos, too, joined this feast, and barked from where he was. Father refused to greet this newborn male. The bull bellowed. Esperanza ignored her bull, nudged the hungry calf, and sent him to her full udder. Tear filled Nuria's eyes. She turned and watched Ignaçio. His face beamed, his eyes glowed.

The resilient male sucked Esperanza's nipples with powerful strokes from his head. Each forceful pull drew a mouthful from her udder. The calf then swallowed that milk and gulped its foam. Little by little, his sunken belly filled. His legs steadied. When he was done with feeding, he withdrew his head from the udder, and moved away from his surrogate mother.

The renewed calf stood still and took in the surroundings. His eyes opened wider. Their sheen brightened. The bull threatened from far. The calf ignored the menace. He was already in his elements on this farm; he set out to discover it with his large eyes and flared nostrils. He saw Esperanza's daughter watching him from the haystack. He lifted his muzzle at the female calf and proceeded on sure feet toward her.

"He would grow into a redoubtable bull," Ignaçio said.

"Nacho," Nuria said. "Stop now."

"Why?"

"The calf just lost his mother."

"I love him."

"You do?" Nuria said. "Then why think along those lines?"

"See his legs and shoulders?"

"He isn't the breed."

"I'll call him Victor."

"Sure," Nuria said. "He has survived death."

"No," Ignaçio said. "He vanquished it."

"You think?"

"Yes."

"Victor stays on this farm."

"We'll see."

Nuria turned toward Father. He still didn't lift his eyes at this new arrival on his farm.

24

3

The arena's orchestra stopped. The bugle ended the morning session. Nuria rearranged her insurance papers, put them in her overnight bag, and placed it on the rack above her seat. She checked her watch. The coaches should leave San Sebastian within thirty minutes if they wanted to reach San Taurino on time for the evening session.

She peeked at Uncle Manu in the driver's seat. He was still napping over the steering wheel; the early lunch had brought out his night's fatigue. These crew members of Willem's tour company stood only at the beginning of the bullfighting season. The coach drivers like her uncle would spend their sleepless nights shuttling tourists between taurine cities. These aged men, robust and resilient, ignored their exhaustion and drove their double-decked coaches night after night without provoking accidents. She brought scalding coffee from the coach's kitchen, pecked Uncle Manu on the cheek, and gave him the smoking cup.

She took a coffee for herself, returned to her seat, and waited for her clients. The half-hour doze had cut her last week's jetlag, but the nap had also stolen the time she could have used to finish the cattle insurance company's paperwork. Father was clueless with legalese, and the depression from losing his best cow wasn't helping him for these forms.

Her clients didn't wait for the bullring's president to finish his closing speech. They rushed out of the arena, ignored the artwork in the city's historic square, and came straight toward their coaches. They wanted to leave San Sebastian and reach San Taurino on time.

From the year's start, Willem had promoted this *mano-a-mano* in all countries across all his channels. These taurine tourists had reserved their sessions before reaching Spain. They didn't want to miss a minute of this duel between Julio and Esteban in San Taurino's bullring. Nuria returned to the kitchen and asked the chef to warm her clients' lunch.

The three coaches pulled away from the arena's square. They joined the city's traffic jammed by its Grand Taurine Week's *feria*. On each deck, her clients sat by four in booths lining its aisle, their faces flushing and their eyes glistening. They ignored the waiters and pored over their cell phones. The bets for the mano-a-mano raged on Willem's all platforms and earned him millions. The two matadors, with their opposing styles and trailing scores, would clash for the first time at this symbolic taurine duel in San Taurino.

The coaches rolled by the city's beaches. Their golden sand, gleaming under the midday sun, watered her inflamed eyes. The vehicles skirted the green butte holding the city's historic lighthouse and then barreled up the hill's flank toward its crest. Nuria returned to her seat and leaned her forehead against the panoramic pane. Mansions and villas lined the steep climb and overlooked the Atlantic's emerald-blue water, glimmering behind a sheer mist drape that refused to lift. Her clients didn't raise their eyes from their phones. They didn't look at what they were eating from their plates or drinking from their glasses.

An altercation started between two tables. Others joined in. The chaos disturbed the crew. Nuria intervened and tried to mediate the dispute; they ignored her. Uncle Manu pulled to the road's shoulder and stopped for the argument's heat to cool. It didn't. He waited.

Finally, one arguer saw the time and urged others to stop. The dispute had cost them three quarters of an hour. If they fought this virtual duel now, they would miss the real one later in San Taurino.

26

The calm ocean swelled from below, splashed the coach's panes, and shocked them. Their quarrel stopped. They wiped their sweat and resumed their lunch.

The food disappeared. The red wine overtook. Adrenaline fell, exhaustion rose. Snores of different decibels left the tables and filled the coach's two floors. Her clients slept oblivious to their cell phones' continuous beeps. The three coaches cruised the ocean-side highway and, at regular intervals, crossed similar coaches carrying similar tourists in the opposite direction. Nuria returned to her seat and sat down.

Since the court ruled corrida's ban as unconstitutional, the taurine tourists' flow into Spain had tripled. San Sebastian's feria drew four million; Pamplona's San Firmin, two times more; Madrid's San Isidro, six times more. The growing bullfighting industry employed the Spanish like her who, in principle, opposed torturing and killing animals in public for human pleasure, but, in practice, were forced to do these jobs. Her rising tours demanded more and challenged her more. Each trip hacked her ethics and chipped her dignity. She didn't know how long she could keep this job without losing sanity.

She wasn't the only Spanish youth caught in this dilemma to earn a living.

Willem employed three thousand youths from her region, and a hundred thousand more from around the nation. Only a tiny fraction of them sided with bullfight's tradition, but they had to swallow their pride and work in his businesses. After the recession, no other industry in the region offered stable employment. On the contrary, this rejuvenated man gave them, with fairness and care, the stability they sought and needed in the unstable job market.

She started working for Willem when she was eighteen. He didn't trick her into a chain of temporary contracts by extending her trial periods. During her eight years with him, she had risen steadily through the ranks, become the chief of his tour operating business in Europe, and received generous compensation that kept her family's boat afloat. Her law school would end in three months. If she cleared her bar exam this summer, she could work for one of the law firms she was planning to interview with. She would face her trial period again at this new job, a number of them as all other fresh graduates did, but those trials would try her conscience less than what she now lived with these taurine tours. After five grueling years of studying law, she was looking forward to changing her life by entering a legal career.

Besides, the court's ruling didn't insure a long life for Spain's bullfights.

Today, bullfighting was sustained by a small fraction of humans that held onto old values handed down to them by their ancestors. A tinier segment of the ambitious young, hungry for dominance and power, joined this blood-bath, but their counterpart outnumbered them. Most bullfight patronage came from countries where laws banned cruelty against animals. These patrons' blood thirst was now being replaced by the new generation's compassion. They saw animals' liberation as their priority. The laws they made showed their growing concern.

The conscious Spanish saw this change. The new trend had already gained foothold in this country. Today's Spaniards embraced the globe's rising conscience for animal welfare. Some regions liberated the bulls and their fighters, both captive to the taurine industry's dollars, and arrested the blood-thirsty tourists' torrent. Their conscientious acts instilled new values.

Meanwhile, Spain's law didn't stand aside and watch its citizens evolve.

A lesson Spain had distilled from Franco's regime was to promote its regional autonomy. Regions' laws respected the national constitution, but the state didn't interfere with their day-to-day running. Corrida's ban on the Canary Islands had endured two decades and a half. The assault on the Catalan ban hadn't prevented Catalonia from keeping bullfights out. Whereas some municipalities didn't renew their toreros' licenses, others diverted their bullfight funds into children's causes. Some favored concerts, art expositions, and seminars in their arenas to taurine shows. Their acts now drew tourists who shunned them earlier for their primal image.

These changes hadn't reached San Taurino yet, but their path was being paved. This historic city, known for its taurine culture, had unique art, architecture, and nature. In her life of twenty-six years, she had traveled to more than a dozen countries; she hadn't seen another city combine its beauties this way. The image this city promoted from its bullfighting tradition prevented conscientious tourists from coming here; they didn't want to spend their money on cruelty. Conscious citizens saw this tradition's drawback. They were acting to change it.

San Taurino wasn't Spain's only city determined for this shift. Other taurine cities of unparallel beauty, whose arenas kept out spectators that didn't want their feet stained from gored bulls' blood, welcomed this change. Their citizens saw the brighter enlightenment they could offer above the dark entertainment from torturing animals. Their governments found other cultural treasures that brought more money to their treasuries, without soaking their arenas' sand in blood and without drenching their cities' faces in shame. These cities now rearranged themselves to lift their images by removing their ancestral taurine burden.

The three coaches skirted Santiago de Compostela, courted pilgrims heading toward the city's welcoming basilica, crossed Vigo's industrial zone, and cruised on the Atlantic's scenic road. If the coastal traffic rolled at this speed, they should reach San Taurino in two hours and a half. That would leave her clients an hour at Willem's taurine bar before going to the arena for the mano-a-mano. Nuria took a water bottle to Uncle Manu at the wheel, then got herself one and returned to her seat.

The coach's drone and the ocean's hum lulled her. She inclined her backrest and stretched her legs. The sun reverberated from the ocean and blocked the view to her right, but, to her left, lush grass and bright herbs shined on fertile pastures. Their swaying forage, dotted with cream-white sheep and black-brown cattle, rolled up the sloping hills, and reached the farms rejuvenated in the hands of new-generation farmers.

These farmers were emerging fast from the country's youths. The recession's bite still sent many reeling away from Spain, but, among those who remained, some traded their grey business suits for organic farmers' green smocks. This new farming sector was sprawling across regions and drawing increasing subsidies from the European Union. These farms' higher profit margins and their farmers' sharper business skills were now pushing Spain's traditional banks to open their vaults and finance this transition with generous loans.

At home, she had brought up this new trend a few times. Their two farms, with no loans on their backs, could switch to organic farming easier than others. But Father didn't want to learn new skills at his age. And for Ignaçio, farming of any kind stayed the last thing on his mind. He seemed happy to leave his parents' farm in her parents' hands.

Ignaçio's growing interest in bullfighting worried her. He topped his veterinary classes, Carlota confirmed his flare for the trade, but the life of a San Taurino's vet didn't shine. Most farmers had little money to pay their vets. Most vets earned their living by treating company animals of the elite and swallowing their insults. Ignaçio saw these every week at Carlota's clinic. On the contrary, a top matador earned millions. That was a thousand times more than what a vet or a farmer earned. But only a few matadors reached the top and earned that sum. The rest lived from working multiple jobs and selling bullfight souvenirs. She couldn't let Ignaçio slide into that glittering path and extinguish his life's light.

Besides, Ignaçio was kind to animals.

He was more than competent with them. In just a week, he had won the heart of newborn Victor and made the male calf feel like a young bull. Victor's growth reassured his surrogate mother, Esperanza, and pleased his adoptive sister, Lorenza. Even Herman, the contending bull, sometimes set aside his disdain and watched Victor with admiring eyes. The calf was progressing fast under Ignaçio's aegis and forging a bond of confidence with him.

Also, Ignaçio's deft at handling animals placed Santos at the right emotional distance from Victor. From staying over-protective of this calf, the dog had become his friend. While he kept an eye from far, he also gave the calf a widening freedom to venture into their farm and explore its remote corners. Victor welcomed this liberty and exploited it for his growth. This soldering confidence, between two animals so close yet so different in their styles, would have never built without Ignaçio's magical hands. He was more than gifted with animals.

Ignaçio's extreme sensibilities would never let him hurt animals. He wasn't indifferent to the fighting bulls' sufferings. While most toreros saw the *lidia* bulls as animals to fight and kill, Ignaçio saw in them something more than bulls. She noticed the shadows that crossed his face when he watched bullfights on television. At times, he did see himself as Spain's next Ortega, but coming close to bullfighting in any way would be a suicidal move for him.

In his younger years, she could distance him from taurine shows. But his growing age and toughening will were eroding her power to dissuade him. The rest of her family didn't care about his shift. Like most Spanish families from their generation, their stance on bullfighting was indifferent at the best. Other survival issues, running in their heads, pushed out all ethical debates on humans fighting bulls in public for whatever reason—art, culture, or economy.

The coaches passed Ignaçio's farm, left the cliff-side highway, and circled down the hills' flanks toward San Taurino. The groaning brakes woke her clients. They sat up and checked their cell phones. The long siesta had calmed their nerves. Those who fought before lunch now became friends. Within half an hour, they could continue their bets at Willem's taurine bar, sip Spain's best sherries he always reserved for them, and head for the mano-a-mano at the city's bullring. Bit by bit, their murmurs drifted from bullfighting to politics. Then they ran out of topics and stared at the taurine city approaching from below.

There was a gathering at the port. From the banners' shapes and colors, Nuria knew who those belonged to. She checked her watch then went up to Uncle Manu. He also confirmed that it was now impossible to turn around and take the alternative route into the city. Besides, there was a good chance that road lay blocked too—like all

32

other roads that brought taurine tourists into the city by carloads, poured them out at designated places during order, and let them loose at any place they could during disorder.

She heard curses and turned around.

Her clients had picked up the blockade on their phones. They were rising from their seats and peering through the windows.

She grabbed the microphone. She reminded them of the hairpin curves they would now turn and of the sharp precipice on the side they were leaning together. They got her message. The agitation stopped. They returned to their seats and kept their eyes on the phones. Silent anger radiated from their flushing faces and raised the closed heat inside the vehicle.

Two rows of vehicles, stalled end to end, blocked the bridge's entry to San Taurino. Uncle Manu cut his coach's engine, left his seat, and stretched his limbs. He had driven nonstop five hours to make up for the time lost in altercation. He stepped outside, lighted a cigarette, and chatted with the other two coaches' chauffeurs. Nuria stayed inside her coach.

Her clients checked their phones and fidgeted in their seats. Some left the coach, jammed the sidewalks, and complained. The taurine duel would begin in less than thirty minutes. The coaches wouldn't reach the arena for the opening parade. Once the first of the six bullfights started, all gates would close and nobody could enter afterward. Nuria went outside, asked Uncle Manu to watch her clients, and trotted toward the bridge.

Miguel stood on the bridge and raised his banner. His foundation's members surrounded him. Last year, he returned from Brussels and started this foundation. Now he had thousands following him from this region and millions from around the nation. Like him, these men and women practiced nonviolent civil disobedience. The police and the civil guards patrolled the bridge, guarded its entries, and protected these activists. Willem's paid thugs waited at the bridge's both ends, folding their arms and vaunting their muscles.

Nuria passed the security barrier and approached the demonstrating group. Miguel noticed her and creased his eyebrows. He left his group and came toward her.

"My clients have their tickets," Nuria said.

"So do others," Miguel said.

"Do you know what you're doing?"

"Do you?"

"What do you gain from this?"

"You don't see?"

"Not all these vehicles are going to the corrida."

"I know," Miguel said. "But yours are."

"You think you're acting fair?"

"You know the answer."

"Do you feel good doing this?"

"Do you?"

"Miguel, listen." She touched his forearm. "You want to stop people from attending this corrida? Go, block the arena's gates."

"We weren't the first to reach there."

"Who's blocking the arena?"

"Go and see."

"Then let us go!"

"The sidewalks are free."

Miguel ignored her glare and returned to his group. Nuria rushed back to her clients and asked them to follow her.

34

Her clients labored down the cramped sidewalks. They hurled invectives at Miguel and his followers. The activists ignored the insults, kept their calm, and held their ground. The taurine tourists gave up, lumbered down the bridge, and reached its city-side exit.

Avenida de Corrida lay blocked, but not by Miguel's followers. From cluttered clusters, Marijuana smoke coiled upward. These people were too stoned to act, shout, or move. Events like today's one provided employment for the recession's rejects. Out of work for months, they had given up hope for jobs. For their smoke, they now accepted pittance from anyone and for any cause. They didn't want to know who they were demonstrating for or for what reason. Some were in their mid thirties to early forties. Most got their meals from soup kitchens then hung around the station, the public squares, and the harbor. Prison provided them food, care, and shelter. The authorities no longer bothered to pick them up.

Nuria ushered her clients into the arena's court. The place brooded silent violence.

The parade opened in the bullring. The orchestra's *paso doble* grew from the arena's acoustics, passed over the third-floor arches, and died between the protestors' cries on one side and the supporters' cheers on the other. At the court's center, edgy collectors crowded the stand that auctioned the six bulls' heads from the morning session. Next to that stand, serene citizens held wicker baskets and queued by the butcher's stall that sold the bulls' vermillion meat and crimson organs, garnished by laurel wreaths, blue and yellow flowers, and purple flesh of split figs. They didn't mind the drama unfolding in the court or in the bullring.

Facing the arena's main entrance, the Roman soldier's bronze statue stood defiled. Its helmet, epaulets, and metal cape, sprayed with scarlet paint, glowed under the sun's shying rays. Red and white tape condemned the statue's pedestal. The police cornered the racketeers in the loggia and ignored the arena's crowded main gate that scared her clients.

Blood draws blood.

This wasn't new. Demonstrations around bloody bullfights drew blood-seeking gangs. They didn't come for bullfighting; they came for violence.

The police saw Nuria waiting with her taurine tourists. Two officers, wearing stern faces, came and cleared the way to the main gate. They avoided looking at her and her clients. They returned to their rank and watched her group with contempt. Among them, she recognized the sergeant hurt from his clash with Willem's goons before her trip to Japan. The bullfighting magnate and his collaborators couldn't win this police force that didn't accept bribes from them and didn't depend on Mayor José for their living.

Elite aficionados, arriving late for the corrida, jammed the main gate; her clients now had to wait. She channeled their impatience into the arcade's boutiques. The Museum of Taurine Arts had pulled down its shutters. The souvenir shop ignored the racket and sold its posters of famous bullfights, miniature bulls of marble and granite, and *banderillas* that tourists would leave at the airport because international aviation laws considered these harpoon-ended darts, covered by bright-colored frills, as assault weapons. The quiet collectors' shop stayed somber at the far end and offered hooves, horns, and tails of renowned bulls, once awarded to their legendary killers and later traded by their needy owners for money.

The orchestra stopped. Pedro's voice rose above the outcries and announced the six parts of the mano-a-mano, about to begin. The stalled aficionados pressed for the gate before the first bugle call cut their rights to enter. At the ticket booth, Mother haggled with a red-faced tourist in her broken English. Nuria asked the gateman to let her clients pass and then went toward the ticket booth.

"Can I help you?" she asked the tourist.

"No."

"Do you have your ticket?"

"No."

"This show is sold out."

"How do you know?"

"Sir," Nuria said. "The woman at the counter is telling you there are no more tickets left for this corrida. This is a huge event. You should have bought your ticket earlier."

"She doesn't speak English."

"I'm telling you this for her."

"Who are you?"

"Someone who knows."

"Are you from the black market?"

"Pardon?"

"Do you have a ticket to sell?"

"No."

"Then get lost."

Nuria called the security guards. They took the angry tourist by the neck and threw him out of the loggia. The bugle announced the first corrida of the six. The arena's gates closed. Nuria thanked the guards and then entered her mother's office.

Mother wiped her tears. Nuria pecked her on the cheeks and then hung her jacket and purse from the peg. She went to the room's far end and peered through its porthole into the arena. Esteban strutted

37

around the bullring, left his footprints on the fresh sand, and saluted his fans waving from the galleries. Pedro fidgeted in the president's box. Below him, Rafaela and Angel sat still on the front row to his right; Willem and Mayor José, to his left. The oval arena had filled to its brim this evening. There wasn't a single place left.

Esteban instructed his three pickers and then called his two lancers on horseback. The descending silence froze the viewers. Their tense faces turned toward the bullpen's closed grill and waited for the first of the six bulls to charge into the bullring.

The bailiff on horseback looked up at the president's box. Pedro took the key out of his pocket and threw it at the bailiff. The man caught the key and prodded his horse toward the bullpen. Esteban positioned his toreros around the bullring. Willem left his seat, came to the wooden barrier, and leaned on its top rail.

Nuria sighed. She pulled down the blinds and returned to her mother.

"I'm worried," Mother said.

"About what?" Nuria asked.

"My job."

"Why?"

"For my English."

"Your English is fine."

"More tourists are complaining."

"Angel said that?"

"No," Mother said. "Willem did."

"You don't work for Willem."

"Angel does."

"No, he doesn't."

"His salary comes from Willem's—"

"Mother," Nuria said. "Trust me."

She reassured her mother. Even though a large part of the bullfighting organizer's funds came from Willem's donations, Angel and Rafaela would never sell their association to this businessman of bullfighting. They knew Willem needed them for his taurine business. Willem didn't own this arena; the city did. The association rented it from the city and managed it for their bullfights. To please Willem, neither the city nor the association would descend so far as to fire a long-term, hard-working, honest employee like her mother. Besides, she would report this rude tourist to the city authorities tomorrow morning. Mother could count on her.

The bugle announced the corrida's first *tercio*.

The bullpen's gate opened, but no virile bull charged out; instead, an adolescent calf's frightened bleats filled the arena. The spectators murmured. Esteban cursed and condemned the immature bull. Mother's forehead creased. Nuria rushed to the window and peeked through the shutter's slats.

The pen-keeper thrust the young bull into the ring. The scared animal ran along the wooden barrier, bleated in horror, and searched for an escape route. Twice it tried to jump the barrier and fell back onto the sand. The toreros provoked the animal with their capes, but the young bull refused, returned to the pen, and stood bleating in front of its closed gate.

Esteban lifted his arm and signaled the mounted lancer near the bullpen.

The lancer walked his horse to the young bull and plunged his lance into the animal's hump. A piercing cry erupted from the wounded bull, magnified from the arena's acoustics, and repelled the blind-folded horse. The viewers protested. The clamor grew; the

39

scared horse reared; the lance came off the bull's flesh. The lancer tugged the reins, stood on the stirrups, and strived to guide his carrier. The panicked horse refused its rider's orders and ran toward the wooden barrier. The bleeding bull stopped bleating, turned its hind toward the ring, and tried to open the pen's gate with its muzzle.

The bugle announced the corrida's second tercio.

A club emerged through the pen's grills and smacked the young bull on the muzzle. The bridge bone cracked. The shocked bull cried out in terror, recoiled from the grills, and reeled toward to the ring's center. One picker met the animal on its way and plunged two color-frilled darts onto its back. The young bull halted in its tracks, stopped crying, but still refused to fight back. The second picker planted two more colored darts into the bull's flesh.

Protests rose from the galleries. The viewers wanted this immature bull out. Pedro took out the green handkerchief and waved it from his box. Esteban spoke up and asked for their patience. He assured the spectators he would bring out this coward bull's bravery. Pedro put away the green handkerchief, brought out the red, and waved it at the crowd. The third picker ran and punished the agonized young bull by planting two black-frilled darts in its flesh.

The bleeding bull stood still, six darts hanging from its flanks, and refused to fight.

The bugle announced the third tercio. Nuria took her mother by the arm and dashed out of the ticket office.

She ran from the corrida, but the corrida ran after her; the arena's acoustics was built for this pursuit. They reached the car and drove away from the parking lot. The farther the car moved, the louder came the corrida's sounds: the matador's roars, the bull's pleas, the viewers' hoots, and Willem's cheers. Another piercing bleat erupted and wore away beat by beat. The arena's orchestra replayed and ended the first corrida of the six.

The crowd shouted for the bull's ears and tail. Pedro granted those as Esteban's prize.

Ole!

Willem hollered for the bull's hooves and horns. Those, too, were granted to Esteban. The elite aficionados sang their anthem. A matador hadn't received such trophies in San Taurino's arena for three decades. Pedro ordered the mutilated bull out of the ring and then bashed the rancher that furnished the coward bull for this coveted mano-a-mano.

Nuria glanced at her mother; her hands trembled on the steering wheel.

"Not a good start for this duel," Mother said.

"The bull didn't come from Rafaela's ranch?"

"No, it was a replacement bull."

"What happened?"

"Her bulls fought others in the corral. One lost its eye. She replaced the injured by another from her ranch, but this evening the vets found the new bull color blind. Another bull couldn't come from her ranch, so they used this one marked for a corrida tomorrow."

"But this bull wasn't legal!"

"Why?"

"A corrida needs a bull at least four years old."

"Do you believe it was a *novillo*?"

"Do I?" Nuria sighed. "What do you think?"

"The vets should know."

"Unless the rancher paid them."

41

A *lidia* bull cost eight to twelve thousand euros to reach its legal age. Ranchers bribed arenas' vets and passed underage bulls as adults. Rafaela never did this. Her bulls came pure-bred and full-grown. The lottery had punished the arena's vets by picking this immature bull, marked for an ordinary corrida, as a replacement bull for the extraordinary mano-a-mano.

After this evening's embarrassment, Pedro would call the government's vets tomorrow and have the dead bull's teeth checked. If those vets found this animal underage, the arena's vets would lose their jobs. Pedro would also ensure that the region and the state stopped this rancher's subsidies.

The bugle announced the second corrida's first tercio. The new bull charged into the ring with a full-blown roar.

Ole!

Julio received the bull with a burst of cheers and then led the animal with his graceful commands. Applause swelled and spilled from the acoustic arena. The city's lights throbbed to its rhythm. The gyrating citizens stopped in their tracks and tuned their ears.

On Plaza de Toreros, expectant fans of both matadors watched this corrida unfold on the high-resolution screen's panorama. The ferocious bull bore the insignia of Rafaela's ranch that elite matadors craved and feared. After each Veronica pass Julio used to divert the bull's furor, the fans pored over their phones and revised their bets. The cheers from Esteban's camp confirmed Julio's exceptional feats with this bull. The bugle call for the second tercio died among the square's thunderous roars and intoxicated howls.

The car left Avenida de Corrida and turned right by the Ruins of Santa Maria. This twelfth-century convent, transformed into a municipal hospice, employed three hundred paramedical professionals like Ines. They hadn't received their salaries for months, yet they returned to work everyday and nursed senior citizens approaching their end. Neither the city nor the state had money to pay these dedicated employees. The region's charity funds didn't cover the hospice's day-to-day expenses. The bullfighting association had pledged its profit from today's taurine duel to lift this hospice from its ruins. Taking a definite stance, for or against bullfighting, was a challenging task for anyone.

The bridge's entrance stood clear. After the arena's gates closed, Miguel's people had no reason to block the city's traffic. The car traversed the bridge then climbed up the hill's flank. The port's noise stayed below. The corrida's sounds came clearer, bounced off the hills, and vibrated the evening's crisp air. The bugle announced the corrida's third tercio. A solemn silence descended on the arena and extinguished its flaming applause. In this final third, Julio would make his signature moves before slaughtering this redoubtable bull.

The bull roared louder. Julio cried out in terror.

Mother jolted the steering wheel. The car veered from its course and jerked toward the shoulder. Commotion rose from the arena, echoed through the hills, and drowned the toreros' outcries. Mother straightened the car, flashed her eyebrows, and kept her eyes on the road. The bull continued to roar. The ring's clamor rose and fell. Nuria leaned her head out and strained her ears. No more sounds came from Julio's voice.

Nuria glanced at her mother: she, too, was holding her breath.

The car climbed the hills, reached the plateau, and cruised the cliff-side highway. The city's lights and sounds didn't reach this place. On their left, across the Atlantic, the orange sun's throbbing heart sank by inches, spread its violet roll on the ocean's undulating

43

water darkening by minutes, and painted the hills on their right in a scarlet glow. At the valley's depth, working farms took shelter in its growing shadows and wound down for the night.

"You should cut your work," Mother said.

"I can't," Nuria said.

"The hours show on you."

"They should."

"Why don't you let Ignaçio work?"

"Nacho is helping Charo."

"Like you, he could work for Willem."

"No."

"Why?"

"Nacho is bright," Nuria said. "I don't want Willem to dim him."

"Ignaçio is handsome too."

"I know."

"See?"

"What?"

"You're still single."

"Mother." Nuria turned. "What are you saying?"

"Ignaçio is an adult," Mother said. "You shouldn't protect him like a child."

"Nacho is an orphan," Nuria said. "I give him the chance he deserves."

"You're saving him for yourself."

"Pardon?"

"You worry me."

"Why?"

"Ignaçio is your dance partner."

"So?"

44

"Flamenco flares passion."

"You believe that cliché?"

"Flames burn."

"Stop!"

"You're crazy."

Mother shook her head and stared ahead. Nuria bit her lip and turned her face toward the window. They reached Ignaçio's farm. The car left the cliff-side road, turned on the mud trail, and descended toward her parents' farm.

The trail's bumps broke the sullen mood. The moist breeze brought the pines' fragrance and dissolved the silent tension. On the hills' darkening slopes, purple shadows of cattle and sheep roamed the slumbering meadows. Last summer, on those high pastures, Yolanda met Victor's father, conceived the calf, and left him last week on their stable's floor.

This orphaned calf deserved more than what he had now. Those pastures belonged to her extended family. Before she left for San Sebastian, she had promised Victor one as his future home with his cows. He would grow to an ardent bull and claim his house of promise.

"Ignaçio should work his parents' farm," Mother said.

"Father is already working that farm."

"The load is too much for Jorge."

"Nacho can't manage his farm."

"Why?"

"He has his studies."

"He can help Jorge."

"Did Elena get her transfer?"

"She did."

"Jaime can help Father then."

"We should find a place to put them up."

"They could use the attic above the barn."

"Ignaçio could move there."

"No," Nuria said. "Nacho stays where he is. That room has served for his home since he moved in with us. He needs stability to finish his degree. He still has three years of hard study and harsh internships. Charo says he's learning fast and doing a great job at her clinic."

"But his room is so close to yours!"

"Mother, we already settled that issue."

"Okay, okay."

"That place above the barn is bigger for the couple," Nuria said. "Jaime could have his privacy there with Elena. There would be enough room for their children later."

"If they decide to have any."

"Why, did Elena take a pay cut for her transfer too?"

"What do you think?"

"Has Jaime lined up a job in San Taurino?"

"Not that I know of."

"He can then work full-time on Nacho's farm."

"What if Ignaçio takes it back from us someday?"

"He won't," Nuria said. "Nacho doesn't have what one needs to run a farm."

"He can sell it, though."

"He won't do that."

"How do you know?"

"Mother, please," Nuria said. "Nacho is grateful to us for what we've done for him. He has trusted his parents' farm in our hands and never asked a question about it. Besides, this farm has belonged to his ancestors for three generations. He'll never sell it to anyone."

"Are you sure?"

"Of course."

"I hear the Euro deputies in Brussels are making noise about Spanish farms."

"They are," Nuria said. "But those noises are against the bull ranches."

"Like Rafaela's?"

"Yes," Nuria said. "They won't cut subsidies for cattle farms like ours."

"But her husband makes those laws."

"Not anymore."

"You think?" Mother said. "Pedro still has his connections in Brussels from his two terms there."

"The Euro deputies today belong to a new generation."

"You think their age makes a difference?"

"I wasn't referring to their age," Nuria said. "I was referring to their values."

"What values?"

"About animals," Nuria said. "This generation has new values. Their deputies want bullfighting out."

"That's what the youths say."

"Not just the young."

"Who among the old?"

"Charo."

"She's the only one I know."

"There can be more."

Mother frowned and stared ahead. Nuria let the message sink.

"Won't Pedro help his wife?" Mother said.

"For what?"

"The subsidies."

"You worry about her?"

"No."

"Good," Nuria said. "Rafaela earned enough money when she was a matador. She doesn't need more. You can see that. As the bullfighting association's president, she draws no salary. Her husband doesn't come from a poor family. They don't depend on anyone's funds."

"But her ranches need money to survive."

"The ranches she runs belong to her husband's family for generations. Like ours, they have no mortgages to pay. Her bulls come expensive and they sell well. They won't starve. Pedro knows his ways around this region and this country."

"That's what worries me."

"Why?"

"Pedro can pass new laws for his region and give more money to the bull ranches."

"He can."

"And the state will follow his footsteps."

"Possible," Nuria said. "Pedro has his clout in the national legislature."

"Cattle farms like ours will get less from the region and the state."

"We'll get more from the Union."

"You think Europe will balance our cuts?"

"Mother."

"Yes?"

"Do you have any control over any of these?"

"No."

"Then why worry?"

"We can hope."

"We have issues we can act on."

"You're right."

"Let's deal with those."

Mother did have a valid concern, though. While the Euro deputies pushed to lower bull ranches' subsidies, the national deputies pushed to raise corrida as Spain's cultural heritage. If Spain adopted this law, bullfighting would receive the protection of a national monument. The state and the regions would then spend more to nurture bullfighting. The cattle farms would receive less.

The Union's directives didn't rule Spain. Europe served only as a loosely held federation for its members. Each sovereign state acted freely, made its laws, and chose its policies. Even the Spanish deputies and executives in Brussels couldn't force Spain to change.

They could only wait and see.

The car reached her parents' farm, rolled under the cattle barrier, and parked before their homestead. Nuria remembered she had left her overnight bag in the coach above her seat; the cattle insurance papers were inside that bag. She took out her cell phone and sent Uncle Manu a message. Santos greeted them wagging his tail and barking his joy. Nuria followed Mother and the dog into their home and then shut the screen door behind them.

In the den, Father sat with Ignaçio and watched the mano-a-mano on television. The duel had finished at the arena, but the station replayed its critical parts: the bull flipping Julio and goring his belly; the paramedics lifting the twenty-nine year old matador from the blood-soaked sand and carrying him toward the door for the dead—away from his sobbing wife of twenty-four, and from their wailing son of three; the mounted bailiff circling the bullring, pushing back shocked spectators, and restoring order; the arena's employees replacing the sand and smoothing it out for the next bullfight. A quiet tension hung in the arena's air. The corrida then resumed under blinding floodlights. Esteban finished the remaining four bulls and performed his *rueda de vuelta.* He ran around the bullring, toasted his victory to his fans, and left with his trophies by the winner's door. Willem stood motionless at his spot by the ring and leaned on its wooden barrier, his blue eyes gleaming and his red face beaming.

Nuria forced her eyes off the television. She pecked her two men on the cheeks. Ines was on call tonight at the hospice. Nuria went into the kitchen and offered to help her mother with cooking. Mother asked her to shower, change clothes, and rest before eating.

By the time Nuria reached the dinner table, an unprecedented violence had erupted in San Taurino's historic city center.

The newscaster recounted the events' order: "Julio died a heroic death in the bullring," launched by his wife on the social media, clashed with "Your husband got what he deserved," and ignited the riot. The camera moved through the city's flames and fumes and then stopped on Plaza de Toreros. Miguel urged both sides to stay calm during this national disaster. The screen split into six windows. Each showed a major Spanish city catching San Taurino's fire and spreading it to others.

"They would never find a matador to replace Julio," Ignaçio said.

"The third in row will now rise," Father said.

"No!"

"Why?"

"Julio was exceptional," Ignaçio said. "Ortega reincarnated as Julio. He combined corrida and choreography in a way nobody could. How do you—"

"Nacho!" Nuria pushed her plate aside. "Can we stop this now?"

"Why?"

"We've had enough of this discussion already."

"We just lost Spain's number two matador."

"Are you thinking of replacing Julio?"

"Someone has to."

"Not you."

Ignaçio rose from his chair. He left his plate and picked up the calico cat. He clacked up the staircase and shut his room's door.

Nuria stared at the empty stairs. This wasn't a new behavior of Ignaçio's. He had behaved this way since he was fifteen if she tried to keep him away from bullfights on television. But in the last few months, he had done this more frequently and more silently. His quiet defiance shattered her authority. She worried for him. He was slipping away from her grip, and her parents' indifference was encouraging his growth in this dangerous direction.

The camera moved to cities in Portugal, France, and Mexico. The exchanges on social networks grew exponential. The youths across the world caught this riot's flames and hurled them across all platforms. Nuria left her plate on the table, bid her parents goodnight, and went up the stairs. Santos sensed her mood and followed her.

She knocked on Ignaçio's door; he didn't reply. She turned the knob; the door wasn't locked. She opened it and stood outside; he didn't lift his eyes. Magdalena purred on his lap. An impulse rose. She wanted to slap his stubborn face and ravage his savage curls. She

51

checked her passion and stayed outside. She watched him fondle the cat. She sighed at his room's disorder. She glared at Ortega's life-size poster. He still refused to look at her.

She told him she loved his art but hated his cruelty. She accepted his chaos but refused his follies. She would have kicked him out if he had another place to go. She asked him to sleep well and then shut his door. She stood in the corridor and waited for him to cry. This time, he didn't. She strutted up and down the corridor. She reproached Santos for following her. She sent the dog down the stairs to her parents. Ignaçio still didn't emerge from his room.

She entered her room, closed the door, and burst into tears.

She lay in bed but couldn't close her eyes. If she did, in her head the underage bull bleated, and dying Julio pleaded.

At some point, she descended into a jetlagged doze and then rose to a young calf's bleats. The cries came from Victor's stall. She checked Ignaçio's door, went down to the barn, and rubbed the motherless calf until he calmed. The taurine duel's clamor still echoed in her head. She wrapped the sweater around her and walked toward the edge of her parents' farm.

She stood at the farm's fence and watched the glistening river. San Taurino's lights glittered in its water and glimmered on the far bank. The rioters had left the city; the racket's notes still lingered in its core. The night's crisp air rang its sorrow. The desolate city ignored her violation, raised her bruised face, and strived to retrieve her dignity.

San Taurino didn't deserve this treatment. Bullfighting didn't originate in this city; it took its origin in Rome.

Rome's coliseum held the first bullfight. Prisoners thrown against hungry lions didn't survive long. Bulls prolonged the shows by slowing death. Romans came to this region two centuries before Christ's birth, when they invaded the Iberian Peninsula from the South. The indigenous fell to Rome, but, up here in the North, Celts and Basques resisted until twenty-two years after Christ's birth. Romans incorporated San Taurino that year and celebrated its birth by holding the city's first bullfight in its public square.

Then the Roman Empire fell.

Afterward, Italy enacted strict animal laws and set Europe's trend. But Rome's taurine tradition endured in San Taurino. The following centuries altered bullfight's form and adopted new norms. Those changes reinforced corrida's presence through the city's evolution.

San Taurino built its arena after Rome's coliseum. This oval-shaped bullring, set on nine acres, measured hundred and seventy-eight meters along its north-south axis; hundred and forty-six along the east-west. The arena's three floors, built with red bricks, cement, and iron clamps, soared thirty-two meters. Sixty arches stood on hundred and twenty columns, topped by marble gargoyles and bronze carvings. From its slaughterhouse, a cobblestone gutter descended the bulls' blood into the river and gave it the name Sangre de Toros. Afterward, changing environmental laws and rising human conscience closed this gutter, but the river retained its name and continued to nourish the rust-brown algae that flourished in its water.

The city then restored and renovated its arena.

Today, under Willem's patronage, the remodeled arena's thirty rows, spread on three levels, sat forty thousand viewers. Its reinforced acoustics amplified the bulls' roars, the toreros' cries, the spectators' hollers, and the orchestras' music louder, raised them higher, and hurled them farther into the city. The sounds echoed in the mind's remote corners hours after the bullfights. They resonated in the head months beyond the bullfighting season. The citizens heard the taurine clamor in their daydreams and nightmares throughout the year.

Willem's arrival had changed this city into a perennial taurine theater.

4

The clashes over Julio's death faded into the city's Roman games.

The Feria of April seized San Taurino while Nuria continued her taurine tours around Spain and job interviews with law firms. Spring birthed more calves on her parents' farm and brought Victor new company. The fast-growing orphan overcame his nightmares, took these latter arrivals under his care, and eased Santos's cow-herding task. The bond between the dog and the calf soldered further and strengthened through their growing collaboration.

The pastures and the hills thickened their green coats. Camellias, begonias, and fuchsias lighted the city's balconies. Jasmines lifted the days' humor; evening primroses deepened the nights' mood. Humans heard the primal inside them and forgot their animals. San Taurino's bullfights followed its ferias and saint days; partisans and protestors stayed out of this mess. Then a week before the Feria of Ascension, Miguel published a piece on social media that resurrected the clash, ended the citizens' complaisance, and stood the city's peace on its head.

By the rules of Spanish bullfighting, a bull that kills its matador enters the books as a *toro loco*—a crazy bull—to be slaughtered after the fight unless the bullring's president pardons the animal. Julio's killer, despite its provenance from Rafaela's ranch, didn't earn this grace from her husband. Pedro couldn't find a reason to grant this bull amnesty.

Against persistent protests from Miguel's foundation and other animal-rights group, the authorities slaughtered this crazy bull and pushed the city's conflict to its peak. Afterward, time's erosion cooled these animal lovers' passion. Their perspective enlarged. They saw the authorities' act from a different angle. Early spring fed these bulls with fresh herbs and grass, which gave them an edge over their fighters, out of practice through the previous autumn and winter. They accepted this slaughter as fair, lowered their banners, and went home.

The Spanish bullfighting rules don't stop there. They also require killing a crazy bull's mother, to finish her lineage and avoid birthing other toro locos. Fearing stronger protests from animal-rights groups, the authorities killed this crazy bull's mother in strict secret and then paid the ranch that sold this bull to Rafaela when it was a calf. The money silenced the rancher. But a crazy teenage neighbor of his called Miguel, led him to this cow's grave, and gave him the video that detailed its slaughter.

Miguel waited until the week before the Feria of Ascension to publish this story.

The cruel video outraged the groups. They abandoned their spring fever and responded to an urgent call for justice. Once more, violence erupted in the city. Once more, Miguel stood up and called for calm. But this time, his calls drowned under outcries from home and abroad. The video ran wild over the net. Tourists canceled trips; countries boycotted Spanish imports. San Taurino opened its feria and waited. No one dared the city's boiling rage. Bullfights still followed their calendar with two daily sessions. Each session filled only a tenth of the arena's seats.

Willem complained to Mayor José. The city sued Miguel's foundation.

5

The professor ended the final exam. Ignaçio shunned the girl peeking at him from two rows ahead, handed in his paper, and left the amphitheater. He heard his name and turned around. The professor was calling him from the hall's door. Ignaçio returned. They shook hands.

"How did the exam go?" the professor asked.

"Fine."

"What are you doing this summer?"

"Working for Charo," Ignaçio said. "Why?"

"The hospital needs help."

"I saw."

"Can you?"

"I'll talk to Charo."

"The state cut our money."

"I know."

"The hours will count toward your internship."

"Charo needs me at her clinic."

"You want me to talk to her?"

"No," Ignaçio said. "Let me do that."

"Carlota said good things about you."

"So you already talked to her."

"I did." The professor held his gaze. "We need you, Ignaçio."

"What did Charo say?"

"She understands."

"Did she agree to split?"

"Yes."

"You don't need to ask me then."

"Thank you."

The persistent girl stood in the hallway. Ignaçio nodded at her, left the building, and walked into the parking lot. Glass slivers crunched under his feet. Broken panes gaped from the second-floor windows; the university still hadn't replaced them. This veterinary hospital was the country's best and cheapest. People used to bring their animals here from all parts of Spain. Then the recession ate their money for travel and pet care. The doctors needed to earn their living elsewhere. He didn't know how his two-year education would help this hospital, but they must be in deep—

"Will you give me a ride?"

Ignaçio turned. The girl was following her.

"Will you?" she asked.

"Where?"

"To town."

"Where's your car?"

"Broke down."

"Here?"

"No," she said. "At home."

"How did you come?"

"On foot."

"You walked the seven kilometers?"

"Yes."

"Why didn't you take the bus?"

"You think they're running?"

"Can you keep your silliness out of my car?"

"I can."

"But will you?"

"Yes."

Ignaçio opened the passenger-side door and stood aside. The girl sat inside and closed the door. Ignaçio went to the driver's side and waited. The girl pulled her skirt over her knees and opened the driver-side door. Ignaçio entered the car and ignored the girl's stare. He revved the engine, rolled down the windows, and drove away from the parking lot.

The car passed by the law school. Their building didn't stand in a better shape. Withered shingles peeled off its façades. The stained walls waited for a paint job. Nuria should pass her bar exam this summer, leave this decaying place, and keep working for Willem. The taurine tours didn't ease her life. Yet her plight stayed a notch higher than a lawyer's—and several notches higher than a vet's. Money had stripped dignity from all professions. The education system didn't breed new professions for its youths.

The car crossed the campus's crumbling gate, sputtered up the tree-lined avenue, and ran parallel to the national highway that connected San Taurino to Madrid. On their left, beyond the vehicles' thickening exhaust, the posh parkway overlooked the ocean's blinding mirror. On their right, sprawling homes embellished the wooded slope and vaunted their gleaming pools and perspiring lawns.

A decade ago, this quarter belonged to San Taurino's middle class. They fell afterward, sold their properties to rich retirees, and raised the city's real-estate price. Today, the jobless couldn't own or rent. In three more years, building a homestead on his parents' farm would be impossible; banks would never lend money to a fresh veterinary-school graduate. His solemn pledge to help the region's poor farms and their animals wouldn't convince them.

He wasn't San Taurino's only youth facing this predicament. Vincente still lived at the firefighters' barracks as a volunteer. Ines's

59

uncertain salary would never buy them a home. The couple could go on living separately for years and then give themselves up to growing old. Only Nuria could afford her own place, but she saved her salary and helped her family. The money she earned from Willem burned her life's both ends. You couldn't change her.

Madrid had opened its San Isidro feria three weeks ago. Nuria should return after that fair, but he wasn't sure. Her clients might want to go to the fairs farther down south. Willem would pay her extra and impose those tours. Nuria could refuse, but she wouldn't. She wanted more money. Working for an employer you don't like is difficult. In this region's shaking economy, most employers cried for the state's bailout; Willem's taurine business defied bankruptcy and provided stability. Whether Nuria liked it or not, he would have to work for Willem someday.

"Ignaçio," The girl said. "I'm leaving school."

"Why?"

"We're too many in this batch."

"I know," Ignaçio said. "The school shouldn't have merged our classes."

"They're raising fees in autumn."

"Again?"

"Mama can't pay anymore."

"She works?"

"She has her salon."

"You'll work with her?"

"She gets no clients."

"What'll you do?"

"Piercing."

"Pardon?"

"Yes."

"After two years of veterinary education?"

"The animal anatomy courses will find their use."

The car joined the traffic on Boulevard de Lidia and stalled before Willem's Taverna de Tauromaquia. This elite bullfighting bar employed San Taurino's poster-fit boys and girls. At the tavern's entrance, two bouncers sweated in black suits under June's punishing rays. On its terrace, taurine tourists tanned under a scorching sun, sipped sherry, and placed their bets.

Farther east, two double-decked coaches unloaded more tourists in front of Willem's Gran Taurino Hotel. Another coach received tourists emerging from the five-star hotel's revolving door. Uncle Manu guided their porters toward his vehicle's trunks. Under the hotel's portico, the concierge in matador's outfit stretched his arm toward the gourmet restaurant next door. Neither the arriving nor the departing tourists took that direction. Beyond the restaurant, the empty golf course's evergreen grass waited for its holes to be filled this season.

The Taurine Academy's chateau rose from the golf course's far side. Since the state raised this bullfighting school to a national monument last year, its dome, façades, and gardens had received a significant facelift. On its front lawn, aspiring first-year students trained with fake bull heads and real capes for their year-end exam. The second-year students had graduated as toreros and left for their cut-throat world, where no godfather guaranteed your place. Only a fraction of these graduates, after their required twenty-five fights with underage bulls, would pass their accreditation, get their confirmation, and earn their matador's titles. The rest would join the trade as *picadors*, *banderilleros*, and *puntilleros*. Or quit their bullfighting career for something else. Or finish their lives in wheelchairs or graves.

"You should try the Taurine Academy," the girl said.

"Sorry?" Ignaçio said.

"You were looking at it."

"I was."

"Do you watch bullfights?"

"Yes."

"At the arena?"

"No," Ignaçio said. "On television."

"Why on television?"

"You see nothing from the sun-facing seats at the back."

"Get a front-row seat behind the barrier."

"Those cost hundreds of euros."

"Your flamenco earns you money."

"Not enough."

"You'll make more from corrida."

"I know."

"And you have what a matador needs."

"You think?"

"Of course!" The girl laughed. "Unless you want to work as an arena's vet and spend your life checking the *lidia* bulls' teeth."

"I don't."

"What are you waiting for?"

"Are you asking me to quit like you?"

"Don't call me a loser."

"I didn't."

"I'm a quitter." The girl sighed. "It's the same."

"What's your name?"

"You don't care."

"Why do you think I'll succeed as a matador?"

"The way you move."

"That's flamenco."

"You don't dance like others."

"Do I dance like a matador?"

"You'll be the next Julio."

The car turned left and reached Plaza de Toreros. On the square, the institutions' officers enjoyed hot lunch from the serving restaurants and cold mist from the sprouting fountain. On the city hall's portico, Mayor José talked with legislator Pedro. They descended the staircase, marched to the regional bullfighting association's office at the far end, and met Rafaela at the building's carriage door. She shook the mayor's hand and kissed her husband on the cheeks.

The passenger-side door opened. Ignaçio slowed. The girl stepped out of the moving car and closed the door. She trotted before the vehicle, turned around, and waved at him. Ignaçio stopped. She ran across the square and joined a group at the bullfighting bar. He recognized this group. He had seen them at the port's tattoo parlor that sold marijuana. Both businesses' owner, also a veterinary-school dropout, drove a sports car now.

The businesses around bullfighting generated more money than bullfights. Willem was sand in some eyes and pain in some necks, but San Taurino's heart throbbed to his taurine empire's beats; they pumped money into the city's economic arteries. His enterprise brought this city thousand times more clients and filled its coffer hundred times more than all other businesses, theaters, cinemas, and football matches combined. You couldn't beat him.

True, bulls died in arenas. So did cattle in slaughterhouses. But before dying, these bulls lived a king's life for four years that the cattle had no rights to. Animal lovers claimed that the *lidia* bull endured torture and death for the city, but a skilled matador knew how to kill a bull without making the animal suffer.

Besides, like their fighters, these bulls were warriors at heart. They fought with pride and pleasure. They met their death with courage, dignity, and valor. They enjoyed the privileges exclusive for their race and then sacrificed their lives for others. Willem took this martial art from ancient Spain and translated it into money for its citizens. Those animal-rights activists like Miguel, who carved their lives from tax-free donations, did nothing to lift Spain's youths from their precarious situation after the recession.

The car turned right on Avenida de Corrida. The traffic didn't slow him at this hour. He turned left from the avenue, crossed the bridge over the Sangre de Toros River, shifted to the lower gear, and bent over the steering wheel for the steep climb. Someday, this ruin of his would end up in the river, and they would have to fish it out with his remains. Flamenco didn't earn him enough money to replace this car. He couldn't ask Nuria or her parents. The revenues from his parents' farm didn't cover his room and food at their home. Since Jaime and Elena joined them two months ago, this family's burden had grown heavier. Nuria bore most of it by staying single. Time had come for him to ease their load by moving out.

His burden wasn't fair on Nuria. She was only five years older than him.

From the day her parents adopted him, she had acted as his surrogate sister, punished him with her eyes and words when he didn't behave, and rewarded him with her tender warmth and firm care when he did. Their relation had evolved through time. She had grown reserved, remote, and rougher from responsibilities piling on her shoulders. Yet her flame to keep harm out of his way had retained its furor. It was difficult not to love this woman. It was difficult not to hate those who hurt her. It was difficult to see her burn from work she didn't like.

Nuria was a woman of solemn dignity. If she worked in law, she would make a great lawyer; she was cut for this profession. But a lawyer's work wasn't what she thought. The law firms she was interviewing with should give her a glimpse of the legal playfield. She wanted to run from the taurine world's pain; the legal world's pain would torture her more. Her ethics would revolt. Her integrity would shatter. Her honesty would turn against her. After suffering in taurine business for eight years, she deserved better from the law.

Ignaçio left the cliff-side road and turned on the trail by his parents' farm. Jaime drove the harvester and collected nettle for compost. The hot breeze brought its stinging scent mixed with manure's odor. Since the young man arrived from Vigo, he had turned this fallow land into a fertile farm. If he continued at this pace, Jorge could bring his cattle here in a month. The fresh feed would boost his animals' yield and give him money for autumn and winter.

The thought lightened Ignaçio. He slowed his car and surveyed his parents' farm. A new grill separated the trimmed pasture from the tilled vegetable patches. Budding shoots peeked from their wet soil. Along the farm's fence, fresh clods surrounded the fruit trees' roots. Their bursting branches welcomed buzzing bees, chirping birds, and skipping squirrels. He couldn't recall seeing so much life on this farm since his parents died. The heron no longer found its solitude in the cottonwood tree by the pond. The solitary bird had bustling company

65

now.

Jaime had gifted hands. He had turned the barn's attic into a loft for Elena and him. He had renovated the farm equipment of Jorge and the neighbors. He had repaired their vehicles, vans, and cars. This skilled go-getter would soon earn his financial independence in San Taurino. The couple would live happier here than in Vigo.

The car turned toward Jorge's farm.

Febrile breath wafted from the river. Ignaçio pushed his hair aside and opened his shirt's top buttons. If the June sun scorched San Taurino's hills this way, what would it do in the South? He hoped Nuria's taurine clients wouldn't drag her to the ferias in Cacéres, Granada, and Sevilla. After Madrid, she should return to the shades of her parents' farm.

Her family was kind to him. His mood swings didn't ease their lives; they understood him and took him as if he were related by blood. He wasn't. In this Pyrenean corridor of avalanche and rockslide, his parents' land had belonged to his Basque ancestors for generations, but only his parents had dared move here and paid with their lives. All other neighbors came from the South. Blood linked them; they resembled and behaved alike. He stood on the pole opposite from Nuria, Jaime, and Ines. Yet Jorge and Paula saw him as their fourth child. Uncle Manu and Aunt Belen considered him their nephew. The recession took its toll from these southern farmers, but they found their contentment in this close-knit community.

On the one hand, he couldn't leave Nuria's family at their financial problem's crux. On the other hand, he couldn't stay with them and sink their finances deeper. His flamenco shows earned little money. He studied veterinary medicine to serve this community, but its farmers had no money for vets. If he had to move to earn his living, he might as well do it now. That would at least help Nuria and her family.

His move would hurt them, but they would see his reason. He would leave his parents' farm in Jorge's hands. Jaime could help him enlarge his cattle, receive more aid from Europe and the state, and reach the economy of scale he still needed to survive in traditional farming. After that fatal landslide, the city reinforced these hills' flanks and built ramparts around their bases. Today, his parents' property was safer. Jaime could build a farmstead there and move in with Elena when they had enough money. The whole family would do better without him and with two farms in their hands.

Nuria, too, would be free to live and work the way she wanted.

He heard Santos's howls before his car reached Jorge's farm. The Pyrenean shepherd leaped across the inundated grass toward the cattle barrier. Boulders fallen from the hills had again deviated the woods' stream. Dried mud cakes peeled off the dog's snow white coat. Ignaçio parked his car behind the stable, uncoiled the watering hose, and cleaned the dog.

The noise brought Victor. Sweat shined the calf's jet-black coat, but he didn't want to be sprayed; he wanted his game. Ignaçio put the watering hose away. After his year-end exam's stress, he too needed this game with the three-month old calf. Magdalena came and rubbed her fur against his leg. He patted the calico cat on the back, ignored her mewls to pick her up, and entered the stable. The cat followed him. He changed into his shoes for the game, lifted the cat in one hand, and came out holding the red cape in the other.

Victor was already heading toward the spot for their game.

Ignaçio closed the gate, placed the cat on her post, and called for *entrada.*

Victor stopped and turned around. The calf lifted his head and pricked his ears; he was waiting for today's *palo*. Ignaçio sang an *alegría* that suited Victor's mood. The calf bobbed his head to the palo's beats. His dewlap swayed to the song's tempo.

Victor was changing fast in appearance and character. In three months since his birth, the calf had grown from twenty-seven to a hundred and seventy-six kilos. You could already see a young bull in him. His rapid growth assured Esperanza and worried her. The adoptive cow was now caught between this precocious calf and her possessive bull. Jorge would soon have to move Victor away from Herman.

The calf no longer bleated; he bellowed. When Herman groaned, Victor groaned back. He learned fast from this bull, but he also rejected the old boy's vices. This independent calf was growing by his own blueprint. Lorenza marveled at her adopted brother's progress. Even old Herman sometimes dropped his defense and watched this black calf bloom into a formidable bull. Santos could now ease on his canine duties and trust his bovine friend's unique course.

Ignaçio started a *pasada de pecho* and ended the pass with a *punta*. Victor mirrored him by passing chest-to-chest and tapping his hooves' tips.

The calf didn't stop there and wait for the next move. He raised his head, lifted his tail, and executed a series of *vuelta*. The donkey brayed in admiration. The calf loved these turns. They added to his repertoire of ruse growing with his muscles and hump. He no longer limited himself to imitating his master. He learned the passes, made them his own, then added his twists and surprised his teacher.

Their games were evolving fast. The calf already saw his master as his equal.

Ignaçio performed a backbend turn and raised the cape. Victor reared up, twirled with his front legs in the air, and charged at the cape. Ignaçio moved from the calf's line of charge. Victor turned, circled him and danced, and then did a back-to-back *pasada de espalda*.

Ole!

Ignaçio finished his palo and switched to *silencio*. Victor regained his calm, but his eyes shined at the cape. Ignaçio bent his knees, quickened his footwork, and thrust his trunk high. Victor responded to this *sentao* by speeding his hooves, lifting his chest, and raising his head higher. He didn't stop there. He leaped and turned a full circle with his hooves off the soil.

Ole!

Santos barked. Magdalena was descending from her post on the fence.

The calico cat came and got in the game's way. Victor didn't appreciate her interruption. The jealous cat didn't see the danger from this calf's killer hooves. Ignaçio withdrew the cape, rubbed Victor's dewlap, and kept the calf calm. Santos dissuaded Magdalena and ushered her out. The cat returned to her post. Ignaçio released Victor and shifted his *palo*.

He sang a fast pace *bulería*, stood face to face with Victor, and held the cape chest high. The calf charged. Ignaçio dropped one hand to his waist, turned in the charge's direction with the cape, and lured the calf around him. Victor brushed past him and braked. Ignaçio spun and faced the calf. Victor turned, burst past his other side, and finished the Veronica pass.

69

Ole!

Ignaçio raised the cape. Victor charged again.

Ignaçio lifted the cape above his head, turned against the charge's direction, and slid the cape over Victor's back. The calf stopped, turned, and groaned. Ignaçio dropped one hand, snapped its fingers, and rotated the cape with the other. Victor's eyes followed the cape, but the calf stayed in his place. Ignaçio lowered the cape to his waist, switched it from one hand to the other behind his back, and then rotated it horizontally around his trunk. Victor stood still and watched this new *serpentina* pass. The calf then stepped back and forth; tossed his head and flapped his ears; shook his tail, swayed his dewlap, and twisted like a serpent.

Ole!

Ignaçio called for the climax and speeded his palo.

He gathered his feet. He raised the cape above his head. He stood on one leg, spun on the spot, and revolved the cape. Victor watched him spin. The calf responded to this *revolvera* pass by striking his hooves, turning in concentric circles, then rearing up and performing a—

Santos barked again.

This time, his bark wasn't for the calico cat. Ignaçio arrested his spin and watched the farm's entry. Nuria's car rolled under the cattle barrier, crunched on the driveway's gravel, and stopped before the farmstead's door. She stayed inside the car, held her head erect, and kept her face turned away from them. The dog didn't dare go and greet her.

Ignaçio folded the cape, stooped, and patted Santos on the head. The dog looked from him to Nuria. Ignaçio urged Santos to go. The dog lowered his head, tucked his tail, and walked on stiff legs toward

Nuria. She ignored the dog, entered their home, and closed the door.

Magdalena mewled. Ignaçio turned. The calico cat jumped down from the fence, held her head and tail high, and marched to him. He ignored her. She rubbed her fur against his boots. Ignaçio sent Victor away with Lorenza, picked up the calico cat, and entered the stable.

He put away the red cape and waited for Nuria. She didn't come.

Ignaçio took his swimming gears, left the stable, and returned to the pasture.

Like him, Victor too was agitated from their game's abrupt end. He rubbed the calf's dewlap until they both calmed and then led him toward the farm's gate. Santos howled and galloped toward them. Victor turned around and welcomed his canine friend. Ignaçio raised the cattle barrier, let them out, and took their favorite trail through the hills toward the river.

He understood Nuria. For the orphaned calf, she had retained her maternal outlook.

But Victor no longer needed a mother. He was growing fast and seeking independence. You could see this growth from the way he now drank from Esperanza's udder. He was a precocious boy who pushed his parents aside to test life's avenues and taste its adventures. Victor preferred his mates to his mother. Like the *lidia* breed calves, he showed his innate fighting streaks by lowering his head before his horns emerged. Marking Victor for meat would do him more than injustice. Jorge still resented him for killing his best cow, but he wouldn't dare take the calf from Nuria's care and send him for slaughter.

Nuria's rigid directive came with her protective side. He couldn't resent her.

They left the mud trail and cut across the meadows. Santos wanted to lead, but Victor knew where he was going; the herbs' aroma didn't change his priority. This calf led his pack on Jorge's farm. He learned from his success and failure. Like the *lidia* breed calves, destined to fight as bulls, he ignored pain and fear. He should get his fair chance at bullrings.

They reached the river's inlet where Victor learned to swim when he was three weeks old. The current no longer frightened him, but he preferred a dip in this quieter bay before entering the river's mainstream. Ignaçio watched the calf splash around with Santos. Then he changed into his swimsuit and plunged into the inviting pool. The mountain's melt-water washed his heat and fatigue. The cold penetrated his skull, cooled his brain, and buried its bubbles.

He floated on his back and admired the surrounding pines. Their canopy cascaded down the hills' slopes and brought the perfume of their needles, barks, and cones. This face of these hills received little grace from the sun; their conifers survived the slaughter that made place for grape vines. Their sublime scent lingered in this bay throughout the year. They eased his breathing in the months when his chest constricted. Their shadows shaded him on the days when life scorched him with its heat. Few souls dared these hills' steep trails. After the ocean swelled and swallowed a couple from a cave, no one explored their flanks on the other side.

This place provided him time and space when he needed solitude and silence.

The twin bells tolled from Iglesia Sacrata di Ser Vivo. Ignaçio turned around and faced the stoic church's back, flanked by the arena's gaiety on the left and by the hospice's sobriety on the right. Except for these bells' peels, the city's din didn't reach this sheltered

72

bay. The surrounding trees camouflaged this pool. They hid him from the telescopes mounted on the fort's rooftop battlement. He could float incognito in this water and soak the city's subtle beauty.

Santos barked. Wakes rolled in and bobbed Ignaçio. He turned on his chest and saw the two animals chase a passing boat. This river hid its undertow from humans, but animals do know. He hollered. Santos understood. He paddled around Victor, barked, and strived to dissuade the calf. Victor defied the dog, pursued the boat, and rode the churning waves.

Ignaçio swam out and brought Victor back to the shore.

By the time they returned to Jorge's farm, he had already milked his cows. Ignaçio took fresh milk in a bucket and held it under Victor's mouth. The calf sniffed the milk, moved from the bucket, and searched for Esperanza. The cow suckled Lorenza on the pasture. Victor went to Esperanza and sucked from her udder. Ignaçio left the milk bucket to Magdalena and Santos, took the outside stairs to his room, and hung his wet swim gears on the balcony's railing.

He was taking off his soiled clothes when someone knocked on his door.

Ignaçio knew the knock.

He pushed the dirty clothes under his bed, wrapped a bath towel around his trunk, and opened the door. He faced Nuria and braced for her attack. This time, she didn't bash him for his game with Victor. She pushed him aside, entered his room, and closed the door.

She stood still and stared at his face. He avoided her gaze.

Each month, this period shined her dark eyes. He couldn't ignore what her dilated pupils held at their depth behind that glow. Her wet black curls, flowing down her sun-tanned shoulders, wafted a floral scent that spun his head. He bit his lip and lowered his face. He took out fresh clothes and started for the bathroom. She blocked the door and lifted his chin.

"How did the exams go?" she asked.

"They're finished."

"When will the results post?"

"In ten days."

"You're halfway through your studies."

"I have three more years left."

"Those will fly."

"I wish they did," Ignaçio said. "The school costs money."

"Your dance earns money."

"They don't cover my expenses."

"Nacho," Nuria said. "This is your home."

"I'm twenty-one."

"So?"

"I should work like you."

"I have good news," Nuria said. "I'm quitting Willem."

"You got the law job?"

"Yes!"

"Will you litigate?"

"I hope."

"You should."

"Why?"

"You'll be a good litigator."

"I see."

"Nuria," Ignaçio said. "I didn't mean—"

"I know what you meant."

"You know too much."

74

"Do I?"

"Can I go now?"

"Not yet." She held out a wad of bills. "Put these away."

"I don't need money."

"Yes, you do."

"For what?"

"A car."

"I have a car."

"That one is going."

"Where?"

"To the junkyard."

"I'm not taking it there."

"Then Jaime will."

"Is this an order?"

"Yes."

Plaza de Toreros teemed with citizens. The stairs of the city hall and the regional legislature had no empty spots. The national legislative initiative's course would be decided this week. If the petition drew the required half million signatures, the deputies at the nation's legislature would have to debate the proposed bill before autumn. The world's aficionados were pouring into the country and betting on this initiative's fate. San Taurino had received its fair share.

The square had no place to park. Nuria left her car on a side street, wedged through the crowd gaping at the television above the fountain, navigated the pro- and anti-corrida groups separated by the police, reached the building of the Regional Association of Bullfighting, and buzzed their intercom. Angel answered her call, descended from his office, and opened the bolstered door. Nuria regarded his face: sober, solemn, serious. The association's secretary held her gaze without a word and then led her up their disfigured mahogany staircase.

Under their feet, the chipping stairs creaked and squeaked. Above the fraying handrail, on the discolored wall, the association's former presidents sweated. Pedro's portrait stood last in line on this dim corridor. The stale air reeked dust, floor wax, and cleaners. Cobwebs covered the overhead air-conditioners. No air came from their vents, no life hummed in them.

They passed the president's office. Rafaela lifted her head, nodded at them, and returned to talking on the phone. Her marriage to Pedro lifted her from bullrings for escorting him at society's events. Two years ago, when he left to head the region's legislature, he placed his wife in his seat and broke the association's code. As its president, she could now be with Angel in this building, without drawing attention from the press. Their discretion would ease Pedro's journey toward the nation's legislature, on a political terrain mined with corruptions, scandals, and games that befriended money, power, and glory. The man had kept his matador wife busy.

Angel ushered Nuria into his cramped office and closed its peeling door. They didn't sit.

"Thanks for coming," Angel said.

"What's it about?" Nuria asked.

"Your resignation."

"Pardon?"

"Willem asked me to talk to you."

"I just saw him."

"I know," Angel said. "He still wants me to talk with you."

"My resignation has nothing to do with bullfighting."

"Why did you resign?"

"The tours."

"Your clients tire you?"

"My bar exams are coming."

"When do you start this law-firm job?"

"End September," Nuria said. "That is, if I pass the bar."

"Is your contract permanent?"

"For six months."

"Is their salary higher?"

"No."

"Are you sure about this job?"

"I'll see after the bar."

"Nuria." Angel leaned forward. "Why are you leaving?"

"It's the hours."

"You're not telling me the truth."

"Don't ask me then."

"Are you fed up with Willem?"

"No more than you are."

"Then please stay."

"You called me here to say this?"

"No."

Angel opened a folder and took out a fax. Willem was offering her a jurist's post and doubling her salary. The permanent contract had no trial period. She would receive a vehicle that she could also drive for personal needs. The job didn't require her to pass the bar exam.

"Thank you," Nuria said. "I still want to pass the bar."

"Of course," Angel said. "When is the exam?"

"Mid September."

"You'll have the first two weeks of September for free."

"Willem isn't offering me this."

"I am."

"I need time to think."

"Nuria." Angel leaned backward. "What's so special about this law firm?"

"Nothing."

"They do have an animal laws division."

"You did your homework."

"Yes," Angel said. "And I read your thesis too."

"You know then."

"Will you turn against us?"

"For bullfights?"

"Yes."

"I can't."

"Then why risk your family for animals?"

"I wish I knew."

"You can't take Miguel's place either."

"I don't want to."

"You know the laws are changing."

"Not yet."

"They will," Angel said. "Do you want me to help your family?"

"How?"

"I can recruit Ignaçio at the arena this summer."

"No, you won't."

"I can talk to Willem about Jaime."

"He's looking after Ignaçio's farm."

"I spoke to Paloma and Juan."

"For what?"

"To sell their flamenco bar."

"To Willem?"

"Yes."

"You must be crazy," Nuria said. "How did they react?"

"They said they'd think about it."

"They're being polite with you."

"They need money to retire."

"I know."

"Does your father need money?"

"Pardon?"

"If Jorge wants, he can sell his farm and—"

"Work for Willem?"

"I didn't say that."

"Do you have anything more to say?"

"No."

"Then I'll go."

She didn't wait for Angel to escort her out of the building.

She reached her car without looking at anyone. She sat inside the vehicle, kept its doors and windows closed; Angel's words still entered her car and vibrated its air. The closed vehicle trapped the late June sun and punished her with its heat. She drove from the square, stopped on the city's terrace, and rolled down the car's windows. The port's febrile breath wafted up from below and choked her with its thick vapor.

She knew a place that would help her breathe.

She drove to the ocean and stopped at the beach where its rip currents kept away citizens and tourists. At a spot sheltered from the passing drivers' eyes, she stripped to her underwear and swam out in the receding water. The smooth sheet stretched into the horizon and grew the ocean's surface. She needed to feel small in order to see what happened in Angel's office.

She saw it.

The words of this disabled matador had hit her three vital spots: the two men she loved more than herself, the ancestral pride of her family's farm, and a cultural legacy from the South she valued. All three were being devoured by another tradition that was emerging as Spain's only heritage by the measure of money.

If this legislative initiative lifted bullfighting to a national monument, it would receive a protection far larger, wider, and deeper than the royal decree granted. Violations would be punished by years in prison and millions of euros in fine. As the bullfighting association's secretary, Angel didn't decide this legal initiative's fate. The thwarted matador was trying to help her and her family in San

80

Taurino's shrinking economy, growing its dependence on the bullfighting industry, flourishing from tourists' money. She couldn't stay angry with him.

Like her, Angel was captive to this economy's impasse. So were Ignaçio and her family. So were the bulls and their fighters. So were San Taurino's all other residents bound to their personal ties. They had to nourish their blood from taurine dollars by offering themselves to this bullfighting empire, growing at the expense of the region's other trades.

Willem didn't initiate this shift; it came from demand meeting supply. Some humans demanded blood; Willem found means to supply it. The blood was real; the means, legal. The shift tarnished Spain's image, but it furnished the Spanish the money they needed to live. The threat to Ignaçio in bullrings, the threat to her family's farm and their financial independence, the threat to Paloma and Juan's flamenco bar and their dignity—all these threats originated from and converged to this single shift in this country, the shift that had become the country's symbol.

Angel didn't need to read her final-year thesis to know that Spain's animals deserved better; that the status of animals in Spain and the penalties for cruelties against them fell far below the European standards; that defending animals or their rights wouldn't earn a lawyer's life in this country. William didn't bring bullfighting with him when he immigrated to Spain. The tradition had lived in this country for centuries.

None of these made her feel any better or worse. But somehow they released her chest from the pressure's grip. She saw she was worrying about things she could do nothing about. She then saw the things she could still do something about. They waited for her to act.

She swam back toward the shore and set priorities for her acts. She came out of the water, dried herself under the sun, then started her car and drove from the beach.

She didn't feel like going home.

She took the alternate route and stopped on the hilltop. The crest overlooked her farmers' community nested among the hills' feet. She left her car and stood on the cornice she used to come with Ignaçio when they were teens. Since then, the city had condemned the caves under her feet for structural instability; their roof still offered an overview of this southern farmers' settlement that no other spot in the Pyrenean range did. On days like today, she needed this expansive view to push her derailing thoughts back to their places.

She saw Ignaçio at his game with Victor, but they looked tiny compared to the rest. This Basque boy, named after their saint, was an exception in her southern community. Yet these dark-skin farmers accepted this fair-skin orphan as one of their own. Victor too, orphaned at birth, had stayed a pariah on her parents' farm for months, until Father finally saw this calf's promise, set aside grudges, and spared him the slaughterhouse for reproduction. Reproductive bulls were now becoming a source of growing revenue for these cattle farms.

These two orphans she had abandoned for her work. They found their nourishment from this game, flourishing between them through her increasing absence. They each needed the other for company. Depriving them of their pleasure, as she did three weeks ago after her taurine tour, was unfair to both. She was wrong to make a big deal of something small.

With Ignaçio, she was making the same mistake Ortega's mother made with her son. This woman, too, was a flamenco dancer. She, too, tried to keep her son away from bullfighting, by drawing him into flamenco. Ortega then fulfilled her wish—and his—by growing into a matador who danced with bulls before killing them.

Ignaçio excelled at his veterinary studies. Unlike her, who struggled to finish her final law-school year, he loved his courses and topped his class. He had finished only his second year; not just Carlota but other clinics and hospitals wanted to hire him. If she steered him away from his innocent games with Victor, she would push him farther in the direction she didn't want him to go. She could stay prudent, but she couldn't let her paranoia destroy his future.

Ignaçio loved to perform: the main reason flamenco drew him. She didn't like to travel; the tours separated her from his moves. At the same time, she needed a stable job that paid well, to help her family and sustain his growth. If she accepted this jurist job, she would have stability and money—and her travel would go. Like him, she loved flamenco. She could do more shows with him and keep him busy. Their shows would help Paloma and Juan. The couple wouldn't have to sell their flamenco bar to Willem.

The jurist job would help everyone.

Victor's growth started on the day he was born. He drank from Esperanza's udder, left his surrogate mother, and met her daughter Lorenza; she became his adoptive sister. He learned from the hooves and horns of the other cows he searched milk from. He saw the bull as his future role model and as someone to avoid now.

His search didn't end there. He had more to discover on this farm and beyond.

His nose on the electric fence defined his limits; he respected them. He observed the mountains that surrounded the farm; they looked too big to approach now. He explored the animals of his size. He did fine with the farm's other calves, but not with the large-horn goat and the bighorn ram. His canine friend, Santos, had to rescue him from these two solitary males that smelled stronger than the bull.

He learned to bray from the donkey. His imitation flattered this animal bigger than him. Each time they brayed, the horse neighed, and Victor did a poor job at imitating the horse. The cacophony angered the bull. Esperanza had to save Victor from her male.

Victor ignored the bull, but the bull didn't; he watched Victor from distance. Victor took the bull's attention for admiration. He approached the bull and offered his friendship on equal terms. The bull groaned and chased him around the farm. Santos had to deploy his tact and dissuade the dominant bull.

These repeated relief operations reinforced the bond between the calf and the dog that started on the day of Victor's birth. He marveled at what this canine friend, smaller than him, could do with larger animals using only his passes and barks. When Victor applied those on others, they brought him disasters. Santos had to rescue him again.

But Victor was learning fast.

He separated centipedes from caterpillars by their hair. He saw black caterpillars go into green cocoons and then come out as yellow butterflies. Some birds flew by day; others hunted at night. All creatures that resembled birds weren't always birds. For example, those bats that hung with their heads down from the trees' branches. They didn't lay eggs. All creatures that laid eggs weren't birds either. For example, snakes and frogs. Snakes ate frogs. All birds had wings, but they didn't always use them to fly. For example, the farm's hens. They beat him with their wings if he annoyed them. Some birds ate other birds. He scared off the two eagles that circled the farm and targeted the henhouse. This won him Maria's heart. The hen stopped pecking his muzzle when he sniffed her chicks.

The hen's favor encouraged Victor's olfactory exploration.

He separated plants that helped him breathe from plants that made him sneeze. By now, he was drinking less milk and eating more grass, but he wanted to expand the range of his diet by tasting food that others of his race didn't dare. The nettle smelled good to his nose but swelled his tongue and inflamed his throat. He decided to watch his elders and learn from them.

His decision didn't last long.

His nose drew him to the red ants that crawled out of their hill. He hoofed the loose earth; the ants flooded out in mass. Their odor grew stronger. He lowered his muzzle and sniffed the ants. They sent him screaming and running around with a new disaster. Santos couldn't help him this time. His biped playmate caught him, thrust a needle into his hind, and pushed two tubes up his nostrils. The burn didn't calm immediately. He had to wait until the next sunrise before he could breathe again through his nose.

From then on, he decided to apply his nose with more care.

He left alone the snails that carried their houses on their backs; they moved too slowly for his games. But he watched the snail-shaped houses-on-wheels that stopped by the farm after sunset, and the bipeds that came out and went in. At night, the bigger bipeds cracked branches and started flames that sizzled and smoked. The flames scorched his coat and burned his nose if he approached the fence. The smaller bipeds lifted the flames, hurled them at each other, and then laughed and danced. Their games didn't inspire him. Yet his instincts told him to stay nearby. He sacrificed his sleep and surveyed these bipeds.

Nothing serious happened to this farm from them.

As time passed, Victor ignored those flames and returned to rest. Then nature changed its colors. The air grew colder. The houses-on-wheels came fewer and fewer and then stopped altogether when the wind started howling through the hills. He didn't miss them.

One by one, the male calves left the farm; only the females remained. He felt odd as the only male calf on this farm. Little by little, Esperanza's milk dried out. She spent less time with him and more time with his half-sister Lorenza and the other cows. The female calves stopped playing with him. His canine friend tried to make up for his loss, but he still felt alone. The sun went down earlier and rose later. Every afternoon, he waited for his biped playmate to return in his house-on-wheels and resume their cape game. But their sessions grew shorter and became fewer. Victor had to find other games to occupy his time.

Then white flakes fell and covered the ground. He ate the fluffy stuff by mouthfuls and sniffed it up his nostrils; they made him sneeze. The farm's bipeds brought the animals into their stalls and they stayed in. Not much happened. He missed his games. He didn't see the sun anymore, and he heard the rain drum on the roof. He learned to wait with Lorenza.

They were let out when days grew longer. The air still stayed cold. Rain's bouts returned between the sun's rays. Fresh grass raised their heads from the pasture. The cows brought new calves on the farm, except for Esperanza. The newborn calves stayed by their mothers, and the older female calves stayed with them. His biped mate came and went. Victor waited for their cape game and swim sessions to resume; they didn't. The dog stayed busy keeping the bull away from the farm's new arrivals. Lorenza ran out of her games with Victor.

Victor watched the bees carry pollen balls in their arms. He learned to stay away from the striped wasps, which were slimmer than the bees around their waist. He noticed that each bee stung once and then died, but a wasp could sting, live, and sting again. From his older mates, he learned to avoid the long green snakes that leaped after frogs. He admired Enrico's songs at dawn, but he left this rooster alone when he mounted Maria and pulled out feathers from her neck. He noticed the bull didn't punish Esperanza this way when he mounted her. And unlike Enrico, the bull protected the calves from creatures with burning eyes that appeared at night behind the bushes. He concluded he had chosen this bull as his right future model.

Then the sun traveled higher and its rays grew hotter. The snail-shaped houses-on-wheels returned and their bipeds ignited the flames again. This time, Victor ignored them and stayed away from the fence.

One night, the wind blew stronger. Sparks flew, reached the barn, and started flames. Two bipeds lived there. Victor woke Santos. The dog's barks woke others and brought them out. They uncoiled the hose and spread the barn. The water didn't stop the flames. More bipeds ran into the farm and sprayed more water. The flames grew and continued to spread.

Then a house-on-wheels of his cape's color arrived screaming and flashing lights. Four bipeds, wearing fluorescent coats, jumped out, uncoiled longer hoses, and sprayed the barn. They sprayed through the night. The flames left at dawn. The sun rose above the farm. The burnt barn still kept smoking.

His biped mate patted Santos on the head and back. The dog lowered his head, tucked his tail, and glanced with guilty eyes at his bovine friend. Victor didn't forget the mistake he had made by ignoring those flames; he didn't want any credit from his canine friend.

The snail-shaped houses-on-wheels didn't return after this fire. But their flames changed this farm's life. The bipeds here didn't stay the same. They yelled at each other. His playmate, lost in thoughts, didn't answer his calls. Their games and swims stopped. The younger female biped grew older. Her smell changed. She left early and returned late. Her fondling came rarer shorter, and rougher. When she spoke in his ears, her voice sounded weak and hoarse. Victor realized he would have to be patient.

He learned patience from dung beetles. As nature took flame's colors and the air grew crisper, he watched these beetles carve dung into balls and then roll them on the pasture. The first white flakes fell and hastened their work. He followed a small beetle rolling a large dung ball toward its burrow. On their way, a swift, sleek tail vanished under a dung cake.

Victor hoofed the caked dung and turned it over. A grey snake, short and striped, lay uncoiled and didn't dare move.

Victor regretted frightening this crawling creature. He only wanted to play. He lowered his head and watched this tiny snake's triangular head he hadn't seen so far. Its pupils were vertical like the cat's. Those pupils didn't move. He couldn't figure the emotion in them.

He lowered his muzzle further and gave the still snake a reassuring sniff. It sprang up and struck him on the nose. Victor recoiled in shock. Then he realized the stroke hadn't hurt him at all; its speed had taken him by surprise. He left this unsocial creeping creature alone and searched for the dung beetle he followed.

He didn't see the beetle anymore. He couldn't see where he was going. He had difficulty breathing, and his muscles started shaking. He tried to put out his tongue and lick the wound on his nose, but his tongue refused to move. His saliva mixed with foam and dripped from his chops. His biped playmate called him for their cape game. Victor turned around and saw his mate everywhere.

His legs buckled. His chest crashed on the ground. His belly's content came up his throat and poured out from his mouth.

Victor tried to rise; his legs wouldn't obey him. His heart pounded against the soil. His throat didn't let the air pass. He strived to keep his head up; his neck lost its will. His brain went liquid. His biped mate hollered and ran toward him. Santos barked and howled. Victor could no longer stay seated. He rolled on his side and closed his eyes.

More bipeds came running and shouting. They lifted him and carried him away. Along his way, the world silenced, and its motions stopped. Victor saw he was slipping down a slope he hadn't seen until now. An abyss lay at its end. He couldn't arrest his slide. The bipeds caught him before he fell off the slope's edge. They pulled him back and placed him on the ground; he knew its soil. His playmate's hands jabbed a needle in his thigh; it didn't hurt. His mate thrust tubes up his nose and throat; the air flowed in. His mate stroked his coat and spoke to him. The firm rub healed, the calm tone soothed. Victor descended the depths of sleep.

The sun rose and set several times. Victor slept on the soil he knew.

He dreamed of his mother. He recognized the stable. He remembered his mother birthing him on this soil and ending her life. He recalled his mock fights with the farm's older steers. He didn't understand why they left and never returned. After each needle pinch, his playmate rubbed his skin and massaged his legs, trunk, and neck. His ears prickled when the younger female biped whispered and fed him a liquid he didn't know. His playmate came more often and stayed longer than the female.

Their care brought him back. When he returned, he saw his world changed.

He sat up. The bipeds didn't put him back in the stall with others. They kept him in the stable. Sometimes, when the white flakes melted, they brought him out and placed him under the sun on the lawn. From their stall, Lorenza called for him, but not Esperanza. Maria came with her grown chicks and picked insects off his coat. From the corral, the donkey brayed for him, and the horse snorted his support. The pig encouraged him by grunting from its pen. The bull groaned but not for him. The billy goat and the ram didn't point their horns at him.

He sat on the lawn with Santos. They watched the female cat dance and play with mice. Their play resembled his game with the

90

biped mate, but the cat killed her mates after their games. Victor didn't find these killings fair. He stopped watching her games.

Little by little, he recovered his strength and stood on his legs. But his biped mate didn't play with him or take him to the river. They didn't put him back into the shed with the other calves and cows. He was kept confined in the stable and within the lawn's limits. He decided to wait and prove himself.

He didn't wait long.

One evening, the bipeds forgot to close the stable's door. Late that night, a thick snow blanket covered and silenced the gravels. A male wild cat emerged from the woods at the back and stalked the female cat chasing a mouse. The male cat ignored Victor sitting in the stable; Victor didn't ignore him. It was one of those big cats, with pointed ears and burning eyes, which prowled behind the bushes for young calves; the bull had to scare them away. This time, the bull was in the shed with his herd, and the dog wasn't nearby.

Victor's larger size didn't scare this male cat. It continued after the female, plunged into her game with the mouse and oblivious to what was coming after her. Victor rose from the ground and followed the stalking predator. The feline male heard the gravel crunch under his hooves and turned its head. It saw him coming but didn't stop. It didn't see an adolescent calf as a danger for a full-grown wild cat. It ignored him and continued to stalk the female.

Victor waited for the offense.

The moment the feline male crept down to attack, Victor reared up like the horse and struck his hooves on the cat's shoulders. The shocked predator shrieked, snarled, and leaped at him. Victor knew his passes better than this cat from his games with the biped. The wild male missed its target and fell on the gravel. Victor reared again and struck it on the belly. Santos galloped into the backyard and leaped into the fight. The wild cat saw the danger from his hooves and didn't take another chance. It limped away from the battleground. Santos ran after the wounded cat and made sure it wouldn't return to this farm.

A firm hand rubbed Victor's shoulders. He didn't know this hand's texture or temperature. He turned his head and looked behind him. The older biped, who never touched him or looked at him, owned this rubbing hand. His playmate stood aside, crossed his arms on the chest, and watched him and the older biped with glowing eyes.

The bull bellowed. The bipeds turned toward the cattle shed. From its gate, flanked by Esperanza and Lorenza, the bull watched Victor with admiring eyes. Victor reached the bull and met his muzzle. This time, the bull didn't jerk his head or sway his horns at him.

At sunrise, his games with his biped mate resumed.

Angel entered his office, opened the square-side window, and scanned the damage on Plaza de Toreros.

The dawn's hot air smelled last night's powder, smoke, and gas. The July sun shined the sweating municipal workers sweeping hand-grenade fragments and tear-gas shells sparkling on the square's paving stones. The national police towed the charred vehicle from the defiled statue's pedestal. Around the fountain, rags and logs smoldered from last night's arson. The state's count for the injured stopped at fifty-seven while the press counted three times more.

Corrida's elevation to a national monument had exploded the country's riots and rackets. But so far, nowhere else a violence of this order had erupted. The summer wouldn't calm this rebellion; these unemployed insurgents didn't have money to leave for vacation. Yesterday, Willem opened his convention to celebrate this monumental victory. Aficionados were still pouring into the city and filling its hotels. San Taurino hadn't seen the worst yet.

Someone rapped his office door.

Angel stepped back from the window. Diego entered the office, placed printouts on the desk, and turned to leave. Angel stopped the tired treasurer.

"How do the books look?" Angel asked.

"Red."

"Again?"

"Yes."

"What's taking us there?"

"The costs."

"Which ones?"

"You have it there."

"Does Rafaela know?"

"No."

"Tell her when she comes."

"You do that."

Diego left. Angel sat at the desk and pored over the accounts.

The anti-corrida events didn't slow the association's revenues, but, in the last five years, its costs to organize bullfights had soared. The steepest was the matadors' fees, two and a half times more than last year's. The riots had swelled the costs of insurance, maintenance, and repairs. This year, the city was raising the arena's rent by fifty percent. The state was hiking value-added tax by two percentage points and social charges by three. Yet they each claimed their empty coffers were crying for money.

Where do all these bullfighting funds go?

The association didn't pay Rafaela for her presidency, but the bulls from her ranches didn't come cheap. Top matadors preferred to fight bulls branded by her. The association used a rising number of her bulls every year to keep Willem's taurine clients content. If donations didn't come in this month, Diego and he wouldn't receive their salaries, and he would have to go on cleaning the association's offices on his off days. This building's exterior shined from the city's money; its interior wouldn't see any renovation or repair.

Angel noted the key figures in his pocketbook, picked up the two suitcases he brought from the arena last night, and left the building. Willem's paid thug escorted him to the deluxe black car with tinted windows, opened the door, and sat him in the backseat. They left.

The insurgence had treated the city's roads no better than its square.

These insurgents didn't belong to Miguel's nonviolent clan. These rebels cared little about the one-and-a-half-million-euro fine and the three-year prison sentence the new law imposed. They knew the state didn't expect them to pay that sum. They also knew the state didn't have money to lodge and feed them in prison for three years. They thought the state had cracked a joke on them when it passed this law. They now played that joke back onto the state.

They saw this law slaughtering their liberty. They claimed the legislative initiative's half million signatures were paid; those signatories didn't represent Spain's people. The deputies who voted for this law had placed their personal priorities above their nation's democracy.

The car passed the Taurine Academy and stopped in front of the Gran Taurino Hotel. Angel thanked the thug-cum-chauffer, lifted the two suitcases, and marched toward the revolving glass door. A dozen more black cars, their panes tinted too, lined the five-star hotel's double-lane driveway. In each car, two hired muscles killed time on cell phones; Willem didn't bet his clients' security. Art performers and business partners; taurine-club presidents and elite-society members; public officials, political figures, and diplomats; high net-worth investors, power brokers, and influencers—they held the key to Willem's global taurine empire. They flew in last night and ignited this riot. Security from the city and the state would never suffice to protect this legion. Willem had to deploy his private force.

The hotel's lobby teemed with elite aficionados and their cohorts. Dressed up goons guarded the three high-speed elevators. Angel greeted the gang and took one to the rooftop terrace. A wired thug received him at the lift's exit and led him to Willem's penthouse. The bullfighting magnate took the two suitcases and ushered him into the salon.

"How much did you bring today?" Willem asked.

"One hundred and forty-six thousand."

"That's all?"

"More people are paying by credit card these days."

"I don't pay my security boys by card."

"Sorry."

"Tell Diego the wire will arrive tomorrow by noon."

"For what amount?"

"Add the monthly allowance."

Willem called his guard, handed him the cash, and gave instructions.

The guard bowed out. Willem went to the cupboard, took out two crystal wine glasses, and poured Marques de Rioja Grand Cru. He brought the two glasses, placed one in front of Angel, and took the other to his leather chair across the desk.

Stuffed bull heads projected from the walls. These bulls had earned *rueda de vuelta* for their bravery in prominent bullrings. Angel saw the bull that killed Julio at the *mano-a-mano* two springs ago. Its head had cost Willem five and a quarter million euros. Six large screens played six different bullfights on the walls: one at the arena this morning, and five from the days before. The matador in the real-time corrida had returned to bullrings after a serious horn injury three months earlier. Facing another bull from Rafaela's ranch, the scared torero acted overcautious and delivered a deceiving fight.

"Remove that loser from your roster," Willem said.

"The guy needs time."

"You want me to lose my clients?"

"He still draws viewers."

"Watch what they're throwing at him."

"I'll see what I can do."

"Get Esteban on more fights."

"I can't," Angel said. "He has become too expensive."

"How much is he asking?"

"Half a million per corrida."

"How many is he scheduled for this summer?"

"Eight."

"Double that figure," Willem said. "I'll wire you twelve million."

"We can't push Esteban for more."

"Why?"

"He'll get injured."

"You're right," Willem said. "We need an alternative."

"A matador like Julio."

"No, like Esteban."

"He's a brute."

"My clients love his sport."

"Bullfighting isn't football."

"That's nonsense."

Willem claimed Belmonte had reincarnated as Esteban and revived the bullfighting sport, dying in taurine artists' hands. The spectators didn't come to bullrings to view art; they came for adrenaline and blood. Esteban was a cold-blooded killer who knew no fear. This champion bullfighter, gored at least a dozen times, took his combat for a serious sport, not art. Each time he returned from the hospital, he had a fiercer fever for blood. Matadors like Julio, who saw themselves as artists, paid for their pretension by their unpretentious death.

"Let's stick to the essential," Willem said. "Since last year, the chaos around this new law has helped us. It will keep helping us in the future. Let's do everything we can to capture *all* the benefits coming out of this disorder."

"This disorder is generating bad publicity for us."

"That's how it helps."

"Pardon?"

"Son," Willem said. "Do you recall last year's chaos?"

"Yes."

"Did it cut your sales?"

"No."

"Have this year's riots raised your sales?"

"Yes."

"Then where's your problem?"

"At the European Union," Angel said. "The deputies in Brussels would now push harder to cut subsidies for bull ranches."

"Those were British deputies, son," Willem said. "You forgot we kicked them out of the Union."

"No," Angel said. "These Euro deputies are Spanish."

"I'll ask Pedro to handle them."

"They won't listen to him."

"That'll help the chaos."

Willem asserted uncertainty helped businesses. You had to know how to turn chaos into cash.

For example, take his betting business. The bets' outcomes didn't earn him money; the uncertainties around them did. The higher their volatility, the pricier their profit. That's how financial tools worked. He didn't invent them; he borrowed them from commodity trading.

During the oil embargo, he made billions by betting his trading firm's money on shipping crude oil to prohibited countries. The bets on the Catalan ban, the bets on the constitutional court's decision, the bets on the legislative initiative's result—all these bets had earned his taurine enterprise hundreds of millions. Now he was betting again by selling tour packages under the piling storm-heads. They would earn him more if the chaos continued to grow.

Angel was rising from his seat; Willem lifted his hand.

"Stay, son," Willem said. "I haven't finished."

"Who will do my work?"

"This is your work," Willem said. "I have something else for you."

"Go ahead."

"I was at the corrida that retired you from bullrings. I was at Pedro's side when Rafaela pushed him to recruit you. And I'm still here to praise you for the great job you've done in growing this bullfighting association."

"Thank you."

"You're welcome," Willem said. "I know you can do better. Call corrida art or sport or whatever you want, but above all, corrida is commerce. This business is growing. And I'm reinvesting *all* my profits to grow it further. I need your help to secure me more places to put up our growing clientele."

"You bought Pedro's property for your next hotel."

"I did," Willem said. "I wanted to reward him for this new law. The push he received toward the national legislature didn't pay him cash. Have you checked Ignaçio's farm? That would make a great spot for the Gran Taurino Villas."

"That farm isn't on a constructible land."

"Don't worry about my building permits, son," Willem said. "I bought a property from the mayor's mother for those."

"Have you asked Nuria?"

"Yes."

"You know the answer then."

"That's why I need you."

"I can't help."

"Angel." Willem lifted an envelope. "Here's a check for you."

"I don't need a check."

"You look tired."

"I am."

"Are you enjoying your work?"

"I need my salary," Angel said. "I'm behind on my mortgage."

"I'll send this check to your bank."

"Don't."

"You want me to call them?"

"No," Angel said. "Make that check for our association."

"I will."

"Thank you."

9

For months, Herman respected Victor for his valor. The bull's respect grew the calf's trust. Then the female calves' odor changed. The bull changed his behavior. He no longer wanted these heifers to play with Victor. By then, the farm's other steers had left, and Victor found himself without any bovine friends. Santos spent more time with him and compensated for this loss. Victor's relation with his canine friend forged a stronger bond.

Over time, Victor's odor changed too: it resembled the bull's. The stronger Victor's smell grew, the moodier Herman became. Now the bull didn't let Victor approach Esperanza. His surrogate mother also pushed him back and spent more time with the females. Sometimes, his adoptive sister stole her way toward him; the bull chased Lorenza away.

Victor found the bull's behavior unfair. Their friendship waned. But he respected Santos's orders and didn't confront Herman.

Spring again brought new calves for Victor's company, but still not from Esperanza. His surrogate mother spent more time with her bull and pushed Lorenza toward the heifers and the newborn calves. As weeks passed and nature bloomed, these heifers' smell grew stronger, and they reacted to Victor's growing odor. Lorenza now sought him more often. The progressive changes aggravated Victor's problem: the bull lost his poise and turned aggressive.

Victor still respected Santos and ignored the bull's aggression.

But he felt sensations he didn't know. Lorenza spent more time beside him. His adoptive sister's presence now had a different effect. More heifers surrounded him. Lorenza dominated them and tried to possess him. Her behavior surprised Victor. He observed Esperanza closer. His surrogate mother didn't do this to her bull or to his other cows.

Victor's muscles grew. The growth arrived faster on his legs, back, neck, and shoulders. A precocious power forged his muscles and fought the currents when he swam. The hills shrank before his eyes. When he called, they yielded and echoed. His spell grew on his heifers, on the younger calves, and on the farm's other animals.

His relation with the biped mate deepened. Their games toughened and lasted longer. The sessions grew into mock combats. They bowed before and after. He discovered his playmate's strengths and weaknesses and then used them to win their games. He learned prudence and applied his force with caution. Unlike him on four legs, his playmate was less stable on two. If he charged with full force and used his shoulders, he toppled his mate and hurt him. He used his power on the billy goat and the ram if they challenged him. They left him alone.

Then his horns grew.

At first, they felt odd on his head; he didn't know what to do with them. If he imitated the bull's use of horns, he ended up with cuts and bumps on his forehead. Santos could no longer help him in his new encounters with Herman. Victor stood at a distance and observed the bull apply his horns on others. The real help came from his biped playmate and the blood-colored cape they used for their games.

His mate now changed this cape's use. If Victor didn't lower his head enough, his mate withdrew the cape and stood aside; Victor had to step back and change his charge for their game to continue. He grappled with his blind spots at the front that his mate didn't have. He used his horns with extra care because his mate now stood closer behind the cape. Once, he drew blood from his mate's thigh. He stopped their game and licked his mate's wound. His mate pushed his muzzle away and urged him to continue their play.

Victor understood his mate. Their art of war came with respect. Pleasure was its goal. Injuries, natural to this art, didn't hurt their friendship. They bowed to each other and resumed their game.

Over time, Victor discovered other frailties in bipeds: they couldn't see on their sides, and they couldn't turn their ears. These were serious drawbacks in a fight. He could surprise them from behind or take them from their sides. Bipeds' forelegs gripped and hurled things—acts he couldn't do—but he had weapons they didn't. Their hind legs did little more than carrying them around. Their feet, heads, and shoulders posed no danger for bulls.

Bipeds were harmless for bulls. They could only be friends.

By now, Victor's heifers had grown. Lorenza led them. The bull no longer bothered about this group. The new herd staked out a niche Lorenza liked and lived in harmony with the rest. Victor was learning new skills from his games with the biped mate. These lessons drew him more than the farm's other animals did. He didn't mind what the bull did with his herd, his cows, and their calves. Those adult affairs didn't concern an adolescent calf like him.

But he did care about his surrogate mother. Esperanza didn't let him approach her; Victor kept an eye on her from distance. This cow had fed him, licked him, and guarded him in his vulnerable days; her safety, security, and wellbeing were important to him. For the most part, Victor trusted Herman for these tasks, but the changing bull no longer cared about her.

Then her belly bulged. Her gait slowed. She spent her time sitting aside from Herman and his herd.

The bull's odor changed. From his withering coat, hair fell off in

103

patches. His aggression rose toward his herd. Several bipeds had to hold him down when Victor's playmate thrust a needle in his thigh. Those shots didn't help Herman. Esperanza grew worried about her bull. Victor could do nothing to help her.

One morning, the needle operation provoked the breakpoint.

The bull shook off the bipeds, flipped Victor's playmate, then ran around the farm and charged everyone. Esperanza rose to her feet and tried to calm Herman. The bull charged her too. She cried out in pain, and Santos couldn't help. She ran from the bull; the bull ran after her. Victor could no longer bear this. He approached the bull and tried to dissuade him. His intervention raised the bull's aggression. Herman left Esperanza and charged Victor.

Victor avoided Herman's charge, but he wasn't facing a biped; he was facing an animal similar to him, larger in size, which didn't have the bipeds' drawbacks. The only edge Victor had over this bull was his repertory of passes, the ones he had learned from his games with the biped mate. Victor now used those passes against Herman.

But his ruse didn't fool the bull. The more he escaped the bull's horns, the more the bull tried to get him. The chase continued around the pasture, sent the scared animals running and screaming, and drove Santos out of his wits. The dog gave up, sat on his haunches, and started howling. The thwarted bull slipped and fell. Victor could have gored Herman's eyes, but the bull was important to Esperanza and a benefactor to the farm's cows and calves. Victor didn't want this bull to suffer any more than what was peeling off his hair and changing his odor.

Besides, Victor was enjoying Herman's chase. Their game felt equal to equal.

The encounter produced thrills Victor never tasted with his biped mate. This new game aroused instincts he hadn't known so far. The bull used his horns with skill. Victor's deft passes didn't always spare him their slashes. But his wounds didn't hurt. Blood oozing from them reassured him. He saw he was robust and resilient to peril. For the first time in his life of two years, Victor felt he was living his elements. His biped mate, bleeding from the bull's horns and standing aside from the chase, confirmed this truth by an admiring gaze. Like him, his mate saw two quadrupeds of different size and experience reaching the same level.

The game tired out the ailing bull. His chase slowed and his moves shred power. The more he lost his coordination, the more energy he spent chasing Victor. Exhaustion overtook the bull. After six more rounds, Herman's legs buckled. The bull bellowed and collapsed. Esperanza walked to her male and licked his sweating coat. The fallen bull didn't resist her. The cow's soothing licks calmed her bull.

A new tongue licked Victor behind the ear.

He turned and saw Lorenza. The growing heifer had a glint in her eyes he hadn't seen until now. Unlike Esperanza, she didn't lick his wounds; she pressed her forehead against his, sniffed his muzzle, and stood at his side. Together, they watched his biped mate ignore his own bleeding wounds and help the exhausted bull recover. Santos stopped his whimpers and welcomed this emerging peace.

The winding down woke Victor's wounds. What didn't hurt during the fight spoke during the peace. Blood had stopped coming out of his cuts, but the raw skin tightened around them. His bruised muscles refused to move. He faced Lorenza and his other heifers. They all lumped into one. His muzzle tingled. The fence turned around him. Buzzing bees blurred his vision. He didn't understand

105

why this short chase had tired him more than his long swims in torpid water did. His legs, flanks, neck, and head shook. He lowered himself and sat on the grass.

The bipeds took him from the pasture and put him again on their front lawn. They cared for him until his wounds healed.

Then, one morning, they came with Santos, Lorenza, and his other heifers. They left the farm and took a mud trail Victor had seen before but never treaded. They proceeded in a file along the fence. Esperanza watched them from far. The bull, his other cows, and their calves ignored them. They turned the corner. The farm Victor knew stayed behind.

A lush pasture with new trees, bushes, and herbs refreshed his eyes. At this pasture's far corner, a home stood; it didn't look big and solid like the one on the other farm. Trees, lining this farm's fence, bent down and offered ripping fruit. The tilled earth held up flowers, plants, berries he didn't know. He heard sounds he knew. But the only living creature he saw on this farm was a heron by the pond. He couldn't figure the bird's emotion from far.

They reached the wooden gate and entered the farm. The heron didn't resist their entry or greet them. The tall-legged bird barely moved when the bipeds ushered the animals onto the pasture's virgin grass. It tilted its head at the approaching herd, opened and closed its long pointed beak, and then returned to watching the pond's inviting water. The heifers spread on the pasture and marked their territories. His biped mate stood beside him, watched the pond and a mound of stones piled on its far shore, then rubbed his coat and spoke in his ear.

Victor didn't know the words his mate spoke. But they moved his heart, slowed its beats, and raised his confidence. He understood his mate was putting him on an important piece of land and trusting him to guard it with his herd. The trust removed Victor's blues and lifted his spirit. He thanked his mate with a nudge from his muzzle. Santos acted edgy. The dog didn't seem reassured. Victor tried, but he couldn't restore his canine friend's poise.

The bipeds started leaving; Santos stayed. They asked the dog to come with them; Santos went back and forth. Victor understood his canine friend. Santos was now caught between the old farm and the new. His biped mate saw the dog's dilemma. He lowered his mouth, spoke in the dog's ear, and patted the troubled animal on the back. His touch and voice calmed Santos. The dog saw his new role and accepted it. He stood on surer feet and barked at Victor and his herd. The biped mate applauded Santos. The dog raised his head and tail and then followed the bipeds toward the other farm. Victor stood at his new farm's gate and watched them disappear down the trail. They didn't look back.

He heard Lorenza calling him from far. He turned his head toward her.

She was staking her territory by the stones piled above the pond. The heron watched her graceful moves. She finished, stopped moving, and waited for him. The heron caught a fish and then flew into the cottonwood tree's foliage. The other heifers found their places on the pasture and tasted its virgin grass and scented herbs. They already saw this farm as their new home.

Victor didn't feel hungry. He turned away from the gate, lifted his muzzle, and went toward Lorenza.

10

The April feria opened in San Taurino with more than usual fanfare.

Corrida's elevation in Spain injected fresh vigor into the bullfighting world. Taurine cities woke from their doubts, revamped their arenas, and multiplied their bullfights. Eight hundred thousand bulls gave their lives to this renewed vigor, in countries that still held their deaths as legal spectacles. Pro-bullfighters celebrated their victory and watched these shows in arenas or on television. Anti-bullfighters went home, lay low, and waited for their coup.

They didn't wait long. Their coup arrived when Europe halved bull ranches' subsidies.

Last year, while Spain raised corrida to a national monument, three Spanish Euro-deputies lobbied in Brussels: they claimed bull ranchers violated the Union's common agricultural policy, by inflicting unnecessary cruelties on their animals. Now, the same deputies revealed the sum going into promoting Europe's bullfights. Other deputies voted and cut subsidies.

Anti-bullfighters saw this cut as a major victory. They emerged, celebrated in streets, and clashed with pro-bullfighters and bull-ranchers crying for relief. The state gave more money to bull ranches. Cattle, dairy, livestock, grain, fruit, and vegetable farms received less. Their farmers poured into streets and protested. The state didn't help them.

The second coup arrived when an occult clique celebrated their saint-day in San Taurino by throwing cats from a building's tenth floor and watching whether these animals brought them luck by landing on four feet. Miguel published the story on his social network, laying the dead cats side-by-side on the pavement. Enraged cat-lovers rushed out and demanded punishment harsher than the law permitted. Their cries drowned pro- and anti-bullfighters; they returned home and watched these cat-lovers settle their accounts with the state.

The cat-lovers didn't get the public stage for long.

The third coup arrived when, during a cat-lovers' protest, an officer fired a lethal shot, killed a transient man's dog, and claimed his act as self-defense. A quiet procession, carrying the animal's corpse, started from the lieu and drew mad dog-lovers from their homes. Their rage filled streets, jammed squares, and sent the cat-lovers home. Pro- and anti-bullfighters avoided this mess around cats and dogs. They stayed indoors and waited for their turn.

Meanwhile, the three coups flooded the treasury of Miguel's foundation. He used this money to multiply his lawsuits against animal abusers; against cities and regions; against the state, for its leniency toward cruelty on animals. The city finally withdrew their charge against his foundation, for releasing a video two years ago and sinking its treasury into penury.

11

Stalled vehicles jammed the bridge's entry into the city. Ignaçio pulled to the shoulder, turned his car around, and took the alternate route to the university.

His classes were again cancelled. If these interruptions continued, his fourth year would never finish on time, and nobody knew how long his final year would take. No hospital or clinic could legally employ him before he received his official degree.

The veterinary school didn't close as an exception. The primary, the secondary, and the high schools closed without notice this spring. They couldn't pay their gas, electricity, and water bills. Libraries and sports centers had shut their doors long ago. Nuria no longer had to face any of this. Ignaçio circled the empty parking lot and then drove out of the campus.

None of this affected the Taurine Academy. Their lawns stayed busy.

He reached Plaza de Toreros. The square squirmed with the city's unpaid workers. Ines and her hospice's colleagues sat in front of the city hall, laying their placards on the paving stones; they looked tired of their slogans. Doctors, nurses, and paramedics huddled in groups and demanded their salaries; the state had not paid them in six months. Parents yelled about absent care from daycare centers. The diseased cried about their sick healthcare. The aged grieved for their dying retirements and for paying taxes on what little they received. All were angry about spending more and getting less for their money.

The police had barricaded the road to the bridge. Employees of the entire public transport network—boats, buses, trains, trams—walked the streets and blocked the city's traffic. Those who still had jobs couldn't reach their work this morning. Elena cleared the jammed road for two ambulances that took away the injured from a fight. Ignaçio waited in a side street, let the ambulances pass, and crawled on Avenida de Corrida for the alternate route.

His car crept before the city's arena. Angry drivers thrust their fists, blew their horns, and hollered at the vehicles ahead. Six double-decked coaches, parked on emergency blinkers in the avenue, unloaded taurine tourists, dressed sharp, yelling in English, and jostling toward the arena's gate. Six more coaches idled behind them, waiting for their turns to pour out.

Hired goons, dressed as civilians, guarded glossy cars, parked on sidewalks. Few bore native plates. Their owners briefed the journalists and ignored the citizens impatient to pass. Among these go-getters, Ignaçio recognized a few models, actors, singers, and entrepreneurs of international renown. These multi-millionaires always placed corrida at football's level and demanded more from matadors. They didn't come to arenas for bullfight's art. They came for cruel combat lessons they could take with them and apply on their peers. They spent without care, and they demanded servitude. The city ignored their debauchery. Merchants ate their insults and filled their demands.

Ignaçio looked at his watch. The arena's morning session would open in forty minutes. He pulled to the roadside and turned on his car's blinkers. He left his vehicle, wedged through the crowd, and entered the arena's souvenir shop.

He found the *estoque* at a bargain price. The fake aluminum sword, seized at the airport, had sustained some damage and found its way to this souvenir shop; it could serve those who didn't need their souvenirs to be perfect. He paid for the sword, brought it back to his

111

car, and hid it under the backseat from Nuria's eyes.

The coaches left. The traffic picked up. The bullring's president opened the *paseillo*.

The orchestra started. The arena's acoustics magnified the parade's pomp and hurled it over the arches. Ignaçio tailed the cars honking to the parade's rhythm. He inched through the jam behind the hospice, the arena, and the church. He merged into the traffic going east on the alternate route and sped out of the turbulent city seized by this taurine frenzy. The city stayed behind, but its clamor remained. The uproar calmed when he reached the hills, crossed their cavernous top, and started descending toward the southern farmers' valley.

A fire truck, blowing its sirens, came from the opposite direction. From the driver-side window, Vincente stretched out his arm and waved at him. Last winter, the barn's fire threw Jaime and Elena out of their attic. On the positive side, the city afterward offered Vincente a paid contract for his service. He would still live in the firefighters' barracks until he and Ines saved enough to move someplace. Jorge received nothing from the insurer to restore his barn and paid three times more after that fire. Willem seized this opportunity and raised his offer for the farm, but Jorge refused to sell. Life wasn't easy for anyone on this farm. Hard times bring the best in humans out. These farmers had proved that more than once.

Ignaçio slowed his car. Nuria was leaving in her service vehicle for work.

She called him and pulled to the side. Ignaçio stopped his car and got out. She descended from her van and kissed him on both cheeks. The strong perfume she now used failed to hide that odor; its trace remained in her whizzing breath. Their paths rarely crossed on their floor. She left before dawn and returned late. Her progressive decline worried him.

"Your school closed again?" she asked.

"Yes," Ignaçio said. "Only the Taurine Academy is open."

"Did you go to that academy?"

"Should I?"

"No," Nuria said. "Your show at the market hall touched me."

"You had time to watch?"

"You're meant for solos."

"Do you still enjoy dancing with me?"

"Nacho, please!"

"How's work?"

"I love it," Nuria said. "I get better everyday at avoiding laws."

"Don't be ironic."

"Willem pays me for that."

"Why don't you quit?"

"What will I do?"

"You passed the bar."

"The law firms don't pay enough."

"Are you working for Willem to cover the fire?"

"No."

"To pay for my studies?"

"No."

"Then why?"

"I don't know."

"Nuria." Ignaçio lifted her chin. "What are these blues for?"

"You."

"Pardon?"

"You worry me."

"Why?"

"For everything."

"Like what?"

"I don't know."

She averted her eyes and bit her lip. He tried to wrap his arm around her shoulders. She pushed him aside and walked away.

"Nuria."

"What?"

"It's not me alone," Ignaçio said. "We both have changed."

"I know."

"Our relation is changing."

"Yes."

"Do you want me to leave this farm?"

"No!"

"Nuria." Ignaçio stepped toward her. "I hurt to see you change like this."

"Then don't look."

"Will you quit working for Willem?"

"No."

"Why?"

"Stop."

"Why don't you let me work for him?"

"Go away!"

She wiped her eyes and climbed into her van. She closed the door and drove away without looking at him. Ignaçio watched her go, got into his car, and started the engine.

The jurist job took her self-esteem and distanced her from flamenco. She did those extra hours not just for money, but also to stay away from home, away from their floor. She wanted him to

114

dance with her but not look too close. The dilemma was tearing her apart. He could do little at this stage to pull her out of this mire. His solos now generated more cash to cover his expenses at her parents' farm, but not enough to lift her family's financial burden. Before he graduated and earned enough to relieve her load, she would sink to a depth beyond rescue.

He reached her parent's farm; the bitter taste remained in his mouth. He searched for Magdalena; the cat wasn't there. He called Santos; the dog didn't come. He looked for Victor and remembered the calf had left this farm. He stood on the pasture and watched life move in Jorge's farm. Every animal followed its course, did its chores, and paid him little attention. He could go from this farm today and nobody here would miss him tomorrow.

He left Jorge's farm and walked up the trail. He didn't know where he was going, but he needed to go somewhere. The farther he went, the closer Jorge's farm felt. Nuria's family bound him by their favor. His swelling needs devoured their shrinking means, as a cuckoo chick did in a swallow nest. The fire had tightened this family's financial squeeze. He would have to earn more money from his shows and help them restore the barn before autumn.

He couldn't accept how Nuria had changed in less than two years as a jurist. Each job has its pitfalls; she should know this by now. She knew what Charo sometimes did for her work. Nuria's change didn't come only from working in law; it also came from her parents' stress, their subsidy cuts, and his growing expense that her salary couldn't meet. She was defying her maximal limits and decaying to death. He could do little to help her now. If he left, he would at least take his pressure off them; at the same time, he would also add to their pain.

Only a year away from graduation, his situation symbolized

Spain's youths living with their guardians. There was no way out of this impasse. These youths didn't create this status quo; it descended on them from their ancestors. These youths held the power to change this system, but they first had to stand on their own feet. The only employer that helped them find their foothold was Willem's taurine empire. But Nuria was laying her life on his path to keep him away from that line of work, no matter what her job took from her.

Someone's gaze stopped him. He saw he was standing beside his parents' farm, and the eyes watching him belonged to Victor. The calf stood by the stones above the pond. Ignaçio called; Victor didn't come. Since the calf moved here with his heifers a month and a half ago, their cape game and swim sessions had ceased. These days, he found little time for Victor. The space between them was growing and filling with sorrow.

Their separation had grown the orphaned calf's pain. True, the mobile home stood at this farm's corner, but Elena left early and returned late, and this year, Jaime again waited tables for Willem to pay their mortgage. The calf, left on this desolate farm, had little contact with the humans he knew. Neither his heifers nor Santos could give him what he missed.

Ignaçio leaned on the farm's gate and watched Victor. The confrontation with the bull broke the calf's barrier. Since he moved to this farm with his herd, the six weeks had grown and matured him. Now he measured six feet from hooves to horns; his muscles and hump, double the size for his age. You could no longer call him a calf; he was already a young bull leading his own herd. Yet a distinctive trait separated him from the rest. That trait wasn't the glistening rolls of his firm dewlap that marked his father's race; that trait was his large black eyes and the soul they held. The harvester's

116

scar on his muzzle heightened their beauty.

This magnificent Victor was still his friend. This majestic animal now lived on his parents' farm. Nuria had promised this miraculous orphan a future home on her family's farm, and this magnanimous misfit had already found that promised home on his parents' land.

This land now belonged to him. He could build a shelter here and live with Victor; this place had everything for them. To live here, they would need nobody's favor. They would be close to the other farm; Nuria's family could come here and see them whenever they wanted. He wouldn't need much money to build a simple shelter on this land with no debts attached. He no longer had the money Nuria gave him for a new car. He had given that money to Jaime for fixing the old car. The couple needed to make down payment for their mobile home. Once he finished his final year and earned a decent salary, he could build his shelter here.

He could also buy this mobile home from Jaime and Elena later. They wouldn't live on his farm for ever; they would find another place and move on. Like Vincente, Elena could get a rent-controlled flat for her service. Jaime was scouting places for his mechanics shop. This couple had already found their bearings in this city. He could learn sustainable farming from Jaime and then continue after they left. His patience would benefit everyone.

The thought lightened his burden. He opened the gate and called Victor. The young bull came in his poised gait and determined steps. Ignaçio led him across the cliff-side road then down the steep trail onto the beach. Victor had heard the ocean but not seen it until now. The sinking sand raised his doubts. Every few steps, he stopped and hoofed. Soon he got this new terrain's feel and treaded with growing confidence. He lifted his muzzle, sniffed the salt and algae drifting in the air, then turned his ears to the ocean and listened to its subdued roar.

The water lapping the shore bothered Victor; he kept his hooves out. He walked along the border and sniffed the skimming foam. The mousse entered his nostrils and made him sneeze. He recoiled from the ripples, stopped at a distance, and gazed at the sandpipers scurrying by the water's edge after skipping insects.

Ignaçio undressed and entered the water. Victor lifted his head. His ears perked, but he didn't come. Ignaçio rolled on his back and swam from the shore. Victor stayed in place and kept his eyes on him. Ignaçio called. The young bull didn't venture into this water he didn't know. Ignaçio left him in peace. Now that Victor lived closer to the ocean than the river, he would come here more often, master this new water, and discover its surprises. They should have brought Santos along. The dog, too, had never seen the ocean, and he enjoyed swimming with his bovine friend. Since Victor left Jorge's farm, the two friends hadn't swum together.

The dense salt stung Ignaçio's back. The water thickened under him. He didn't have to swim to stay afloat. The growing cold seeped into his muscles and toned their nerves and fibers. The brine's iodine brightened his spirit. He lifted his head but didn't see Victor on the sand. The young bull must have gone bored, left the beach, and returned the way he came. The algae's smell retrieved souvenirs from his memory's mist. Ignaçio stopped swimming, sprawled his limbs, and watched seabirds circle above him and move toward the shore.

The birds' movement bothered Ignaçio. They didn't flap their wings or glide on the air. Yet their circular trajectories moved toward the shore. He realized what was happening with these birds. Their shifting toward the shore meant he was moving away from it. He

118

turned on his chest and saw he was caught in a current.

This wasn't a rip current he could escape by swimming parallel to the shore. He was in a marine current that was carrying him toward the large. He couldn't escape this current without leaving its corridor, and he couldn't see how wide this corridor was. He was already far from the shore. He didn't see any humans on the beach or on the cliffs; if there were, they wouldn't see him here. The current was pulling him fast. Even if they saw him, they could do little to help him now. He would have to find his own way out of this current.

No waves came from the large and pushed him toward the shore. He had to conserve his energy. He swam across the current's corridor, from one side to the other. The current still held him and carried him farther. He couldn't swim against this current. Without some help, he could do nothing. He stopped swimming, closed his eyes, and rolled on his back.

The situation didn't panic him. It was a natural way out of his impasse. He didn't provoke this end; if it came to him now, this must be the right time for him to go. Others would benefit from his departure. His testament willed his assets to Nuria. They would find that holographic will in his room and do the required. He wasn't leaving behind any debts for them to pay. His farm would pay his debt to her and to her family.

The ocean warmed to his thoughts. Its undulations rocked him like a child on its mother's lap. The soothing water sang in his ears and lulled him to sleep.

He tried to recall his days with his parents; those days hid behind time's haze. He tried to see his games with Nuria from their teenage days; those games faded behind a mist's veil. He tried to forget building a shelter on his farm and living there with Victor; the young bull shook his head and startled him. He had to live for Victor. He couldn't leave life now with his lame excuse. He turned on his chest and swam toward the shore. The relentless current held him.

Then the current started turning. He struggled to keep his head above the water, but its downward pull grew. Twice he choked under water. He managed to come up and breathe. The third pull sucked him deeper and kept him there. He stopped trying and accepted the defeat.

A dark silhouette approached him underwater. The fins swayed, the belly bulged, and the breath bellowed.

But this shark's speed didn't belong to its species.

As the animal neared, he discerned its four legs threshing like a galloping stallion's. He saw the dewlap's folds sway from the animal's thrusts. He recognized Victor's approaching neck, head, and shoulders. He stretched his arms and grabbed the young bull's hump.

Victor swam to the surface, raised his head above the water, and waited for his mate to catch his breath.

Then the power strokes started again and carried them toward the shore.

12

Angel stopped the video clip. These cameras weren't just high-tech; they also hid from the arena's public zone. That didn't surprise him. The videos wanted to show what happened to the bulls before and after corridas, outside spectators' view. What did surprise him was the time the investigators were taking to locate these cameras. The arena had seen the national police only once. The municipal police had no jurisdiction. Meanwhile, Miguel's clips were spreading the polemic's wildfire. The city had no choice but to wait.

Commotion rose again from Plaza de Toreros. Angel closed the square-side window, returned to his desk, and buried his face in his hands. The bull's suppressed moan from this morning's clip still rang in his ears. He wasn't just surprised by Miguel's videos; he was shocked by what they showed. This cruel treatment had happened at the arena he managed. This bull couldn't be the first to live this torture routine before and after the fight.

Angel replayed this morning's video and paused the clip. He still couldn't believe his eyes and ears. He leaned back in his chair, crossed his fingers, and strived to regain his bearings. He couldn't. The slaughtered animal lay on the screen and pumped blood in his temples. This bull had come from Rafaela's ranch. He didn't dare go and talk to her now. He knew what he would see on her face. She must be devastated. He left his seat, paced his office, and grappled with her cold wrath coming through the wall.

Lidia bulls' maltreatment before corrida was known in taurine circles.

After he renewed this arena's lease fifteen years ago, he took strict measures to ensure these bulls were treated with the care and respect they deserved. Now, these videos revealed facts that surpassed his imagination and silenced his indignation. Before he gave himself to anger, he should make sure these raw clips were real.

The sandman was real. The bull was real. The corral was real.

These videos were real.

He replayed the horn-shaving part from the first day's clip: the horn tips' filing was real, the bone marrow's removal was real, the horn ends' repacking was real. These sophisticated cameras, high resolution and hypersensitive, had picked up the right details at right moments. Miguel must have obtained them from his obscure connection in deep surveillance. They still lay in ambush at the arena. Nobody knew how many. The taurine shows couldn't reopen until the police found them. The officers were taking their time to search. At this month's end, the city wouldn't wait a day more to kick the association for the arena's rent, four months late.

Angel forced his eyes away from the screen. He resented Miguel. At the same time, he thanked this activist for his clips. The lidia bull symbolized masculinity. Man's sanctified adversary on equal footings. These bulls were to be fought on fair a ground and treated with dignity before, during, and after their corridas. The code stated this. Its rules applied as much to toreros as to bullrings' employees. The sandman, the slaughterer, and the vet—these three would immediately leave the arena. The city had suspended their jobs. They would never find work in another bullring. The corrida's president had revoked the bribing matador's trophies. He would now make sure this torero's title was stripped. Rafaela would haul the four of them to the court and place them at the foot of justice.

He replayed the second day's clip and fast-forwarded to the surgical operation. The gloved hands lifted the red rosette and the tricolor ribbon from the bull's shoulder, removed the pin that attached the ranch's emblem to the bull's coat, and thrust a three-inch harpoon end into the bull's nape. Its muscles convulsed. Its neck writhed. Its hump twitched. The bull roared, tossed its head, and swayed its horns. A sandbag hit the animal on the head and on the loin. The groan stopped. The bull passed out. The gloved hands pushed the double-barbed dart deeper into the fallen bull's neck. Blood streamed from the torn flesh and dripped onto the pen's soil. The gloved hands stitched the bleeding wound, covered the stitches with the ranch's logo, and removed the blood from the bull's coat.

The same gloved hands, on the third-day clip, stuffed cotton balls into the bull's ears, shoved wet tissues up its nostrils, and smeared petroleum jelly in its eyes. The clip's infra-red parts revealed that the bull, kept in the dark pen for three full days and nights, hadn't eaten, drunk, or slept a minute. The stimulants, shot at regular intervals on the bull's hindquarters, had ensured the animal never sat down.

Angel replayed the corrida's video. The bull's odd behavior in the arena now fit these clandestine clips. The brave bull fought the coward matador till the end, was dragged around the ring for its lap of honor, and then removed from the public view. The slaughterhouse's video showed a butcher's knife slitting the bull's throat. Its legs threshed, its head tossed. The animal, two chains still wrapped around its trunk and six *banderillas* still projecting from its flanks, rolled on the floor in a growing blood pool. The slaughterhouse couldn't have killed this bull in another way. They weren't equipped with legal instruments of painless killing. The bulls that entered their walls were supposed to be dead.

This wasn't just breaking bullfight's rules; this was an outright violation of its laws. An outrage on these animals' dignity. This was an assault on a sacred institution the citizens had enshrined by legislative polling. This sacrilege happened in a city whose taurine tradition had endured two thousand years; in an arena he took under his aegis a decade and a half ago and then revamped with care. He took out the coward matador's contract, crumpled it into a ball, and hurled it through the door.

Rafaela picked it up and entered his office.

She didn't look at him. The cold furor radiated from her eyelids. She threw the contract into the trash, opened the square-side window, and leaned on its ledge.

The swollen carotid throbbed on her glistening neck. This martial-art black-belt had little respect for toreros that didn't see the bull as their equal; she threw them out. She lifted these bulls and their beauty to divinity. She saw each bull's death as a magnificent tragedy for the man and a sacred sacrifice by the animal. This coward matador, desperate to rise and replace Julio, had slammed her faith and defiled her brand. No words could calm her woes.

A voice hooted from below. Rafaela shut the window and moved back. Angel checked the time: they should leave in fifteen minutes. He didn't want to cross this bristling sea of humans growing on the square. Diego tapped on the door and avoided looking at them. Rafaela glared at him. The sullen treasurer announced that Mayor José was on the line for them.

Angel picked up the call and turned on the speaker.

"I'm taking Miguel to court," the mayor said.

"For trespassing?" Angel asked.

"Yes."

"The police questioned him and let him go."

"They're on his side."

124

"Pardon?"

"Who do you think gave him those cameras?"

"No!" Angel said. "What proof do you have?"

"Don't quote me on that."

"You're stretching too far."

"I'm not," the mayor said. "I'm meeting Judge Emilio this afternoon."

"For the police?"

"No," the mayor said. "I'll get an arrest warrant for Miguel."

"Who says he placed the cameras there?"

"Have you seen his last video?"

"Those depress me."

"He has his tail caught now."

Angel hung up the call and opened the latest video. The forty-three-second clip showed two men leaving the bullpen's gate, cutting across the arena's sand, and climbing the stairs by the president's box. One of them was Miguel. A pull-down mask covered the other man's head and face. The two reached the landing above the ticket booths, opened the sliding glass door, and entered the hall. The clip ended at that point. From there, a staircase would lead them to the street; only a few employees had keys for that exit door.

"Miguel gave himself up," Angel said. "What is he trying to do?"

"Prove his authenticity."

"Pardon?"

"The press is questioning his videos."

"The law can now put him behind the bars."

"The court won't."

"Why?"

"Not after this polemic."

"You think the other man is from the police?"

"See the color of his trousers? His harness? His boots?" Rafaela said. "Who do you think those belong to?

"Firefighters."

"See my point?"

"No."

"You think Miguel can climb and install those cameras?"

"Okay, okay," Angel said. "But why would a firefighter help Miguel?"

"Why would the police give him those cameras?"

"Come on!"

"You think I'm joking?"

"Why did that firefighter go in wearing his uniform?"

"He's speaking for his colleagues."

"Why didn't they leave by the fire escape?"

"What do you think?"

"They're saying they have a key for that door."

"Good."

"No, Rafaela," Angel said. "This doesn't smell good."

"It could smell worse."

"Who gave them the key?"

"Are you asking me to find that out?"

"No, I will."

"Do it soon."

Rafaela left his office. Angel informed Diego they would go for a couple of hours. The treasurer carried blue-black pouches under his eyes; they didn't come from insomnia. Diego's stance on bullfighting was changing. Miguel's videos wouldn't reverse it. The forces of order were growing their opposition. Those who earned their salaries

126

from bullfight's money were sick of its mess. The videos showed their wish for this long-revered tradition.

Rafaela emerged from her office with her car key and purse. Angel took Willem's fax and the two farms' papers and then followed her measured steps down the creaking staircase.

Plaza de Toreros now stood quiet for its crowd. Differing groups assembled at different places. You could feel the calm before the storm: tight and tense. Those who calmed storms hadn't come this morning. From the throng near the fountain, a man nodded at them— a cop disguised as a civilian. This officer was hurt by Willem's thugs last summer.

But the officer didn't carry his firearm under his clothes. He wasn't here on duty. Angel checked the group's other members. None of them belonged to the police. All of them stood tormented. Angel nodded back at the officer and then moved on looking ahead.

Rafaela touched him on the arm and pointed her chin at the bullfighting bar. A man was leaving its terrace and rushing toward them. Angel recognized Ishmael. The regional paper's chief editor ran a column on bullfights and another on gossips. After Miguel's videos, Angel didn't want to meet this journalist. Shriveling subscriptions and dwindling ads were killing this paper and making its editors desperate. Aficionados got their news from social media. Gossipers got their juice from free tabloids. Even Willem had cut his budget for this paper. Angel wanted to rush, but Rafaela didn't change her gait.

They reached her car and opened its doors. The chief editor caught up with them and begged for a minute.

"Who are you pitching for today?" Angel asked. "The pro or the anti?"

"The pro," Ishmael said.

"For how long?"

"Don't know."

"Consider switching camp."

"Why?"

"Miguel has more money for ads."

"He doesn't need us."

"We don't either."

"Thanks," Ishmael said. "Will you take *one* question from me?"

"On what?"

"The treatment of bulls."

"Shoot."

"Does it fit El Codigo?"

"El Cossio."

"You're right."

"Do you have a copy of his treaties?"

"I do."

"Read it."

"Thank you," Ishmael said. "Do your people really treat—"

"Trust the videos."

"You agree then?"

"I'll fix it."

"You didn't know?"

"I promised one answer," Angel said. "I've given three."

"I see the Gold Lady in the driver's seat."

"This is her car."

"You don't drive?"

"No."

"The injury from the horns?"

"Yes."

"Does it also affect your relation with—"

"Stop!" Rafaela said. "You've asked enough."

"Have I?"

"Did anyone say you're a coward?"

"No."

"Stupid?"

"No."

"Boring?"

"No."

"I say you are."

"Which one?"

"All three."

"Thank you."

"You can go now."

13

Ignaçio took the pet owners' names and phone numbers and told them Carlota would call this afternoon. Today was a dog-day for dogs. He gave a painkiller shot to the Labrador carrying six *banderillas* on its back and then entered Carlota's office. She still haggled with Willem's publicist who came with a court order to euthanize her dog. The repeat offender, by nature a gentle breed, perked its ears, narrowed its pupils, and listened to their heated exchange.

"This dog doesn't need to die," Carlota said. "He needs to change owner."

"Pardon?" the woman said. "How dare you?"

"You stress him."

"What?"

"I'll call the judge."

"No!"

"Listen," Carlota said. "This dog doesn't deserve to die."

"He has caused me enough troubles."

"Do you take him out?"

"I have no time."

"See?" Carlota said. "Change your job."

"I can't."

"Pay someone to walk him."

"I've tried."

"Put him up for adoption."

"Nobody wants him."

Carlota asserted she wouldn't put this dog to sleep. She would write to the judge, get the sentence commuted to castration, and find someone to adopt this dog. She asked the owner to see a psychiatrist and get help if she didn't want to leave Willem. The publicist accused her of verbal assault, threatened legal action, and then dragged the confused dog out of her office.

Carlota received the Labrador and its owner. The colored frills of the harpoon-ended darts, folded at their joints and hanging from the dog's flanks, were soaked in blood. The painkiller shot hadn't killed the tormented animal's pain; the dog's owner was now in agony.

"Who did this to your dog?" Carlota asked.

"My son," the woman said.

"How old is he?"

"Nine years."

"Why didn't you bring him?"

"He's suffering."

"He should."

"They arrested his father."

The woman explained. Her ex-husband was the arena's vet. Miguel's videos had sent him behind the bars. She had little control over what he taught the boy on his days of guard. The brutal arrest had left her son disoriented. The aspiring torero had relieved his stress by playing with her dog. She didn't want her son to kill bulls or die in a bullring. She would now use Carlota's report to sever the boy's guard from his father. He was violent with their son.

The tortured dog required three more shots before the six banderillas could be removed from its flesh. The animal lost a liter and a half of blood. Its mutilated ligaments and tendons would never heal despite the stitches. Its sheared nerves would impede its vital functions and leave the animal dependent on its owner for life. The woman still wanted her dog.

The operation ended. Ignaçio helped the woman load the sleeping dog into her van and then returned to the clinic. They were about to close for lunch when an emaciated dog limped in through the open door and stood on three legs. No one followed this dog into the clinic.

Carlota froze in place. Ignaçio left the counter and kneeled before the dog. The animal blinked, ducked its head, and wagged its tail. It didn't lower its fourth leg. Ignaçio patted the dog's head with one hand and extended the other in front of its raised leg. The animal sniffed his hand and lowered its swollen paw on his palm. Its skeletal chest heaved to breathe.

The dog was running a fever. The animal's watering eyes and putrid breath warned Ignaçio. He lifted the suffering paw and examined underneath: a bone splinter, lodged in the crushed flesh, had started the gangrene. The injured ankle would have to go.

Ignaçio raised his eyes at Carlota. She was biting her lip.

"The poor animal can't wait," Carlota said. "Put him on the table."

"We should call his owner."

"Do you know his owner?"

"I don't," Ignaçio said. "If you want, I can look."

"Do you see a collar on him?"

"No."

"Which month are we in?"

"July."

"What happens to dogs in July and August?"

"Okay, okay," Ignaçio said. "But to walk in here like that, the dog must know this place. I can search your computer and see if someone—"

"I know every animal I treat."

"Then why did he come here?"

"What do you think?"

"Charo, please!"

"Shut your mouth and get him on the table."

The infected paw went. Ignaçio wrapped up the amputated leg and wondered what Carlota would now do with this handicapped dog. The abandoned animal must belong to this quarter. It must have seen other animals enter this clinic to know this place helped them. The dog's owner must have kicked it out before leaving for vacation. The animal must have stayed in this quarter because this was the only place it knew. The shelters for abandoned animals filled fast in summer. Even if they found this dog a place somewhere, the mutilated animal wouldn't survive a week. Ignaçio's appetite deserted him.

"Nacho," Carlota said. "How is Victor?"

"Two-thirds of the heifers are pregnant," Ignaçio said. "They'll birth this winter."

"He's doing his job then."

"We need equipment."

"Use Jorge's."

"We can't," Ignaçio said. "We do organic dairy."

"Who are 'we'?"

"Ines, Jaime, and me."

"Get your own equipment."

"We need money."

"Come on," Carlota said. "Were you three expecting Victor to wait until you buy your equipment?"

"No."

"Go, eat your lunch."

"I don't feel like eating."

"Then get out of here."

"You need me for that dog."

"I told you to leave."

Ignaçio disinfected his hands, changed his clothes, and left with his backpack.

Outside, the July sun bounced off the ragged grey paving stones and flared the tumbling buildings' peeling colors. As usual, the market street ignored the sorrow in Carlota's clinic and retained its gaiety. Since the city closed this street's traffic, the vibrant pedestrian life had returned to this ancient quarter and pushed its modern silence and solitude out. If you sought company, you found it here at all hours of day and night, from all ages and affiliations; you didn't wait long. This quarter gave its contagious care and compassion to anyone needy.

The street's oaks rattled. The palms and planes rustled. They muffled the city's clatter, softened its bustle, and slowed its breathing. A soothing breeze cooled the city's fever and condensed its breath on humans. Ignaçio wiped his face, nodded at the street hawkers, and shook their hands. At the street's mouth, the public bath shot sulfur spumes. They coiled above the heads surrounding the marble basin and wafted toward the market. San Taurino's suspension hadn't stopped these gamblers from betting on other taurine cities' corridas.

He reached the covered market. Its etched glass and iron latticework, its buzzing hall and humming crowd, its spilling shops and hailing merchants—they lifted San Taurino's citizens from their time and placed them in the epoch the structure was built. He navigated through the bursting stalls and the rushing shoppers. He smelled cherries, strawberries, and plums on one side; meat grilled with rosemary, sage, and thyme on the other. He emerged from the gyrating mass, drenched in sweat and ready to eat, and searched for a place to buy his lunch.

A female voice giggled above and shouted his name. Ignaçio stopped and looked up.

A rusted clothesline traversed the street from one window to another. The wire carried white cardboard boxes, tied with gold ribbons, from one girl to another. The girl on his left, wearing a low-neck blue blouse, sent him a flying kiss and pruned her lips. The girl on his right, wearing a blood-red maiden's dress, opened her arms and sang a love song. Ignaçio lowered his eyes and passed under the traveling line.

A spinning wreath flew at him and settled around his neck. It smelled of dry laurels and summer flowers. The street applauded. The windows ululated. The wreath's launcher moved forward and stood akimbo. Ignaçio tried to pass. She spread her arms and blocked his path.

"Pay your exit," she said.

"How much?" he asked.

"One sevillana."

"With you?"

"No."

"Your mother?"

"No."

"Your grandmother?"

"No."

"With whom then?"

"My sister."

"Why?"

"It's her birthday."

"Where's she?"

"Behind you."

Ignaçio turned. The sister grinned and lifted her hands. The other girl took his backpack, held it against her chest, and started a *palo*.

> *Your sorrow sings through my artery*
> *Come to me, I'll dance to your rhythm*
> *I can't feed on your leaves for eternity*
> *You're a tree that lives one autumn*

He danced with the birthday girl. She followed his footwork and mirrored his hand moves. The circle drew tighter and clapped to the palo.

> *Life is cruel, life is kind*
> *Open your eyes and raise your neck*
> *I can sail when the sea has no wind*
> *I'll stand storms when our ties break*

He raised her arm and twirled her around him. He rolled her on his back and flipped her above his head. He laid her on one shoulder and rolled her to the other. Applause soared, neighbors emerged, shoppers shouted. Hawkers forgot their stands and filmed the dance.

He hitched her up and launched her over his head. He spun around, caught her, and stood her on his knees. Cheers burst, ululates swelled. Bouquets flew and exploded. Blue, orange, red, and yellow petals covered their hair and clothes and then settled on the pavement.

> *Summer is here, winter comes later*
> *I'll recall our dance and heal my remorse*
> *Free your heart and give me life's water*
> *I'll treasure your gift and preserve its force*

Ignaçio let the reeling girl go. She sat on the street, covered her face, and quaked from laughs and tears. He rubbed her head, slung the backpack on his shoulders, and turned his back toward her. The circled opened and let him pass. The applause continued.

Near the hot spring, he smelled jasmine and saw he was still wearing the wreath. He took it off his neck and stopped in front of the basin. The betters paid him no attention. He hung the wreath on the infirmary's carriage door and saw in its corridor the ancient lady sitting with her two creels. She raised her eyes and gave him her toothless grin. He removed the wreath from the infirmary's knocker and placed it around her neck. She lifted a slice of tortilla from one basket and a box of paella from the other. He took out his wallet to pay. She shook her head and waved him off. He bowed to her and walked away.

He opened his car's door and sat inside to eat. The heat cooked him. He rolled down the windows, drove up Avenida de Corrida, and reached Plaza de Toreros. The teeming square buzzed with anti-bullfighting groups of different creeds. He didn't see Miguel or his followers among them. The police must have booked this pro-animalist. He broke the law. At the same time, he revealed the truth. This bull's torture, in the arena's obscurity, denied all measures of humanity. The cruelty discredited humans, destroyed civility, denigrated dignity.

But Miguel could have done better. Instead of posting those videos on the social network, he could have taken them to the authorities. They would have ignored his trespassing and done the necessary. His foundation would now need all the donations it received from those videos to save him from the law's grip.

Those videos divided this city. Anti-bullfighting sentiment wasn't

137

new among the forces of order—corridas always caused them headaches—but the videos also revealed the division among the arena's employees. In Nuria's family, the clips' revelations drew silence from Ines and Vincente, Elena and Jaime, and Paula. Only Jorge claimed bulls should reproduce, not fight or entertain humans, and then returned to watching bullfights on television.

His car inched with the traffic. On his left, the city's terrace was as usual taken by painters oblivious to all events. Beside them, both footpaths bristled with taurine tourists who couldn't get seats in other cities' bullrings. They wanted San Taurino's arena to open. Their insolence sent Nuria to hell. Her jurist job didn't spare her their threats.

He crossed the bridge on the Sangre de Toros River, drove up the hills' flanks, and felt his hunger's pangs. He pulled to the side, opened his car's doors, and savored the tortilla and the paella. Across the rust-colored river, on the city's southern edge, the arena slept with its gates closed while the frenzied tourists jammed the museum of taurine arts, the souvenir shop, and the tax-free luxury outlets that sold clothes, jewelry, and perfumes. Farther south, the rolling meadow glimpsed between the church's belfries and revealed the grazing *lidia* bulls.

He finished his food and walked to the cliff's edge. Below, on the river's opposite bank, the port's quarter slumbered. Its clients had packed and left for other taurine cities. The open shops, restaurants, and bars found no one to invite. This remodeled port depended on taurine tourists. Only the flamenco bar of Paloma and Juan had a few regulars on their patio.

The church's bell peeled thrice. He had two more hours before reporting at the hospital. He should go and see Victor. The rescue from the ocean had grown them both and drawn them closer. The rising demand from his internship and flamenco didn't leave them enough time together. He could give these two hours to Victor. That would do them good.

14

"Did you send them his revised offer?" Rafaela asked.

"Yesterday," Angel said.

"Have you called them?"

"No."

"How will they react?"

"How do I know?"

"Do we have to do this for Willem?"

"We aren't doing it for him."

"Why are we going then?"

"You forgot?"

"Yes," Rafaela said. "Sorry."

"Ignore those clips."

"The bull was mine."

"Justice is straightening the vet."

"Who straightens the slaughterhouse?"

"The mayor."

"Have you fired the sandman?"

"Rafaela," Angel said. "These people work for the city."

"Who stole the keys?"

"You think I know?"

"What do you know then?"

"Our association is heading for bankruptcy."

"We're trying to save it."

"Let's do that."

Their car left Plaza de Toreros, turned west on Avenida de Corrida, and cruised by the city's terrace overlooking the napping port, the sleeping estuary, and the slumbering ocean. Only the street artists ignored the July sun's midday scorch and painted the suspended city's desolate arena. Angel turned his face away from the painters and stared straight ahead.

On the avenue's other side, the luxury-good outlets sweated to meet their customers' nonstop flow. Miguel's videos had stopped the city's corridas and blessed these merchants. The suspension had exploded their business from taurine tourists waiting in this city for its arena to reopen. The extra shopping took their steam and reined in their violence.

Last year, corrida's coronation extended the bullfighting season by a month on each end and re-birthed these tax-free shops. Wealthy tourists kept them busy. This year, the region's unemployment fell two percentage points. These merchants now employed more citizens in spring, summer, and autumn. Only for the winter, their employees sought the state's aid. The regional legislature wanted to extend corrida into winter. If Pedro convinced his legislators, these shops would never close their doors and count on the state to pay their leases.

"Angel," Rafaela asked. "Will Ignaçio agree?"

"He refused before."

"For the performance too?"

"That I don't know."

"Why do we have to go through Paloma and Juan?"

"They represent him."

"Have you informed Willem of your plan?"

"No."

"Will his clients like this show?"

"We'll see."

"What if they ask for refund?"

141

"They have," Angel said. "William told me."

"He's eating the loss?"

"He can."

"We shouldn't lean on him."

"We don't."

"You think?" Rafaela sniffed. "Why are we pitching for him then?"

"The two farms will help our association."

"They'll serve Willem."

"His villas' clients will be ours."

"His bulls will threaten mine."

"Don't mix personal with professional."

"I'm not," Rafaela said. "If Willem raises bulls, he'll destroy bullfighting."

"We won't let him."

"Why are we going then?"

"Wait and see!"

"I don't understand you."

"Then don't try."

Rafaela shook her head and glared ahead. Angel understood her worries but didn't agree. If Willem bought cattle farms and converted them into bull ranches, more *lidia* bulls would come onto the market, but they wouldn't compete with hers; those who wanted her pure-bred bulls would continue to ask for her brand. The bullfighting magnate wouldn't raise his bulls for love; he would raise them for blood. His bulls would never replace hers.

True, their association's finance shouldn't depend on Willem's patronage. But he couldn't see how. The arena's prime seats cost at least two hundred euros. Those below the president's box and in the

VIP gallery cost three to six times more. After the financial crisis, the Spanish couldn't afford them. Those prices paid the city, the ranchers, and the matador's agents. Their bills didn't come cheap. The downturn had plunged rates, but the association's books couldn't refinance its mortgage. They would keep paying their high interest rate for the five remaining years unless the bank evicted them for not paying the last four installments.

Willem knew this fact. He used it. His grace didn't come free. He used his knowledge's lever to enter their association and enforce his rules. His bid for the flamenco bar, his offers for the two farms, his demand for a new matador of Esteban's breed before the running season ended—they signaled only the beginning. When it came to acquiring power and exercising it, this senior strategist knew how to play his patience game.

The car passed the thermal bath, reached the station, and parked at the port. Rafaela stayed inside the vehicle. Angel walked along the waterfront, reached the flamenco bar, and stood below its patio. Paloma saw him and squinted. She strutted into the bar and returned with Juan.

"This *tablao* isn't for sale," Juan said.

"I know," Angel said. "I don't work for Willem."

"What brings you here?"

"Can we go inside?"

"After you tell me."

Angel revealed his plan. The arena would stay closed for taurine shows until the police investigation completed, but it could hold other performances. He would replace each corrida by a flamenco show. He came to them because they were the region's best. He regretted the pressure Willem put on them. In his association's crisis, he counted on their collaboration.

"Flamenco for corrida?" Juan asked.

"Yes," Angel said. "Spain's equal legacies."

"The law doesn't see that way."

"Do you?"

"Ask Paloma."

"Then let me."

"Come in."

Juan escorted him to the counter. Paloma raised her chin and served him sherry. Juan drew her aside and whispered in her ear. She listened, nodded, and frowned. She grimaced, tossed her head, and flung her hand. She tapped Juan on the chest and pointed her index at his face.

Juan held his poise and listened to Paloma. Her glare cooled. Her face smoothed. She leaned on the counter and plunged into her thoughts. Juan didn't interrupt her. She lifted her head, ordered her man, and left the bar. Juan exhaled, poured a glass of wine, and returned.

"Ignaçio's solos may work," Juan said.

"It will," Angel said. "He has the *lidia* bull's poise, strength, and grace."

"And the energy."

"Can you get him to do this for us?"

"I've to ask him first."

"Will he agree?"

"We'll see."

Angel laid down his offer. The association's insurance covered eighty-five percent of the canceled bullfights' cost. He would give the couple the entire sum if they pulled him from this impasse. He would also make sure Willem didn't bug them further for their flamenco bar.

"I'll deal with Willem," Juan said. "Anything more?"

"No."

"How is Rafaela?"

"She's in her car."

"Why?"

"She didn't want to offend you."

"Tell her she can count on us."

"Thank you."

Juan confided that Ignaçio had little time for extra shows, but he would try his best to fit a few at the arena. Angel produced the contract. Juan pushed it aside and reminded him the heat was melting Rafaela in her car. He led Angel outside and shook his hand. They parted.

Angel walked by the port's bullfighting bar. The owner franchised it from Willem and drove a racing car. The man and his girlfriend smoked under the blazing sun; marijuana wafted in the stiff air. Their bar had no one else, inside or outside. No customers treaded the waterfront restaurants and shops. Their clients were raising hell in other taurine cities after San Taurino's suspension. Since the legislature passed the national-monument law, these cities had seen a six-fold rise of violence and violations that targeted their young adults and under-aged youths. The law enforcers didn't applaud the lawmakers for this sacrilege.

Angel reached Rafaela's car. She was on the phone. He waited until she finished her call and then sat in the passenger's seat.

"Will they do it?" Rafaela asked.

"They'll try."

"The money will save their bar."

"I hope."

"The court will protect them."

"Willem's goons won't."

"He already has troubles with the law."

The car left the port and reached the station. Passengers descending from the airport bus merged with travelers leaving the station. These tourists didn't bring taurine energy with them. Their arrival changed the city's face and renewed its soul. Only a week's suspension had pushed San Taurino back to where it stood a decade and a half ago when he arrived here. The car passed the poised tourists, turned left on Avenida de Corrida, and climbed uphill.

"Will Jorge agree to sell?" Rafaela asked.

"No."

"Then why go?"

"Why?" Angel said. "To stop Willem."

"How'll Jorge help?"

"Wait and see!"

"I don't understand you."

"Then don't try."

"Willem incorporated his matadors' club and agency," Rafaela said. "He's selling shares of both to his investors."

"Can you stop him?"

"No."

"Then why talk about it?"

"Angel," Rafaela said. "What's happening to you?"

"Get real."

"And take corrida for football?"

"We need a matador like Julio."

"There isn't one."

"Do you want me to return to the ring?"

"Can you?"

"Rafaela!"

"I regret saying that."

Her lips quivered. She squeezed the steering wheel and stared straight ahead. Veins throbbed on her temple; muscles stiffened on her jaw. He understood her frustration. Their association could do nothing to stop Willem from turning corrida's art into bloodbath.

The bullfight industrialist ranked matadors by profitability. His patronage placed Esteban-like brutes at the top and pushed other matadors to change their styles for money. If Willem acquired cattle farms and turned them into bull ranches, he would create crossbreeds to shed more blood. Other ranchers would take his money and produce his breeds; no one replaced their lost European subsidy.

Seventeen years ago, when he traded the suit of light for the suit of grey, he didn't know what he would discover in this business. The year before, his crippling accident had thrown him out of bullrings; joining this association reopened the only door for him to stay close to bullfighting. He didn't regret Rafaela's favor. He regretted this rising pressure that shrunk corrida's quality and tainted their relation. They could do little to stop this slaughter.

Rafaela did have a valid concern. Bullrings weren't slaughterhouses in the open. The bulls should preserve their race's grace; the matadors, their trade's pride. Their encounters should produce art, not just blood. Corrida was losing aesthetics to aggression. Bulls were turning into brutes; matadors, into murderers. If this became the norm, the taurine academies would change their curriculum and kill a millennial heritage.

Preserving financial independence was crucial. Replacing Julio was essential. He had no control over what Willem did elsewhere, but for San Taurino's arena, the matadors' agents signed their contracts with his association. In this symbolic city, he would never let another Esteban-like matador rob Julio's place.

The car turned left from Avenida de Corrida, crossed the bridge over the Sangre de Toros River, and climbed the northern hills' flanks. Rafaela shifted to a lower gear. The back of her hand pressed his thigh. She kept her hand on the gear-stick and drove with the other. He felt her remorse. He glanced at her; she looked ahead. The fault, by no means, was hers. He left his thigh against her hand and turned his face toward the window.

"Angel," Rafaela said. "I don't blame you for how the arena treated my bulls."

"I should have checked."

"You've fixed the problem."

"Not sure."

"Why?"

"The problem is Willem."

"Yes," Rafaela said. "But the solution isn't Miguel."

"His videos revealed."

"He broke laws."

"He thought we knew."

"He wanted attention."

"Attention brings money."

"Pedro will fix that flaw."

The car reached a plateau. Farms perched on the surrounding hills' slopes. These farmers didn't like bull ranchers. He didn't know how to approach Jorge, but he needed this southern farmer to stop Willem. Jorge had his clout in this valley. The man should be dealt with care. Angel asked Rafaela to pull to the side and let him out; he didn't want her to face Jorge.

15

Ignaçio wore his flat shoes, took the real cape and the fake sword, and shut his room's door. Across the corridor, Nuria's room waited with its door open; the arena's scandal kept her away most nights. He closed her door, picked up Magdalena, and went down the stairs. The wafting scent watered his mouth. Grilled almonds and hazelnuts, ripe apricots and peaches, warm cinnamon and licorice rose from the living room and lightened his mood.

He reached the den. Paula sat with Jorge at the dining table and shared a fruitcake.

"Juan called," Paula said.

"Why?" Ignaçio asked.

"He didn't say."

"I'll call him later."

"He said it was important."

"Then it isn't."

"What are you rushing for?"

"The hospital."

"With your cape and sword?"

"I have an appointment before."

"Don't take the cat with you."

"Victor doesn't like her."

Ignaçio put Magdalena down. The cat jumped on Paula's lap and mewed for the cake. He rubbed Jorge's head and kissed Paula's cheeks. She sliced the cake. Ignaçio picked two, held one in his mouth, and left with the other.

Outside, Santos waited by his car. Since the cattle went to the high pastures for summer, the dog had lost his job. Ignaçio sat him in the passenger's seat, threw the sword and the cape on the backseat, and offered him the other slice. The aging dog ate it from his hand. Ignaçio waited until Santos finished his part, revved the engine, and left with the dog.

Halfway up the caked mud trail, Santos barked. Nuria's service vehicle turned and rolled downhill. Ignaçio pulled to the side to let her pass; she stopped beside his car and lowered her window. Her breath smelled alcohol. Ignaçio averted his eyes and looked straight ahead.

"Santos is going to the hospital with you?" Nuria asked.

"No," Ignaçio said. "He's going to see Victor."

"With his cape and sword?"

"Right."

"How's life?"

"I was going to ask you that."

"Don't."

"Have they given you a decent room in their hotel?"

"I have what I need."

"Nuria."

"Yes!"

"Willem is devouring you alive."

"I'll see you later."

Nuria raised her window and drove down the trail. Ignaçio watched her car disappear in his rearview mirror and then continued up the trail toward his farm. On his right, the farm's fig trees bent over the barrier and vaunted their growing fruit. The passersby would eat them in September. Bees and wasps fought on the ripe apricots, plums, and peaches. They opened their hearts to anyone who dared their scents. Swifts and swallows, starlings and sparrows, jays and martins and squirrels ignored the invasive parrots and feasted on the bursting fruit.

Ignaçio parked the car at his farm's gate and let Santos out. The dog howled and swayed his hind. Victor stood erect and alert by the pond. His heifers lifted their heads and perked their ears. Ignaçio took the cape and the sword. The dog trotted toward the young bull.

Lorenza came and stood beside Victor. Other heifers surrounded them. Santos cleared the arena's center and placed the spectators around the ring. The heron, perched on its nest in the cottonwood tree, raised its head and rose to its feet. Santos climbed the stone pile and sat on his privileged post. The dog now wanted his preferred show.

Ignaçio held the cape and sword under his armpit, brought his feet together, and bowed before the heron. The bird clacked its beak and shook its head. Ignaçio took off his *montero*, dedicated the day's performance to the heron, and tossed the broad-brimmed hat toward the arena's center. The bird tilted its head and watched the hat land on its brim. Ignaçio circled the ring, finished toasting, and placed the sword at the cottonwood tree's foot.

He brought the cape to the center and faced Victor. The virile bull squared his shoulders, lifted his head, and held his dewlap still.

From his hooves to horns, Victor now measured six and a half feet and weighed twelve hundred ninety-eight pounds. At twenty-seven months, he was already this valley's legend, three to four years away from his full size. This farm's grass and herbs—tasty, nutritious, and abundant—hastened his development for now. After his heifers birthed their calves, this place would limit his growth. Next summer, he should move with his herd to a higher pasture.

They each bowed to the other and then started their performance.

152

Ignaçio held the cape to his side and invited Victor to charge. The confident bull roared and passed closer than usual. Ignaçio spun on the spot and switched the cape to the other side. Victor leaped at him, turned three times, and brushed past the cape.

Ole!

Ignaçio drew the cape closer and narrowed the *paso.* Victor spun faster and passed nearer. The turns quickened; the passes shortened; the gap closed. Victor matched the paso's rhythm, retained his poise and balance, and never brushed his mate. Lorenza mooed; Santos yowled.

Ole!

The bull's flare at blending agility, precision, and speed was becoming his niche.

Ignaçio kneeled on the ground and stretched the cape low. Victor lowered his head and charged. Ignaçio raised the cape and slid it from the bull's horns to the tail. Victor braked. Ignaçio leaped, flipped in the air, kneeled on his other knee, and stretched the cape. The bull turned and charged. Ignaçio hitched the cape and rotated it above them. The bull whooshed under. Ignaçio flung the cape, flipped to his right, and stood at the center. Victor reared up, caught the cape on his horns, turned a full circle in the air, and brought it to his mate.

The heron squawked; Santos barked.

Ole!

Ignaçio took the cape, held it at his waist, and stretched it to the right. Victor charged. Ignaçio spun the cape and flung it above them. As Victor passed under, Ignaçio flipped over the bull's back, caught the cape on the other side, and stretched it to his left. The bull hitched the cape, flung it higher, turned three full circles in the air, and then caught it on his horns.

153

Ole! Ole! Ole!

Ignaçio cart-wheeled to Victor, tucked the cape under his arm, and walked away.

Victor groaned: the bull didn't want this game to end. He followed his mate and nudged him from behind. Ignaçio left the cape by the sword and returned to the center. The heifers stirred, shuffled, and moved. Lorenza stood still and waited for the *desplante.*

Each performer stepped back from the other. Movements stopped, sounds ceased. Ignaçio kneeled before Victor. The bull lowered his muzzle. Lorenza raised her nose and heaved.

Ignaçio opened his shirt, thrust his chest out, and shouted for the climax. The bull pointed his horns and rushed straight at his mate. Ignaçio leaped and grabbed his horns. Victor tossed his head and hoisted his mate. Ignaçio soared above the bull and flipped thrice in the air. The bull turned. Ignaçio vaulted off Victor's back, spun around, and faced him.

Victor roared; Lorenza bellowed.

Ole!

The bull charged from the right. Ignaçio leaped from his left foot and kicked his right leg high. Victor passed under his thigh. Ignaçio spun on the spot, leaped from his right foot, and kicked his left leg high. Victor charged from behind, passed under his thigh, and spun at the front. Santos rose to his feet, pointed his snout at the sky, and bayed at the passing gulls.

Ole!

Ignaçio cart-wheeled around Victor, leaped over him, flipped forward and backward. The bull stood still. Ignaçio somersaulted—sprang, rose, spread his arms—then landed on his bent knees and bowed to the heron. Victor nudged him and pointed his muzzle at the

154

sword.

The bull wanted the finale.

Angel walked along the sheer cliffs and surveyed the surroundings.

To his left, a fog layer, as thick as the one covering his association's future, hid the Atlantic and forbade the flaming sun to touch its water. The thwarted flames turned on the hills to his right, flared them in burning colors, and scorched the cattle seeking refuge in the parched meadows. The rising heat drew the ocean's cool draft. A perfumed breeze descended from the hills and pushed his head above the anxiety's clouds. He could count on one finger his trips to this suburb in seventeen years, but now he saw why Rafaela took her Egyptian stallion to these hills two or three times a week. This panorama was the heaven for Zeus.

The panorama would also make the paradise for Willem's taurine clients. His proposed Gran Taurino Villas, an ambitious misfit for this stunning nature, would destroy its treasure. Angel hoped Mayor José wouldn't lose his head and grant Willem the permit for money.

From his right, a mud trail left the asphalt road and sloped down into the valley. At their intersection, a beaten-down car blocked the worn-out gate of an abandoned ranch gone wild. A new mobile home stood at this ranch's far right corner. On its left, a ruined home's stones piled above a reed-lined pond. In front of its gleaming water, under a blooming cottonwood tree, a herd of cows, calves, and heifers surrounded the young rancher, dressed in a flamenco shirt and matador's pants, and a black bovine creature whose dewlap's folds almost touched the ground. The rancher carried a red cape and an aluminum sword under his armpit.

He couldn't recall seeing a bovine animal like this one before.

Was it a buffalo?

No. The buffalo had neither a coat nor a dewlap. And their horns always curved over their heads. This bovine animal could be an exotic bull brought from Africa to mate with European cows. Young farmers into organic farming were now doing these crossbreeds in Spain. This rancher, in his eccentric outfit, fit that organic category. The young man wouldn't know this valley's traditional farmers from the South; he didn't belong to this suburb.

Angel crossed the road and peered into the valley. At the hills' feet, a stone breastwork shielded the cattle farms delineated by thick dark hedges. The sun's glare simmered their bare pastures. Their cattle grazed on the hills' naked slopes, searching for fodder, water, and shade. Despite its parched desolation, a sense of community reigned in this valley. Willem couldn't snatch these farms from these southerners, living here for six generations, and build his bull ranches. Besides, the *lidia* breed required strict measures to preserve their traits.

Angel returned to Rafaela's car, got in the vehicle, and told her they wouldn't meet Jorge for the two farms. She applauded his decision. She drove up and turned her car around. She frowned at the vehicle parked at the intersection, blocking the ranch's gate. She craned her neck above the ruined car, peered into the wild ranch, and pulled to the side of the trail.

"What are you doing?" Angel asked.

"You don't see?" she said. "That's him."

"Who?"

"Ignaçio."

"Under that tree?"

"Yes."

"Playing with those animals?"

"Yes!"

"Are you sure?"

"Do you watch his flamenco?"

"Do I have the time?"

"Then trust me."

They left her car and stood at the ranch's gate. Angel put on his shades, leaned on the top rail, and squinted at the game's participants above the pond.

Rafaela was right.

This young rancher, dressed in a dancer's shirt and torero's pants, was indeed Ignaçio. The last time he saw a performance by this flamenco miracle was five years ago when Ignaçio was a teen. Since then, his legend had grown with his spin. How this dancer could slow, stop, and speed on the ball of one foot—without putting down the other or moving his arms—had carried his reputation beyond Spain and established him as flamenco's emblem. At twenty-three or twenty-four, this Basque youth was the country's culture symbol around the globe.

But what he saw now wasn't just flamenco. This virile dancer— vivid, vigorous, and vibrant—borrowed leaps from ballet, turns from jazz, and flips and vaults from gymnastics. He fused those moves with corrida's *paso*s and passes. He used his choreography in this mock combat with that bovine creature and constituted his *pellizco*. This young Basque man, from his unique niche, would no doubt make up for the arena's lost bullfight shows.

"Did you see Ignaçio bow to his bull?" Rafaela asked.

"Is that a bull?"

"Look, the bull bowed back to him."

"You want matadors to bow to your bulls?"

"Corrida is a martial art."

"Your bulls won't bow back."

"They should," Rafaela said. "I'll now train them."

"Can we go back to the office?"

"Call him."

"For what?"

"You'll see."

She ignored his stare, pushed up her sunglasses, and watched the performance unfolding under the cottonwood tree.

Then he saw her reason. They could wait for Paloma and Juan. Or they could ask Ignaçio right here and now. Flamenco never happened in Spain's arenas. This could be the first time. Besides, this cape-and-sword game with that strange bull meant Ignaçio adored bullfighting. He might feel for their association's plight. They hadn't expected this result from their trip, but this was an outcome they couldn't throw.

This meeting of sheer chance had more to it. Since Julio died two years ago, the scout to replace him had produced no matador of his caliber. Meanwhile, Willem's pressure had turned corrida from an art show to a cruel throe. This flamenco star's covert desire they had stumbled upon this afternoon came to the bullfighting art as a thrust from the divine hand. Nobody would question Ignaçio's dance talent. His cape moves and passes with this bull revealed his skills in taurine art. If Ignaçio came on board, Julio would fade into history.

Angel stood tall and lifted his arm. He was about to call Ignaçio, when Rafaela's hand covered his mouth. She pulled down his arm. He turned and watched her. She ignored his gaze and looked straight ahead. Her cheeks lifted in a smile and her eyes beamed.

She never smiled this way. He returned to watching Ignaçio and

158

the bull.

Their game was shifting.

The heron squawked. The *faena* ended. Time had come for *el momento de la verdad*. Ignaçio marched to the cottonwood tree, fetched the cape and the sword from its base, and returned to the arena's center. Santos barked. The dog didn't call for their game. Ignaçio turned. A couple stood at his farm's gate and scanned its occupants.

Lorenza mooed. The pregnant heifer wanted the moment of truth. Younger calves moved back and bleated for the *suerte de muerte*.

Victor stood at the ring's edge. The young bull again wanted their luck of death to finish at the arena's center. This *al natural* exit broke his frontiers and offered their honored guests his bravery's full show. Victor's destiny was now confined to reproducing on this farm. This fake moment of truth was the closest this brave bull could get to a real bullfight's honor. He was justified in demanding this exit from his mate.

Ignaçio positioned himself at the ring's center. Sounds and movements stopped again. He pointed the sword to his right, stretched the cape to his left, then cried out and stepped toward Victor. The bull lowered his horns and charged. Ignaçio flung the cape, leaped above the bull and split his legs, and touched the sword's tip between the bull's shoulder blades.

Victor roared and passed under him.

Ole!

Ignaçio landed behind the bull, spun around, and stopped to watch. Victor leaped, caught the cape on his horns, and turned thrice in the air. Ignaçio ducked. The bull reared and leaped over him.

Ignaçio turned around and spun on the spot. Victor held the cape upright, danced to his left and right, and then ran around the ring performing *la rueda de vuelta*.

Ole!

Lorenza bellowed. Ignaçio carried the sword to the center and waited for Victor to finish his laps of honor.

Victor joined his mate. Ignaçio took the cape from his horns and tucked it with the sword. They stood side-by-side and bowed to the heron. The young bull, still excited from living his moment of truth, groaned and grew restless. Ignaçio rubbed Victor's dewlap and calmed the bull. Santos descended from his post, ended the show, and ushered the herd to their pasture.

A male voice, strident and resonant, shouted his name.

Ignaçio turned. The couple still stood at his farm's gate. The man lifted his arm and waved his hand. Ignaçio couldn't place them in his memory. He sent Victor to his herd and checked the time. He was scheduled to report at the hospital in thirty-five minutes. He folded the cape, held it with the sword under his armpit, and marched toward the couple.

What he saw ahead slowed his steps. The woman—streamlined fit and flaming blond—was the elite *rejoneadora* Rafaela, the former champion matadora on horseback. The man next to her—muscular, dark-haired, and fair-skinned—was the star matador Angel, retired from bullrings. Ignaçio couldn't figure what they were doing here at this hour. This valley's southern farmers didn't welcome their bullfighting association or their northern origin.

"We came to ask for a favor," Angel said.

"From me?" Ignaçio asked.

"For your solo."

"Where?"

"At the arena."

"It's closed."

"Not for flamenco."

Ignaçio scanned their faces. They seemed serious.

"You have to ask Juan," Ignaçio said.

"We did."

"Did he agree?"

"He'll confirm."

"Wait for him."

"Ignaçio."

"Juan is my agent."

Rafaela raised her chin at Victor. "Is that beautiful bull yours?"

"No," Ignaçio said. "It's Jorge's."

"What breed is he?"

"His father came from New Mexico."

"And the mother?"

"Spain."

"He has poise, power, and grace."

"He does."

Angel pointed to his cape and sword. "You seek the true?"

"No," Ignaçio said. "Not really."

"You should."

"Why?"

"You're better than good."

"I can't."

"Why?"

"I'll hurt someone."

"Someone close?"

"Yes."

"That's a pity."

"It is."

Ignaçio looked at Rafaela. She was watching Victor and his herd. Angel rubbed his neck and opened his mouth to speak; Rafaela reached out and pulled him by the arm. They moved back from his farm's gate and walked toward their car parked beside the trail. Ignaçio opened his car's door, threw the cape and the sword at the back, and sat in the driver's seat.

Inside their car, Angel spoke with Rafaela and shook his head.

Ignaçio started his car. Rafaela backed up their vehicle and stopped beside his car. From the passenger-side window, Angel stretched his arm and held out a business card.

"Keep this," Angel said.

"Why?" Ignaçio asked.

"How did your exams go?"

"They aren't finished yet."

"Call me after they are."

"For what?"

"Where's Jorge's farm?"

"At the end of this trail."

"Is he home?"

"Not sure."

"Good luck for your final year."

"Thanks."

"See you later."

Angel thrust the card into Ignaçio's hand. Their car rolled down the mud trail. Ignaçio watched them turn the corner and then stared at the stark business card. Its sober lettering marked only the name and the cell phone number of the bullfighting association's secretary. He shoved the card into the glove compartment and found his mobile phone there.

He pulled out his phone and dialed Juan's number.

16

The piercing light cut Victor's nap. The beam streamed from the biped couple's home. The female's silhouette crossed the window and left their sleeping room. One by one, the lights came on and put out his sleep. Victor rose to his feet and surveyed his herd.

His movements woke Lorenza. The pregnant cow struggled to rise; sleep held her down. He waited until she found her feet and then they left for a walk around the farm. Last night's agitation followed him. He couldn't see its source.

The pond's odor calmed him.

But its static water contained little surprise. Its depth didn't even submerge his full height. When he entered this reservoir, he ruined the heron's luck. He missed the river's turmoil and the ocean's rolls. He longed for his biped playmate to take him to the wild. The female owl screeched from the oak tree. The male owl hooted back from the mountains. Their calls woke the heron and stirred the other cows. Victor went to the pond, quenched his thirst, and joined his herd with Lorenza.

The female biped emerged from their home and fixed the holster on her belt. Her manners changed when she carried that weapon around her waist. Tonight, her male companion wasn't home, and she walked more with his gait. She reached her vehicle without looking at the farm or its animals. She spurted the vehicle's engine, revved it, and drove away along the ocean's front. The cows lowered their heads and returned to grazing. The dawn's rays peeked between the mountains and colored the clouds above the ocean in violet, orange, yellow, and red.

The rooster crowed on the other farm. Victor turned. The hills blocked the rising sun, but its beams shined their crests, reflected from the clouds, and lightened the forest that separated the two farms. Chatters, rasps, squeaks, and tweets filled the forest's canopy. Cries, crunches, groans, and swishes woke its undergrowth. Lives treaded with caution and crawled about with hesitation. A stiff breeze drifted from the ocean and silenced them.

Santos howled from the other farm. The dog's wary call drew the horse's nervous neigh. The donkey brayed and woke their chickens. The goats bleated, the pigs snorted. On that farm, Santos herded more animals than cows, but the bipeds there also mounted guard. On this farm, the bull herded cows and kept predators out. More of them came these days, and they weren't always lynxes. This farm's both bipeds cared little about these predators.

But this farm also had a lot to offer: its grass, herbs, and flowers; its fruit, vegetables, and berries; its trees, bushes, and reeds. If the dog tried them, he would know what he was missing and come here more often. He understood his canine friend's burden. Santos had his duty for the other farm, had to split his time between the two, and couldn't always be with his bovine friend. The dog trusted Victor's herd to give him company. That was reasonable.

Yet bovine friends don't always suffice. An active bull needs more to stay busy. Not much happened on this farm. His canine friend knew this and didn't come often. Victor reached a bunch of ripening grapes and saw a spinning spider freeze on its web. He left that bunch to the panicked insect, walked to the farm's fence by the trail, and waited there for the car.

An odd biped appeared in the trail's dark and approached the farm's fence. Victor strained his eyes but couldn't recognize this stranger. He sniffed the air: the biped smelled male. The biped saw him and stopped. He held a lasso in one hand and a club in the other. Victor moved closer and scanned the biped. He didn't like what he saw. He rumbled and swayed his horns. The odd biped didn't leave. Victor stayed at the farm's limit and warned his cows.

Muffled cracks came up the trail. The strange biped rushed into a thicket and merged into its mass. A shining van emerged from the dark. The other farm's young female biped drove up the trail and passed by him, leaning forward, looking ahead, and talking to herself. Her new odor, of fermenting fodder and aging molasses, lingered after the burning gas.

Victor sighed. After he moved to this farm, she came only once. She talked to the biped couple that lived here, glanced at him and his biped mate at their game, and then left without waiting for them to finish. She wore dark rings around her eyes, like the raccoon that drank from the pond at night. Her chin, jaws, and cheek bones sank in her swollen face, now round like the owl's. She didn't seem at ease on this farm, neither with herself nor with anyone.

Victor waited by the barrier. The odd biped didn't emerge from the bush. He turned to join his herd. Another vehicle sputtered up the trail. He knew its sound. It approached fast. He rushed, thrust his neck out, and turned his head toward the car. The vehicle sped by blowing its fumes. His playmate didn't wave or look at him. Victor recoiled from the fence and ran toward the gate. His mate didn't stop there. The car turned on the ocean-side road, followed the young female biped's vehicle, and left behind its coiling smoke. Victor stood at the gate, watched the smoke clear, then lowered his head and ears and trudged toward the pond.

He had to be patient. His playmate might stop by this evening for their game.

The heron stood still at its spot among the reeds. This patient bird had no problem waiting daily. He should learn patience from this heron. For this bird, rewards came few and far; when they did, they thrilled. The rescue from the ocean had grown him and his mate. Their games had evolved with them. Their sessions now resembled combats, yet the tact they used forged their trust. They tricked, tripped, toppled, and tumbled. His mate stabbed him with the metal bar. He lifted his mate on his horns, flung him, and then watched him flip head-over-heels and land on his two feet. From his playmate, he learned to dance; to twist and turn; to leap, spin, and land. But he couldn't keel head-over-hooves; his mate still had an edge on this one.

Now every session drew some blood. They ignored their hurts, bowed to each other, and resumed their combat. The thrill renewed their relation and reinforced it further. Their game descended them into their deeper depths. When they rose, they weren't the same.

The heron squawked.

A vehicle groaned near the farm's gate. Victor turned and pricked up his ears. A van for transporting steers backed up and stopped against the gate's rails. There were no steers to be lifted from this farm. Lorenza came and stood at his side. The other cows turned and pointed their muzzles.

The heron squawked twice. Santos barked.

A smaller vehicle descended from the ocean-side road, stopped beside the larger one, and blocked the trail. Six bipeds descended from the two vehicles. They scanned the farm and its surroundings. Victor recognized the strange biped with the lasso and the club; he didn't know the others. He gathered his herd and pushed them backward. Lorenza held her ground beside him. Three bipeds forced

167

the gate. The other three returned and entered their vehicles.

The heron squawked thrice. Santos bayed and left the other farm.

The gate gave away. The odd biped returned to the larger vehicle, released the hasp on its backdoor, and opened its panels. He threw the lasso inside, pulled out a pole, and held it in his other hand. The pole's triangular top, narrowed to a pointed tip, shined in the dawn. His mates climbed into the vehicle and lowered a machine used for transferring bales. The strange biped kept the club and gave the pole to one mate. His other mate mounted the machine and rolled it to the gate. The three bipeds entered the farm and came toward Lorenza and him.

The heron squawked nonstop. Santos barked and rushed through the forest.

Victor nudged Lorenza and reminded her of the life growing in her womb. The fearless cow ignored his warning, tossed her head, and charged at the intruders. Victor ran after her. Lorenza reached them before him. The odd biped swung the club and aimed it at Lorenza's head. Victor leaped in between and took the blow on his hump.

The impact flung the club off the odd biped's hands. Victor thrust him on the shoulder, threw him onto the ground, and pressed him down with his horns. The fallen biped labored to breathe. His reddening eyes pleaded. Victor released the pressure and stood over him.

Santos galloped across the pasture. His ears bled; bloodspots covered his fur. The dog circled Lorenza and barked. The stubborn cow didn't step back. She lowered her horns and pointed them at the dog. Victor left the bipeds, ran to Lorenza and Santos, and helped the dog push the pregnant cow back to their herd.

A metal tip pierced his skull's base. Victor shook his head; the tip dug deeper into his flesh. The sting numbed his face and blurred his eyes. His playmate never picked him at this place. His instincts told him this spot was vital. Further digging would leave him permanent damage. He rolled his eyes to the side and saw the hand that held the pole. The odd biped's watering eyes glittered. His face hardened. His crooked smile constricted his pupils.

Victor saw his mistake in turning his back to these bipeds. He stood still. The metal tip didn't dig deeper. A needle pinched him at the shoulder on the other side. He rolled his eyes to that side. A pair of hands pulled back a syringe larger than the ones he knew. The needle's shot fluttered his heart, slowed his breathing, and reeled his head. His muzzle lowered. The metal tip withdrew from his skull's base. His knees buckled, his legs gave away. He collapsed to the ground and struggled to raise his head. His eyelids drooped. He heard Santos's barks, but he could no longer see what the dog was doing with the cows.

The machine reached him. Its forks slid under him, lifted him off the ground, and moved him away from his herd. He tried to turn his head; his neck didn't move. The machine carried him toward the gate. Lorenza bellowed behind him. Her hooves rushed toward them. He hung his neck and strained his eyes. The strange biped raised the pole and aimed its tip at Lorenza. The desperate dog ran after the belligerent cow. Victor regretted sparing this crooked biped from his horns. He strived to rise. His attempts failed. He groaned at the merciless biped.

Santos howled in despair. The heron squawked and assured the dog. The bird's calls came closer and grew sharper. Its wings flapped harder and faster. Lorenza braked. The cruel biped forged ahead. The heron swooped down. Before the metal tip hit Lorenza at the chest, the bird slammed into the biped and struck him on the face.

The pole dropped from the biped's hands. He covered his face and fell to the ground. The heron's wings slapped him; its claws scratched him; its beak pecked his head. Another biped lifted the pole. The heron flew and chased him. Santos circled Lorenza and barked nonstop. This time, the cow didn't resist the dog. She recoiled, stood aside, and trusted Santos.

The machine crossed the gate and carried Victor to the larger vehicle. It hoisted him and loaded him into the vehicle's back. He heard two more bipeds at its front. The loading biped descended, shut the backdoor's panels, and latched its hasp. Santos barked at him. The biped ignored and climbed at the front. The vehicle fired its engine and rolled away from the gate.

Santos bayed and circled the vehicle. The bipeds maneuvered it through his barks and turned on the ocean-side road. Santos ran after them and howled. The vehicle sped. The dog jumped onto its back and bit the door's hasp. The vehicle ran faster. The relentless dog held onto the hasp and scratched the vehicle's door.

The vehicle braked, jerked, and leaped forward. Santos fell off and hit the pavement.

The thwarted dog yipped, yelped, and yapped. The vehicle revved and sped away. The dog's barks faded into whimpers. Another vehicle rushed from behind and screamed at the fallen dog. Victor strained his neck, raised his head, and perked his ears. The vehicle behind roared, honked, screeched, and drowned the dog's cries.

Victor closed his eyes and pricked up his ears. No more sound came from his canine friend.

Victor lowered his head, rolled on his flank, and stretched his legs.

"Your internship requirements are finished," The vet-in-charge signed the release certificate and gave it to Ignaçio. "Have you chosen your final-year thesis?"

"Not yet," Ignaçio said. "Charo has talked to me."

"I saw her testify before the legislature."

"She's hot for company animals."

"She's reasonable."

"You know what she's after now?"

"The fighting bulls," the doctor said. "Excellent topic for your thesis."

"Are you serious?" Ignaçio said. "She claims they're farm animals!"

"They are."

"You believe that?"

"Sure."

"Then you, too, are crazy."

The doctor ignored the jab. He proclaimed the *lidia* bull might have descended from a savage breed that roamed the Iberian Peninsula in another epoch, but since then, humans had captured them, re-engineered them, and bred them in captivity for centuries. No wild streaks were left in their genes. Like all other herbivorous animals, these bulls could survive in nature without humans, but that trait alone didn't label them as wild. They weren't averse to humans. Carlota was revving her research to prove this fact. He agreed with her claim.

"Pair up with her," the doctor said. "She's solid."

"I've to leave."

"You know Europe slashed the bull ranches' subsidies?"

"They should," Ignaçio said. "Those bulls aren't farm animals."

"The Union didn't cut for that reason," the vet said. "They cut for the cruelty committed on these bulls, in the arenas and on the ranches."

"I'll go now."

"Talk to Carlota."

"I have."

"Her investigation is worthy."

"Let me decide."

Ignaçio took his internship certificate, left the hospital, and drove out of the parking lot. He disagreed with the vet-in-charge. The Union was right to cut subsidies, but the reasons they gave were wrong. These bulls were still savage. Their breeding and rearing, according to *The Treaties*, guaranteed this trait. Europe's common codes for treating farm animals didn't apply to this breed. He passed the campus's main gate. August's taurine fair still jammed the city's arteries. Time pressed him for the port. He drove toward the interchange. He paid toll and headed north on Madrid-San Taurino highway.

The debate on farm animals versus fighting bulls wasn't new. Their plights competed in all human courts. The battle always centered on who suffered more and ended in the same quagmire. If Charo planned to improve the fighting bulls' luck by classifying them as farm animals, she ignored what the farm animals went through. The fighting bulls at least got four free years to roam and feed in nature before dying a glorious death in bullrings.

The status quo's essence was this: All animals suffered in human hands.

173

Even the animals of company. He saw this everyday, at the hospital and at Charo's clinic. Dogs in therapy demonstrated their owners. No animals were left wild anywhere in the world, not just in Europe; humans had stripped all animals of their wilderness by changing their natural habits and habitats. The vet-in-charge might be right about re-engineering the *lidia* breed for bullfights, but these bulls faced no more or no less constraints than all other animals that served humans. Animals today depended on humans to live. Our species had constrained them to extract servitude. Charo didn't need her high-flying research to show this truth.

The port's parking lot was seized by valets and chauffeurs. Ignaçio parked illegally on a side street and then squeezed through the loitering crowd killing time on the waterfront before their session at the arena. The bullfighting bar spilled its adrenaline addicts onto the street's cobblestones. Some sweated in fake matador's suits and real tuxedos on the sidewalk; others smoked marijuana and cooled their heat under August's midday sun. The girl who quit the veterinary school two years ago owned this lucrative bar with her partner now. She noticed him coming, greeted him with a polite smile, and settled accounts with her clients.

Ignaçio reached the *tablao*. Heads turned on the flamenco bar's patio. Mouths stopped eating and talking. His two weeks' dance solos at the arena now brought Paloma and Juan taurine clients, but he wasn't expecting them here after the suspension ended. The last four weeks had revived the city's corrida. The journalist who covered the arena's flamenco solos lifted his arm and left his table. Paloma pushed Ishmael back and hurried toward him.

"You're late," she said.

"I got busy."

"Have you eaten?"

"No."

"You must be hungry."

"I'm not."

"Then eat something."

Juan saw him from the counter and took out his books. Paloma slapped him on the wrist and shoved away the books. She led Ignaçio to the back, ushered him into their office, and asked him to stay there. She went out and shut the door.

Ignaçio washed his face and neck at the basin. He sat in the new chair at their old desk and observed the remodeled room's renewed furniture. The walls smelled fresh paint. The ceiling hung new fixtures. On the floor, crisp terracotta tiles surrounded their refurbished Andalusian mosaic. A panoramic painting of their southern landscape stood above the restored mantel.

Paloma entered. She held a summer salad and a water pitcher.

"When were these done?" Ignaçio asked.

"Last week."

"Did Willem send someone?"

"He came."

"And?"

"Left."

She placed his food on the desk, stood aside, and fanned herself.

"The *farruca* ran hot in the bullring," Paloma said.

"They loved the cape."

"Forget Nuria."

"Pardon?"

"She's your woman," Paloma said. "But not for dancing."

"Stop."

175

"Nacho, listen to me."

"Then don't talk nonsense."

"For now, leave Nuria aside."

"She has no time."

"Farruca is male."

"Farruca is solo."

"You're better off alone."

"That I agree."

Juan thumped on the door. "Are you done with your son?"

"Not yet," Paloma said. "Who told you to barge in?"

"Who looks after the bar?"

"What are you doing?"

"Who serves the tables?"

"Have you paid Nacho?"

"Did you let me?"

"Do now."

"Thank you."

Paloma left. Juan opened his books and laid out the accounts. The two weeks' net from the arena alone exceeded last full year's by four times and a half. The *tablao*'s share would silence Willem for the couple's life. Ignaçio signed the papers and savored this moment of truth. Paloma returned with a coffee and gave the cup to him.

"Are you done with Nacho?" she asked.

"Yes."

"Go, defend the bar."

"From Willem's people?"

"The press!"

"What do they want?"

"Nacho."

176

"I leave him to you."

Paloma dodged Ishmael. She escorted Ignaçio to his car, kissed him on the cheeks, and sent him away with a slap on his hindquarters. She waited until he drove away from the port, passed the station, and turned on Avenida de Corrida. The taurine crowd, in varying states of sobriety, lumbered up the avenue for their afternoon session. He wanted to take Victor and Santos out for a swim before high tides covered the beaches this afternoon, but he couldn't drive quicker through this parade's floats. He switched to a lower gear and leaned back.

This morning, when he was leaving for work, he saw Victor's head poking over his farm's fence; he didn't have time to stop and talk to the bull. The rescue from the ocean had grown Victor into a full-blown bull—poised, patient, and potent. Other than impregnating his cows and protecting his herd, this virile animal found few outlets for his exceptional strength and energy on this farm. Their games and swims removed Victor's ruts. They broke his barriers, opened his horizon, and stretched his limits. For these, the bull needed his mate.

His extras at the arena had helped a few and hurt this bull. Both his internships were now finished. Two more weeks remained before his final year started. He would spend more time with Victor and compensate for his loss. He would also tend the vegetable patches and the fruit orchards on his farm; the taurine tours left Jaime little time for them.

His car inched past the thermal bath and crawled by the city's terrace. He picked up the papers from Juan and held them on the steering wheel. He still couldn't believe the amount marked for bank transfer, but he was relieved to see the flamenco bar freed from Willem's grip. This *tablao* was Paloma and Juan's lifeblood.

177

Flamenco was their religion. The couple had come a long way since they started their career in the South. Their life still centered on this performance art they cherished and nourished. Paloma was right on *farruca*'s appeal to taurine tourists, but she failed to see the vital: this flamenco's style suited him the best.

Farruca was special to Spain. People from the South built it for those they loved in the North; you could see that love in how its *pasos* fit its *palos*. Corrida divided the country; farruca united it. What Ramon and Francisco started in the South, Antonio and Molenito carried to the North and spread beyond Spain. He saw this unity in how Angel and Rafaela connected with Juan and Paloma at the arena—before, during, and after his farruca solos.

He loved farruca: it breathed freedom.

Freedom to move, freedom to show, freedom to tell.

No other flamenco style evoked this liberty. Its lyrics, rhythms, and tones thrilled his blood. Its poses, bursts, and pauses freed his spirit. Its crests, troughs, and craters poised his heart and silenced his soul. The jumps, the turns, the twists, the flips, the spins—they drained his energy, nourished his whole, filled his nerves, muscles, and sinews with the new. Each performance grew him, in a way he couldn't tell. He saw this growth in how his handwork, footwork, and face work changed during the show. The audience grew with him. He felt their growth in how they connected with his farruca. They took his affinity and made it theirs.

Farruca wasn't meant to be male; farruca was meant to be solo. It took the man and the woman in a human, united the two, and then put the union out. It permitted expressions one gender denied the other. It took moves from one gender and fit the other. It allowed intensity, inventions, and interjections that united both. A woman could wear a man's pants, perform the dance, and stay a woman. In this integration, complicity ruled over competition.

Nuria wasn't cut for this unity. She needed a man to balance the woman in her. And that complicated matters by mixing feelings. You can't stay a brother and furnish a lover; you have to choose. True, they lived under the same roof as siblings and shared the same parents, but the dance drew them closer than they thought; they knew they weren't related by blood. The conflict hurt both. Their dance revealed that hurt. It stuck them in an impasse.

The jurist job's demand had removed Nuria from their dance shows. Their separation now forced him to go solo. Leaving their home would help them, but his final year's load wouldn't permit his move. His solos' money would restore their barn and buy the dairy equipment for his farm. He would also need money to buy Charo's clinic next year. If he didn't want to live on Nuria's floor, he could buy Jaime and Elena's mobile home after they left this winter for their rent-controlled apartment in the city. Until then, he needed to save money.

He drove east along the city's terrace. Since the arena reopened for bullfights four weeks ago, Avenida de Corrida had stayed jammed in varying degrees from anti-bullfighting moves of different sorts; the city's force couldn't keep this thoroughfare clear. Demonstrations mired Plaza de Toreros. Miguel's partisans weren't there on this square. No more videos came from his foundation. The activist must be lying low to avoid the justice. Ignaçio turned north from the avenue, crossed the river's bridge guarded by Willem's private security force, and started his climb along the hills' flanks.

He returned to his solos at the arena.

The two weeks had confirmed his flair for farruca and revealed something he didn't know: the oval ring confined its performers. Its soaring walls and arching vaults, its sloping galleries and shouting spectators, its shining barrier and circling rails—they impressed when you were outside and intimidated when inside. They suffocated you when you stood at the ring's center. You couldn't leave the place; there was no escape route. After the solos ended, when Angel pushed him to join San Taurino's bullfighting academy, he couldn't say yes.

He couldn't see himself fighting a bull in that ring. He couldn't see Victor in that bullring fighting a human. They were freer on his farm with their simulated corridas. Corrida was art; so was flamenco. Victor's reproductive mark stood above the region's bulls'. They both fared better outside bullrings. Fate's turns were revealing this truth.

Nuria would be relieved to know this shift of his view.

The thought lightened his heart and lifted his spirit. He trolled a *buleriá* tune and whistled along. The financial problem was now solved. Jaime and he could build that shed on his farm and get their dairy equipment before Victor's cows birthed. They would trust this line to Ines; the woman had knack for dairy. His solos' funds would help everyone. He would finish his school, take Charo's clinic, and continue his farruca shows. She would surely replace him at the clinic when he left for tours. He would go with her for his final-year thesis.

He saw Santos on the pavement and pressed the brake. The car screeched, skidded, and groaned. Santos lifted his neck, turned his head, but didn't move. He couldn't see what the dog was doing there, sitting in the middle of the road, and turning his back toward the farm. Ignaçio pulled to the side, stopped the car, and ran toward Santos.

Santos rose on three legs and folded the fourth. Ignaçio could see bloodspots on the dog's fur and the tear marks on his muzzle. He

180

reached Santos, lifted the dog off the pavement, and examined the folded leg. The dog turned his muzzle toward the farm and emitted a mournful howl. Ignaçio understood Santos. He carried the wounded dog toward his farm.

The farm's gate stood ajar. A heavy vehicle's tires marked their ruts on the soil. At two different spots, dried blood patches stained the scorched grass. The stains' colors and textures confirmed they didn't come from the same animal. Signs of struggle lay scattered around the area. Two animals had left this farm against their will; he knew at least one. Ignaçio returned to his car, pulled out his cell phone, and left a message for Elena.

He sat Santos near the gate and went farther inside the farm. Lorenza confirmed his fear. The lead cow waited by the pond and stared at the gate. The sorrow in her eyes revealed what she knew: her male would not return. The other cows spread around the pasture and stood in different states of disarray and despair. Ignaçio checked them one by one, counted one heifer missing, and found the rebel behind the mobile home. Her smell and gestures announced her pregnancy; before leaving, the bull had completed his work.

The other stain might have come from Santos. He returned to the dog and rechecked his wounds: the blood didn't come from him. He went to the trampled grass and pored over the two blood patches. One looked thicker than the other; he couldn't tell if it came from Victor. He was no longer sure of the two blood stains. They might have come from—

His cell phone rang; he answered without checking the caller.

"Nacho," Nuria said. "Are you all right?"

"Elena told you?"

"Yes."

"What else she said?"

"She's coming."

"Nuria," Ignaçio said. "I need you here."

"I've to ask Willem."

"Tell him off."

"Please."

"Come *now*."

"Nacho," Nuria said. "I can't find your Victor."

"You can mobilize our neighbors."

"How is Santos doing now?"

"He broke a leg."

"Did he?"

"I'm dealing with him."

"Ok, I'll come."

"I hope."

Ignaçio hung up and called Carlota's clinic. After a dozen rings, nobody answered. He checked the time: Charo must have left for the day. He tried her cell phone twice; she didn't answer. He couldn't leave Santos's leg untreated; he should take the dog to the emergency.

He backed his car to the gate, loaded the dog at the back, and sat in the driver's seat. His phone beeped. A text message from Elena informed him she was coming with her colleagues; he shouldn't trample or tamper the scene. He tossed the phone aside and started the car. His phone rang. The call came from Charo. He stopped the engine and picked up his phone.

"Nacho," Charo said. "Are you okay?"

"Yes."

"Why did you call?"

"Can I use your clinic?"

182

"Now?"

"Yes."

"Why?"

"Santos has a fractured front leg."

"He broke it himself?"

"No."

"You know who did it?"

"Not yet."

"Find out."

"Charo!"

"Bring the dog."

18

The night's search didn't find Victor but forged the farmers' bond. Jorge was away selling his steers. His neighbors combed the hills, their valleys, the forests, the planes despite what they thought of the bull's fate. Since the financial downturn, stealing animals from grazing lands and selling them at illegal markets had grown into a nationwide problem. These farmers made frequent rounds and watched their animals. But this was the first time an animal disappeared from someone's farm in the valley.

The farmers assured Ignaçio they would watch Victor's cows until Jaime returned and fixed the farm's broken gate. Their bleared eyes didn't stop their search at dawn. Ignaçio pleaded them to return to their farms and feed their animals. They left only after all hopes of finding Victor extinguished one by one. Exhausted Vincente still continued his search.

Nuria stayed home this morning. She warned the region's slaughterhouses about their responsibility for verifying the origin of cattle brought to them. She reminded the border officials of their duty in cases like Victor's. She ignored calls from her work. Her allure and aura pushed others back without words. You had to notice the tremor on her fingers and the scribbles on her notepad to know what was happening inside her. Ignaçio asked her to take a break; she told him to do his part while she did hers. Ignaçio left her alone and went out.

He stopped at their farm's fence. The daylight revealed Santos's fur on the barbed wire. The dog must have squeezed through there and rushed to his farm. Ignaçio widened the gap, passed between the wires, and followed the dog's traces through the forest's undergrowth. Cracks stopped him in his tracks. Chestnuts burst and fell from the foliage. No other sounds came. Santos's shortcut brought him to his farm's intact barrier. The wires again showed the dog's hair. He crawled under the barrier and reached the vegetable patch. The earth wasn't trampled. The vegetables weren't crushed. Victor hadn't come to this part. Ignaçio walked to the guarding neighbor, thanked the old farmer, and released him from his duty.

He replayed last morning's events. He walked up to the barrier lining the trail. He found the place Victor poked his head from and watched his mate leave for work. Across the trail, the bush lay trampled; its branches, pushed apart. Was the bull really watching his mate or someone else coming through that gap? Santos spent most of his time on the other farm. Victor took the responsibility for surveying this one and did his regular rounds.

What brought the dog here in such a rush?

Ignaçio went to the mobile home and sat on its stoop. Victor wouldn't call for Santos's help unless the situation slid beyond his limits. The elements did point in that direction.

But Victor didn't call like other bulls. When he bellowed, his voice resounded from the hills and reached the neighbors. His urgent call would have pulled them out too. Besides, his farm bordered a busy highway. No intruder could load a resisting bull and drive away without drawing attention. Signs of harsh struggle lay strewn everywhere. Victor's call had brought Santos here from the other farm. Yet nobody heard or saw anything.

A crucial piece was missing from this scene.

He walked to the taped area. He stood at its perimeter and scanned every inch of the grass. He still found nothing that solved the puzzle.

A wet muzzle nudged his hand from behind. He turned and saw

185

Lorenza. Her puffed eyes, circled by dark rings, glowed red from crying. Ignaçio kneeled in front of the cow, took out his handkerchief, and wiped her tears. The pregnant cow put out her tongue and licked his face. Ignaçio closed his eyes and stayed in place. Her snuffs and sobs told him what she was going through. He rose to his feet and rubbed her belly. The proud cow refused his pity and swayed away from him. This belligerent female was feeling her guilt after seeing her male lifted from his farm before her eyes. She must have given Victor's lifters a serious trouble.

But Lorenza showed no signs of struggle on her.

What could have happened?

The sun was passing over the zenith. Ignaçio looked at his watch and felt his head reeling. Each passing hour pushed his hope's light farther. If what Nuria's acts implied was right, by now Victor could be anywhere in Spain.

Or in Europe.

Or in the processing chain of a—

Spasms rose from his stomach and stopped his thoughts. He turned his back to the spot and walked toward the mobile home.

The door wasn't locked. Elena had left it open for them. Ignaçio sat in their living room, took a stock of the place, and strived to keep his mind away from Victor. This two-bedroom trailer should suffice for him after the couple moved to their downtown apartment. The shed he and Jaime planned to attach to this mobile home should suffice for Ines's dairy for now. Later, when their cattle grew, they would enlarge their operation and buy another trailer.

But Victor was no longer with them.

They couldn't carry out their plan without Victor. He couldn't see another bull taking Victor's place on his farm. His chest tightened, his throat choked. For the first time after Victor moved to this farm, he saw how much of their plan depended on this exceptional bull. The animal's absence since yesterday was already loosening the earth under their plan. If they couldn't find Victor and bring him back alive, only a few more days would sink their plan into the ground. He rose from the chair, splashed cold water on his face, then leaned on the basin and stared at the farm's gate.

No Victor came in through that gate.

Ignaçio moved back from the window and lay on the sofa. He closed his eyes and tried to rest. The images of Victor, in different stages of slaughter, rushed into his brain and wrung his nerves. The fatigue from the search and the lack of sleep weren't helping him.

Fighting these images wouldn't work. He rose from the sofa and tried his trusted protocol. He stood on one leg, evened his breath, and observed the invading images. They left one after another. He stood on the other leg and watched his obtruding thoughts. They, too, vanished. He was able to hear sounds, smell odors, and see things as they were around him.

He returned to the sofa, sat upright, and strived to stay awake.

A phone rang. Ignaçio rolled over and fell from the sofa.

The rings vibrated in his back-pocket. He pulled out his cell phone and focused his blurred eyes on its screen. The call came from Elena.

"You found Victor?" Ignaçio asked.

"No," she said. "But I have the results."

"For what?"

"The lab tests."

"Oh."

"Ignaçio!"

"Yes?"

"Be patient."

"I'm trying."

"We're doing our best."

"I know," Ignaçio said. "What do the results say?"

"The blood came from two sources."

"That I already know."

"One of them was a man's."

"That too."

"How?"

"Only one animal was stolen," Ignaçio said. "I know Santos's blood. No other animal bled on this farm. The blood that didn't come from Victor had to come from the thief. One of the thieves. At least a dozen. I can't see how they could do their job otherwise. Neither Victor, nor Lorenza, nor Santos would have made life easy for them."

"You want to join the police?"

"No."

"Are you assuming there was a struggle?"

"The blood proves it."

"What if they anesthetized the bull?"

"You mean: they gave him a shot?"

"Yes."

"Impossible," Ignaçio said. "Victor won't let a stranger do that."

"They could have fired the shot from far."

"That's possible."

"They used a forklift to carry him to their van. The tire prints at the gate came from a mid-size truck, but all his ravishers didn't come in the same vehicle. The oil marks left on the road pavement indicate the presence of an old sedan."

"Can you locate the man?"

"From his blood?"

"Yes."

"He's not in our database," Elena said. "But we have his eyeball."

"Pardon?"

"The man lost an eye."

"You think Victor gored it?"

"Who else?"

"Then the bull wasn't anesthetized."

"That's why I'm calling you."

She wanted to know if an immobilized bull could lift its head, use its horns with precision, and aim at someone's eye. Ignaçio explained: it depended on the shot's potency. To load Victor on a forklift, they would have used a shot strong enough to immobilize the bull's neck, not just his legs. The eye must have been gored before the shot. If that were the case, Victor wouldn't have stopped at plucking his ravisher's eye; he would have killed the man or caused more extensive damage. Lorenza didn't do this job; there was no blood on her.

"Victor probably couldn't," Elena said. "Others got in his way."

"I doubt."

"The shoe prints show at least four accomplices," she said. "Probably there were more in both vehicles."

"Victor would have fought them."

"Unless they hurt him first."

"Did they?"

"You said it: the blood came from Victor."

"I suppose," Ignaçio said. "I don't know for sure."

"It came from a bovine male."

"How did the blind get away?"

"In the sedan," she said. "There was a driver."

"All this happened in silence?"

"Before daylight."

"I saw Victor at dawn."

"It happened shortly after sunrise."

"Are you sure?"

"Yes."

"Did you check the hospitals?"

"No one came with a lost eye."

"Living or dead?"

"Yes."

"Incredible," Ignaçio said. "There had to be a vet involved."

"Pardon?"

"If they fired a shot to immobilize Victor, someone decided its potency."

"You think this theft was orchestrated?"

"How else?" Ignaçio said. "Victor is no ordinary bull."

"Someone who knew him?"

"Someone who also knew his weight."

"Who knows his weight?"

"Me, Charo, and Jorge."

"Where's Jorge?"

"Down south."

"Doing what?"

"Selling his steers."

"When did he leave?"

"Two days ago."

"When does he return?"

"Tomorrow."

"Does he know?"

"Nuria must have told him."

"Anyone else knows the bull's weight?"

"No."

"Are you sure?"

"Yes."

"Who weighs the bull?"

"You're right," Ignaçio said. "I'll ask the weighing station."

"The one between the port and the train station?"

"That's the only one."

"I'll call them."

"Elena."

"Yes?"

"Lorenza wasn't hurt at all."

"Why would they hurt that cow?"

"She wouldn't let strangers load Victor on a forklift."

"Who said they were strangers?"

"What are you saying?"

"Nothing," Elena said. "We have to stay open."

"Are you sure the bovine blood came from Victor?"

"Who else could it come from?"

"Was it from a bull?"

"I told you: it came from a male."

"You can't know for sure if that male was Victor."

"No, we can't," Elena said. "Not until one of his cows gives birth."

"That would be too late."

191

"Why?"

"I don't know."

"How is the dog doing now?"

"Santos dislocated a shoulder."

"You think they beat the dog?"

"He fell from somewhere."

"How do you know?"

"The X-rays."

"Someplace high?"

"No."

"That's strange."

"I found him on the road."

Ignaçio explained. The X-rays showed a vertical impact on the dog's femur. The scrapes on him came from falling off a running vehicle. They must have loaded Santos in their vehicle too, but the dog had escaped somehow and returned to the farm.

Elena asked him to sit tight and hold onto his hope. The entire lifting operation must have completed within minutes for no one to hear or see anything. In one way or another, the thief would turn up somewhere, injured or dead. The man's DNA was now in their database. She would run a check across Europe and search for a match. By wounding one, Victor had left behind a precious trail; she promised to follow it. The bull would no doubt return to his farm. In the mean time, Jaime would install surveillance to protect Victor's herd; she had already spoken to her husband about this. Jaime was returning tonight; Ignaçio could rest now.

Ignaçio washed his face, drank from the tap, and stepped out of the couple's home.

The sun was sinking below the farm's gate and painting its rails crimson. It wasn't so long ago that Victor first stopped at this gate, sniffed its rust, and rubbed his hooves on the soil before leading in his herd. After that move, each day passed grew the bull, matured his cows, and enlarged this farm. Their growth had marked every part of his land. Within a day after Victor's disappearance, all that growth had shrunk to zero. Whoever robbed this bull had also stolen this farm's soul. The cattle barely moved now. The shadows took longer to grow. The ocean's breeze didn't bother to come here. The life Victor brought here had left with him. No more promises on this land. The desolate farm waited as it did after that killer landslide.

The setting sun drenched the cottonwood tree's flowers in yellow, orange, and red. The pond's reeds glowed violet. Ignaçio climbed the stone pile and sat on Santos's seat. The dog chose this place for a good reason. The heron made its nest on this tree for a good reason. His parents built their home on this spot for a good reason. He recalled the last meal he ate with his parents before going to Nuria's place, but he couldn't remember their faces.

That wasn't so long ago either. These stones hadn't moved an inch since.

The heron sat in its nest. The sun colored the bird's feathers saffron, but the plumes on its chest glimmered purple. Ignaçio descended from the stone pile and then walked toward the cottonwood tree. The heron lifted its neck and tilted its head; its beak's tip glowed violet. Since last evening, he had passed by the pond at least a dozen times, but he hadn't seen this bird once at its spot in the water. That was unusual for this heron.

Was it sick? Injured? Vomiting blood?

He stood under the tree and peered at the heron's nest. The bird rose to its full height and spread out its wings. No injuries. A fish from this pond couldn't hurt a bird of this size. The blood on its chest and beak came from another source. Whatever stained this bird with blood had also prevented it from fishing; otherwise, water would have cleaned its beak.

Ignaçio lifted his arms and waved at the heron. The bird squawked, lowered its beak, and lifted something from its nest.

Ignaçio approached the bird. The blood's source was in the heron's beak: the bird was trying to tell him something. The heron's eyes explained why it didn't fish. The same sorrow also prevented Santos and Lorenza from eating. They had seen more and known more, yet they could tell nothing.

If you saw your kin stolen and couldn't tell anyone, how would you feel?

He studied veterinary medicine. He was supposed to know animals. Yet he read so few of their messages, understood so little of their emotions. He should have seen these animals' signs. Their gestures confirmed Victor's ravishers weren't regulars to this farm. They didn't belong to this community. They were marauders from a strange land. They broke into this farm and took Victor against his will. One more of them left behind an eye to this heron.

Ignaçio pulled out his phone and dialed Elena's number. The heron opened its beak and swallowed the eyeball. Ignaçio hung up the call and watched the bird's moving throat. If Elena called back now, he couldn't explain this bird's act. She would never understand.

Killing this heron and recovering the eyeball might help find Victor but would do serious injustice to this bird. One perpetrator's genetic code was already in the police database. If they caught this one, they would find the others. After what this bird had lived, it needed peace to find its feet. Ignaçio put the phone in his pocket, bowed to the heron, and left his farm.

Three-quarters down the trail, he heard a vehicle behind and turned. A car coming toward him slowed. He didn't know this vehicle. It didn't belong to this valley.

At the trail's fork, the car turned and followed him. He could now see the vehicle's front. Its model was as old as his; its chassis, more worn-out and more beaten-down. The car was going to Jorge's farm. Ignaçio stopped at the farm's gate, raised the cattle barrier, and waited for the vehicle to pass. The car stopped and cut its engine. Its driver stepped out.

Ignaçio recognized the driver. His muscles tensed.

"Is Paula home?" Miguel asked.

"I don't know."

"Can I see her?"

"For what?"

"I have something for her."

"I'll take it."

"I've to talk to her."

"About the bull?"

"Which bull?"

"Wait here."

Ignaçio went and informed Paula. Her forehead creased and her face darkened. Nuria stiffened. Paula resumed her normal air and asked him to bring Miguel. Nuria frowned at her mother, rose from her seat, and peered through the den's window. Miguel hadn't moved; he stood behind the gate and surveyed the farm. The calm activist showed no tension.

Ignaçio returned and asked Miguel to follow.

Paula held the door open. Miguel bowed to her and stood on the patio. Nuria fidgeted in the den. She coiled her fringe and chewed her lip.

"I went to the booth," Miguel said. "You had left the arena."

"You should have called," Paula said.

"I don't have your number."

"What is it now?"

"The key."

"Couldn't it wait?"

"No."

"Why?"

"I'll be booked tomorrow."

"Come in."

Miguel entered the den and apologized for his intrusion. A search & seizure warrant was now out; he didn't want to keep her key in his place. He took out an envelope and held it to Paula. Nuria seized the envelope and flung it across the floor.

"How dare you?" Nuria blew. "You think you're above the law?"

"Sorry," Miguel said. "I didn't coax or coerce Paula."

"She offered it to you?"

"Yes."

"For money?"

"Don't insult your mother."

"How could you do this to her?"

"She wanted to help."

"I don't believe you."

"Ask her."

Nuria glared at her mother. Paula held her daughter's gaze and kept her face stern. Nuria finally gave in and looked away. She

196

walked across the floor, picked up the envelope, and kept it in her hand. Her jaws tightened. Her chest heaved. Her other hand reached to tear the envelope. Paula warned her. Nuria gave the envelope to Ignaçio and asked him to open it.

Ignaçio broke the seal and peeked inside: a key and a letter.

Nuria asked him to read the letter.

Dear Paula,

Many claim they're against bullfighting. Their stance is more cerebral than visceral. You never announce yours; your one act shows more than a million words. If this key's truth ever leaks, I'll take the blame. I'll say I stole it from you. From the way I work, nobody will doubt my words. You served the *lidia* bull by loaning me your key.

Thank you.

Miguel

Ignaçio lifted his eyes and looked at Nuria. She gazed far and bit her lip. Her eyes didn't blink. Her face didn't flinch. Tear welled from her eyes, rolled down her cheeks, and fell on the tiles. Ignaçio slid the letter inside the envelope and gave it to Paula. She took it without changing her face or moving her lips. Everyone's breath sounded in the den except his.

Miguel bowed to them and turned toward the door.

Ignaçio opened it for him.

19

Along the way, the vehicle's door opened twice and loaded two more steers.

Victor sat up but couldn't rise to his feet. The moving vehicle's closed heat parched his tongue and drenched his coat. Sweat trickled down his flanks and dripped onto the floor. The metal room had no water or food. Only a few dry grass stems lay scattered. Victor left those stalks to the two scared steers; they chewed those for their reassurance.

These two males were smaller and younger than him. They had a distinct odor he didn't know—and a streak of aggression he never saw before. They left him alone and clacked their horns for the grass stalks. After the stock finished, they staged a full-blown clash. One nearly gored the other. Victor rose to his feet and stood between them. The dominant one turned its wrath on him. Victor didn't need his horns to push this rebel back to its corner. Afterward, no conflict followed. Both steers deferred to him.

They rolled through hollering bipeds and honking vehicles. They climbed uphill, sped downhill, and ran through planes. They went straight. They turned right and left. They braked and backed up. The bipeds at the vehicle's front cursed, thumped, and yelled. They stopped, but not for long. Two bipeds descended and switched sides; the other stayed in. The vehicle rolled, regained its speed, and ran its course. The noise outside faded. The air inside heated. The two steers heaved and reeled from the heat.

The bipeds didn't bring them any food or water. Nobody cleared their waste. The heat grew the stench and choked their nostrils. The two steers abandoned their rivalry, sat in their corners, and hung out their red tongues. Victor moved to the vehicle's back and breathed through its door's crack.

Light outside dimmed. The heat cooled and the air freshened. Other vehicles came few and far. Theirs sped through the dark. No more vehicles arrived from behind or front. Theirs left the paved road and rolled on a mud trail. The air outside thickened with dust, humidity, and scents. He recognized the pines, oaks, and chestnuts but not the other trees and herbs. The grass and the soil of this parched land smelled pungent. An ocean breeze came, heavier with salt and lighter with algae. This ocean didn't roar like the one he knew. Birds here flapped their wings harder and squealed louder. The animals along the trail smelled sour and cried longer. Their calls lingered. Their desperate notes dominated this desolate land.

The wild's desolation gave way to farms' warmth. Cows mooed, calves bleated, bulls bellowed. The two steers inside lifted their heads but didn't rise to their feet. The vehicle passed several farms, and their dogs ran after it. Lorenza, Santos, and the heron appeared before Victor's eyes; he pushed their images aside. His instincts told him their journey was reaching its end and his old friends couldn't help him face this new predicament. He had to survive this challenge and return to his herd. The two steers glowered at each other and then clashed again. This time, Victor left them to solve their problem.

The vehicle slowed. More biped voices came from outside. Some ran along its side and shouted to the two inside at its front; others went to the back and hollered. The vehicle shook, groaned, vibrated, and halted. Its drone died. The three bipeds descended from its front, met the others at its side, and then went toward the back.

The door opened. The burning sun dazzled Victor and bleared his eyes.

The two steers darted past him and leaped from the vehicle. They didn't go far. Bipeds on horseback ran after them, swung their lassos, and brought them back. The ropes choked both steers and bulged their eyes. The mounted bipeds raised their pressure until each steer crashed to the soil and threshed its legs.

The rebels didn't fight back. The bipeds loosened their ropes. The steers rose to their feet, lowered their heads, and stood still. The bipeds on horseback whipped them and drove them away from the vehicle. Victor didn't hear or see the two steers again.

The vehicle's bipeds came for Victor. They were prepared, and he knew better. He let them lower him to the ground and lead his way. They walked him alongside a farm's fence, its parched pasture larger than the two he knew. Behind its stakes, on a lush patch around a large reservoir, bovine forms stood scattered: all were males. The bulls saw him, lifted their heads, and perked their ears. The hot breeze brought their odor. They smelled like the rebel steers, but they didn't come toward the fence to fight with him. They just watched him.

These bulls didn't fight with each other. They stood together like brothers, as he used to do with other steers before their adolescence. The air reeked of bulls only; he didn't see or smell any cows on this pasture. Peace ruled this farm. The males had no females to compete for. Sensations from his previous farm were leaving him. He was already changing. He didn't like this change, yet it was freeing him from a burden and reviving another trait of his.

Three bipeds opened the gate. Victor struck his hooves on the soil and then walked into this all-male farm that he knew would be his new home.

One biped took his hoof strikes for rebellion. He lifted a pole and hit Victor on the leg. Victor ignored the blow. The biped took

Victor's poise for defiance and continued to strike. Victor stepped forward and swayed his horns. The biped sprang back and swung the pole at his head. Victor ducked. The pole struck his horns and shattered to pieces.

Victor reared up and roared. The disarmed biped fled with one of his mates. The one who remained returned to the vehicle, pulled out the metal-tipped pole, and pointed it at Victor. The bipeds on horseback returned with their lassos and whips. They surrounded him from behind. Victor knew the one to keep his eyes on. He stood still and faced the biped holding the lance.

The other bulls approached. They stood apart and watched the fight. A thrill Victor didn't know welled from within him. His heart pumped, his head throbbed, his lungs bellowed. He didn't invite this thrill, but it grew. It flowed along his nerves, flooded his vessels and sinews, and charged his muscles with an explosive force. He resisted the explosion and waited.

The mounted bipeds left, returned with picks, and met his hooves. They fell to the ground, and their horses fled. Victor ignored the fallen bipeds and kept his eyes on the lancer.

The lancer glared at him. Victor warned him with a rumble. The biped refused to back down or lower his lance. A virtue Victor believed in and valued so far was now leaving him. He still resisted his impulse and waited for the offense. His poise inflamed this biped.

The lancer charged, lunged forward, and launched the lance at his head. Victor ducked. The lance flew between his horns, hit the farm's fence, and pierced its stakes. Victor reared up, leaped, and struck his hooves on the lancer's collarbones. The bones cracked. The lancer crashed to the ground. Victor stood over him and pinned him with his horns.

A voice within him warned it was enough. Another spoke louder and claimed it wasn't. The two voices fought while Victor stood still, and the lancer clutched his chest and writhed on the soil. One voice vanquished the other. Victor fought the vanquisher and lost the battle. If he wanted to live in dignity on this new farm, he would have to listen to this winning voice from now on. On his old farm, he made a mistake by pardoning one lancer; here, he couldn't make the same mistake by pardoning another. Life never gives you the same chance twice. *An enemy shouldn't be left behind alive.* Victor positioned his horns' tips on the lancer's chest and pressed down on his lungs.

A female biped cried from far. A male horse neighed.

Victor released the lancer, lifted his head, and looked in the sounds' direction. The female biped, wearing the sun on her hair, almost stood on a rust-colored stallion galloping toward this farm. He recalled her silhouette but couldn't place her. No biped he knew rode a horse so fast, with so few moves and jerks, and with so little effort. The two leaped like one animal.

The stallion slowed and stopped before this farm's gate. The biped female descended without stirring the animal. She moved the stallion with her eyes and without his reins. They stopped at the gate and didn't gaze at him. Victor now remembered where he first saw this female biped and when. On that day, this stallion wasn't beside her; a biped male was.

She opened the gate, stepped onto the pasture, and closed the gate behind her. The stallion stayed outside and kept its eyes on him. An impulse rose in Victor to charge at her, but the rules of bulls dictated they couldn't attack or hurt females. She came closer, stopped in front of him, and watched him without fear. Her mouth didn't move. Her eyes admired his stature. The other bulls gathered behind her and

202

stood ready to defend. Victor watched the stallion. The horse's steady gaze shifted between him and her. This stallion, too, would defend her.

Victor applauded these animals' guard. Their defense removed his doubts. He raised his head, lifted his muzzle, and tilted his horns backward. His gestures relaxed her animals.

She raised her arm and reassured the stallion. She turned toward the bulls and sent them away by a move of her hand. She returned to the gate, opened it, and brought her stallion in. She scanned the fallen bipeds and regarded his state: no glare from her eyes, no reproach from her mouth, no reprimand from her gestures. Victor understood why these animals obeyed her and stood by her on their own will. He appreciated their voluntary deference.

She used her phone, spoke to someone, and returned to him. She examined his wounds one by one. She didn't fondle him or speak to him in soft words. Her rub came firm, yet it brought tender warmth. What left him earlier returned to him now in a different form.

She went to the tool-shed and returned with a box he knew. She opened the toolbox and dressed his wounds. The fallen bipeds moaned, moved, and rolled on the ground. She ignored them and tended him. Her treating hand felt as sure as his biped playmate's back home.

The treatment's odor stirred her stallion and drew her bulls. They must have received her care more than once. They stood still, but their eyes followed her moves. Back home, he did the same with his biped mate. He missed his old farm. He missed his playmate. He missed their games.

This female biped resembled his male playmate in many ways: how she touched him or looked at him; how she walked, turned, and moved; how she carried herself, held her head, and used her limbs. He could see her leap, jump, vault, and flip like his mate. Yet something was missing from her. He couldn't point his muzzle at it. That missing piece endeared her to these animals—her horse, her bulls, and now him—and enforced her mastery over them. She didn't have to use any physical, visual, or verbal force.

She owned her horse, but she was the mistress of her bulls.

The thought lightened his heart and brightened his mood. Victor lowered his mouth to the ground and chewed a few grass strands. The Mistress of Bulls stopped her hands. She went to the shed, returned with a pail of water, and held it before his muzzle.

He drank from her hands.

She uttered a word. He lifted his head and pricked up his ears.

Her mouth opened: "Mors."

Victor didn't know this command. He had never heard this word. He stood still and watched her face and eyes; they gave him no clues. He returned to drinking, finished the water, and received two more bucketfuls. They quenched his thirst and soothed his burn.

The Mistress of Bulls held his gaze and drew out the word: "M-O-R-S."

This time, Victor understood her.

20

Jorge walked into the barn holding the saddle in one hand and a thick envelope in the other. Santos raised his neck and perked his ears. Since his accident six weeks ago, the dog hadn't seen the high pasture. Ignaçio lifted Santos's healing leg and examined the peeling plaster.

"Came by registered post." Jorge raised the envelope. "I signed for you."

"I'll send it back," Ignaçio said. "Willem won't stop."

"The taurine association sent it."

"What do they want?"

"Open and see."

"Angel works for Willem," Ignaçio said. "I'm not selling my farm."

"Then deal with both."

"Did they call you?"

"They won't dare."

"Are you bringing your cattle down today?"

"Only the steers," Jorge said. "How's the dog's leg?"

"Should have healed."

"Would heal faster if he stayed home."

"You know Santos."

"Did Jaime fix your farm's gate?"

"Long ago," Ignaçio said. "He finished the doghouse too."

"Santos won't stay in a kennel."

"Did you try Lorenza again?"

"That cow gives me the horns."

"Leave her on my farm."

"I'll add a few calves today."

"There's place for more."

"Did you check the neighbor's bull?"

"I did," Ignaçio said. "The wounds didn't come from a bear."

"Was it a lynx?"

"Not sure."

"Those thieves are professional."

"Anyone else lost calves?"

"Six more."

"Male and female?"

"Male."

"Sells for meat."

"Not always," Jorge said. "Some reproduce."

"How many more steers you got?"

"Seventeen."

"All mature?"

"Yes."

"Sell soon."

"I'll."

"When?"

"This morning."

"Good luck."

"See you."

Jorge scanned his barn's restored interior, placed the envelope on the new steel rack, and left with his horse's gears.

Ignaçio removed the plaster from Santos's leg. He disinfected the closed wound, cleaned the growing skin, and asked the dog to rise to his feet. The dog rose on three legs and licked the fourth. Ignaçio encouraged Santos. The dog lowered his fourth leg onto the ground and then transferred his weight. Ignaçio rubbed the healed leg and the shoulder. This time, the muscles didn't tighten, and the skin didn't flinch. The dog had overcome his trauma.

Santos withdrew his leg, walked on four in his regular gait, and left the barn. The dog stood behind the farm's barrier, lifted his muzzle, and barked at the other farm. The heron replied. After six weeks, these two animals still held onto their hope for Victor.

Lorenza, too, held her ground on the other farm and refused to move here with her herd. Humans think animals forget their companies and move on with their lives. Neither Santos, nor Lorenza, nor the heron would agree. He couldn't compensate for their loss.

Charo saw the fighting bulls as farm animals. If she widened her vision, she would see a bull could become a company animal for some and play a role more important than a cat or dog did for a human. The bull's disappearance could turn a known place into a strange land and leave a permanent void for a cow, a dog, and a heron that no one could fill. That farm no longer felt his. He couldn't go there. Animals' emotions aren't superficial as Darwin claims. Over time, they sink deeper, grow their roots, and persist. He would work with Charo and prove this truth in his final-year thesis. He owed this duty to both these farms' animals.

The school opened next week. His dance tours would limit to weekends. After Victor left, the tours to Catalonia, Canaries, and Balearic Islands provided only short escapes from this desolate place; he couldn't go farther leaving Santos on three legs. Now the dog was standing on his four feet. The tours abroad should resume. Distance removes deception and enlarges vision. He needed a clearer head to decide on the hospital's offer and his final-year courses.

Farruca was taking up a larger space in his life. It was no longer a question of recovering what missed from his sphere; it was now a question of furnishing what veterinary medicine couldn't. He loved animals, he loved facts, he loved truths. But he also loved to grapple the irrational that science refused. Flamenco lived beyond the rational. Farruca thrived in the irrational. The hospital would limit his liberty and cut his dance. Charo's clinic would retain his tours. She counted on his purchasing her clinic. After giving forty-five years of her life to this trade, she deserved a break from its routines to do something else she cherished.

The tug between the hospital and the clinic was now resolved. He would accept the loan from Willem's bank on preferential terms as long as the man didn't press him to sell his farm. The senior bullfighting magnate was good at heart; otherwise, he wouldn't help Jaime with the mortgage to buy that mechanic's garage. This revived go-getter's business provided San Taurino's youths what the region and the nation couldn't. He wasn't the devil's advocate as some claimed. You just had to know how to keep his ambitions within limits.

His farruca shows were entering other arenas and drawing larger crowds. If he could handle their demand, he wouldn't need the loan to buy Charo's clinic. Nuria wouldn't seek Willem's favor and fear for her family's farm. His flamenco would free everyone.

The past two weeks had seen the barn restored without begging money from the bank or bullying the insurance company. This week had seen him buying Jaime and Elena's mobile home at an above-market price. The couple would now use the extra money to furnish their downtown flat. Next month, he would move to his farm and liberate Nuria's space. Something was developing between her and Miguel; she often saw him in jail. Life had changed for some and was still changing. The dairy equipment would wait until Victor returned to his herd.

Life *is* change; he would go with it.

He left Santos outside, returned to the barn, and packed his medical tools. He saw the registered letter on the shelf. He picked it up and went to his room. He sat at his desk, opened the envelope, and peeked inside: a thick stack of pages. His heart fluttered, his hand hesitated. He left his desk, went to the balcony, and smelled the flowering creepers below.

The scent honed his senses. His breath hastened, his eyes sharpened. His head reeled. He searched beyond the farm's barrier but didn't find anything to grab. He went to Nuria's room, knocked on her door, and recalled she was at work. He returned to his desk. He sat before the open envelope and closed his eyes. The envelope didn't go away.

He pulled out the pages and placed them before him. He stared at the stack: on its top, sat a holographic letter from the taurine association's secretary.

Dear Ignaçio,

Despite your refusal, I took the liberty to recommend you to our Academy of Taurine Arts. Enclosed, please find their response. Their two-year program commences next month. The decision belongs to you.

Sincerely,

Angel

The admission came with a full scholarship and a free residency. Credits for the anatomy and physiology courses, transferred from the veterinary school, would shorten his term by six months. The taurine association's secretary offered to serve as his mentor.

Ignaçio closed the envelope and rose from his desk. He had already given his decision at the end of his farruca shows in the arena. He wasn't going back on that decision now. Higher priorities lay ahead for him and for those he loved. He couldn't be distracted by opportunities like this offer. He closed his room's door, went downstairs, and searched for Santos.

The dog wasn't on this farm; he must be on the other.

The offer returned to his mind. Staying near the letter wouldn't help. He left Jorge's farm and walked for his. At the trail's fork, his feet hesitated; they wouldn't go toward his farm. He left the trail, climbed the mount, and went toward the river. Before Victor moved to his farm, they used to take this path for their swim. A year and a half isn't long. Yet these past eighteen months had altered a few lives; the twelve ahead would change more. At the mount's knee, he shunned their usual path through the meadow and climbed a hill's flank he didn't know.

Below, the familiar meadow greeted him with an unfamiliar face. The goldenrods' batons beat the flowering yuccas' ivory stalks and lost to the heathers and lilacs. The trilliums' pink and red gazed from the heath's tapestry, glowing with daffodils, daisies, and dandelions. The dogwoods' cream defied their yellow, soaked the sun's burning colors, and burst into saffron, orange, and crimson. The hazel pines shined their copper, gold, and purple robes. Their leaves swayed and sent their raisin's scent. Aspens fluttered beside alders. Willows, birches, oaks swung their catkins among maples, beeches, cottonwoods. At the hill's terrace, prickly pears sat with pincushions and cocklebur thistles. They flashed their blooming violet flowers and offered their ripening scarlet fruit. Bumblebees, monarch butterflies, cecropia moths ignored their thorny spines and feasted on their offers.

A grackle called. A partridge and a pheasant replied. A hawk swooped down and snatched a shrew from its burrow. A meadowlark sang. A mockingbird imitated the song. A nuthatch scurried down a hawthorn's trunk and clashed with a wren skittering up, pointing its tail. A golden eagle squealed above the meadow and silenced a woodpecker working on an oak. A squirrel peeped from the tree's trunk, defied the eagle, and skippered up the oak's limbs.

Ignaçio reached the peak and walked east along the hill's crest. Down in the valley, a creek broke away from the river, turned into a bayou, and lost itself among the marshes and swamps. The willow's dripping green hid the creek's water from view. Two condors circled above the wetland and scanned its decaying mass. When Victor was two and a half months old, a racer snake impressed him there with its speed, and he ran after it. They both loved that hidden place; each, for a different reason. Ignaçio descended through the pine grove, stepping over fallen trunks, crunching on cones and needles, and reached the river's bay they knew.

This bay, too, had changed. Lily pads floated in the place of watercress and offered their white, pink, and red patchwork. Cattails and *kans* grass took the reeds' place. Their cream-white stalks bent down and kissed the lichen gleaming orange and yellow. The sun's fingers pierced the green canopy, reached the forest's floor, and painted glowing patterns of hope.

Across the river, inside the belfry of Iglesia Sacrata di Ser Vivo, early autumn dimmed the stork's nest. The adult bird stood with its offspring on the church's steeple and planned their flight south for the winter. The city' rush didn't change their plan. The arena's howls, growls, roars, groans, moans didn't break their trance. They cared little about what humans did.

Ignaçio sat on the culvert and watched the stream drain the marsh. The water gabbled and gurgled. Dace danced in the pool's twirl. The rush stems ignored their rust and fluttered their leaves to the breeze. A luna moth flew from a buckeye to a bittersweet and chased away a bluebottle. A bunting lifted its head from a buttercup cluster and watched a bullfinch feast on blackberry brambles. A bighorn descended from the pine grove and hid behind a birch. A black widow crawled up a wild dill's stalk and scared a flycatcher admiring a bluebell.

The morass creaked, squeaked, screeched, and squawked. Life rasped, rattled, and rustled through this wetland. The seconds moved, the sounds changed. Not a single moment stood still. The new drowned the old. The fresh removed the pale. The brave ate the coward. This magic land hid its surprise. Anything could happen here any moment. Nobody would guess. Victor could watch you from a thicket of maidenhair fern and you would never know.

You leave your security's tendrils back home. You come here and go with its flow.

Security didn't court his life. What seemed secure slipped away. This happened with his parents, this happened with Victor, and this was happening with Nuria. His entire life was an accident, a series of rare events. Only one could have deviated from its course, and his life's trajectory would be entirely different. Fate stands on a flimsy balance.

He loved this imbalance. At every tipping point, a new hand emerged from somewhere, helped him find his feet, and adjusted him to the shift. His life was shifting again.

His chest swelled, his breath surged. He rose to his feet and darted through the swamp. He dashed up the magnolia, wisteria, and grape vines. He heaved to the hill's crest. He ran on its ridge and crossed its pass. He reached the condemned caves he used to explore with Nuria.

At the hills' darkening feet, the dusk's hands reached the valley's farms and painted them orange and mauve. This southern farmers' community had also changed. He didn't go down the hiking trail he used to take with Nuria. He turned away from the valley he knew. He ran farther and descended into one he didn't know. He fled that valley, crossed another pass, and heard the ocean. He knew its sound. He stopped running and walked toward the ocean.

The glimmering sun inched downward and kissed the glittering waves. The retiring rays flared the trees' burning suits of light and flashed their dancing jewels. The saline air defied the fall's colors, rushed into the hill's corridor, and lost its brine to the sage, rosemary, thyme, spearmint, basil. Milkweeds burst their fluffs and softened the mesquites. Pitcher plants and Venus flytraps hid among poison hemlocks and waited for unwary bees and wasps. A praying mantis saw him coming, reared up on its hind, and covered its head with the front limbs.

Blue, red, and black berries garnished the uphill trail. Ignacio picked a few and heard a running animal's hoof strokes. He dropped the currants, sprang up, and spun around. The strokes came from a galloping horse, not a running bull. A cocoa-colored Arabian stallion carried a streamlined blond woman, standing on the stirrups and bouncing to the horse's rhythm. The two approached. The woman sat back on the saddle and tossed her head to the side. Long strands of golden hair swiped her shoulder and twisted at her widow's peak.

Ignacio recognized Rafaela. Nearing him, her Egyptian stallion

213

slowed to a canter. She nodded at him and squeezed the horse's flanks. The stallion lifted its muzzle and neighed at the ocean. She stood on the stirrups and galloped away. The taurine association's president wasn't known for her warmth, words, or expressions. She never smiled at anyone.

A pheasant crossed the stallion's trail. From a shrub, a wild piglet appeared and offered its friendship to the bird. The pheasant ignored the pig cub and continued its journey. An ocelot descended from a cypress and crept after the two. Wild boars emerged from the thicket and chased the predator. The feline stalker abandoned its preys and ran up a Lebanese cedar.

Ignacio reached the corridor's mouth and descended onto the shore. He never came to these beaches because they drew bathing beauties who pointed their breasts to the sun and turned with it. Now the autumn sun traveled lower. The descending fall chilled the air. The late tides swept the sand and left no place for idle sunbathers. Seasoned surfers treaded the turbulent water and courted its swelling waves.

The tidal waves called him. Their muffled roars lured him. He wanted to play with them. The shimmering sun descended further. The glittering waves swelled, raised translucent walls, and wore foaming cream caps. Gulls, loons, terns screamed and circled the swells. Skimmers planed and skimmed their surf. The tumbling walls toppled, collapsed, and rolled. The waves splashed the glowing sand and fizzed under his feet. Sandpipers ran after the flying foam and foraged the twitching insects. Ignacio picked up a writhing stingray and threw it in a sizzling pool. The reverse tide scooped the pool, lifted the fish, and carried it back into the ocean.

The sun's disk sank lower. Its robe changed from yellow to

saffron to orange. The wind calmed, the swells subsided, the seabirds stopped crying. The surfers floated on the water and waited for their feats. Ignaçio stripped to his underwear and entered the inviting ocean.

The water kneaded his thighs. The cold revived his vessels. The smell released his nerves. He plodded waist-deep and waded along the shore. The yielding sand massaged his feet and relieved his sinews. Waves greeted him one after another. He frolicked under their cover and then continued to walk. The salt's iodine toned his brain and honed his senses. He saw clearer, heard sharper, smelled stronger. He turned around and plodded back toward his clothes.

The surfers hollered. The water sank and sucked in. A wave rose and raised a wall. White froth crowned its top. The water sank deeper and shrank back farther. The swell rose higher, built a mound, and projected a brim. The mount's crest toppled; its slope rolled toward him.

Ignaçio leaped and plunged into the roll.

The breaker caught him. The wave robed him into its folds, rolled him in its barrel, and hurled him onto the sand. The returning tide whooshed past him. The slithering sand sizzled. A starfish twitched, a whelk rolled, a nautilus slid in the draining water. One by one, Ignaçio lifted the disoriented animals and threw them into the receding water's sheet.

The rolls left him in vertigo. This vertigo didn't nauseate him; it whetted his appetite. The hunger woke his heart, lightened his head, and sharpened his spirit. His heart pumped. His lungs heaved. His muscles throbbed. He returned to the water and waited for more.

The ocean gave it to him.

She grabbed him in her arms and raised him above her head. She rolled him, flipped him, turned him on her lap. She held him in her embrace, sang in his ears, and let him dance. He forgot who he was. Each breaker broke one tie from his past. Each roller rolled him farther from his present. Each whitecap capped his fear and pushed him to explore the future. He saw who he was now. He saw who he was becoming. He saw who he could be. A breaker returned him to the beach. He leaped from the sand, dashed into the ocean, and gave himself to her.

The wild ocean played with him until her passion ran out.

She lifted him to her bosom, brought him to the beach, and lowered him there. He sat up on the sand, wrapped his arms around the trunk, and watched her slip away. The setting sun sparked her headdress and shined her jewels in rainbow colors. He waited; she didn't come.

But she had left him renewed.

A renewal he couldn't figure but sensed in him. The beach didn't look the same. The air didn't smell the same. The rays didn't feel the same. He heard sounds he didn't know. He felt impulses alien to him. He saw the world with a stranger's eyes. This world appeared strange.

He was a stranger in this world: born to Basque parents, raised by Andalusian farmers, and dancing flamenco in Galician style. Life granted him the liberty that uncertainty opened and certainty closed. Yet he was running after stability—by studying medicine, by learning to farm, and by securing a home for his future family. He was setting himself up for traps that wrought life out of living. He was surrounded by people who accepted his differences. They loved him and cared for him. He loved them and enjoyed their company. But they raised a wall that suffocated him, limited his moves, and killed his freedom. He would crush those barriers, break those routines, and leave those certainties. He would embrace uncertainty.

He wore his clothes, took out his cell phone, and called Nuria.

At dinner, he offered them his farm; they refused. He listed his farm's benefits for them; they didn't listen. Nobody touched the food. Nobody breathed. Nobody moved a limb.

"So," Nuria said. "You move from healing animals to killing them?"

"These bulls are raised to fight," Ignaçio said. "They should fight."

"You believe that?"

"Yes."

"They can kill you."

"Reward requires risk."

"Nacho." She swallowed. "What about me?"

"What about you?"

"How do I feel now?"

"About my move?"

"About us!"

"That's why I'm leaving."

Nuria pushed her plate and left the table. She clacked up the stairs and clattered down the corridor. She entered her room and slammed its door. Jorge placed his hands on the table and started to rise. Paula pressed her palms on her husband's hands and kept him at the table.

They remained seated. No more sounds came from upstairs.

Paula rose from her seat and put away the plates. Jorge reached for the television set, but then he changed his mind and lit a cigarette. Paula wiped the table, opened the window, and sat next to her husband. Outside, dark descended its cover fast over the farm. The

217

moon rose faster and lifted the night's blanket. Ignaçio saw Santos returning from his farm. The dog now walked normally on four legs and no longer needed his care. He was free to leave.

Paula spoke:

They were sad to see him go, but they understood him. She didn't agree with his fighting the *lidia* bulls, but, if this was what he wanted to do for his living, she would go with it. They wouldn't use the money from his dance shows. They would run his farm and keep its funds in a separate account. He could claim that money from them at any moment. She would leave Nuria alone for tonight and deal with her feelings tomorrow. He didn't need to worry.

And, of course, their door would always stay open for him.

21

The rooster crowed. The dawn's break brought no new hopes. Ignaçio closed Nuria's door, lifted Magdalena from the corridor, and entered his room. He lowered the cat on his bed, opened the door to his balcony, leaned against its railing, and scanned the sleeping farm.

Wind brought the cattle's smell from the gleaming pasture. Their silhouettes quivered on the dappled patches shimmering under the descending moon. The forest's canopy stirred. A warbler sang in the cycad's palms. A nightingale crooned from the barn. The air announced a thirsty day. He lifted his pitcher, filled it in the bathroom, and watered the balcony's plants.

The jasmines sent their scent from the patio. The bougainvilleas crept on the wall. These plants needed water. Ignaçio took his pitcher and went downstairs. He watered the creepers, the hyacinths, the elderberries, and the privets. Their perfumes grew and asked him to stay.

He refilled the pitcher and drenched the forsythias, the gardenias, the gladioluses; the morning glories, the narcissuses, the nasturtiums; the peonies, the poinsettias, the primroses; the azaleas, the fuchsias, the carnations. They didn't take long. The cacti refused his water.

He stood holding the empty pitcher and searched for more plants to water. The lilies, the marigolds, the dahlias, and the black-eyed-Susans beckoned him from the barrier's rails. He gave them more water than they needed and then found nothing else to do on this farm.

The morning glories opened their petals for the day.

They asked him to leave.

Ignaçio checked his watch. Jorge and Paula would soon rise and

219

feed their animals. He didn't want them to see him go. He had loaded his car last night to avoid waking their pain this morning. He should leave now before they woke. They might wake Nuria too.

He returned to his room and placed the leaking pitcher on his desk. He patted the sleeping cat, took his wallet and documents, and descended the balcony's stairs. The farm now smelled stronger. Its contours grew sharper. Its animals felt dearer. He recalled feeling this way before lowering his parents into their grave. This farm had raised him for seventeen years. Time had come for him to leave. He ignored its lures and marched toward his car by the farm's gate.

He reached his car. He sat inside the vehicle and resisted looking back. He held his breath, closed his eyes, and prayed for this farm. The cape and the sword floated in his vision. He had forgotten them on the barn's shelf. They didn't belong to this farm. They should go with him.

He returned to the barn and found Santos sleeping on its floor. The dog lifted his head and perked his ears. Ignaçio took the cape and the sword from the shelf. The dog stood, shook off his sleep, and wagged his tail. Ignaçio crouched beside him and explained the reason. The dog wouldn't listen. Ignaçio left the barn. Santos overtook him and reached his car.

Ignaçio opened the passenger-side door and made room for Santos. He sat in the driver's seat, started the engine, and peered into the side-view mirror. The farm looked far and small. He rolled, reached the trail's fork, and glanced at the mirror. The farm's gate seemed no more than a row of bars; the rest hid in the dark. He checked the rearview mirror and saw nothing over his luggage. He turned at the fork, changed gear, and sped uphill without looking back.

The car reached the trail's end.

Ignaçio stopped at his farm's gate and let Santos out. The dog now knew the reason. He didn't wait for the cape and the sword. He jumped the barrier and ran for his round. Ignaçio hesitated, opened the gate, and scanned his farm. He didn't see the dog anywhere.

A silver-grey cloud sailed from east and covered the moon above the ocean.

A bovine figure stirred under the cedar. Ignaçio recognized Lorenza. He crossed the pasture and walked to her. The pregnant cow was holding out well. The bulge now showed on her belly. If all went right, she would birth her calf this December. The grouse called under the persimmon. A ptarmigan responded from the forest and skittered away. A nighthawk squealed and woke the badger. The raccoon finished drinking and left the pond.

Ignaçio walked the moonlit alleys through the pussy willows. Their shadows hid him from the moon. They never concealed him from Victor's eyes. Somehow, the bull always knew. No matter which way he went, he would always end up face-to-face with the bull. Today, he hid behind Victor's favorite trees, but the bull didn't come looking for him. Only the farm's owl screeched overhead and flew toward its nest in the oak tree.

Ignaçio emerged from the shadows. From the weeping willow, he broke a few branches and weaved them into a wreath. He held the garland in his raised hands and marched toward the pond. He climbed the mound and reached the stone pile. He kneeled before the pile, placed the wreath at its foot, and traced a cross on his chest. He closed his eyes, raised his head, and recited his trusted prayer. The silent stones listened to him.

He finished his prayer, rose to his feet, and climbed the stone pile.

221

He was moving from this real place to someplace unreal. To do something unreal. He needed to find his anchor. These stones felt real. This pond, the musk rats, the shamrocks looked real. The basil, the dill, the oregano smelled real. The heron dwelled in its real nest. The oaks and birches, the maples and chestnuts, the figs and prunes, the plums and apples, the grapes and currants—they all lived on his farm's real soil. Their moving shadows were real. Victor could emerge from any of them at any moment. The bull would still feel real.

But Victor wouldn't appear again on his farm.

That, too, was real.

The breaking sun colored four cloud rows. They raced over his farm and merged above the ocean like a straight highway's parallel lanes. An oriole woke, peeked from its hanging nest, and stared at him as if he were a stranger on his farm. A jay laughed from the willows. A crow cawed from the mobile home. A mole peeped from its hole, sensed him on the stones, and slid back into its burrow. A jackal howled, a wild cat yowled. Santos barked and silenced both. The dog was doing his duty on this farm and not looking for the bull. The heron woke in its nest, left the cottonwood tree, and took its place among the reeds in the pond.

Only humans repent their losses for this long and treasure them as souvenirs.

This barren land contained the comfort of sorrow. He was standing on this stone pile and wallowing in that comfort. He needed to go. He still owed an explanation to Charo. He would send her a text message first and then call her tomorrow. He would surprise Paloma and Juan at their *tablao* this morning and give them his plan for the remaining shows. After hearing the news, they might cancel

222

those. He would thank the hospital for their generous job.

He descended from the stone pile and marched toward his farm's gate; he didn't look back once. He crossed the gate, reached his car, and started its engine; he still didn't look back. He turned the car, backed it up, and checked the rearview mirror. Victor's head still didn't appear above the farm's gate. He rolled his car, climbed the paved road, and heard a mournful howl. His foot pressed the brake and slowed the car. He bit his lip and shook his head. He pulled to the side and peeked at the side-view mirror. Santos stood at the gate and pointed his snout.

But the dog seemed smaller than real in the mirror.

And far.

The rays lit her eyes; they warmed. Nuria stretched her arm and found his place empty. She opened her eyes and sat up on her bed.

This wasn't a dream; this was real. His smell filled her room.

She left her bed and stood at the window. Dawn flowed between the hills and bathed the heath behind their farm. At the valley's mouth, on Uncle Manu's farm, his harvester cut the hay for winter. Despite his taurine tours, her uncle never stopped working his farm.

The chickens clucked below her window. The cuckoo cooed from the back, and the nightingale crooned from the cypress. Bees sang and danced on blooming heathers, irises, dandelions, roses, and melons. They foraged before the air chilled and welcomed winter.

After what happened last night, she couldn't return to sleep now. She tied the cardigan around her shoulders, left her room, and shut the door. Across the corridor, silence oozed from Ignaçio's closed room. She tapped the door and waited outside. He didn't rise. She pressed her ear against the panel, heard only purrs inside, and pushed the door.

The door opened. Magdalena lay in his place. The cat had the whole bed to herself.

Ortega's poster was gone from his bed's foot. The empty room sat stark, stripped bare except for the cracked pitcher leaking on his desk. He had cleaned the floor's tiles and left the balcony's door open. Nuria crossed the wet floor, went to the balcony, and leaned over its railing. His car was gone from its place. At least, he had taken the vehicle with him.

Brewed coffee wafted from the kitchen window. Her parents spoke in the den; she didn't want to hear them. The watered plants glittered on the balcony and waited with their scents. He had forgotten the zinnias, the roses, and the *belles-de-nuit* closing for the day.

She returned to his room. She lifted the empty pitcher, filled it in their bathroom, and quenched the plants' thirst. She held the pitcher to her bosom and surveyed his room. He had occupied it for more than a decade and a half. Now, no traces of his were left in this place. A rivulet dripped from his desk. She wiped the water, mopped the floor, and left the room.

She didn't want to meet her parents. She didn't want to leave for work. She didn't want to call Willem and ask for a leave of absence. She knew Ignaçio wouldn't be on his farm, yet her eyes needed to see to believe. Before leaving, he might have stopped at his farm and checked the cows. He might have found one or several sick. He might have stayed to treat them. The taurine academy's offer couldn't harden that part of Ignaçio's heart. She went down by the balcony's stairs and left for his farm.

Santos came down the trail. The dog's lowered head, ears, and tail warned her; she knew what she would find on Ignaçio's farm. She bent down and patted Santos on the head. The dog didn't stay. He slipped from her hands and trudged down his path. These six weeks since Victor left had transformed both farms' lives; one didn't have to look close to see the change. Everyone, except her, had changed life.

Humans make radical leaps at turning points. She was a human.

She reached Ignaçio's farm. Elena was leaving for work. She saw Nuria and backed her vehicle. Nuria hesitated to tell her about Ignaçio's departure: it felt too early to say.

"We saw him this dawn," Elena said.

"Nacho?" Nuria asked.

225

"Yes."

"What was he doing?"

"His usual round."

"It wasn't usual."

"I know," Elena said. "Paula called."

"This morning?"

"Last night."

"What did she say?"

"Do you really want to know?"

"No."

"She wasn't the only one to help Miguel."

"Pardon?"

"The cameras came from me."

"Elena!"

"The firefighter on that video was Vincente."

"Mother told you all this?"

"No," Elena said. "I'm telling you."

"Will she be in trouble for the key?"

"No."

"Are you sure?"

"I work for the police."

"Has Miguel confessed?"

"He doesn't need to," Elena said. "We're working to pull him out."

"What about you and Vincente?"

"What about us?"

"Will you get in trouble?"

"We'll see."

"Does Mother know all this?"

"What do you think?"

"Elena," Nuria said. "I can't think anymore."

"Then believe me."

"You people worked as a team?"

"Yes."

"And never told me?"

"We couldn't."

"Why?"

"You had no time."

"I'll have now."

"You think?"

"Yes."

"How?"

"You'll see."

"Let's hope," Elena said. "It's good Ignaçio left."

"Mother said that?"

"No."

"You're saying this?"

"Yes."

"Why?"

"He switched camp."

"You told him?"

"I won't."

"This is crazy."

"I agree."

Elena left. Nuria didn't enter Ignaçio's farm. She wouldn't return to her work. This job had removed her from home. She was still discovering the distance it had built between her and her people. Another serious issue hovered above her family. She would fix it before it got them. Today was the occasion. She left Ignaçio's farm and walked toward her parents'.

She tried hard but couldn't stop resenting Ignaçio.

He could have taken the hospital's offer if he didn't want Carlota's clinic. He was among the top five in his class and only a year away from graduation. His flamenco shows broke his ruts and brought money that helped everyone. He had no reason to see himself as a burden on her family; no reason to feel guilty for her, her parents, or anyone else. Yet he flung all this in the air and dived for a bet he saw as a sure win. He left those who loved him, nurtured him, and stood by him holding their bags in vertigo. Only he was capable of hurling such follies.

Good, he had left with his nonsense. She wouldn't worry about him.

She should have known. She had seen him grow. As early as eight, Ignaçio was drawn to bullfights; she couldn't keep him from watching corrida on television. It was lamentable that a state didn't protect its minors from watching these public shows of violence, gore, and death; that its laws permitted to destroy its future citizens by arousing their passion for violence. She had channeled his bursting energy into flamenco. He had embraced this art and excelled in it. Yet the lure of violence won at the end.

Ignaçio was wild but not violent. The taurine academy would turn him into a brute he wasn't. He would kill by the wrong passion and get killed for the wrong reason. It was one thing to simulate corrida with Victor; it was another to fight the *lidia* bulls. He had hot blood, not harsh temper. His parents had left him a void she couldn't fill. His *farruca* solos gave him the attention he needed. They brought him the power, glory, and status he craved. Yet he pushed all this aside and went for the bloodshed.

Violence has its pull for the deprived. Love can't resist that pull.

Mother's car came up the trail. She slowed the vehicle and lowered her window. Nuria didn't want to talk to her; she kept walking. Mother pulled to the side and stopped the car.

"Charo called," Mother said.

"About Nacho?"

"For Santos."

"Did you tell her about Nacho?"

"She knew."

"How?"

"She asked you to call her."

Mother left. Nuria reached her parents' farm but didn't feel like calling Carlota. She went to her room; it still smelled of Ignaçio. She didn't want to be in this room. She made her bed, showered and changed, then took her parents' accounts and went downstairs.

Father glanced at the farm's books in her hands. He sat down but didn't look at her. Nuria placed the folders on the table, separated the third quarter's figures, and laid them in front of his eyes. He didn't react. She highlighted the puzzling amount and pushed the sheet toward him.

"This fifty thousand," she said. "Where did it come from?"

"Insurance."

"No."

"You called them?"

"Yes."

"The subsidies then."

"From the state or the Union?"

"Both."

"Impossible," Nuria said. "The amount came as a single transfer."

"Who needs all this explanation?"

"The fiscal authorities."

"They never ask."

"They *will* for this amount."

"I'll check when I have time."

"Father."

"What?"

"We have money now," Nuria said. "Why do this?"

"Everyone does."

"On cash."

"Not for that sum."

"Exactly," Nuria said. "See my point?"

"Yes."

"Who paid you?"

"A buyer."

"Where is the invoice?"

"Ask your mother."

"I did," Nuria said. "She doesn't know."

"Where did the wire come from?"

"A bank up north."

"A friend."

"When did you sell him your cattle?"

"Before the crash."

"And he paid this late?"

"He couldn't before."

"I don't see an unpaid invoice in your books."

"We didn't make one."

"Father."

"Are we done?"

"Not yet," Nuria said. "One more question."

"Shoot."

"Did Miguel pay you for the key?"

"Pardon!"

"Did he?"

"What do you take us for?"

"Be careful with money."

"Watch your words."

Father left the living room, went outside, and lit a cigarette. Nuria regretted. Her face burned. She combed the first two quarters' accounts. She found no other figures that jumped to her eyes. Her vision clouded. She gathered the papers and returned to her room.

She sat at her desk and checked their accounts since the markets burst. She found no other anomalies. Her parents were honest farmers. They played by the rules. She was harsh to doubt their honesty from a single error. By no means, she was justified to suspect them for accepting a bribe from Miguel. She was insulting her parents and Miguel.

She was refusing to see the status quo of farmers like her parents.

After the economic downturn, the state left its citizens to their banks, collected taxes as before, and filled its coffers. The farming chain's actors had to look after themselves. They did this by trusting each other in good faith. Their play seemed fair. Their acts strengthened their bonds. Her parents had acted by this common faith. She couldn't resent them.

You have to take the dog with its fleas.

Victor's disappearance had revealed how humane her family members were; how much courage they carried despite their limited

231

means; how much compassion they possessed, and how modest they stayed about it. If she had a fraction of their qualities, her life today would be different. Many other lives would suffer less.

Besides, if she questioned her parents' integrity, she herself was faring worse. She was earning her living by helping Willem skirt laws. The man fed Spain and its people, but his roads were often illegal. The three legal units of his that she led—business, tax, real estate—always had something to hide from someone. These hide-and-seek games lowered her self-regard. Each legal project, done illegally, left her moral a little lower. Over time, the effects added up and stopped her from looking in the mirror. She no longer needed this job. She still did it because she had no time or energy to look for another.

Thoughts provoke change. She never thought because she feared change.

She had no reasons to fear. This farm was doing far better than before. Everyone here had worked hard, and their efforts had pulled them out. Stability now reigned in this family. The members were free to do what they wanted. They didn't have to worry about their next meal or shelter. Some were already giving their hearts to what they loved. She could do the same and permit her soul the rewards it deserved.

The new laws for company animals had created fresh demand. Most law firms were now opening their animal laws division. The Union's pressure was rising on Spain, to tighten its animal laws further. These lawyers would have more work coming to them. She had turned down the firm that offered her a job in animal laws two years earlier. They were now going stronger. They might still take her if she called them. If they didn't, there would be others. Her thesis on animal laws and her experience as Willem's jurist shouldn't leave her out of work for long. She would take this risk.

Willem's contract required a three-month notice. If she resigned now, she could start a new job in January. She would lose her service vehicle from Willem, but she could take back her old car from Jaime. His new garage was now in service; he would need a larger vehicle. Today was the occasion for this move.

Her cell phone rang.

The call didn't come from her work; it came from Carlota's clinic. She picked up the call, went to the balcony, and searched for Santos. She didn't see the dog on this farm.

"What's this now?" Carlota said. "Another of Ignaçio's jokes?"

"Who told you?"

"Paloma and Juan."

"Nacho is with them?"

"Where else?"

"Sorry, Charo," Nuria said. "Nacho ditched everyone, not just you."

"You believe that?"

"Did he leave us a choice?"

"Are you blind?"

"About what?"

"Do you see him killing bulls?"

"I didn't before."

"Just wait."

"I hope you're right."

Carlota hung up. Nuria stared at the phone until her eyes blurred. She returned to her room and gazed from her window. The sun, crossing her family's farm, marked it in sharp stripes of light and shadow. Between them, she couldn't find any grey to hide from the cruel rays.

Life would be easier to deal with if it came this way: in perfect black and white patches; with no ambiguity, no impurity, no uncertainty. But life is imperfect. A perfect perception is imperfect. The imperfect can still go somewhere. The perfect have no further place to go.

She, herself, wasn't perfect. She couldn't expect others to be.

She lifted her phone and called Willem.

Part II

23

The academy's bus, carrying the sixty-two students without a car, left for the *tienta*. Ignaçio slung the duffle bag on his shoulder, left the hostel, and walked toward the parking lot. The April sun sparked the lawn's dewdrops and shined the academy's dome. The spring *feria* had canceled this week's classes. The students not at the bull ranch this morning would help the municipal workers open the taurine fair. The twin bells rang the hour from Iglesia Sacrata di Ser Vivo, pumped the city's heart, and raised its beats. After the two failed years, the mayor now pushed hard to rebuild his mark; the last few days had tripled the city's tourists.

Ignaçio entered his sports car and noticed his bank statement. This car cost eighty percent of his monthly stipend, but it also saved him time to reach the ranches for his practice. Those ranches weren't close to the city. The leather seat made the long drives comfortable.

He checked the time. The vet wanted his help before the tienta. If he took the expressway, he should reach the ranch before the bus arrived by the country roads. These days, only a few ranchers wanted the academy's students to sever, select, and brand their yearlings; the rector didn't want his first-year students to disrupt this ranch's work. Ignaçio left the parking lot, greeted the security guarding the academy, and waited at the gate for the traffic to clear.

Four deluxe coaches of Willem carried their tourist loads toward his Gran Taurino Hotel. Boulevard de Lidia stood jammed from one end to the other. Ignaçio turned right on Paseo de Aficionados, skirted the jam through the side-streets, and drove east toward the city center.

The traffic stalled by Plaza de Toreros. While the city prepared for this evening's bull-run, Miguel and other animal-rights activists built their stands on the square and rubbed shoulders with the police, the firefighters, the national and civil guards. Nuria wasn't with Miguel. The crowd shuffled and shouted. The legislature and the court ignored them. At the far end, sturdy grills guarded the bullfighting association's building and reflected the streaming sun's festive spirit. Angel leaned from his office window and soaked the square's action. Ignaçio honked and waved; his mentor didn't hear or see him. The retired matador looked troubled.

Ignaçio understood his mentor's dilemma. Angel knew his trade and valued his work. He didn't want Willem to hurt bullfight's art. Esteban was a butcher, not a bullfighter. If Angel didn't intervene, Willem's favorites would model matadors' style. Rafaela's force, strength, and toughness kept their association on track, but Angel's tact and stamina balanced corrida's business with art. This wounded matador held Willem's zeal for blood at bay.

Despite his pressure, Angel had proved a reliable mentor. Crossing bullfight's labyrinths and surviving its ambushes required long luck and short shrifts. An aspiring matador needed an inspired guide. Horns alone didn't comprise this trade's dangers. Corruption's spines and competition's thorns, long and sharp and poisonous, waited at every turn, caught the unwary and the inexperienced, extinguished their lives' flames, and devoured them alive.

Angel knew this maze of sleaze. His insights taught more than the academy's classes, both for business and art. Their busy schedules left them little time to meet. But when they did, their meetings produced precious treasures. Angel didn't do this only to help him; he did this also to preserve the bullfighting art. His mentor was counting on him to lead the change.

His foot pressed the brake pedal. At the square's far end, on

Avenida de Corrida, Nuria's old car inched along. She sat inside the ruined vehicle, rounding her shoulders and leaning on the steering wheel. This wasn't the first time he saw her stooping inside this beaten down car she took back from Jaime after returning her sturdy service vehicle to Willem. Her new job at the downtown law firm offered cars only to their experienced partners. She had left her eleven years' seniority with Willem to start at this firm's bottom rung. Only Nuria could do this.

Seven months had passed since he left her family's home. Their paths crossed here and there; they didn't stop to talk or slow to look. But the last eight weeks had dropped her rigid shoulders and lowered her stubborn head. This wasn't the Nuria he knew. Willem's tyranny had never crushed her this way. Trading the jurist job to defend animals was ruining her. By now, she must have seen what these firms did with the laws made for defending animals. She must have seen she was faring worse with this law firm by earning less and committing more crimes. For an ethical woman like her, these blows on her conscience were showing on her figure and posture. He waited for her to pass and then joined the traffic crawling west.

San Taurino ignored others' affairs and dressed up for her spring *feria*. The city's terrace buzzed with painters and burst in blooming colors. Along the avenue's footpaths, palms and planes rattled their leaves; cherries, magnolias, oranges shook their flowers and offered their scents. Farther down, on the market street, vapor rose from the thermal bath and veiled the old quarter's leaning buildings and their peeling façades. The sun pierced that veil and danced on their crumbling balconies' flowers: on morning glories, marigolds, and forsythias; on phloxes, peonies, and pansies; on jasmines, hibiscuses, and hollyhocks; on bougainvilleas, carnations, and camellias.

Past the fort's decorated gate, the intoxicated station clattered and clacked, screeched and squealed, groaned and thumped. Trains arrived, taxied, and left. Above, poised gliders sailed the city's air and dragged their gold-lit banners. Piercing jets sliced the azure sky into equal squares. The blazing sun burned the jets' tips and drenched their expanding trails in scarlet.

Ignaçio turned left after the station and sped for the highway. He passed the police station and the firefighters' barracks and then slowed before Jaime's mechanics shop. In his garage, Jaime stood beside a dismounted car and showed its parts to his trainees; all six came from his community of Andalusian farmers. This proactive, go-getter had delivered his promise to this community that sheltered him on his return from Vigo. Ignaçio pressed the gas pedal harder. Jaime heard the sports car's sputters, looked up, and waved at him. The trainees turned and gaped at his car. Ignaçio changed lane, merged in the mad traffic, and escaped fast.

The rough highway hid him in its cover. The harsh speed soothed his woes. The sharp wind thawed his blues.

Excess ferments poison; gratitude obeys this rule. He had repaid Nuria's family and their community what they gave him. He couldn't stay with them for life, like a piece of driftwood caught in their current and flowing in their predictable ways. He had to leave them behind to live his own life. His presence was, by no means, indispensable for them. Those farmers and their cattle were doing well without him. His absence hadn't ruined them or their community. If he had stayed with them, he would have erred on the side of excess. They didn't miss him.

On the contrary, he had lost his community. The taurine academy didn't foster cohesion among its students. Of his classmates, seventy-

239

two came from abroad; twenty-nine fought the language barrier. The cut-throat competition made one student's gain another's loss and left no room for compassion. He had luck. Angel's aegis ensured fair treatment from the academy. His mock fights with Victor gave him an edge and placed him before other students. He didn't face the artificial horns on his classmates; he went to bull ranches and faced the real. Using his courses transferred from the veterinary school, he could shorten his term, but he would stay its full duration and master this trade's rules. He loved his training at this school.

You can't accelerate your natural growth. Those who climb fast crash faster. Their rush doesn't prepare them for their success's weight. If you want to rise to the top and stay there for your due time, you pay with your patience. Diligence doesn't take any short-cuts.

The academy's life came with its luxury—a form of luxury odd for someone emerging from penury, yet essential to fit the elite bullfight niche. The academy inserted you into this niche and trained you in its lifestyle. As long as you watched its downward slope, you didn't slip into debauchery. So far he had avoided this slope. He had no reason to go toward it. He missed simple life. Once he graduated and earned his renown, he would leave this luxury.

His mood lifted. He shifted gear, left the highway, and entered the country road. On each side, cereal fields, vegetable patches, and fruit orchards flourished and garnished the farmers' hamlets. Cows mooed, bulls bellowed, pigs grunted. Calves bleated and suckled under their mothers' udders. Roosters crowed, hens clucked, turkeys gobbled. Rugged kids, dressed in rags, ran by the tumbling farmsteads. They chased their dogs, rolled in the dirt, and savored the spring's arrival. They heard his car's firing. They stopped their games and dashed to the fences. Ignaçio slowed his car and threw candies at them. They caught those and hollered.

Tienta was a big event for a bull ranch. Bull raisers tested their calves' bravery. Although ranchers belonged to a cooperative, their competition was stiff. A poorly selected batch could ruin their reputation and kill their ranches fast. A fighting bull cost three to four times more to mature than an ordinary one. Ranchers selected only those bulls that shined their names. They invited apprentice toreros to their tientas to test their calves' courage, skills, and bravery.

Tienta was also a big event for aspiring bullfighters. They could impress the agents who would recruit them after graduation and launch their career as *novilleros*. A wrong attitude, a wrong gesture, a wrong step, a wrong turn could kill a potential torero's budding future. All students knew this trade's cruel reality and deferred to their future agents.

Not all students would qualify for today's tienta. This rancher wanted those who handled horses well. A calf that met a human on foot during tienta remembered the encounter and used it later in a bullring. Your skills with bulls alone didn't place you ahead in this game.

He reached the ranch. The academy's bus was delayed. The students who came with their own transport stood at the barrier. He saw the fresh graduate who had successfully completed twenty-four *novilladas* and would do his final one this afternoon in the village. These students would go to this bullfight. The young bull for this reduced-scale corrida would come from this ranch. The novillero had brought his family of toreros to check this ranch's bulls.

Ignaçio shook hands with the aspiring matador, his uncles, and his cousins. Three of them would assist him this afternoon in the arena. The young man seemed troubled. Ignaçio wished him good luck, entered the ranch, and walked toward the vet waiting for him.

Men on horseback severed the yearlings from their mothers, gathered them at a corner, and made room for selecting the two- and three-year old calves. Those that failed the test would go straight to the slaughterhouse. An eighteen-wheeler waited for them at the ranch's gate. Their mothers would accompany them to the same slaughterhouse.

Ignaçio helped the vet sort out the color-blind calves; they left for the waiting truck. He measured the older calves' horns, checked their shapes, and tested their necks and shoulders. Those that didn't meet *The Treaties*' standard left for the truck. Their progenitor was a brave bull pardoned at a corrida last summer to reproduce. He had failed to transmit his traits to his progeny. He, too, left with his cows for slaughter. Only a sixth of the calves remained. They would now be tested with capes and picks by the academy's selected students.

"You're good for this work," the vet said. "You should return to the veterinary school and finish your degree."

"Pardon?" Ignaçio said.

"I didn't mean now."

"Why would I return to the veterinary school?"

"Matadors don't last in bullrings for ever."

"You're thinking too far out."

"I'm not," the vet said. "Most finish in their thirties. Then they have thirty more years to spend. They become the industry's slaves. If you get your veterinary degree, you can work at arenas or teach at academies like I do."

"I'll think about it."

"The veterinary school was sad to see you go."

The rancher called the vet. Desperate yearlings, choked by lassos and burnt by branding irons, needed urgent care. Ignaçio offered to help. The doctor asked him to prepare the tienta and left for the wailing calves. Ignaçio stood and watched his professor. The aged president of the regional taurine veterinarian association crossed the ranch's pasture on sure feet.

The students called his class "The Anatomy of Killing." Despite his global renown for his research on the fighting bulls' anatomy, physiology, and trauma, this doctor carried a humane side. He didn't treat his students as dispensable actors on bullfight's stage; he warned them of a reality the toreros' boiling blood ignored. The man didn't want him to finish like Angel; he was spreading a safety net for a student he knew from the veterinary school.

But the alternative didn't attract him. He had escaped one safety net to embrace life's perils; he wasn't going back to another for safety. A vagabond lives rare events. These events, unpredictable and unconnected, have a predictable connection: the flame. It lightened his soul. A secure net would suffocate this flame, extinguish it, and ensure his death.

Security kills with certainty. That is the worst form of death.

The rancher called him. The tienta would start for the selected calves. The man wanted his input for matching the students to the horses.

In bullfighting terms, a *lidia* bull that shows no interest in fighting is a *manso*: a coward. But the *novillero* was mistaking this three-year old bull's moves for cowardice. Ignaçio glanced at the rancher standing against the ring's barrier. The man's smile confirmed the bull's trap.

This ranch didn't raise coward bulls; it raised bulls that were dangerous: *peligroso*.

You could see that danger in the way this bull had entered the ring. You could see that danger in the way this bull had picked its target from the beginning. You could see that danger in the way this bull had ignored the picks and kept its eyes fixed on the target.

And that target wasn't the cape.

A pure-bred bull, like one from Rafaela's ranch, was a noble creature that came endowed with a wide range of emotions. You could dance with such a bull, play with it, lead it by your moves, and move it by your emotions. It wouldn't box itself into a single-minded goal or trick you with an undercover scheme to achieve its purpose. It would see you as its equal and fight you by the fair rules. Such a bull made a dignified adversary, worthy of facing and fighting.

This young bull didn't descend from the pure-bred. It descended from a selective breeding method that favored the trade's virulent traits. It emerged from a genetic engineering toolbox that honed these traits to their worst for toreros. This ranch specialized in these bulls. The law didn't regulate their fabrication. The result was this pure devil taken for a coward.

The bleeding bull stopped looking at the novillero. It lowered its head and pointed its ears backward. The agents leaned over the barrier and murmured. The aspiring torero switched the sword to his right hand and swayed the cape with his left. The bull didn't respond to his cape moves. The animal dug the soil, sniffed the sand, and snorted. The three assistants took their turns to provoke the animal. The stubborn bull stood still and refused to charge them.

The president announced the *novillada*'s last three minutes.

The desperate novillero lost his poise. He cried out and lunged at the bull. The animal was waiting for this face-to-face move. It raised its muzzle, thrust its head at the young bullfighter, and hit him on the

244

chest. His bones cracked. The teenage boy flew to the ring's side. The bull charged, lifted him and flung him, and crushed him against the ring's barrier. The assistants rushed to help the broken bullfighter. They couldn't dissuade the bull or distract its fury.

On the golden sand, the blood patch grew around the young victim.

Ignaçio exited the highway and entered San Taurino. The city was bristling.

Citizens gathered in pockets and boiled over the *novillero*'s death at the bullring; the boy was nineteen years old. The taurine fair's decors were torn down; the streetlights, broken; the city's arteries, clogged. He drove through the dark side-streets, lost his orientation, and turned in a tortuous grid. The mob closed in. His sports car wouldn't escape unscathed. He found a secluded alley, parked his car in the elms' shadow, and walked to the Gran Taurino Hotel.

Angel received him at the Taverna de Tauromaquia, escorted him into the bullfighting bar, and left him with Esteban at the counter. The awkward seconds took minutes to pass. A hired beauty cat-walked to Esteban and offered him her bare arm. Esteban took her by the shoulder and paraded through the aisle, through the rows of palms, toward the bar's back.

Six silent screens cast corridas on three walls, in real time from Spain and abroad. At the tables and on the sofas, bets flew high among state dignitaries, overseas diplomats, taurine-club directors, bullfighting executives, and real-estate barons. Their *tapas* and *copas* waited untouched. They speculated on these bullfights: the hits and misses; the wins and losses; the honors, awards, and exits on shoulders; the matadors' ranks, contracts, and revenues.

Among their high-flying gamble, a poised Asian beauty sat erect, wearing a cream-white choker, her ink-black hair tied up in a pony tail. Silver ear-hoops sparkled against her glowing tan-brown face. The woman's profile evoked a shadow. Ignaçio couldn't recall where he had seen her. From time to time, she glanced in his direction, her contours tensed. Ignaçio moved from her line of view and turned toward the bar's wall free of bullfighting screens and bets.

The portrait of a nineteenth-century classic bullfight covered that wall. Underneath that portrait, Rafaela directed her group: it consisted of her husband, Pedro; Mayor José and his wife, Margarita; Judge Emilio and his wife, Soledad; and Angel. The two women, deputies at Pedro's legislature, listened to Rafaela and nodded at her husband. Snacks and drinks served on their table also waited untouched. They ignored the bar's other occupants and their bets.

Willem huddled with his cohorts at a corner and observed Rafaela. Her measured words, reserved gestures, and long pauses troubled the bullfighting magnate. He watched her group's sober manners, grave expressions, and upright poses. The taut air thickened above their table and spread in the bar. Willem noticed him at the counter and lifted his hand. Ignaçio nodded.

A voice he knew called him from the bar's door. Ignaçio turned.

Ishmael, the editor-in-chief of *El Periódico de San Taurino*, entered the bar and came to the counter.

"Were you at that *novillada* this afternoon?" Ishmael asked.

"Yes," Ignaçio said. "I saw you."

"Did you take photos?"

"You did."

"You should have too."

"Why?"

"You'll see."

"Hey, Ishmael." Willem marched to the counter. "How are you this evening?"

"I love this party."

"Who invited you?"

"Nobody."

"You just walked in?"

"Yes."

"For fun?"

"No," the editor said. "I report for my paper."

"There's nothing to report here."

"Are you sure?"

"You'll have to leave."

"Why?"

"I'll make announcements."

"I want to hear them."

"They're private."

"For these public figures?"

"Just go."

Ishmael left. Willem went to the center-stage, adjusted the microphone on his lapel, and announced the seven-course dinner to be served with a list of vintage wines from France. His cohorts sat up straight and shuffled for space. Some came to the counter and got their drinks. Ignaçio moved to the end and made space for them.

A waiter brought him a sizzling platter: shrimps and squids, swordfish and shark cubes, lobsters and other rare creatures drained from the sea, boiled and broiled, garnished with rare relishes, and served with delicate care. He refused the platter and took the glass of water. The closed air thickened. Food, wine, and smoke courted

247

cackles, clutters, and croaks. The bar's heat rose. The odor stuffed his nose. The noise thumped his temples and numbed his head. His face flushed. Sweat dripped from his sideburns, streamed down his neck, and drenched his collar. He opened his shirt's top buttons and moved closer to the door.

The Asian beauty left her seat and walked toward him. He recognized her subtle gait. The Japanese came to Spain for flamenco, not for corrida. There was bullfighting in Japan, but it was between two bulls. He couldn't figure what she was doing in this bullfighting bar.

"I heard you switched," Naomi said. "What a surprise!"

"Who told you?" Ignaçio asked.

"Willem."

"You know him?"

"My boyfriend does."

"I don't see anyone else from Japan."

"He isn't Japanese," Naomi said. "He's from the Middle East."

"A diplomat?"

"He owns a taurine club."

"I see."

"And he invests in Willem's business."

"Real estate?"

"In everything," she said. "He knows Willem from his oil trading days."

"Willem traded oil before?"

"Among other things."

"I didn't know that."

"Now you do."

"I wish you a great evening."

"See you soon."

Naomi returned to her Middle Eastern man. Willem rose from his seat and declared he had news for his investors. He thanked them for attending his private gala, deplored the city's turn of events this evening, and promised to make their *feria* safe. Claps rose and broke his speech. He bowed to his guests, waited till their applause ceased, and resumed his announcement.

He was incorporating a new holding company, headquartered in Lichtenstein's tax haven. This company would hold three new businesses under its umbrella: one, an exclusive agency for matadors with the highest profitability; two, a taurine club for aficionados with at least ten million euros; three, an estate for the highest quality fighting bulls that the genetic engineering could produce. These three units would span the entire taurine world.

Of this new company's equity, sixty-five percent would come from his pocket. For the remaining thirty-five, he counted on his long-dated friends to trust his usual business sense.

He also wanted to add a fourth business unit that would own the globe's best-performing arenas. In most countries, these arenas were classified as national monuments. His bids faced fierce resistance from their laws. Tonight, he was urging his overseas patrons to help him create this unit by straightening their unfavorable laws in his favor.

Rafaela rose. She lifted her purse, left her seat, and strutted toward the door. Heads turned, eyes followed her moves; she ignored them. Willem stopped and bowed to her; she continued. Angel ran after her; she didn't look back. Willem resumed his speech. The mayor left with his wife. After a while, Pedro filed out and followed them.

Only Judge Emilio and his wife remained.

Ignaçio pulled into the parking lot of Iglesia Sacrata di Ser Vivo. Angel thanked him for the ride but didn't leave the car. The man seemed lost in thoughts.

Ignaçio cut the engine. He saw his mentor's dilemma. The taurine association's heftiest donor was Willem's empire. Rafaela's walk-out from the gala this evening wouldn't help his patronage. The two entities fed each other. The projects Willem revealed at this party would kill their relation. If the bullfighting magnate succeeded in acquiring the monopoly he sought, all taurine actors would prostrate at his feet. Corrida's art would lose to bullfight's butchery. Like his mentor, he would have to leave bullfighting if he didn't buy Willem's rules.

But he couldn't see Angel and Rafaela giving up so soon.

"The *novillero*'s strategy this afternoon cost his life," Angel said. "The boy should have used a mounted picador for that young bull."

"He wanted to impress the agents," Ignaçio said.

"He paid for it."

"Wasn't he scheduled for accreditation in San Taurino?"

"Yes, two weeks after the *feria*," Angel said. "Esteban would have served as his godfather at the ceremony."

"That explains the boy's moves."

"He isn't the only one."

"I know."

"Would you behave like him?"

"No."

"I count on your word."

"You can."

Angel left the car and limped toward his home. It wasn't a permanent limp; it came out when he worried. But he held his head erect. He crossed the paved square, opened his home, and entered on surer feet. The bells tolled above the church. Ignaçio sat inside his car and counted the twenty-two strokes. The din rang in his ears long after the bells stopped.

His head reeled. This recurrent vertigo didn't pass by lying down or eating a sugar cube; for it to leave, he had to keep moving. He started the engine, pulled away from the car park, but didn't want to return to his room on campus. He drove through the revolting streets. He watched the city's order disrupt by the hour. He forgot his fear and cruised in the forbidden zones. He scoured the upheaval's rubbles without knowing what he was searching for.

Time eroded the disruption from the city, but not the chaos from his head.

On the city's terrace, at a deserted spot where the lights were out, three young men surrounded a *lidia* bull tethered to a plane tree's trunk. Another cord tied the animal's head and muzzle to a broken lamppost. Two torches blazed in one youth's hands. Under their crackling fire's glare, the two other young men shaved the immobilized bull's horns, using a pair of carpenter's files. At their feet, four metal collars glimmered red on the pavement.

Ignaçio couldn't figure how these three men could have brought this massive bull, packed with muscles, up to this terrace and constrain it for torture. He pulled to the roadside, got out of his car, and saw the answer. A dozen more youths, male and female, hid in a parked truck's shadow and watched their comrades working on this bull. The thick air reeked of marijuana and harsh spirits. They saw him coming and warned him in a language he didn't understand.

Ignaçio stopped. He pulled out his cell phone and called the police station. No one picked up his call; the force of order must still be out clearing the city's disorder from this evening. He approached the three men surrounding the bull and asked them to stop the torture. They bared their teeth and brandished their daggers. He recoiled from the three drunkards. He called the national emergency line and reported their abuse to a sergeant.

The two young men finished filing the bull's horns. Each lifted a metal collar and slid it down the horn he bled. The bull groaned. The man holding the torches stepped forward and shoved their stems into the collars' holders. The brutal thrust forced the collars further down the horns and brought the flames closer to the bull's head. The shocked animal roared. The hiding youths clapped and cheered. The mad bull strained its neck and kicked the air.

Ignaçio's cell phone rang: an officer wanted the exact location.

One young man pulled out a dirk and approached the bull's head. Wind blew from the port and fanned the torches. The flames singed the bull's nape and hump. The animal twisted, turned, and tugged its muzzle. The odor of burnt hair and flesh filled the air. The jerks slid the torches further down the bull's horns. The desperate animal wrenched off its muzzle, tossed its head, and leaped in frenzy. The blazing torches still didn't come off its bleeding horns.

The bull's torsion tore the cord's strands. The rope broke and freed the animal.

The man holding the knife recoiled. The bull crushed him against the plane tree and flung the other two youths onto the pavement. Ignaçio dodged the mad animal's charge. The raging bull leaped to the truck and leveled the hiding young men and women. It bellowed across the avenue, galloped to the terrace's edge, and jumped at the

252

port's water.

Ignaçio dashed to his car and rushed to the port. He couldn't save the broken bull.

The two torches went on blazing from the animal's unbroken horns.

24

"Don't go to the city this morning," Mother said.

"I have to," Nuria asked. "Why?"

"Have you seen the news?"

"Yes."

"Take a day off."

"I'm still on probation."

"Work from home."

"You can't during trial period."

"We aren't desperate for money."

"When does the arena open?"

"Who knows?" Mother said. "I'll go and see Belen."

"Did Uncle Manu get home last night?"

"They closed the roads."

"The city will cancel the *feria*."

"I hear Ignaçio got caught up with the *correbus* last night."

"Who told you?"

"Elena."

"You asked her about him?"

"She called."

"To tell you that?"

"Yes."

"I don't believe you."

"He's in the news."

"Nacho left us," Nuria said. "And you're still after him."

"He'll return."

"I don't want him to."

"Nuria!"

"What?"

"You shouldn't be angry with him."

"Don't tell me how to feel."

"People learn from their mistakes."

"No," Nuria said. "Nacho isn't learning."

"How do you know?"

"Jaime tells me."

"See?" Mother said. "You're not indifferent to Ignaçio."

"I'll leave now."

"They closed the bridge to the city."

"The alternate route is open."

"Stay at Miguel's place if you have to."

"Pardon?"

"Don't kill yourself to return home."

"I'll see."

Nuria left for work. The alternate route didn't help her.

The revolting city shot its tumult into the suburb. The uproar soared, spread, and shook the surroundings. The desperate vehicles inched through the jam, each impatient to get ahead of others and beat this new predicament. Thumps and booms accompanied microphones. The dissonance reflected from the hills, reverberated through their valleys, rocked the cars, buses, coaches, trucks, and vans stalled on the interchange. No one looked at, spoke with, or yielded to another. Nobody could turn back. Silent anger seethed and charged the tense air.

By the time Nuria entered San Taurino, the clock had ticked past ten-thirty. Burnt shops gaped along the road. The arson's odor permeated the city. The arena quivered behind the security's barricade. The church and the hospice braced behind their closed doors. Farther ahead, Avenida de Corrida lay clogged. Last night's disastrous *correbus* had closed two of its four lanes. The jammed side-streets didn't promise a quicker route to her office.

On Plaza de Toreros, the army guarded the city hall, the regional legislature, and the national tribunal. Citizens demanded justice for last night's vandals, arsonists, and racketeers. Everyone remonstrated; no one listened. The crowd grew and spilled from the square. The human mass choked the avenue and halted its flow. Exhaust rose and thickened the air. Nuria closed her car's windows, eased on the gas pedal, and crawled with the traffic.

She rehashed the three cases she would debrief this morning. They didn't inspire her to continue and report at work.

On January second this year, when she first reported at this law firm, she went with a different vision of her work. Since then, the past three months and a half had revealed the reality of practicing animal laws. She still stood two and a half months away from her trial period's end. Even if she passed her probation, she was no longer sure she could hold onto this line of work. She didn't see her plight improving or her assignments getting better.

Spain trudged behind Europe for animals—not just for fighting bulls, but for all animals. Cruelty committed on them drew penalty half of the European norm. Most Spaniards now saw their animals as sentient beings, but Spain still saw its nonhuman animals as the object of law, not as its subject. The Spanish laws favored seeing animals as their owners' properties. The Union was tightening its pressure on these laws, opening opportunities for firms like hers, but these firms used those laws to target humans, not serve animals. Lawsuits to extort money or seek revenge were exploding and clogging the country's tribunals.

Her car reached the western end of the city's terrace. Red and white tapes surrounded the parts where the *correbus* last night had turned into a disaster. The charred truck, used by the delinquent youths to bring the unfortunate bull, waited on the pavement, its crushed chassis still fuming. The broken rope, tied to the plane tree's trunk, swayed in the port's breeze. The security tapes had preserved the night's frost from trampling feet. Around the tree's base, where April's early sun warmed the paving stones and thawed their frost patches, scarlet blood oozed and turned crimson at their borders. Nuria averted her eyes.

Last night, the gored racketeer died on the spot. This morning, his two accomplices lay in coma at the hospital and sank fast toward death. Six more youths—treated for broken bones, dislocated hips and shoulders, and internal hemorrhage—would pay regular fines in Spain for an ordinary public disorder and return to their home country. The law would ignore what the dead bull suffered last night—before, during, and after the torturous correbus.

The law would also overlook the *novillero*'s death in the bullring last afternoon. In the code's eyes, this incident occurred while honoring a long-revered tradition, now legalized as a national heritage, even if the teenager's death thwarted the *feria*, started a riot that killed four citizens and injured six officers, ruined public and private properties, and murdered Spain on the international stage. The law would see these causes and their consequences as legal.

She reached the terrace's end and turned into the historic district. Rebels, rioters, and racketeers always spared this quarter shielded from churning actions. The lukewarm rays streamed onto the bourgeois homes and lighted their balconies. Spring flowers—red and yellow, blue and purple, orange and white—flared their railings. They lured tweeting birds and humming bees, hurrying to feed their progeny. They didn't care about the city's riot.

Kids of all ages and status filled the refurbished daycare center's colorful courtyard. Some frolicked, laughed, and screamed at the jungle gym; others played hide-and-seek and chased their favorites through the tropical labyrinth. Among the elite's sumptuous, sober homes, the brave new low-income building rose and bowed to the thirty-five floor steel-and-glass tower that replaced the abandoned convention center. It held her law firm and a dozen companies. It housed an Olympic-size swimming pool in its basement, accessible to San Taurino's citizens regardless of their social standing. They didn't get involved in San Taurino's taurine life.

Nuria parked by the swimming pool's entrance. She sat inside her car and calmed her mind. She collected her thoughts and gathered her papers. She got out, took her time to walk around the tower, and then paused before its revolving doors. She greeted the security officers and chatted with them. She passed the turnstiles, avoided the elevators, and took the stairs to the eleventh floor. She stood before her firm, watched its door, and entered its corridor.

The managing partner saw her coming. He checked his watch but didn't utter a word or make any gestures. Nuria went to her office she shared with five other junior lawyers; they didn't lift their heads or glance at her. She reorganized her desk and rearranged her old case files. She opened the new ones, booted her computer, and started typing their briefs.

The manager rapped on her door and asked her to come to his office.

"I read your court proceedings," the manager said. "You're a tough litigator and your arguments are sharp."

"Thank you."

"How are the new cases going?"

"Not good."

"Why?"

"The evidence sucks," Nuria said. "The pieces don't add up."

"For all three?"

"Yes."

"How do you know?"

"A vet I trust checked the animals."

"A vet we use?"

"No."

"You shouldn't have," the manger said. "What's your strategy now?"

"Drop these cases."

"Do you know who these clients are?"

"I do."

"And you want us to drop them."

"I'm tired of these made-up cases. I'm tired of humans who use animals as means to serve their ends. I wish these animals spoke our language. I wish these animals told the court truths about their company humans."

"That sounds like your master's thesis."

"It does," Nuria said. "And that *is* the problem."

"You aren't tired of Miguel?"

"Pardon?"

"He uses bulls to serve his end."

"No, he doesn't."

"Let's get this straight," the manager said. "Do you know how many aficionados we have on our roster? How many families of toreros? How many politicians, entrepreneurs, investors, and business executives from the bullfighting industry? How many of San Taurino's elites?"

"Should I?"

"Do you know what your affiliation with Miguel does to our firm?"

"Are you asking me to leave him?"

"Yes," the manager said. "You should have told us before."

"That's my private life!"

"It hurts our profession."

"I thought you defended animals."

"We defend humans."

"Even those who hurt animals?"

"As long as they pay, yes," the manager said. "We're a firm that specializes in animal laws. Those are laws related to animals. We defend anyone who comes to us and pays our fees, for their rightful wrongs or their wrongful rights. Everyone has a right to defense."

"Thank you for the insight."

"I thought you already knew."

She returned to her office and resumed her typing. Her fingers raced. When the briefs finished, she was burning. She needed a target for her fists, feet, and teeth. There was no one in her office. Her colleagues had left early fearing another riot in the city. She stepped outside. The corridor's carpet recoiled from her shoes. She stopped at her manager's office and glared through the glass pane. He, too, had fled her fury.

She rushed to her office and grabbed her sports bag. She dashed down the eleven floors, changed into her swimsuit, and splashed into the sleeping pool.

The pool woke. The cold water took what she wanted to give. The vigorous laps drained her passion and refilled her poise. After a kilometer and a half, she climbed out, showered and dressed, and took the silent elevator to her deserted floor. The sun sank into the ocean and flooded her office in orange. The warm glow soothed her soul and revived her spirit. Across the water, the north hills soaked up the rays and drenched her farmers' community in the valley. Their incandescence looked divine.

She shut her computer, gathered her bags, and left her office.

Outside, the city had ceased its uproar and silenced its microphones. She pulled away from the curb, turned in the middle of the street, and braked before bumping into another car. Ignaçio pulled back and let her pass; he didn't look at her or utter a word. She slowed her car and peered into the rearview mirror. He sped his sports car and disappeared from her view.

This wasn't the first time she ran into him. This wasn't the first time he avoided her. This wouldn't be the last time she saw him go around and vaunt his car. Soon he would boast his killing skills, his trophies, his other exploits. Until one of those bulls got him by the—

She slapped the steering wheel and cut that line of thought. The pain stabbed her chest and stung her throat. She pulled to the roadside and opened the windows. The air didn't help. On her phone, she watched again last night's video: Ignaçio trying to save the burnt bull, fallen on the port's pavement. In his eyes and moves, she didn't find any special sympathy for this unfortunate bull. He only did what another veterinarian would do to save an injured animal.

No, she wasn't so sure of his gestures. She replayed the clip and watched it closer. Now it seemed he did less than required. He knew he would soon kill these bulls. She didn't know this egoist stranger

261

anymore. She was happy the distance between them had grown. She threw the phone into her purse, pulled away from the curb, and sped toward the city center.

The speed broke her cyclic thoughts and enlarged her vision. Her anger left. She saw her manager's viewpoint from a different angle.

She didn't agree with him, but she understood his concern for their firm. Animals didn't pay; humans did. Animals didn't need money; humans did. Like other firms, hers used laws made for protecting animals to exploit humans for earning money. They weren't evil.

But the state enacted incoherent laws. On the one hand, they protected company animals as sentient beings, capable of feelings; on the other hand, they excluded fighting bulls as non-sentient beings, incapable of feelings. This exclusion served humans to torture and kill these bulls in public, in the name of art, and sacrifice them for money. That wasn't civil.

Animals didn't make laws; humans did. If these bulls were elected at the legislature, they wouldn't vote for this exclusion. Yet these laws generated money for the economy—money that built her office, paid her salary, and renovated the district where she worked. Elites like Willem invested big sums in these renovations. That was civil.

After the financial downturn, San Taurino left its historic district to the ruins. Then laws elevated bullfighting to a national monument. The season of bullfighting extended on both sides. The city's arena held two sessions per day throughout the season. Twelve bulls gave their lives daily to this arena; four hundred, per month; four thousand, for the ten-month season. The money they fetched from tourists, the investments they drew from businesses, the donations they received from aficionados—these funds churned the city and fueled its growth; built its low-rent apartments for the unemployed, underemployed, and destitute; erected its daycare center for children of the poor; revived its hospice, hospital, libraries, and schools.

These funds renovated the city's long-ill, debt-ridden public transport that the senior, the minor, and the jobless used for free. They reopened the schools and public libraries. They converted the city's failed convention center into a host of thriving enterprises like her law firm; like those hi- and bio-tech entrepreneurs with a global outreach; like that avant-garde sports complex in its basement, which trained the city's youths for international events.

Willem took a thirty-percent stake in most projects. His investments in this taurine city lifted its citizens' quality of life. Only the stadium rejected his patronage because he wanted a second arena at its centerfield outside the football season. The football clubs, their fans, and the stadium's managing company resisted Willem because they didn't need his money.

Nuria exited the historic district and turned on Avenida de Corrida. The security tape and the charred truck were gone from the ill-fated *correbus*'s site on the city's terrace. The broken rope still hung from the plane tree and swung in the breeze. Below the rope's torn ends, at the tree's foot, blood-red candles burned and encircled the dead bull's portrait leaning against the trunk. Their flickering flames simmered the two torches blazing from the fallen animal's intact horns. Traffic slowed at this spot, picked up speed, and moved along the avenue.

Plaza de Toreros had thinned its throngs. Nuria entered the square, parked by the fountain, and got out of her car. The dusk's colors left the city; its broken streetlights didn't pick up the relay. At

Miguel's camp, under torches and headlamps, his foundation's members worked on their laptops, prepared meals, and served anyone hungry for food or words.

The city's homeless queued before the makeshift tables. Among them, Nuria saw Xavier, the elite matador fallen from grace; after his gore, he switched side, traveled to taurine cities, and traded his story. This evening, he didn't queue for food or drink; he listened to a young girl talking to Miguel and wiping her eyes. Nuria recognized Theresa from last night's news: the girlfriend of the teenage *novillero* who died in the bullring. Miguel typed the girl's story. Nuria left him with Xavier and Theresa and joined the members that served meals.

A police van entered the square and stopped in front of Miguel's camp. Elena came out, took a coffee from her, and called her to the side.

"You should have seen," Elena said, "Ignaçio wasn't himself last night."

"Where did you see Nacho?" Nuria asked.

"At the port."

"With that bull?"

"Yes."

"Was he drunk?"

"Why?"

"He wasn't walking straight," Nuria said. "His hands were shaking."

"He looked sick."

"Did he talk to you?"

"No," Elena said. "He yelled at Charo for not reviving the dead bull."

"He woke Charo?"

264

"Sure."

"He has lost his civility."

"Charo didn't mind," Elena said. "She regretted his plight. Paloma and Juan came out too. They tried to pull him into their tablao. He broke off and ran like a mad bull. He almost fell in the water. I ran after him, but he fired away in his sports car."

"I saw him drive today," Nuria said. "He looked fine."

"I don't know where he'll sleep tonight."

"He has his room at the taurine academy."

"They emptied their campus."

"Why?"

"You haven't heard?"

"Just tell me."

"Protestors have broken the academy's gate."

"For the dead bull?"

"For the dead novillero."

Nuria went to the techs' table and scanned the news feeds. The media counted a hundred and sixty-seven demonstrations in Spain; three hundred and forty-two across Europe; sixteen hundred and eighty-nine around the globe. An eighth demonstrated for the young bullfighter's death; the rest, for the tortured bull dead from the *correbus*. The video of that fatal *novillada*, furnished by Vincente's barracks, had drawn twelve and a half million views; the video of the disastrous correbus, furnished by Elena's station, exceeded thirty million. The story from the novillero's girlfriend, written by Miguel and fed by his techs, went live on the net and caught fire before her eyes. Nuria returned to the cooks' table and resumed serving food and drinks.

"Paula called Ignaçio this morning," Elena said.

"Mother shouldn't," Nuria said.

"She wanted to lodge him."

"On our farm?"

"Yes."

"Nacho has your mobile home now."

"We cut water, electricity, and gas before leaving," Elena said. "Jaime called him, but he wouldn't stay with us. He refused Vincente and Ines. He didn't return the calls from Paloma and Juan. Charo thinks he's showing signs of depression and—"

"Why are you telling me all this?"

"You don't care?"

"No."

"I don't believe you."

"Then don't!" Nuria said. "He had people loving him, caring for him, looking after him. See how he paid them back? He believes he's an orphan and behaves like one. He thinks he has no responsibility for others. Let him be an orphan! Let him stay and starve in his mobile home. Let him sleep in his sports car. He loves his stupid vehicle more than he loves anyone. Leave that egoist behind! And leave me alone."

"Nuria."

"What are you trying to do?"

"Next year, this dead novillero could be Ignaçio."

"Stop!"

"I'm serious."

"Don't take me down that route."

A fire-truck pulled to the square's end. The driver-side door opened. Vincente descended from the truck and trudged to the stall. Water dripped from his helmet and work uniform; both were specked with burnt hay and charred wood. Nuria offered him coffee. He pushed the cup aside and asked for a bowl of warm soup; he was hungry and cold.

"Another arson?" Elena said.

"Yes," Vincente said.

"Where was it?"

"At a bull ranch."

"Which one?"

"The one that sold that bull."

"For the *correbus*?"

"Yes."

"How bad is the damage?"

"The farmstead collapsed. The bulls broke the ranch's barriers and fled the fire. Now they're running free in the valley. The arsonist's car caught fire. He was stranded without clothes in the open and—"

"Did he leave his clothes in the vehicle?"

"Yes."

"Was there a camera mounted on its roof?"

"Yes," Vincente said. "You know him?"

"How old is he?"

"In his twenties."

"I'll call my station."

"Why?"

"He's that fugitive," Elena said. "He burned two slaughterhouses in the South."

"He won't burn another again."

"Why?"

"The bulls gored him on their way out."

267

"Is he dead?"

"We left him in the hospital."

Nuria heard a voice she didn't like. She turned and saw Ishmael. The chief editor of *El Periódico de San Taurino* was talking to Miguel. The pro-bullfighting journalist's presence meant troubles for Miguel's foundation. His articles fell far below journalism's civility and dignity. She strained her ears but couldn't hear what the editor wanted. She left the serving table, walked to Miguel, and stood beside him.

Ishmael bowed to her; she ignored him. The journalist's practiced smile failed to hide his anxiety.

"I roughed you up in the past," Ishmael told Miguel. "I won't waste your time now with lame apologies. Feel how you want to feel about me and my articles. This evening, I come to you for something else. Can we talk?"

"Sure," Miguel said.

"A group wants to demonstrate on this square next week."

"The square belongs to everyone."

"They're foreigners."

"I'm foreign too."

"They're pro-animal like you."

"And they came to you?"

"Yes," Ishmael said. "They want *you* with them."

"They didn't contact me."

"They didn't dare."

"Why?"

"Their demonstration is topless."

"On this public square?"

"Yes?"

"You should know my answer."

"I do," Ishmael said. "I already told them."

"The discussion is closed then."

"Not yet."

"We're busy."

"Let me explain."

This occult clique called themselves warriors for animals. Made of elite foreign youths, they wanted immediate exposure. They would take a full-page ad in his paper if he showed a bleeding bull agonizing to death. They would pay a six-figure sum if he convinced Miguel to diffuse their demonstration on his foundation's social network. His paper would do the work and cover this demonstration; Miguel didn't have to be present at this event. He would cut a deal with them if Miguel agreed to diffuse the news feed to his subscribers.

"The show won't hurt your paper?" Miguel asked.

"No," Ishmael said. "It will help."

"Are you switching side?"

"I report what I see."

"My subscribers won't watch this show."

"Let them decide."

"Why are you doing this?"

"I'll tell you."

A journalist, by the trade's code, was supposed to be impartial. He wasn't. He descended from an artists' family that painted bullfights and played orchestra at corridas. Six years ago, after finishing his studies, he started reporting bullfights by his family's values, but they no longer felt right for him. His sail now turned toward the opposition; he forced it back toward his origin. The result was a fake paper, reporting fake events. It lacked life. His subscribers smelled his paper's death. They had stopped reading his articles and buying ad spaces. This approaching death didn't come from the digital age. His regional paper was digitally more equipped than most national newspapers. The problem lay not in his paper, but at his core. The pro-bullfighting stuff had stopped motivating him long ago. He couldn't do better.

"What motivates you in this demonstration?" Miguel asked.

"Not the topless part," Ishmael said. "What lies beyond this demonstration."

"I need to see your article first."

"We'll write it together."

"Where will the topless come from?"

"Outside Spain."

"The youths will bring them?"

"Their talent agency will."

"The city will allow this show?"

"It's not against the law."

"The citizens won't approve it."

"They don't have to attend."

"What about their children?" Miguel said. "They'll see it on television."

"They see bullfights on television."

"You're shifting your sail!"

"Will you collaborate?"

"Not sure."

"Think."

Ishmael left. Nuria grabbed Miguel by the wrist and pulled him away from his camp.

"He used you before," she said. "Use him now."

"He wants to save his paper."

"Help him."

"Why?"

"This time, he isn't lying," Nuria said. "An enemy changing side serves better than an ally. His writing carries charge. We'll use his prose; its poise, strength, and power."

"What's happening to you?"

"Go with his flow."

"You, too, are changing!"

"Trust me for this move."

"Are you sure?"

"You'll see."

25

She wanted to lose at least one case; she lost all three. She was tired of this business of animal laws. Now she would be relieved from this parody. Nuria didn't ignore her glaring clients; she stared back at them. Her cold gaze told them what she thought of their cases. She thanked the presiding judge, gathered her case files, and marched out of the tribunal.

In Plaza de Toreros, the catwalk before the regional legislature had finished. The topless now posed at the square's center, in three rows by their assets, and exhibited the clique's logo on their body parts they most treasured. Those lying on the pavement raised the logo's banner on their arched chests. Those sitting on folded knees tied the logo's belt around their waists. Those standing tall wore the logo's band on their thighs. Ishmael moved his equipment and filmed them from every angle. The passersby ignored them and their warriors for animals.

Nuria reached her car, pulled away from the square, and drove to her law firm.

Her office floor hummed with meetings. The managing partner sat alone at his desk and sweated behind six tall piles of thick case files. Nuria tapped on the closed door and entered his office. The manager's face froze in a scowl; he quickly recovered his smoothness.

"I heard," the manager said. "Your clients called."

"Do you want me to leave?" Nuria asked.

"No."

"I don't like these cases."

"I have something else for you."

"What?"

"A corporate."

"A client of this firm?"

"Not yet," the manger said. "We would like to have them."

"Which one?"

"You know them."

"How?"

"You worked for their head."

"Willem?"

"Yes."

"No way!"

Nuria rose from her seat, gathered her files, and turned toward the door.

"Wait." The manager stood up. "Willem called and asked for you. He said you were good and he would retain our service if you—"

"I don't want to work for him."

"You'll work for us."

"It will be the same."

"No," the manager said. "You won't work with animal laws. You'll work with tax, real estate, and business laws."

"That's what I meant."

"You already did this work for him."

"He wants to buy me back."

"He didn't put it that way."

"Did he make an offer?"

"Yes."

"Have you sold me to him?"

"Not yet."

"Don't."

"Nuria, please listen," the manager said. "We can end your trial period now, raise you to an associate, and give you a personal office. Willem wants you only, no one else. His account will be yours. We'll give you a new car. If you can retain him for five years, we'll make you a partner, and you'll have other perks."

"Stop!"

"You're wild."

"I have reasons to be."

"Go home, think over, sleep on it."

"My decision won't change."

"We'll meet again tomorrow."

"Let's hope."

She sent a text message to Miguel and then drove away from her office building. She didn't look in the rearview mirror. She didn't turn her head to either side. She sped through Avenida de Corrida, turned on the bridge over the Sangre de Toros River, and climbed up the north hills' flanks. Wakes from her impulsive act followed her and hit her on the plateau.

Her frenzied drive slowed. She peered at her community's farms. Their threadbare homes contrasted the spring's burgeoning valley. These farmers were still holding out.

Her parents' situation was now different.

Last year, the insurer settled for their barn's fire. The company also reimbursed them for Victor's theft, and for Esperanza's and Herman's deaths. This year, their farm's renegotiated loans cost three times less in interest. Subsidies came at regular intervals, from the region and from Europe, in quantities larger than past years'. The municipality offered tax breaks to this community's farmers. Her parents' finances no longer squeezed them. If she wanted now, she could set herself up as an entrepreneur, use Ignaçio's empty room for her office, and practice honest law from home while serving her community. She didn't need this law firm's job.

She could now serve animals. The upgraded laws didn't create enough work to employ a specialized prosecutor. As in this morning's session, the tribunal contracted private lawyers for prosecution. She had seen the defense side. She could use her insight to prosecute owners that abused their animals or abandoned them. The pay wouldn't be high, but the work would be real. At least, these animals, under her aegis, could benefit from the laws humans made in their name. She might even find some free time to return to her dance.

The thoughts erased her doubts and cleared her vision. She rolled down the windows, sang a *sevillana* song, and drove along the cliff-side road. On her left, the quicksilver ocean sparkled and danced to her tune. The saline breeze soothed her face, opened her chest, and eased her breath. The muffled roar raised its voice and confirmed her decision.

She left the cliff-side road and turned on the mud trail toward her parent's farm. At the gate of Ignaçio's farm, Lorenza and her male calf stood and watched the road's traffic. The rust-brown calf, three and a half months old, had Victor's pendulous dewlap: Mother's reason to name this calf Victor the Second. Nuria stopped at the gate and got out of her car.

The calf stretched his neck and peered into her eyes. His large irises—dark, still, and shining—showed her tired face's haggard contour. She bent above the calf and stroked his dewlap. He tossed his head and smacked her nose.

Lorenza shook her head. The cow's eyes apologized for her calf's misbehavior.

Nuria let the calf go; he hadn't inherited his father's kind side. Victor the Second returned to his mother and suckled from her udder. Nuria reached out and rubbed Lorenza's forehead. The cow raised her muzzle, sniffed her knuckles, and returned to licking her calf. Victor the Second had inherited his mother's pride: Lorenza didn't welcome touches from everyone.

Nuria stayed at the gate and watched the other cows. All had healthy calves that measured larger and weighed heavier for their age. They would ease her parents' finances further. This farm, after sleeping for a decade and a half, yielded exceptional fruit, vegetables, and honey. Aunt Belen and Ines sold them at the farmers' market on Sundays, along with the curd and cream, the butter and cheese, the yogurts and desserts they made from this farm's milk.

Ignaçio's desertion hadn't disrupted his farm. His mobile home served for the dairy. His money earned interest in a separate account at her parents' bank. In a few years, the newborn females would start producing milk; by then, Jaime would have anchored his mechanics shop and enlarged this dairy. If she worked for herself, she would have time, energy, and liberty to join their enterprise of sustainable farming. Ignaçio had no talent to run his revived farm.

Her cell phone rang in the car.

The call didn't come from her law firm; it came from Miguel. She picked up her phone, sat in the driver's seat, and answered the call.

"Got your message," Miguel said. "I stand by your decision."

"I shouldn't have pushed you for the topless demonstration."

"Why?"

"I saw it die on the square."

"Not on the net."

"How many clicks so far?"

276

"Six hundred thousand from Spain. A million and a half from Europe. Four million and seven hundred ninety thousand from around the globe."

"Are your subscribers offended?"

"No," Miguel said. "They're amused."

"And you?"

"Shocked."

"I'm sorry," Nuria said. "I should have thought better."

"Have you resigned?"

"Not yet."

"I have work for you."

"A job?"

"Let me explain."

He wanted a team of lawyers to pursue animal abusers on behalf of his foundation. Lack of funds hadn't permitted him to employ anyone so far. These clicks had already generated sufficient funds to pay a lawyer for a year and a half. He was offering this post to Nuria.

"I would accept it," Nuria said, "but not as your employee."

"Why?"

"I want to work for myself."

"You'll have to pay social charges then."

"They're worth my freedom."

"Fair enough."

"When do you want me to start?"

"This evening."

"You'll wait till next week."

"Why?"

"I'll incorporate my business first."

26

Miguel's subscribers relayed Ishmael's video beyond the topless show's scope.

Views grew exponentially. By the week's end, they drew forty-four million clicks. The occult warriors for animals broke into the open and remained on the world stage. Their clique became a household name among aficionados of the topless. Not a single defender of animals or their rights joined their clan. The warriors didn't care. They got the exposure they wanted.

Discussion threads, centered on the girls' vital statistics, spun for two more weeks on the web and turned the regional *El Periódico de San Taurino* into renowned international media. The aspiring girls entered celebrity databases. They signed six- to seven-figure contracts for acting, modeling, hosting, and other derivative services. The clicks earned eighteen million euros. The sum split between Miguel's foundation and Ishmael' paper. Miguel secured his team of lawyers for animals. Ishmael didn't bow to anyone again for money.

Everyone gained from this demonstration except for the bulls.

They kept fighting humans.

27

The polemic spread on Miguel's network, but the catalyst article was signed by Ishmael.

Angel knew the editor had switched side since Willem threw him out from that gala. The front-page ad with that bleeding bull and the topless demonstration's glaring coverage in his paper proved his switch. Yet this full-blown attack on the bullfighting industry wasn't a mere sequel to his previous publication. To report the taurine underworld in such details, the editor must have insider connections.

Willem came to bullfighting from commodity trading. In that world, direct bribes risked sanctions, but indirect bribes brought durable reward. He earned the commodity-rich nations' favor by buying their rulers' properties at inflated price. He imported this tool to bullfighting industry and used it to ease laws in his favor and procure his building permits. He paid three and a half times more for Pedro's family estate and rewarded the legislator for pushing corrida from a nation's tradition to a national monument. The abandoned farm he bought from Mayor José's mother wasn't on a constructible land; he paid six times more for it and obtained the city's permit to build there his Gran Taurino Villas. His bribing innovations didn't end there.

Judge Emilio's brother owned the arena's souvenir shop, among his many in the taurine world. Their family-run business manufactured genuine bullfighting articles for the informed aficionados and fake ones for the uninformed. Both types sold through their souvenir shops. They auctioned the bull-heads after corridas. Their business's largest investor was Willem's shell company in South America. The same company laundered the cash skimmed from their shops—and from San Taurino's arena, leased and managed by the bullfighting association.

These revelations wouldn't crush Willem's empire. His collaborators gained from these operations. The bullfighting association, on the contrary, depended also on honest aficionados for their donations, not just on Willem. They wouldn't appreciate these leaks from Ishmael.

Ishmael had tied the association to Willem's shell company. The editor's article listed by years the cash skimmed from the arena and matched those amounts to the association's bank account entrees. The arena's booth and the bank must have furnished him those details.

The association's dependence on Willem's donations would now rise. The consequence would exceed the financials. The bullfighting magnate would turn the lever in his favor. He would wedge deeper and force his ways on corrida. The bloodhound never read a line of *El Cossio*, yet he aspired to preside over San Taurino's bullring someday. If he succeeded, corrida's art would die in his hands. This taurine city's legacy would enter the tomb.

Rafaela was at her ranch in the South for *tienta*. She hated interruption during her calves' selection. This morning's revelations called for her disruption. Angel lifted his cell phone and dialed Rafaela's number. She answered on the first ring.

"I saw the article," Rafaela said. "Fire Diego."

"Pardon?"

"He gave our account details to Ishmael."

"Are you sure?"

"Who handles our treasury?"

"I'll let you fire him."

"Angel!"

"Yes?"

"Fire that ingrate this minute."

28

Animal sacrifice is Man's primal tradition. In some epochs, humans projected their evils onto animals they abhorred and sacrificed them for purging. In others, humans traded animals they loved and procured their gods' goodwill. Ancient cultures had this tradition before civilization dawned on them. Afterward, most of them framed laws and banned their practice. Only a few sects held onto this tradition and continued their clandestine sacrifice.

This particular sect was San Taurino's exception. On their saint days, they offered black cats to their sacrificial pyre and then consumed the roasted meat with the sanctified spirit they brewed in their cellars. During this particular autumn night, they had broken into the city's stadium, celebrated their holy feast on the football field, and invited themselves this morning before the justice's altar. The jurors, supposed to leave after their verdict, sat still in the jury box and grappled with this case's facts.

A jury trial for cruelty against animals was rare. This time, the court took a judicial step forward by granting her eight jurors and a judge. None owned cats; all handed down the eighteen-month sentence. Their unanimous verdict set a historic precedence for San Taurino's citizens. Nuria thanked the jurors and the judge and then left the courtroom.

Plaza de Toreros had turned into a shrine for company- and farm-animal lovers. These animal-rights activists didn't lift beasts by lowering humans. They believed the earth belonged to every being and wanted fair treatment for animals. They never gave into violence. They never dived into excess. They never sought perfection. They wanted an imperfect world where humans' opposing forces found a reasonable balance.

Miguel's foundation didn't camp with these balanced activists. Nuria found him behind the fountain, surrounded by ardent youths who defended farm animals from slaughter. Miguel stood on a chair and explained how vegetarianism benefited both animals and humans.

He claimed, on Earth, animals raised for consumption surpassed humans by three times. Even the kindest farmers couldn't raise their animals in a humane manner. Farm animals would stop suffering if humans didn't eat them. Humans belonged to primates. Their large intestine's length and functions resembled vegetarian animals'. Meat's rejects stayed in human colon longer than carnivorous animals', long enough to cause cancer.

Everyone watched him speak. No one listened to his words. The Spanish would never quit their meat for Miguel. Humans are omnivorous animals. Like others of this kind, they also eat some meat for survival. That's all right. What's pervert about bullfighting is the bulls' torture for human pleasure. No animal does this to others. Only humans do this to other animals.

Nuria stood aside and ignored Miguel's speech.

Among the farm animals' defenders, she noticed youths from anti-bullfighting groups and supporters of sustainable farming. Their age spanned from late twenties to mid thirties. There were also traditional farmers from Father's generation who believed bulls should breed, not fight humans. Tradition doesn't stay still; it moves with time. These citizens had eschewed their old values for the new. Many of them were rising to the region's power. Once they replaced the tradition's incumbent, bullfighting would disappear from this region.

In Spain, bullfight's landscape had already changed. More than ninety percent citizens didn't attend or support bullfighting. The Spanish today went far beyond believing bullfights should be abolished and Spain should change laws to eliminate them. Thousands of activists now came forward and fought for this change. The abolition process was riding a bumpy road, normal for all movements, and progressing in a continuous and consistent manner.

Progress comes in a cycle of wins and losses. The cycle doesn't turn in place. The wheels' rolls advance the cycle and change the rider's landscape. The bullfighting movements now rode faster on a steeper and bumpier course. Today's status quo stood far from a decade ago. She wasn't at the start of a rapid change; she was in its middle. The cycle was gaining speed.

She took that as her departing point. Changes had come in the past. Changes were now coming. Changes would continue to come. This morning's trial for the burnt cats promised this change. She would extend that promise to the bulls and learn patience from Miguel.

Miguel finished his speech, descended from the chair, and kissed her on both cheeks. Nuria briefed him on this morning's trial and gave him her bill for the case. Miguel thanked her for convicting the cat burners and told her he would wire her fees this afternoon.

"I would have asked for a longer sentence," Nuria said. "Eighteen months is the maximum in Spain. We're far behind Europe."

"Laws move," Miguel said.

"Not on their own."

"Money moves them."

"That's your vision."

"You want to change laws?"

"Yes."

284

"They'll revert."

"No," Nuria said. "Not if the constitution is amended."

"You'll amend the constitution for the bulls?"

"For all animals."

"What change will you make?"

"Enter animals as nonhuman persons."

"You'll become vegetarian?"

"No."

"But you're asking the slaughterhouses to close!"

Miguel claimed that a constitutional amendment wouldn't help animals. The constitution didn't serve as their sanctuary. He cited India for example.

This country's constitution saw animals as nonhuman persons, placed them at par with humans, and demanded compassion and kind treatment. Yet every year, hundreds of festivals sacrificed thousands of male goats in public. At meat markets, live poultry hung upside down for hours before some saw their heads chopped off; others dangled from bikes' carriers and cracked their necks between turning spokes. Butchers didn't take animals to slaughterhouses for painless killing. They took them behind their stalls, shut their snouts, and slit their throats. The public saw these done before their eyes. Yet they bought meat from these stalls. Humans mandated to make, interpret, and apply laws closed their eyes on these delinquents.

The same country placed bulls and cows above humans. Yet its bovine race didn't escape money's blade. There, you couldn't hurt or kill a member of this race for thrill, but you could slaughter them in secret and sell their meat to other countries. Boasting an annual trade of five billion dollars, India was the world's second largest beef exporter after Brazil. The clandestine slaughterhouses that supplied this meat didn't see the cattle coming to them as above humans, or at par, and treat them with kindness and compassion. Their slaughterers didn't believe the European norms of painless killing. They saw themselves as superior to these animals.

If people around the world stopped eating beef, the cattle would never reach abattoirs, legal or illegal. If humans stopped eating meat, all animals would become nonhuman persons. There would be no need to make or change laws; or to amend any country's constitution.

Laws don't work bias free. A law's fairness limits to those who birth it. A law's design benefits its benefactors—those who convene, draft, and vote the bill—whether it applies to humans or nonhumans. The incentive behind all laws is financial. To humans, money means sustenance. Money drives lives' trades and treatments, whether those lives belong to humans, animals, or plants. Demand for lives makes room for money.

No laws can stop this human behavior. Laws made by some to help are used by others to exploit. When demand dries up, supply dries up too; there is no room to make money. At that point, laws lose their relevance. Trades and treatments gain fairness by themselves.

The key to fair laws doesn't lie in legislators' hands; it lies in consumers' conscience, in their conscious choices for consumption. That's why he organized these demonstrations—to educate people, to raise their awareness, to make them conscious of what they consumed, and to help them see what their consumption choice caused for consequence.

He cited bullfighting for example.

Spain didn't have money to continue bullfights. Tourists' money kept this industry alive. There was demand from some for taurine blood; there was room for others to supply it and earn money. His

286

foundation raised global awareness about the realities behind this trade for a practical reason: if you attended a bullfight in Spain, then returned home with your shots and showed them to your neighbors, they would punch you in the face, grab you by the neck, and throw you out of their homes. These taurine tourists would then regain their common sense and stop coming to Spain for bullfights. At that point, laws would lose their relevance.

"That's awful," Nuria said. "You're advocating violence."

"I'm not," Miguel said. "My reference to violence was figurative."

"You're slaughtering the legal system."

"I respect its laws."

"Enough public opinion already exists against bullfights," Nuria said. "Forming more will yield less."

"What do you want me to do?"

"Conserve your energy, join the legislators, change the laws."

"Laws will change when bullfights stop."

"Spain is a parliamentary monarchy."

"So?"

"The citizens make the laws," Nuria said. "The citizens see that bullfighting is cruel. The citizens know that every bull killed in an arena also kills the country's image."

"Then why don't they change these laws?"

"People's lives depend on bullfights."

"See?"

"But that can change."

"How?"

"It needs time!"

"Don't spend your time on laws," Miguel said. "Spend it on

exclusions."

"Exclusions?"

"From Europe," Miguel said. "Organize trade embargos and international boycotts."

"You're going too far."

"I'm not."

"Only nine percent in Spain favor bullfighting."

"The other ninety-one percent vote for it."

"Have you seen a plenary session?"

"No."

"Go and see one."

"Why?"

"You'll see how laws are made."

An argument won is a relation lost. Nuria left Miguel with his followers. She pulled away from the square and drove toward the bridge.

She regretted challenging Miguel. Her abrasion took its source from her impatience. Both would harm her in what she wanted to do with the law. The youths she counted on to elect her at the regional legislature belonged to Miguel's camp. They wouldn't tolerate her behavior or temper. Like Miguel, they preferred the force tranquil to the nervous, noisy, and aggressive.

She could understand Miguel's defense for farm animals. He studied agro-engineering and then worked in Brussels at the common agricultural policies for a decade and half. He must be sick of the high-profitability industrial farming that saw animals as plants and treated them as plants. She could understand his sensitivity for the bovine race. After his birth, his parents left him on a field; he was saved by a cow's grace. She didn't need to oppose Miguel's views.

His love for farm animals didn't concern her. She could steer his love for the bovine race to help her achieve what she wanted for the *lidia* bulls.

Company animals weren't left to dry on a clothesline. Farm animals were slaughtered by painless norms. Laws already governed the treatment of both. Only the fighting bull, stranded outside these laws, suffered helpless. Their cruel treatment for others' pleasure was unfair and unreasonable. Their exclusion should be excluded from the code. Miguel wanted to protect all animals from pain. The fighting bull's ordeal—what they lived outside rings, what they lived inside rings, what they lived in slaughterhouses—symbolized all pains inflicted on animals by humans.

The act symbolized human civility. This violence happened in the open, before civilized citizens' eyes, in arenas and on television. Whether we applauded this act for art, bravery, or pleasure; whether we tolerated its cruelty for jobs, economy, or money; whether we preserved its exclusion for culture, heritage, or tradition—we validated this slow, systematic torture of a living being and its destruction in full public view as an acceptable show, ethical and legal.

She would target that part of the code.

A fighting bull wasn't a savage animal, dangerous for humans, as the code claimed. These bulls no longer roamed the Iberian Peninsula freely, as they used to do in another epoch. They were now bred and raised by humans, on well-defined ranches and by well-specified norms, for the sole purpose of fighting, as cattle are bred and raised solely for consumption. Business or art, culture or tradition, entertainment or enlightenment—label bullfighting as you want; a fighting bull was still a farm animal made by humans, engineered by

289

humans, consumed by humans. These bulls fulfilled the psychological hunger of only a small fraction of humans.

A fair law, voted to protect farm animals from undue tortures and unnecessary sufferings, shouldn't exclude the *lidia* bull from its scope. If their meat was tasty and healthy for humans, they should be raised only for their meat and then slaughtered by the norms for all other farm animals. These bulls had no reasons to undergo a prolonged torture—before, during, and after corrida—to serve as food for humans.

She reached Ignaçio's farm and turned on the mud trail. Charo's service vehicle waited at the farm's gate. Father stood with the vet by the pond. They watched Lorenza and her eleven-month old calf, Victor the Second. Nuria stopped her car. For the whole summer, this rebel cow had resisted the new bull on the high pasture. All other cows from this herd had accepted that Victor would never return to this farm and fallen pregnant from that other bull.

Charo opened her satchel and pulled out her tools for artificial insemination. Lorenza swayed her horns at the vet, and Victor the Second backed away from his mother. Father moved forward and held Lorenza by her collar. Charo took her instrument and placed herself behind the cow. The male calf walked around them and positioned himself behind the vet.

Charo strapped the cow's hind legs and lifted her tail. The poised calf recoiled farther and lowered his head at the vet.

Lorenza groaned. Victor the Second charged and hit Charo on the buttocks. The shocked vet jerked forward, grabbed her hindquarters, and turned around with a gaping mouth. The calf recoiled again and lowered his head at Charo; Father stepped in and stood between them. Charo threw up her hands, gave up on the calf's mother, and gathered her stuff.

Nuria smiled. She started her car and drove down the trail.

Her foot pressed the brake pedal. Her nose followed the scent; her eyes, the hums and buzzes. The branch that invited these insects with its perfume hung above the farm's barrier. Ignaçio's orchard was bursting with over-ripe mid-autumn figs. She stopped her car by the fence, reached the branch from her window, and grabbed a handful of figs.

Their spirit-like scent reeled her head and watered her mouth. She removed the fleas from one fig, split it open, and stared at its meat-red flesh. She was in that part of her month when she desired the raw—its texture, taste, and smell. She placed the whole fig into her mouth, closed her eyes, and bit its tender pulp.

The grains crunched. The pulp melted. The juice flowed. Their tender touch flooded her mouth and revived memories she no longer craved. She threw the figs over the farm's barrier, started her car, and drove toward her parents' farm. Those memories wouldn't leave her.

She sped her car and forced her thoughts toward Miguel.

He was pushing his limits. No sane individual, institution, or nation would sanction Spain to this extent for bullfights on its soil. True, the taurine industry's global worth now exceeded fifteen billion dollars. But it was still held by a few like Willem. They didn't represent Spain. Spaniards shouldn't be punished for the acts of these few.

Miguel was not an extreme person by nature. His passion for animals blinded his views. Yet his international ambition had opened a legal path she could pursue. Without his insight, she wouldn't have seen this route.

Not so long ago, the pedophiles that perpetrated their crimes

291

abroad and escaped overseas authorities could live under their home countries' protective umbrellas. All sovereign nations granted their citizens impunity and refused their extradition. That legal quagmire had dried. Today, most countries held a global pact. They punished their citizens at home for crimes committed on children in other countries.

Most tourists who attended Spain's bullfights came from countries that labeled cruelty on animals as a crime; performing or assisting it on their soils was punished by years in prison. On the Atlantic's far side, a state that supplied Willem's carloads of taurine clients imprisoned their delinquents for decades. On this side, a state that hosted Europe's most taurine clubs and sent their aficionados to Spain for taurine blood applied similar laws for offenses on its soil.

If she convinced these countries to collaborate with her, to pursue their citizens at home for attending or organizing taurine events in Spain, the bullfighting business would die on Spain's soil within a year or two. The few Spaniards that still attended these shows could never keep this business alive.

This international collaboration didn't lie beyond her reach. The nations that held or supported bullfights had renewed their leadership. These leaders came from a generation of new values. Their ancestors might have indoctrinated them into taurine shows along with football matches, but they now saw their world from their eyes using today's values; they didn't place corrida at par with football. They didn't take the status quo's longevity for its validity. They had the audacity to question their ancestors' ways. They had the vision and skills to go beyond the existing and create the new. They had the intelligence, diligence, energy, and drive. They could dream, design, and implement the right for their epoch.

That's where lay her hope.

The thought cleared her blues. She sang a tune, reached her parents' farm, and stopped at its gate. She raised the cattle barrier, passed her car under it, and rolled on the driveway. The crunching gravel brought Santos out from the barn. The sad dog no longer ran toward anyone, wagged his tail, and barked with joy to greet; Victor's disappearance and Ignaçio's departure had left their indelible prints on his soul. Santos watched her silently from far and waited by the homestead. She reached the dog, patted him on the head and the back, and held the door open for him. The dog didn't go in with her.

She stopped at the dinner table and picked up the messages left by Mother.

All messages came from pet owners and farms. Except for one. The man had left only his first name and cell phone number. She scanned her memory; she couldn't place him. She set him aside, gathered the rest, and went upstairs.

She opened her office and sat at her desk. The new furniture and the fresh decor kept Ignaçio out of this room; it belonged to her now. This home office had given her the liberty she needed to practice honest law. From this place, she would push for the new law, build international collaboration, and end bullfighting. She opened the balcony's door and stood against its railings. She watched the cattle. They seemed content on their regenerated pasture in this renovated farm. Santos, too, could choose to forget Ignaçio and Victor, to live happily here. The dog didn't have to see this lively and beautiful farm only as his place of work.

The pasture's grass stirred. The cattle's odor came over the bougainvillea creepers. The jasmines, the lilies, the marigolds, and the fuchsias turned their stems, opened their heads, and spread their petals. A tanager sang on the cycad. She stared at the bird; it nodded at her.

29

The city hall delayed her meeting till late afternoon but didn't cancel it. For the reelected mayor to maintain this meeting in his first week, his business with her must be important and urgent. Nuria checked the time. The three hours would cut her work's backlog. She rehashed the week's trials and scanned the people she wanted to call for her bill.

Only one person seemed worth calling. This woman, also a private lawyer for animals' causes, had written articles against bullfighting that aligned with the bill's proposition. Her inputs could cover the bill's blind spots before it reached the congressional committee. Nuria reviewed the woman's last three articles, called her, and explained what she was seeking.

"What do I gain from collaborating?" the lawyer asked.

"Pardon?"

"You'll get help for your bill," the lawyer said. "What do I get in return?"

"You help the bulls!"

"They don't help me."

"They do," Nuria said. "Your articles bring you clients."

"Can we cut a deal?"

"For this bill?"

"You want my help?" the woman said. "You've to help me."

"How?"

"Get Ishmael and Miguel to talk about me."

"About your anti-bullfighting stance?"

"About my law practice."

"That's awful."

"Do you want my input for your bill?"

"No."

Nuria hung up the call and stared at her phone.

She saw her mistake. Their exchange also revealed a crucial point she had so far ignored. Among the legislature's deputies, there were many lawyers. Quite a few had anti-bullfighting stance. If she wanted to push this bill, she should collaborate with them. They wanted to help the bulls. Their collaboration would win their support. If she sought their inputs, they would share her bill's ownership and push it during the debate. They would have their stakes.

But she was acting way ahead. She hadn't even entered the legislature; she was already seeking collaboration for her bill. Her fight for the bulls would take long. If she wanted to help them, she should practice patience. The meeting with Mayor José and Judge Emilio this afternoon was important. Their spouses sat on the legislature. Both women were likely to be re-elected in two weeks, whereas her election wasn't guaranteed. These two women would never vote for her anti-bullfighting bill, but she should know her opponents' arguments. She could use this meeting with their husbands to discover their stance against her bill.

A new email arrived on her computer. The mail's header connected it to her exchanges with one of the international authorities. The time indicated the message's origin from the Atlantic's far side. She checked her list of contacts; she didn't recognize the sender.

Until now, all countries had confirmed they couldn't prosecute their citizens at home for attending bullfights in Spain unless the Spanish law defined bullfighting on its soil as a crime. They saw her stance as a legal avant-garde. They regretted their laws couldn't help her cause now. They hoped the pro-animal tides that swelled around the globe would force their nations to revise their laws and pursue their citizens for attending bullfights in countries that still saw these violent shows as lawful. This new email's first line didn't signal such a form response. Nuria opened the message. It came from a Latin American legislator she didn't know.

The legislator highlighted a grey zone for animals in their amended constitution. Eleven judges would convene, reinterpret this shadowed area, and reexamine their code for corrida's legitimacy in their arenas. Afterward, the legislator would lead a commission, hold a plenary session, and harmonize their code with the amended constitution. This work would take time, but she could count on their collaboration. The legislator ended the mail by thanking Miguel for bringing this shaded legal zone to their attention six months earlier.

Nuria gaped at the mail's last line. Miguel had not only thought about this collaboration between international authorities before her, but he had also taken a concrete step toward it.

She couldn't believe what her eyes were seeing. She closed the mail and reopened it. She reread the mail and checked Miguel's full name. The content was real, the name was real. She wasn't seeing a mirage in this legal desert. Even Miguel believed in law's power.

She opened the Latin American country's amended constitution. She skimmed their code and scanned its relevant sections. Miguel had his reason: the grey zone was there. In her zeal to prosecute tourists in their home countries, she had missed these legal anomalies in a nation that boasted the world's largest bullring. She checked Spain's revised constitution and reread the code's sections that regulated bullfights: no anomalies, no ambiguities, no grey zones. The lawmakers had foreseen this problem and taken preventive measures. The constitution's view on animals was laid down in black and white. The bulls couldn't escape its scope.

Nuria checked her watch. She had forgotten her meeting at the city hall.

For once, the clear roads brought her to the city with no further delay. In Plaza de Toreros, the legislative election's candidates delivered fiery pitches on their pet causes. Nuria parked beside the stand that pitched for her, thanked the volunteers for their support, then ran across the square and climbed the city hall's staircase. As an independent candidate, she should have stayed with these youths at her stand and spoken with her citizens. At the same time, these go-getters pitched her cause better than she would have.

A man in a navy-blue suit bowed and held the door for her. Nuria recognized this animal-loving businessman-cum-politician; she had dodged him several times. The election of San Taurino's executives was finished. After losing the regional, Alejandro was now targeting the national, using his same pitch on cruelty-free products, made by his multinational cosmetic company, which earned him big sums from abroad and little attention at home.

"Thank you," Nuria said. "I'm running late for a meeting."

"Ten seconds, please," Alejandro said.

"Five."

"My party needs Miguel."

"Ask him."

"I did," Alejandro said. "I wired him money, he refused."

"He has his rights."

"You're his influencer."

"I'm his lawyer."

"Miguel can lead my party," Alejandro said. "I'll pay him

whatever—"

"Tell him."

"He doesn't want formal authority."

"Then respect his choice."

Nuria passed the door, cleared security, and reached the mayor's cabinet. The secretary informed him and then led her into his office. Judge Emilio sat with Mayor José. Both looked tense. Nuria took her seat, apologized for her delay, and congratulated the mayor on his reelection.

"Yours is coming," the mayor said. "We thought we should talk to you."

"Right," the judge said. "We should."

"Margarita and Soledad," the mayor said. "You know them, right?"

"I know of them," Nuria said.

"They would soon be your colleagues."

"If I get elected."

"We'll make sure you do."

"What's this meeting for?"

"Patience, Nuria," the mayor said. "We're coming to it."

"Nuria," the judge said. "Have you met our wives?"

"No."

"You should," the mayor said. "They're reliable women."

"They're solid like you," the judge said. "Citizens trust them."

"They're stable and stalwart," the mayor said. "They'll be your good friends."

"We'll see," Nuria said. "Why did you want us to meet?"

"We know you'll push to remove the exclusion?"

"Good you know," Nuria said. "These bulls shouldn't be

excluded."

"You'll need our wives at your side."

"They won't help me."

"Not if you—"

"José." The judge nudged the mayor. "Can I take over this conversation?"

"Sure, Emilio." The mayor lifted his eyebrows. "You're the judge here."

"Nuria," the judge said. "Can I get this short and straight?"

"Please."

"We're opening a company of vegan foods. Margarita and Soledad will be on its board of directors, and we want you as our legal counsel. We each have a twenty percent stake in this business. The remaining sixty will come from Willem."

"I don't want anything to do with Willem."

"We understand you," the judge said. "You'll work for us."

"I'll work for no one."

"Did you know Willem is vegetarian?"

"No."

"You should," the mayor said. "Miguel would love to know."

"Tell him."

"We will," the judge said, "when we meet Miguel."

"You're meeting Miguel?"

"Not yet," the mayor said. "We need him to get our company known."

"He doesn't sponsor anyone."

"We know," the mayor said. "That's why we need you."

"José," the judge said. "Can I keep the lead today?"

"Yes, my friend." The mayor sighed. "Please do."

"Thank you," the judge said. "Nuria, we're not asking you to manipulate Miguel."

"I won't."

"We want to cut a deal that will benefit all sides. You convince Miguel to diffuse our brand, and we make life easy for you both."

"We aren't seeking easy life," Nuria said. "I won't push Miguel to bend his rules."

"Our company will produce food by Miguel's principles," the judge said. "If he wants vegan food to be everyone's staple, he should bend his rules and help our brand."

"Why don't you ask Miguel?"

"You're his—" The mayor groaned. "Emilio, that hurts!"

"You're his lawyer, Nuria," the judge said. "That's what José meant to say."

"Have we finished?" Nuria asked.

"Are you rushing us?"

"I need to work."

"This is work."

"See you."

Nuria left the city hall. She walked across Plaza de Toreros, sat at the fountain's base, and inhaled the square's vibes. They closed an exciting autumn and opened a promising winter. The crisp air chilled her throat, soothed her lungs, and toned her vessels, nerves, and sinews. Her stagnant heat ventilated. Her boiling blood cooled. Her blues changed into hopes.

The sun arched low over the city and revived the autumn's departing colors. On the south hills' slopes, the rays flared the ranks of beeches, birches, and oaks and darkened the clusters of cedars, cypresses, and pines. Under their shade, forty-three summers ago,

301

Miguel's parents left him at birth, to escape Franco's executions at forced-labor camps. During the Cold War years, like other South American migrants, they had fallen to the Spanish Miracle's lure, met the White Terror, and fled the country. On their way out, they must have ended their journey in a communal grave with thousand other escapees. The cow that found Miguel sheltered him under her udder, kept him warm, fed him milk, and protected him from buzzards circling the hills until a farmer found him, took him to the city's church, and gave him to the nuns.

She could see his personal stake in the bovine race. She could understand his stance against their slaughter. She could feel his soft spot for cows. She could relate to his drive behind the video he released on the slaughter of the mother of that bull that killed Julio.

Miguel had his faults. Those faults came rather from lacking experience than embracing ignorance. Life had failed to birth in this orphaned philosopher a sense of priority and focus to achieve his goal. But he was a genuine human: honest and humane. He symbolized virtue.

Unlike other foundations, the overheads of his were close to zero. His was domiciled at home, and he never traveled. His workplace was virtual; his work, real. He drew no salary for his work. His associates were volunteers. He shunned personal wealth, power, and glory. He lived simply, in a ruin that could fall upon him any minute. He lived from his former savings. His monk-like existence made him the beacon for those youths who turned their sails away from the wind of material excess, luxury travels, and other artifices that blew their previous generations. Like him, they solved their existential issues by giving themselves to the work they loved. They expected nothing else in return except for nurturing their souls.

That was the reason Miguel could stay calm, and she couldn't. That was the reason he could keep his poise and win collaborations, and she failed. That was the reason she needed him, and not for preparing the bill to remove the bullfighting exclusion from the code.

She was wrong. She also needed him to prepare the bill. Miguel wasn't a lawyer, but he was competent in law.

In theory, she sided with Miguel. From human viewpoint, humans are the most important creatures on Earth. But from Earth's viewpoint, a human is no more important than a spider. Whereas bees fertilize flowers, worms ventilate the soil, and plants clean the air, humans ruin other lives, rob their habitats, and repay Earth with pollution. A human corpse doesn't return to Earth, feed its soil, and birth new lives; it kills more trees for its burial or incineration. His insight carried theoretical weight. In practice, it lacked power to influence humans or initiate changes. Humans alter their behavior only if the results of their change directly benefit them. The blind philosopher had failed to grasp this simple truth.

No direct benefits would come to humans from stopping bullfights. Paid research rather proved the contrary: the fighting bulls entertained humans and invigorated the economy. Like all other animals bred for consumption or company, these bulls served humans by quenching the blood-thirst of some and by extinguishing the hunger of others. In this respect, the code saw these bulls at par with farm- and company-animals; the bulls' exclusion from the law's realm allowed them to serve humans. These animals had no rights to exist for themselves on their own. The law faculty had taken five years to indoctrinate her into this line of thinking. She might see Miguel's principles from his philosopher's vision, but she disagreed with his actions for practical reasons.

Nevertheless, the status quo was changing fast. The tide now swelled in animals' favor. She could ride this tide and reconcile her approach with Miguel's.

Humans made laws, humans changed laws. The fighting bull symbolized the suffering animal. If she wanted to stop bullfighting, she couldn't disperse herself like Miguel; she had to narrow her focus and prove that eliminating bullfights would help humans. Given Spain's economy after the financial downturn, given the money bullfights brought to this economy, searching for arguments to stop bullfighting would send her down a tortuous and torturous path. In her pursuit, she might lose her support at the legislature and find herself alone. She should minimize her conflicts with Miguel and retain his structure's support.

Besides, she believed Miguel: if citizens elected her, she wouldn't be alone.

His words instilled hope.

She needed to brief Miguel on a few cases. They had no meeting planned this evening. He worked from home. She wasn't aware of any events that could keep him out. She checked her watch, took out her cell phone, and then changed her mind.

She would surprise him at his door.

30

Her first day at the legislature was squeezed with meetings. Nuria finished dressing, opened her bedroom's shutters, and checked the orientation day's agenda. The sun peeked between the snow-capped peaks and flooded her room in yellow and orange. She went to the window and peered at the obscure valley.

Dawn's fingers reached the frozen pastures and lifted their dark cover. The farms' outlines emerged, fought the cold, and welcomed the warmth. Uncle Manu drove his tractor and tilled his land for winter. Since the bullfighting season ended two and a half weeks ago, he had worked his farm nonstop without taking a day off. He was a farmer at heart; driving Willem's coaches couldn't change him. Like all other farmers in this community from the South, he saw his three-generation old farm as his ancestors' shrine and devoted himself to it.

The region owed these farmers more. Once the bullfighting exclusion was removed, she would push the region's deputies to vote for more funds. She uttered a prayer, gathered her official papers, and joined her parents at breakfast.

"You look sharp in that suit," Father said. "Are you ready to battle?"

"Not yet," Nuria said. "Soon."

"We count on you."

"Father, please."

"The region is cutting our aid."

"The Union is raising it."

"The city gave a million and a half to the bullring."

"Rafaela sits on the city council."

"Those funds could have gone to our farmers."

"Father," Nuria said. "Are you expecting me to change this?"

"Yes."

"Don't," Nuria said. "I have my priorities."

"You became a deputy only to stop bullfighting?"

"No."

"Good luck with Pedro."

"He only mediates debates," Nuria said. "The legislature's president has no special power to make or change laws."

"That's what you think."

"Can we talk about something else?"

"Like what?"

"Lorenza, for example."

"Don't talk to me about that stubborn cow!"

"Jorge," Mother said. "Forget Lorenza for now."

"Why?"

"She's still holding onto Victor."

"Who're you trying to fool?"

"Trust me," Mother said. "She'll get over her bull soon."

"Victor left a year and a half ago," Father said. "That cow's memory is stronger than yours. If she doesn't forget her bull this winter, she's going to the slaughter—"

"Father," Nuria said. "Stop."

"You want me to feed her and take her kicks?"

"Leave her alone for one more year."

"That cow is useless."

"Are you sure?"

"Yes."

"Why have you saved Victor the Second?"

"We need a bull."

"See?"

"What?"

"Lorenza is useful."

"She won't change next year."

"Wait and see," Nuria said. "Victor's other calves have earned us enough. We aren't hard-pressed for money. We can give Lorenza some time to breathe."

"Jorge," Mother said. "Bring Victor the Second to this farm."

"Why?"

"That calf is big enough to leave his mother. If you sever him this winter, Lorenza will accept insemination next summer. Victor the Second needs to feel like a bull. He'll fit easier with his new herd while he's still young."

"You're right," Father said. "Charo advised me too."

"Then do it," Mother said. "And let Lorenza live."

"Thank you, Mother," Nuria said. "See you this evening."

"Wait," Mother said. "Give me Ignaçio's number."

"Why?"

"You don't need to know."

"Of course, I do."

"I'll call him for Christmas dinner."

"Pardon?"

"He didn't come last year."

"You called him last year?"

"It's his home, right?"

"No, it isn't," Nuria said. "I'll make sure he doesn't come this year."

"Nuria," Mother said. "Give me Nacho's number!"

"You have it," Nuria said. "How did you call him last year?"

"I lost his number."

"I lost it too."

"Will you give me his number?"

"I don't have it."

"I'll get it from Elena or Charo."

"Mother," Nuria said. "What are you trying to do?"

"I want him only for the dinner."

"That killer of bulls?"

"He hasn't killed one yet."

"He'll soon."

"I want him to dine with us this year."

"Sure," Nuria said. "And you'll dine without me."

"Nuria, that kid has no one."

"He's no longer a kid."

"He grew with us."

"He left us."

"You're inhumane."

"You drive me insane."

Nuria left the table, went out, and sat inside her car.

She didn't understand her mother. When Ignaçio lived at home, Mother wanted him out. Now that he was out, Mother wanted him in. She didn't need this nonsense from her parents; she had priorities waiting for her. Santos scratched the passenger-side door. Nuria let the dog in, sat him in his seat, and drove away from her parents' farm.

She patted Santos on the back. The dog sat up and looked ahead.

Eighteen months had passed since Victor left Ignaçio's farm; Santos still held onto his guilt for the bull. Ignaçio's abrupt departure hadn't helped the dog either. The work on the two farms should keep this dog busy and leave him no time for blues. Instead, the double loss was withering him fast and ruining his passion for life. At seven, for his breed, Santos wasn't even halfway through his life. You could smell his sorrow when you sat next to him.

She dropped Santos in front of Ignaçio's farm. The dog didn't jump over the gate as he used to do before; he went under it. Nuria watched Santos trudge toward the cattle. The dog didn't look back at her. She turned left on the cliff-side road and drove toward San Taurino.

The snow didn't block the bridge. The downward slope felt slippery; she should have put on her snow tires. She stayed in low gear and crawled with the traffic. The new deputies, sworn this morning, would return to the legislature in January. She had work to finish before they reported. A driver recognized her, gave her a thumb-up, and overtook her. She resisted her impulse to shout, cased on the gas pedal, and leaned back on her seat. If she wanted to remove the bullfight exclusion from the code, she should stay humane with her citizens.

The removal required tact. Those who installed the exclusion knew these bulls were living beings. Yet they voted for this exclusion because they didn't feel for these bulls. The same voters would never permit similar torture on their company animals, for the economy or for their pleasure, inside a bullring or outside. They weren't close to these bulls. They saw these fighting bulls as incapable of feelings. That should be the departing point of her bill.

The absence of consent was the other key point. Before two boxers pummeled each other in a ring, they signed a contract and agreed to bleed; the bulls didn't. The boxers got paid for their pain; the bulls didn't. The bulls got shoved into rings against their will and then tortured and bled to death. Their four free years of roaming and feeding didn't compensate for this.

These bulls were forced to fight—not one human but six. If their consent were sought, they would never agree. Most of them tried to escape before fighting for self-defense. The court accepted this coercion and permitted this violence because these fighting bulls didn't qualify for the animals the laws protected. The ravaged bulls didn't propagate Spain's art, culture, or heritage. Their plight ravished Spain's image in the international arena.

The situation wasn't hopeless. Spain allowed regional autonomy its neighbors didn't. Franco's successors had ensured regions' liberty to make and apply laws, as long as they didn't violate the constitution. Several regions had already applied this legacy and removed bullfights from their arenas. The court's disapproval couldn't reinstate their bullfighting.

She had studied their proceedings. For a symbolic city like San Taurino, the cessation might be difficult but not impossible. Her election proved her citizens' stance: if they didn't want bullfighting to end, they wouldn't give her their voice. She had failed to draw outside lawyers to help her bill, but the lawyers inside the legislature had helped her. These deputies respected Carlota. Her endorsement would influence their votes during the debate.

This bill would take the whole of her and more. She would have to do further research. She would have to consult experts. She would have to call witnesses for the congressional committee before the bill went for debate. She would have to perform her other tasks at the legislature the deputies were paid for. She would have to counsel Miguel on his foundation's cases. If she didn't keep the peripheral stuff away, her core would burn out.

Ignaçio now belonged to her periphery. He would stay out.

She reached Plaza de Toreros. She parked at the deputies' space and entered the building. The high dome lifted her pressure and expanded her chest. She stood at the cupola's center and soaked its vibes and hums. The queue at the booth eroded. She gave her official papers to the receptionist. He registered her and gave her the office number.

The debate hall opened. The deputies reelected Pedro as their president. He thanked them for their trust and enumerated his duties. He promised to make their work agreeable, fruitful, and memorable. He swore in the deputies and elaborated their responsibilities. He announced January's agenda and ended the session.

Nuria left the debate hall. Pedro followed her and invited her to his office.

"Congratulations!" Pedro said. "You're first in our legislature's long history to be elected without a political party."

"Thank you," Nuria said. "I'll leave when my work finishes."

"Not so soon."

"I don't expect you to vote for my bill."

"I won't," Pedro said. "But count on me for conducting a fair debate. Both sides would have their voices heard before they cast their votes. They represent our citizens. You'll hear and see what our citizens think of bullfighting."

"I hope."

"As the legislature's president, it's my duty to help you draft your bill and submit it before the committee. Can I do something for you?"

"I'll go now."

"Will you ask me?"

"No."

"Nuria," Pedro said. "Wait."

"I have work—"

"This concerns Miguel," Pedro said. "The Union's exclusion, the trade sanctions, the international boycotts—our citizens aren't taking any of this in the right spirit."

"I didn't push him for these."

"I know," Pedro said. "But these noises would hurt your bill."

"I can't stop Miguel."

"He doesn't listen to you?"

"No."

"This doesn't fall in my premise," Pedro said. "But as you represent him, I thought you should know. Something serious is brewing in the capital."

"Against Miguel?"

"No."

"Against his foundation?"

"Yes."

"They can't close it."

"They might."

"Miguel's foundation is legal," Nuria said. "What he does is legal."

"Not always."

"Are you referring to his trespassing?"

"No."

"Why are you telling me this?"

"You could get in trouble."

"Me!" Nuria said. "Because I'm his lawyer?"

"You're more."

"You're stretching too far."

"I'm not."

312

"See you later."

"Be careful."

31

The beeps didn't come from her dream; they came from her cell phone. The commotion downstairs sounded real. Nuria rubbed her eyes and checked the time: ten past two in the morning. She pushed aside her blanket, put on her clothes, and ran down the stairs.

Both her parents, in night robes, stood silent in front of the television. They didn't turn or look at her. Nuria crossed the den, folded her arms, and squinted at the shimmering images. The blazing flames, the deafening clamor, the flying shells told her the reason for the city's nightmare. Her head reeled. She wrapped a shawl around herself and sat on the sofa's arm.

From the bullfighting association's burnt façade, the camera shifted to the littered stairs of the city hall, the regional legislature, and the national tribunal, moved to the taurine academy and its battered entrance, and then stopped on the market road's grilles for the bull-run. Two of the grilles lay flat on the sidewalk among signs of a stampede. Security tapes encircled the zone.

The shops in the arena's arcade stood smashed; the Roman soldier's statue in the arena's court, disfigured. A teenage girl, disheveled and disoriented, cried behind the defiled statue. In Plaza de Toreros, Miguel separated the clashing groups and hailed for peace. Nuria wore her shoes and took her car key. Father blocked her path and bolted the door.

"Don't stop me," Nuria said. "Let me go."

"You can't enter the city," Father said. "The special force has blocked all roads. They don't want the molesters to escape."

"Both Elena and Vincente got injured," Mother said.

"Miguel will get hurt," Nuria said.

"Call him."

"He won't hear."

"Try."

Miguel didn't answer his phone. Nuria pressed her temples and stared at the television. Projectiles left both sides. They flew above poised Miguel and exploded at their destinations. Fire rose; smoke blurred the scene. Behind the smog's veil, Ishmael moved around with his equipment. The fearless editor held his camera upright, turned its range from one side to the other, and then focused on Miguel's maneuvers. They both ignored their peril.

Her parents' landline rang. Mother answered it, switched off the television, and turned on the phone's speaker.

"They caught those kids," Jaime said. "The police broke into their apartment."

"How's Elena doing now?"

"She'll be alright."

"And Vincente?"

"Ines needs to take care of him."

"These riots are ruining this city," Mother said. "Three springs in a row!"

"They'll cancel this *feria* again."

"Who's that girl?"

"Judge Emilio's niece."

"Pardon?"

"Her father owns the arena's souvenir shop," Jaime said. "She was taking his dinner to him. Those boys caught her before she reached."

"How many boys?"

"Six."

"The poor girl!"

"One of them is an ambassador's son."

"And the rest?"

"Friends visiting him for the feria."

"They got the wrong girl."

"That's what the ambassador claims," Jaime said. "He's evoking political immunity, but that applies only to him, not to his family."

"Keep me informed on Elena and Vincente."

"I will."

"Any news about Ignaçio?"

"No."

"Ask him to stay in."

"Mother," Nuria said. "Do you have to—"

"Shut up!"

"Pardon?"

"You heard it."

"Two family members are hurt," Nuria said. "And you worry about that ingrate?"

"Nacho belongs to this family."

"He doesn't think so."

"Take your nonsense upstairs."

"I'll go to the city."

"You stay right here."

"Mother!"

"Quiet," Mother said. "Jaime, I've to leave you."

"Tell Nuria I'm with Miguel."

"Are you?"

"Tell her he's fine."

"You leave right now."

"Mother," Jaime said. "I'm waiting for Ines."

"In that square?"

"Yes."

"Why?"

"The squad is treating Vincente."

"What's happening with him?"

"He'll come around."

"Where's Ines?"

"I don't know."

"Go, find her."

"That's what I'm doing."

"God, help us!"

Mother hung up the call and broke in tears. Father stood immobile and stared at the blank television. Nuria wanted to turn it on but didn't dare. She brought Mother to the sofa and sat next to her. Father put on his coat, picked up his keys, and marched toward the door.

"Jorge," Mother said. "Where are you going?"

"To get my children."

"Are you nuts?"

"You are."

"Get back here."

"I'm not your child."

"Jorge!"

"See you soon."

Father revved his vehicle and drove away.

"Mother," Nuria said. "Let him go."

"What can he do?"

"Nothing."

"How'll he reach the city?"

"He won't."

"Then why go?"

"He'll return."

"I can't take this anymore."

"Mother," Nuria said. "Please."

"I'm sorry."

"Don't be."

"God, please calm me."

"Just try."

"You go and rest."

"I'll stay."

Mother's sobs faded into sleep. Nuria laid her on the couch and then covered her with the shawl. Father didn't return. Nuria made coffee and switched on her laptop. She dimmed the den's light, muted the computer's speaker, and went onto Ishmael's website. The journalist had logged the riot's videos by its events' order. She scrolled to the bottom, found the video of last evening's bull-run, and clicked on the clip.

Rafaela's six bulls left the port. Runners chased them on the route. Spectators leaned over metal barriers and applauded the accelerating race. The confused bulls cantered and groaned. More runners joined the race. The commotion grew. At the station's corner, the disoriented bulls halted and clashed. Trumpets blew behind them. Firecrackers sizzled, flared, and burst. The frightened bulls separated, bellowed, and galloped up the avenue toward the arena.

They didn't reach their destination.

Before the market street, tourists hollered and intercepted the bull-run. The metal grilles, moved from the roadside, leaned against the thermal bath. The thwarted bulls deviated from their course and veered into the quarter's paved street. A woman and her daughter stood on the pavement and waved a red cape at the bulls.

The lead bull leaped at the two women. They withdrew the cape and recoiled in haste. The bull hit them and flung them across the street. The crowd cried and ran. The six fraught bulls trampled the fallen and galloped after the fleeing. On the market hall's stoop, six blond youths sat, smoked, and watched the stampede. Among these drunkards, Nuria saw the ambassador's son, now all over the news.

The bulls raced to the street's end, turned left, and vanished from the view. The camera shifted to the teenage girl crying in the arena's court. Nuria didn't want to see or hear this part. She stopped the video and closed her computer. She returned with her coffee and sat next to Mother. Father was still out doing whatever he wanted to do.

Her cell phone beeped: a message from Miguel.

She opened the message. It contained only a link to his foundation's website. She paused, hesitated, and then clicked on the link.

The authorities announced the two gored women's death at the hospital. The news spread like wildfire on the web. Clicks leaped by hundreds before her eyes. Comments left the linear trajectory for an exponential spree. The deceased women's country hurled invectives at Spain. They added fuel to the riot's fire and fanned its flames.

Nuria answered Miguel's message, muted her phone, and lay next to Mother.

The gravel's crunch woke Nuria.

Mother had left the sofa; she was preparing breakfast for them. Father walked into the living room. Frost covered his hair, face, and coat. His pants and boots dripped water. His fingers shivered, but his eyes smiled.

"Jorge," Mother said. "What did you do?"

"Went downtown."

"How?"

"Took Manu's rowboat to the port."

"They let you in?"

"I made them."

"You're stubborn like your children."

"You knew that," Father said. "That's why you married me."

"How's Elena?"

"At home."

"And Vincente?"

"We'll soon know."

"They took him to the hospital?"

"He's at the barracks."

"And Ines?"

"With him."

"He'll survive then," Mother said. "What got you wet?"

"Those barges."

"You fell in the water?"

"I love swimming."

"Holy God!"

"Do I get some coffee?"

"After you shower and change."

Nuria's eyes watered. She left the sofa, crossed the den, and stood at the open door.

The April sun peeked through the forest's foliage, hurled its nascent rays at this waking farm, and flooded its pasture's frosted grass. The frozen dewdrops, hanging from the fence's wires, caught the rolling rays and glittered. The burgeoning leaves breathed the dawn's light and glistened on the creepers.

The beams hit the frozen stairs and shined their iced tiles. Their frigid cover melted. On the gravel's frost, the crushed crust sparkled. Warm radiance left their sweating sheen and sprayed the spinning cobwebs under the eaves.

They soaked the incandescence and glowed with hope.

32

"The family of the dead has sued for two and a half million," Rafaela said.

"The city will pay that bill," Angel said.

"The mayor passed it to us."

"We don't maintain security."

"Those two women provoked my bulls."

"I know, "Angel said. "Did you tell Judge Emilio?"

"He saw the video."

"How's his niece doing?"

"He didn't tell me."

"Willem called," Angel said. "He wants to cover us for the canceled *feria*."

"We don't need his money," Rafaela said. "We have our insurance."

"Esteban wants his part now."

"He'll wait."

"Are they taking your bulls for slaughter?"

"No," Rafaela said. "They return to my ranch in the South."

"The mayor agreed?"

"Judge Emilio did."

"Their alliance is dissolving."

"It already has."

The ambassador's son broke his electronic bracelet and escaped home detention. The police couldn't identify the car that took the boy to the airport or the private jet that shipped him out of the country. Both were owned by a Bahamas-based shell company, not tied to an individual or enterprise. Judge Emilio issued an international arrest warrant for the boy. He pushed for a search & seizure at his parents' home and subpoenaed them for complicity. The ambassador evoked his political immunity and dodged both.

Rumors grew about Willem's hand. Nothing tied him to them.

The police and the firefighters declared strike. Some officers wore their uniforms and demonstrated with anti-bullfighting groups. The region's audacity inflamed the national authorities. They sanctioned the rebelling officers and suspended them from work. More officers joined the strike and destroyed the city's law and order. The regional government stepped in and pushed back the national. The rebel officers calmed and returned to work.

A week later, Mayor José gave an interview to Ishmael's paper.

"Corrida performs catharsis for humans," the mayor said. "The Greeks used bullfights to purge their violence. The bull's tragedy helps the human's health."

"That was true in another epoch," Ishmael said.

"The principle still holds."

"Violence doesn't attract violence?"

"No."

"What explains the girl's molestation?"

"That exception isn't the norm."

"Thank you," the journalist said. "I have another question."

"You can ask more."

"You say tragedy is good for humans?"

"Yes."

"Why not let two humans fight to death?"

"That's not ethical."

"Why?"

"We live in a civilized society," the mayor said. "We've carried

323

our culture's torch across the world. We've served as civilization's vanguard throughout human history. On our nation's soil, we can't let two humans hurt and kill each other. If we did, we would kill our legacy."

"But we can let six humans torture and kill a bull in our arenas."

"Of course."

"Why?"

"Bulls are not humans."

Ishmael published the interview on his site. Miguel relayed it on his foundation's network. A fresh battle surged between pro- and anti-bullfighting camps, swept the commotion around the ambassador's son, and swayed the city's priorities. Judge Emilio retained Mayor José's "exception" about the molested girl, ignored the city's chaos, and pursued Willem's trail.

33

Victor started transforming into Mors the day he arrived at this bull ranch.

The place felt different. Unlike his previous farm, this ranch didn't have a sea at one end; steep mountains surrounded its all sides. In the morning, the sun found a narrow pass between the peaks to reach the bulls and wake them. Later, when it crossed this farm, it traveled higher and sent them more light and warmth. The place smelled different. Air, thicker with salt, came sometimes but didn't bring any odor of algae or mist. If a sea lay behind those mountains, it didn't roar like the one he knew beside his former farm. The peaks here held back the wind.

The sky above this ranch was clearer and bluer. Its dome rose higher and wore more stars at night. Buzzards didn't circle these peaks. Owls didn't hoot at night. Rabbits didn't frolic, romp, and run on this ranch. Green birds, with forked tails and hooked beaks, dove from the trees and flew close to the ground. They caught lizards, snakes, and frogs. They scoured the pasture, scared its insects, and panicked the squirrels. They quarreled and fought for the nuts, seeds, and berries. The plants and bushes here lay lower. The thickets hid longer snakes and larger spiders. White flakes didn't fall from the sky on this ranch to cover the grass and send its hidden dangers to sleep. All lives on this ranch slept with their eyes half-open.

The bees here grew bigger, wore more colors, and worked harder. They started earlier and finished later. This ranch's reservoir held more water than Mors and his brothers needed. No heron fished among its rushes, reeds, and thickets. On hot days, the water receded faster. The morass didn't let the bulls approach the lake for a swim.

The gulls here laughed at them. The cormorants spread their wings wider but not for friendship. The animals on this ranch fended for themselves and didn't mix with others. Mors had to content himself with his brothers.

The warmer sun and the regular care healed his shoulder and repaired his coat, but Mors remembered the lance's hurt. The wound from a lance's tip reaches deeper, stays longer, and stings sharper. The lance isn't a weapon to ignore: its blade causes more harm than just pain. A lance-bearing biped is a vicious animal. Mors didn't see again the two bipeds that hurt him with their lances, but he decided he would never trust another biped holding this weapon.

Vehicles came and went. They brought scared steers and took sad bulls. The brothers that left never returned. When the sun traveled higher and stayed longer in the sky, other vehicles brought cows to this ranch. These females stayed on a separate side, met his brothers, and left when the trees wore flaming colors. These cows didn't smell like Lorenza. They didn't look at him with her eyes. No dogs herded them. These females didn't seek or need protection. Mors left them to his brothers and stayed away from them. On this ranch, there was nothing else to do except eating, drinking, and roaming. He slept early and woke late.

For most part, his brothers left him alone. He looked different from them, and he behaved differently from them. He couldn't know his brothers for long. After they spent some time on this ranch and attained a certain stature, they left and didn't return. Only he remained on this ranch through its seasons and watched younger brothers come and older brothers go.

His brothers didn't exclude him. He moved from one group to another. He shared their pains and pleasures. This ranch's vast space

326

gave everyone enough room to breathe. The herbs here grew taller; the thorns, lustier. The grey snakes with catlike eyes and the black spiders with red belly didn't pardon anyone. The bulls had to learn to live with them.

He grew bigger than his brothers, twice as large. His growth imposed nature's law; his brothers respected his stature and deferred to his status. When he drank at the reservoir with them, he saw what differentiated him from the rest: his legs and dewlap, his head and horns, his hump and hooves, his muscles and their power. He never applied his strength, speed, or leaps on his brothers. Their differences set limits, preserved peace, and kept them safe.

Nevertheless, Mors found a steady friend on this ranch. The Mistress of Bulls always came on her slim coco-brown stallion that contrasted her mane and matched her erectness, elegance, and grace. She called this stallion Zeus. During the weeks she treated Mors for his lance wound, this majestic horse—poised, patient, and potent like her—waited by the fence, eyed him with compassion, and confirmed his worth. Their friendship started. They touched muzzles and forged their bond. Each visit grew their friendship.

The Mistress of Bulls was the mistress of Zeus. Yet she didn't connect with her stallion the way she did with her bulls; she had something special for bulls. And she didn't connect with her other bulls the way she did with Mors; she had something special for him.

She never smiled at Mors or spoke in his ears. He could see her feelings for him in her firm care. She didn't come often. When she did, she stayed long and rubbed his coat, as his biped playmate used to do after their cape-and-sword games. Her posture, gait, gestures, and regard resembled his former mate's, yet she never danced or played with him. Her care grew him further and maintained their

327

distance. Their sober relation turned him more solemn.

Her eyes never beamed at anyone. Her pupils narrowed at no one. Often she gazed far, sighed, and swallowed like cows whose calves were taken. Her hormones smelled like the young biped female's on his previous farm. And like that female, The Mistress of Bulls never bore any offspring and always lived in her blues. If he tried to lick her hand, she pushed his muzzle away. Like his biped playmate, The Mistress of Bulls preferred firmer feelings.

Nature changed its coat and color twice. Nothing special happened on this ranch.

Then the air warmed fast and fresh shoots peeked from the earth. One morning, six of his best brothers left the ranch in six separate vehicles. Like all other departing bulls, these brothers weren't expected to return, but they did after the sun rose and set seven times. They were no longer the same, neither in appearance nor in behavior. They seemed strange. They saw their brothers as strangers. As soon as the bipeds released them on this ranch, the six bulls ran in six different directions and hid from the rest. Mors and his brothers left them alone.

The Mistress of Bulls came afterward. These six bulls didn't approach her or obey her orders. They wore their troubled air. They avoided bipeds and bulls. They didn't trust each other and form a group. Mors approached them; they gave him their horns. His brothers shook their heads and observed them from far. These deranged bulls didn't want anyone's help.

The air warmed further. The sun traveled higher. One lonesome morning, when the tired leaves sweated and the withered herbs exhaled, The Mistress of Bulls arrived on her stallion, followed by a red house-on-wheels. Mors and his brothers stopped grazing. They

328

lifted their heads, perked their ears, and peered at this decorated vehicle they didn't know. The vehicle rolled to their ranch's gate, stopped behind Zeus, and waited for the stallion to move.

The stallion didn't.

The Mistress of Bulls descended from Zeus and pulled him by his reins. The stallion refused to budge. Mors reached the fence and extended his muzzle over the stakes. Zeus shook his head, lifted his muzzle, and emitted a long neigh. The Mistress of Bulls left her stallion outside and entered the ranch. Mors moved toward her. She didn't lift her eyes and meet his gaze. She took a rosette, pinned it on his shoulder, and stood aside.

Two biped males left the red vehicle and came toward the gate. Zeus blocked their path and struck his hooves on the earth. The bipeds stopped. The Mistress of Bulls went to Zeus, caught his reins, and coaxed him to move. The stallion stayed near the gate and kept his eyes on both bipeds. The other bulls approached and stared at them. The bipeds didn't enter the ranch.

Mors waited.

The Mistress of Bulls left the gate open, entered the ranch, and came toward him.

Mors understood. He nodded at his brothers; they didn't nod back. He looked at Zeus; the stallion shook his head. Mors watched The Mistress of Bulls. Her eyes didn't meet his, but her face looked sure, and her steps seemed stable.

She reached him, touched his shoulder, and then led him out of the ranch.

Her firm touch assured Mors. He followed her to the red vehicle. His brothers reached the fence and groaned at him. Mors turned toward them, lifted his head, and bellowed. His call didn't reassure his brothers. They raised their muzzles and roared at The Mistress of Bulls. She ignored their uproar, left him near the vehicle, and marched toward Zeus. The bulls followed her and continued to roar. She reached Zeus and leaped onto the stallion's back.

Zeus reared up, tossed his head, and neighed. She caught his reins, stood on the stirrups, and spoke in his ears.

The stallion calmed.

Mors felt reassured. The bipeds loaded him into the red vehicle. Its inside didn't resemble the one's that brought him to this ranch. It looked tidy and smelled clean. It gave him enough room to stand, sit, or lie. It contained a bucket of water, a trough with grass, and vents for air. The bipeds closed the backdoor, removed its top slats, and climbed at the front.

The vehicle moved. Mors came to the door and peered through its gap. His brothers stood still and stared at him. Mors nodded. They lowered their heads and ears, turned, and trudged toward the reservoir. Mors sighed. The trail's dust rose, blurred his vision, and hid them.

The Mistress of Bulls followed the vehicle. Dust covered her hair and Zeus's mane. Mors couldn't see her face or the stallion's muzzle. The vehicle reached the trail's end and turned onto a paved road. Zeus wanted to follow the vehicle. The Mistress of Bulls pulled his reins and held him back. The stallion reared up, tossed his head, and neighed. She leaned forward, spoke in his ears, and calmed him. They stood at the intersection and watched the vehicle go.

The vehicle rattled, sputtered, and sped. Mors stood at the door. Zeus and The Mistress of Bulls shrank and then vanished from his sight.

Mors recognized this road he took two years ago. He reckoned the farms, the people, and the animals along the way. He recalled the sounds, the smells, and the texture of the soil. They were taking him back to his previous farm. He didn't want to leave this place. He didn't want to leave his brothers. He didn't want to leave Zeus and The Mistress of Bulls.

But he had friends on his previous farm too, friends he hadn't seen for long.

Would they recognize him now? He didn't know. If they recognized him, would they accept him now? He didn't know. Did he recall them? Yes. If they accepted him, would he want to stay with them now? He didn't know.

Like him, they certainly had changed. He remembered Santos falling off the truck. Did the dog survive the fall? He hoped. If the dog lived but sustained injuries, could he take care of his herd? Or did they get another dog afterward? Did his biped mate find another bull to dance and play with? Did that bull treat his cows well? Did Lorenza forget him and accept that bull?

When he left, Lorenza was pregnant. Did she birth her calf afterward? If she did, was it a male or female? What would that calf look like now? Would Lorenza want him near her calf or chase him away? How would he deal with her and her calf? Why were these two bipeds taking him back to his old farm now? Did he really want to go back there? He didn't know.

He missed his playmate on that farm. He missed their games. The Mistress of Bulls never played with him. He had more in common with his mate than her. Their severance had left him a void she and his brothers couldn't fill. Did his mate feel the same way about him? About his absence? His mate differed from other bipeds. His mate shared his differences with him. In many ways, his mate was closer to bulls than bipeds. They understood each other in silence. That made their relation special. He didn't understand The Mistress of Bulls.

The vehicle left the known path and entered an unknown city.

Mors compared this city to the one he knew: the two had little in common. Yet this city's bipeds resembled those on that farm he was returning to. Orange trees lined its narrow streets and hung their maturing fruit. Mors stretched his neck and caught a few. They didn't smell or taste like the oranges that grew on his previous farm. This city's houses lay lower. They wore whiter walls and brighter red roofs. Thicker creepers covered their wider balconies, façades, and fronts. They wafted smells he didn't know.

The vehicle reached a square, turned around, and backed up toward a fort.

The fort's gate creaked; its panels split open.

The vehicle entered the fort, drove to its back, and stopped at a corral. Five more bulls waited there; Mors didn't know them. The bipeds unloaded him and left him in the corral. The other bulls moved aside and made room for him.

Mors waited three sunrises and sunsets in this corral. Nothing happened.

At the fourth sunrise, new bipeds came and led him out. They didn't load him into the red vehicle; they put him in a pen and turned off its lights. They brought him food and water. He didn't touch those or sit down. He couldn't figure why they left him in this dark room.

The darkness honed his eyes and sharpened his ears. Outside, music played and bugles blew, bipeds cried and bulls roared. Some bipeds hurled his playmate's commands but in an aggressive tone. These bulls, fierce and furious, didn't respect these bipeds' words or enjoy their games. They suffered much and lacked breath. At regular intervals, an agonized bull cried for life, fell silent, and raised other bipeds' applause. Shortly after, the music replayed, the bugles blew, and a new bull charged in and started the old game. They continued.

The last game ended. The fort fell silent. Mors sighed in relief.

A door opened at the back of his pen. This wasn't the door that let him into this pen. Mors walked out; the blazing sun blinded him. When his eyes adjusted to the piercing light, he saw he was facing an arena—not of inviting grass, but of burning sand. At this arena's center, a biped wearing the colors of light stood defiant, holding a cape in one hand and a sword in the other. This biped's attitude and stance didn't resemble his playmate's.

Mors bowed to this biped; the biped didn't.

Mors watched him closer. The biped invited him with the cape for a game. Mors accepted the invitation and stepped onto the hot sand.

He halted: The Mistress of Bulls sat behind the wooden barrier.

She wasn't alone. Above her, a male biped sat in a box, holding a piece of white cloth. Other bipeds sat on her both sides and behind her in three rows. Farther behind, more rows, filled with bipeds, rose above them and leaned outward. Mors marveled at this arena: so many spectators, sitting so close to each other, looking so different. The sun streamed on them and shined their glistening faces. Some held their hands above their eyes and peered at him. Others wore dark sunglasses or broad-brimmed hats and fanned themselves.

Two horses, blindfolded, entered the arena. Colored quilts covered their flanks. Their gaits seemed unsure; their moves, hesitant. They didn't carry Zeus's poise and grace. They seemed troubled. They cantered around the arena, faltered several times, and stood aside. Their riders each carried a lance. Both lances were longer than the ones he saw on two other occasions. Their blades spanned larger and shined sharper. Their bearers seemed more vicious than the two other lancers he met in the past.

These riders carried a nervous energy that scared their horses. The animals wanted to leave; there was no way out for them. Both riders forced their horses by whipping, spurring, and kicking. Their ways with these horses didn't please The Mistress of Bulls. Three more bipeds entered the arena on foot and stood facing the horses. They each held two pointed darts; colored frills flashed around their stalks. Mors didn't know these tools. He didn't know how to play a game with six bipeds and two horses at once. He didn't know this game's rules, moves, or order. He stared at the biped in the suit of light. The biped glared back at him.

A bugle blew.

The biped above The Mistress of Bulls waved the white cloth. The biped wearing the suit of light stepped toward Mors, held out the cape and the sword, and shouted a command. Mors knew this command. He lowered his head, pointed his horns, and charged at the cape.

Turbulence rose at his side and arrested his charge. One of the horses neighed and tried to jump the wooden barrier. The mounted biped kicked the horse and backed it from the barrier. Mors lifted his head and scanned the rider's face: his pupils, narrow and vertical, resembled the snake's that bit him on the muzzle. The cruel rider whipped the scared horse, tugged his reins, and spurred his flanks. Mors now knew the game he would play with these bipeds.

The rider raised his lance and thrust its tip at him. Mors dodged the blade but received the shaft on his muzzle. The blow stung his nose and blurred his vision. The rider raised the lance higher and thrust it again at him. Mors ducked. The blade caught him and pierced his hump.

Applause rose from the galleries. The shearing pain traveled down his neck, reached his brain, and reeled his head. Mors shook his shoulders and tried to disengage the blade. The rider leaned forward and pressed down on the shaft. Mors lowered his head, aimed his horns at the biped, and tried to get him without hurting the horse. The biped swung his stirrup and struck Mors on the muzzle. The metal clanged and broke his nose. Mors stood still.

The Mistress of Bulls rose and shouted at the rider. The biped above her waved the white cloth. Their gestures told Mors the mounted biped had broken this game's rules. He waited for their command. The rider ignored them and dug the lance's blade deeper into his flesh. They didn't enter the arena and stop the game. Mors ignored his pain and made up his mind.

One biped rushed from the opposite side and planted two colored darts on his back. This biped left one eye on Mors's horn and fell on the sand. Another biped charged with two more darts; Mors got him before he planted those. This biped, too, hit the sand and covered his face. The Mistress of Bulls and the biped above her stayed silent.

Hoots came from the viewing galleries. Mors ignored their cries and kept his focus.

By now, he knew what to do with the other four bipeds. He decided to take them by the order of danger they posed.

The mounted biped pressed down further on the lance's shaft and grappled for a firmer hold. Mors led him by a ruse to the left. As the lancer took the bait, Mors veered to the right and freed his hump from the blade. The force wrenched the lance off the rider's hands.

The lancer jerked forward and strived to regain his balance. Mors reared up, aimed his hooves, and struck the lancer on the head. His skull cracked. The lancer fell off his horse and prostrated on the sand. Mors reared up again and struck the fallen biped on the chest. His ribs smashed. His panicked horse jumped the barrier and dashed down the alley.

The other horse threw its rider and fled from the arena. The third biped, holding two more colored darts, rushed toward Mors; a kick from his hind leg broke this biped's neck, lifted him off the sand, and sent him above the ring's barrier. The biped wearing the suit of light dropped his cape and sword, dashed to the barrier, and tried to jump over. His leg broke. He caught his foot between the rails and hung head-down like a bat. Mors spared this fleeing coward.

The crushed lancer lay immobile on the sand. Mors raised him on his horns, brought him to The Mistress of Bulls, and laid him before her.

The Mistress of Bulls lifted her eyes and smiled at Mors.

She spoke to the biped above her. He listened to her and nodded. He took an orange cloth and waved it at the galleries. The bipeds there stood and applauded. The biped above her held a metal piece to his mouth and spoke to the galleries. A band wearing spring's colors came to the arena's barrier and played their joyful music.

The game ended. The Mistress of Bulls entered the arena. Another male biped, wearing a white coat and carrying a leather satchel he knew, followed her. Mors stood still and watched. She signaled him to sit on the sand. The biped took out a syringe and a bottle. The injection stopped his shearing pain. The biped removed the two colored darts from his back and laid them on the sand. Mors saw their barbed ends. The biped dressed his wounds and stitched his coat. Blood still dripped from the lance wound and oozed from the other two.

The biped finished his work and packed his tools. Mors strained his neck, lifted his head, and saw his blood on the sand. The amount reeled his head. He lowered his muzzle and rested his chin. The Mistress of Bulls rubbed his head, neck, and back. Her firm touch broke his taut resistance. His pressure released, his tension melted. His vigilance waned, his awareness dimmed. He abandoned himself to her hands, lay on his side, and closed his eyes.

They lifted him from the arena and loaded him into another vehicle. This time, he didn't travel alone; The Mistress of Bulls stayed with him.

The vehicle didn't haul him to her ranch; it took him to another place he didn't know. They kept him in a stall, made him sleep, and treated his wounds. These wounds took longer to close and healed slower than the previous ones. Neither the snake's bite, nor the weeder's cut, nor the other bull's horns had caused so much pain and did such serious damage.

This deeper wound from the larger lance paralyzed his shoulders. He couldn't lift his head to eat or turn his neck to look. The bipeds wearing white coats helped him eat, drink, and move. He ate food he didn't know. The Mistress of Bulls came more often and stayed longer with him. They took him out to exercise in fields, swim in a pool, and brought him back to his stall. They cleaned his stall several times a day and made sure no dirt stayed on his coat.

The lance stayed in his head as an instrument of torture, punishment, and pain. For him, it became the symbol of hurt. He compared the lance to his playmate's sword, with the club, and with the picks: in terms of danger, none came close to the lance. He would never trust a lance or a biped holding it. A biped armed with a lance should be killed.

Yet the act of killing didn't feel right.

Mors replayed the scene at the arena. The battle there didn't start as a fair play. The biped wearing the suit of light didn't return his bow. Six bipeds fought one bull; all six were armed. Mors refused to fight until he was forced; the bipeds didn't leave him a choice. Blindfolding the two horses and forcing them into the fight weren't fair. Their riders kicked and whipped them if they didn't want to move. Like bulls, horses are pacific animals; they avoid fighting and hurting others. These two horses found no escapes from their riders' torture.

Although the biped wearing the suit of light didn't bow back, Mors was going to play the cape and sword game with him. He didn't see why that mounted lancer got in their way and hurt him with the lance. He didn't see why that other biped rushed on him and planted those colored darts on his back. Those darts stuck to his flesh, hung on his sides, and hurt him every time he moved. The lance was already shearing his flesh and leaking enough blood. He didn't see why this biped had to stab two more darts beside the lance, sharpen his pain, and quicken his blood loss. He couldn't justify this game's rules as fair.

The rules of this game were more than unfair: they were cruel.

During the battle, The Mistress of Bulls confirmed this cruelty. She who barely spoke, moved, or gestured went wild to stop this torture. She was a fair biped who despised cruelty. She punished the unfair and rewarded the fair. Those six bipeds didn't listen to her; they got what they deserved. At the battle's end, when he placed the dead lancer at her feet, she lifted her eyes and beamed. That was the first time The Mistress of Bulls smiled at anyone.

Her smile confirmed that his act was right.

The Mistress of Bulls didn't stop at smiling. She spoke to that biped above her. This biped waved the orange cloth at the galleries. The bipeds there applauded Mors's act and declared it as right. The biped above her called that colorful band to the ring's barrier. They played music and celebrated Mors's victory. Nobody questioned the fairness of his act.

Mors distilled the battle's lessons in his stall and waited for The Mistress of Bulls' return. She never failed to come. Each visit brought them closer. Their love deepened. But her distant regard, frequent sighs, and silent swallows remained; he could do nothing to remove those. He vowed he would never disobey her; never ignore her feelings; never betray her; or never leave her unless she wanted him to. He looked forward to seeing her smile again.

Mors missed Zeus. When The Mistress of Bulls came, she didn't bring her stallion with her. Mors missed her ranch. He missed his brothers. One morning, the bipeds came and took him from his stall. They walked him out of their building and loaded him into the red vehicle he knew. Mors waited; The Mistress of Bulls didn't mount with him. The vehicle was taking him back to his previous farm. Mors didn't want to go there.

He turned out to be wrong.

The Mistress of Bulls followed the red vehicle with hers. They traveled back the road that brought him to this fort. Along the way, she kept her eyes on him. They reached her ranch and unloaded him onto its pasture. He didn't see Zeus anywhere. His brothers came in a group and received him. He lowered his head and ears and then followed their steps. This time, those six bulls that lived apart from the rest lifted their heads and locked eyes with him. Mors saw their strange behavior's source and felt their pain. He lifted his head and bellowed at them. The six bulls bellowed back and confirmed they understood him.

The bellows brought another response: a neigh.

Mors stopped. He turned his head and pricked up his ears. On the ranch's far side, under the generous oak tree that fed the squirrels and sheltered them in its trunk, the stallion stood; its dark silhouette barely moved. Mors bellowed again; Zeus didn't come to him.

Mors broke away from his brothers. He wanted to leap, but he knew he had to restrain his feet. He ambled toward the stallion and stopped along his way to eat. Zeus, too, moved from that tree's shadow, nibbled the grass, and then stopped in his tracks.

Mors waited.

The stallion didn't approach; instead, he walked to the reservoir, stood at its edge, and looked into its water.

Mors understood.

He reached the reservoir and stood next to Zeus.

34

The congressional committee approved her bill before summer. Pedro scheduled the debate for winter; no slot was left for autumn. He asked Nuria to choose three witnesses and submit their names for background checks before the legislature closed. Nuria agreed. She thanked him for his fairness and left for the day.

Outside, dusk receded from Plaza de Toreros. Taurine tourists filled the square. Citizens rushed for higher mountains or lower seashores. Some took this summer month as their paid vacation and escaped the grinding city's taurine fever; others used this month for doing their overtime, worked as seasonal employees in the taurine industry, and made their ends meet. She would use this month to prepare for her debate and catch up with Miguel's cases.

The tranquility on her parents' farm and its surrounding beauty allowed them to vacation at home; she didn't need to go away. If her parents agreed, she might shelter Miguel from the city's two peak weeks and their sweltering heat. She pulled away from the square and drove toward the bridge.

For testimony, her options were limited. She couldn't call Miguel and enrage some of the deputies; her association with him already served as a bone of contention for them. In theory, the deputies voted freely; in practice, interests restricted their votes. Citizens would watch this debate in the hall or on television. If she wanted these deputies to support her bill, she should choose her witnesses carefully. No one from outside could help her in this process.

Theresa, the dead *novillero*'s girlfriend was her number one choice. This teenage girl, although rough, controlled her emotions, spoke well, and behaved in public. After that fatal *novillada* took her boyfriend last year, she formed an anti-bullfighting group that stood apart from extreme movements. Citizens appreciated these youths' civility, dignity, and humility. Even the unfavorable deputies showed sympathy for this girl, felt sorry for her boyfriend, and appreciated her stance.

For her second witness, she would have to choose between Julio's widow and Xavier, the homeless matador. Julio's wife and their fatherless toddler would draw more sympathy from the deputies than Xavier could, although she was no longer sure about Julio's widow's stance; rumors ran she was seeing another elite matador. Xavier would recite how his bullring injury ruined his life, what changed his bullfighting stance, but most citizens saw his conversion as a logical switch after his injury. His anti-bullfighting speech lacked credibility. Besides, she didn't know how the deputies would react toward a homeless man on the witness stand before them, even if she cleared the legal obstacles for registering a transient man for testimony.

The most important testimony would come from Carlota.

Charo's reputation spread beyond the country. Despite her age, she continued her research on fighting bulls and published her articles in renowned medical journals at home and abroad. All regions that stopped bullfights had called for her expertise. Her poignant speech— short, sharp, and solid—had done the job.

No other veterinary surgeon commanded such respect. No other science professional's diction possessed such power. No other human heart contained such compassion for animals. The deputies that took their animals to her clinic saw her beyond a service provider. She was their beacon. Charo's hold on San Taurino's citizens knew no precedence. Even those who favored bullfights venerated her presence. This woman spoke little. When she did, her every word counted. Charo was the only vet who knew corrida's intricacies and technicalities, the ins and outs of *The Treaties*, and the legal framework that governed Spain's bullfights.

Nuria reached her parents' farm. A state vehicle blocked their gate. She got out of her car and went to the van's front. It belonged to the authorities that regulated the region's bullfights. At the driveway's far end, in front of their homestead, Father stood folding his arms over his chest and nodded at four officers. Mother leaned against the door and listened to them. Santos sat on his haunches and pointed his snout at the bullfighting officials.

Nuria backed her car, parked on the trail's side, and marched down the driveway. The officers finished with Father, shook his hand, and then went by her toward their vehicle. They didn't lift their eyes or nod at her. Among them, she recognized the senior officer from the video Miguel released four years ago, after Julio died in the city's ring from a bull's horns.

"What were they doing here?" Nuria asked her parents.

"They came for Yolanda," Mother said. "Victor killed someone."

"Victor!" Nuria said. "Where?"

"In the South."

"Why would they want his mother?"

"He killed a torero."

"Pardon?"

"Jorge," Mother said. "Do you want to explain?"

"Why me?" Father said. "I didn't do this alone."

"Rafaela came to buy Victor from you."

"And you decided with me to sell him."

"Didn't she tell you what she was buying him for?"

"No!" Father said. "Victor wasn't even the breed."

343

"How could she use him for a corrida?"

"How do I know?"

"She makes her rules!"

"If I knew, I would never sell him."

"Did they kill Victor?"

"Of course!"

"The poor bull."

Nuria didn't want to hear anymore. She walked past her parents, entered their house, and went straight up the stairs to her room. She placed her handbag on the bed, opened the hillside window, and peered at the far mountains. The sun sank behind their peaks, slashed the cloud fluffs, and painted them blood red. Their scarlet glow reached the valley, drenched the farms' pastures and exposed their cattle, and darkened the bushes that hid stalkers lying in ambush.

A lynx screeched. Dogs barked and bayed. Nuria moved back from the window, sat on her bed, and buried her face in her hands.

She couldn't hide from this glaring reality. She couldn't suppress her boiling emotions. She strutted to her office, pulled out her parents' accounts, and checked that unexplained amount. The year matched. Yet fifty thousand euros was too large a sum to pay for a bull.

She believed her father would have never sold Victor for bullfighting: he was against bulls fighting humans. Also, he must have thought someone like Rafaela would never send Victor to a bullfight, because she used only her pure bred *lidia* bulls. How could Victor end up serving for a corrida in the South? She stepped onto the balcony and found her father still standing outside. She went downstairs and stood facing him.

"Sorry, I lied to you," Father said. "I needed money to fix the

344

barn."

"You should have used Nacho's money," Nuria said.

"That's so easy to say now," Father said. "What if he stops his bullfighting nonsense today and returns to us? What if he finishes his veterinary degree and buys Charo's clinic? Who would give him money then? Do you want him to go to Willem and beg for money?"

"Nacho won't return."

"You want that, right?"

"Father," Nuria said. "What nonsense is this?"

"We don't want Ignaçio to die in a bullring."

"Then why did you send him away?"

"We sent him away?"

"Father, don't you see?" Nuria said. "Your selling Victor took Nacho from this farm. Victor wasn't just a bull, Father! Victor was Nacho's animal of company. How could you do this to Nacho? How could you sacrifice Nacho to fix your barn? How could you—"

Nuria broke into a sob and ran to her car.

Father blocked her path.

"Move away!" Nuria said. "Let me go."

"Nuria, listen."

"Nacho was happy studying and dancing. Nacho was happy playing with Victor. Nacho was happy tending his farm. If Victor stayed, Nacho would never leave. You ruined Nacho's life, Father! You ruined Santos's life too. Do you see the dog's state now? If Victor stayed, Santos would never reach this stage. Do you think your farm is doing better now?"

"Nuria, please."

"Your farm was doing fine, Father," Nuria said. "You didn't have to do this to us."

"You weren't happy working for Willem."

"Am I happier now?"

"What do you want me to do?"

"Don't try to bring back Nacho. Don't try to change him. Let him die in a bullring."

"Stop!"

"Get out of my way."

"We made a mistake," Father said. "Pardon us."

"Too late, Father," Nuria said. "Victor is now dead."

"Will you tell Nacho?"

"You tell him."

"I will."

"Don't ask him to return."

"He can't kill bulls."

"He will, if you tell him."

"I won't then."

Father claimed he didn't appreciate Rafaela's act. Two years ago, when she offered that sum to buy Victor, she didn't specify the purpose of her purchase. He knew of her family's farm in Galicia. Given Victor wasn't the *lidia* breed, he thought she was buying the bull from him for reproduction. He was surprised by the money Rafaela offered him for that bull. At the same time, given Victor's race and reproductive potential, the bull was worth that sum.

Victor stayed on Ignaçio's farm. Father swore he didn't see their special relation. If he did, he wouldn't sell that bull. Ignaçio's departure had left them bewildered and bereaved. Now he believed his daughter's words, saw the truth, and regretted his act.

Father pleaded her to believe him. He would never sell Victor if he knew the bull was going for a bullring. He swore his refrain didn't

346

come only from his principles. As a cattle farmer, if he raised a single bull for fighting, he could lose his subsidies from the Union. She knew this rule as much as he did. He would never take that risk on his farm and denigrate his ancestors' names. Rafaela never spoke much to anyone. Her deliberate omission of the truth violated his trust and jeopardized his farm. If they didn't slaughter Victor as a crazy bull, he would leave now and bring that animal back to where it belonged.

Nuria saw the sorrow in her father's eyes. She left her car and returned home.

She didn't recognize this bullring. She didn't recognize these galleries. She didn't recognize this taurine city she had brought her clients to. But she recognized this gored matador lying face down on the sand. She recognized this wounded bull standing at the ring's center and shedding tears on the dead matador. Among the exulting spectators, she recognized the senior aficionado leaning against the ring's barrier, complaining to the corrida's president, and asking for more blood.

Another matador entered the ring and pushed Ignaçio's corpse aside.

Two mounted lancers and three pickers surrounded bleeding Victor. The six toreros took their time and bled him more. They turned the bull in circles and drained his energy. Victor roared, fought, and collapsed. The coward matador towered over the brave bull and plunged the sword behind his head.

Victor still didn't die.

Two mules dragged the bull out of the ring and took him into the slaughterhouse. Three men, in butcher's garb, came with ropes and tied his muzzle. Victor threshed his legs, lifted his head, and groaned at them. Two of them held the bull's flailing head. The third brought a butcher's knife and slit his throat. Blood flowed from the slaughterhouse, flooded the ring's sand, and revived the dead matador.

Ignaçio sprang to his feet and shouted at—

***

Nuria sat up on her bed and clutched her throbbing head. The scared cat jumped off and hid under the bedspring. Lightning flashed through the shutters. Thunder cracked, roared, and rolled. The still air grew stiff. Nuria opened the window and leaned against its rail.

She saw a truth she had missed until now.

Corrida, in action, induces hallucination. As long as we haven't seen any bullfights, we may claim indifference, take positions neither for nor against. But when we do see one, the gore's shock revolts us; our moral pointer turns wild. We're forced to choose one side or the other, by our temperament. Corrida's theater incarnates the brute; its actors harbor Death.

The act's impacts go far beyond removing neutrality. Whoever attends a corrida is shaken throughout. The core transmutes. Corrida's issues—ethical, social, or cultural—center on this gore; on this bloodshed and death, not just of the bulls but also of the humans. These humans serve as the role model for youths, the unstable young seeking their stability in money, power, status, and glory. Bullfighting industry ignores these issues and goes for their financial kill.

She needed to show this truth to the deputies; she didn't know how.

The breeze cooled and brought the parched valley's odor. Storm clouds stacked above the mountain range and flattened the pile's bottom into an anvil. The cloud stack descended and kissed the

348

range's crest. Sparks flashed. A lightning fork pierced the ridge, sliced the peaks, and stabbed the valley. Thunder bolted and boomed. The storm head burst. A ragged torrent poured from its bottom and quenched the valley's thirst.

A vapor column rose from the valley, flared at the top, and exploded above the farms. The storm clouds descended further. Rain sheets swept the valley's pastures, drenched her parents' farm, and sprayed her at the window. Nuria leaned forward and stretched her neck. The harsh raindrops slapped her face, stung her eyes and earlobes, and washed her febrile heat.

The pressure left her temples. The fizz stopped in her head. The lump melted, freed her throat, and opened her chest.

She cried.

She cried for Victor. She cried for Ignaçio. She cried for her parents. She cried for their farm; she cried for Santos; she cried for herself. She cried through the downpour that built into a hailstorm, eased into a drizzle, and then stopped. She remained at the window and inhaled the warm vapor wafting from the soil. The scents revived memories she treasured but no longer wanted. She confronted each image, cried, and discarded it.

The long cry hurt her eyes. The tears rinsed her brain. She saw what she had missed.

Victor was dead. But before dying, the bull had done his work. His male calves, instead of going to the slaughterhouse, had gone to reproduce in this community's farms and far beyond. They each had fetched three times more than a steer for meat did. His female calves promised more than this year's batch from that other bull and artificial insemination. Victor the Second was continuing his father's promise on her parents' farm. If Victor lived, his tradition would stretch farther. But she understood her parent's drive behind selling him for that sum. They were down-to-earth cattle farmers. A bull was no more than a bull for them. They wanted to help Ignaçio but failed to see Victor's other roles. She could pardon them.

The path to Nacho's return was now closed.

Should she call and tell him?

No. There was no point. She wasn't sure he would feel the same way toward Victor. To make a living by killing bulls, he certainly didn't feel for them. From his animal of company, the bull had become his enemy. She couldn't blame her parents alone for his metamorphosis. Spain's taurine culture indoctrinated its youths and took their lives early. If this was Nacho's destiny, let it be; she couldn't change it. She didn't want to change it.

She took her phone and erased Ignaçio's number. She erased his photos and Victor's. She erased the videos of their games. Her eyes watered, her vision blurred. She wiped her tears and purged the rest from her phone. The purging lightened her chest and eased her breathing. She opened her drawers and shredded Ignaçio's drawings, poems, and letters. She carried the torn pieces to the courtyard and burned them in the barbecue.

Her spirit lifted. Her soul liberated. She was free to do what counted for her the most.

Below corrida's unethical skin, a pernicious disease hid in bullfights driving an economy: its vulnerability. The downturn had revealed this frailty. Taurine tourists' blood thirst didn't belong to basic necessities; it belonged to luxury. In penury, they did without bullfights. But the citizens who lived from bullfights couldn't do without their basic needs.

An economy that banks on tourism stands on collapsible sand; its economic success is a mirage. A region that depends on bullfights for its living doesn't live long. Those regions that learned their lessons from the recession had reorganized themselves, reinvented other trades, and reinforced their economy. She could site at least six such regions to support her bill. But for this region, she would have to back her claim by facts and arguments. The deputies who disagreed with bullfight's principle voted to retain its practice for economic reasons.

The people she required didn't work during summer. Afterward, the four working months before the debate wouldn't suffice to do the research and build her arguments. She needed to change her perspective and clear her mind. She took a long cold shower and then packed her essential needs into a suitcase. She wrote an email to Pedro confirming her three witnesses. She sent a message to Miguel informing him what she was going to do. She left a note for her parents, loaded the suitcase into her car, and then drove away from their farm.

She had to leave San Taurino for what she wanted to do.

35

Before his second spring at the taurine academy, Ignaçio finished his required twenty-five amateur bullfights. In summer, he received his accreditation from San Taurino; in autumn, his confirmation from Madrid. For both ceremonies, Esteban served as his godfather.

In the same week Ignaçio entered the official register of matadors, he received a call from Willem. The bullfighting magnate offered him a subsidized mortgage if he joined the man's new agency for matadors. Ignaçio consulted Angel. His mentor recommended it. Given this agency's growing clout in Spain and abroad, joining them would jumpstart his career.

Ignaçio joined Willem's agency, accepted the mortgage, and acquired a penthouse on the square of Iglesia Sacrata di Ser Vivo. The flat overlooked his mentor's home across the paved square. From the shop in the arena's loggia, he bought nineteenth-century bullfighting gears, a leather-bound collectors' copy of *The Treaties* by de Cossio, and a life-size framed portrait of Ortega, all on credit from the same bank that held his mortgage, and decorated his panoramic den, which opened onto the arena on one side and onto the church on the other.

By then, he had signed for two dozen bullfights in Spain, including a prestigious corrida in the South. He struggled to cope with the agency's growing demand.

His troubles didn't arise only from his bullfighting schedule.

He suffered from persistent tremor, recurrent headaches, vertigo, and visual disturbances. At first, he discarded them as transient symptoms of stress. Then they worsened after each bullfight. His appetite waned, his sleep ebbed. His temper grew an irascible edge.

He lived nightmares and feared the bed. He stayed awake at night and fell asleep during the day.

His mentor sent him to a doctor of sports medicine. The doctor diagnosed him with juvenile hypertension.

Ignaçio started taking medicine for blood pressure. The pills lowered his pressure for a few days and then raised it higher. The doctor increased the medicine's dose. Ignaçio excelled at bullfights, but outside arenas, he walked like a ghost. He lost his grace. He lost his flair for dance. His style changed and leaned toward Esteban's. That suited Willem better.

Ignaçio's sleep degraded further. His volatile mood swung between highs and lows. He was diagnosed with depression.

The anti-depressants aggravated his hypertension. His blood-pressure medicine's dose rose with his pressure's rise. When he sank deeper into depression, stronger anti-depressants pulled him out and raised his blood pressure higher. He carried around his pills.

At that revered corrida in the South, Ignaçio received the round of honor and exited on four shoulders by the royal door. The following month, further down south, he fought six bulls in a single afternoon and won. Willem attended this historic feat and congratulated him. That evening, Ignaçio gave an exclusive interview on Willem's television. The bullfighting channel diffused both shows throughout the taurine world. Willem's agency sold him for dozens of bullfights across Latin America. He would go there after Europe's season ended.

Awards, trophies, souvenirs blocked his den's panorama and choked its air.

His blood pressure kept rising.

Part III

36

The lawsuit over the two women's death broke the trio's alliance.

Rafaela left the city council. Pedro separated from the mayor. Judge Emilio, angered by Mayor José's comment about his niece's molestation, didn't dismiss the case against the city. The lawsuit dragged through the autumn and exhausted the lawyers on both sides. In the end, they settled out of court and emptied the city's treasury.

None of this surprised Angel. What seized him unwary in the winter and held him gaping for months afterward was the bullfighting industry's frailty: how vulnerable this multibillion-euro business was to nature's unforeseeable forces.

Late autumn was closing its final bullfights through the city's tumbling finance, when it saw the pandemic arrive from abroad and claim six lives within a week. The city responded by locking herself. The deceived tourists deserted the country. The following week, the state closed its frontiers. Desperate citizens scrambled to return home before Christmas. Within a week, the city's life came to a standstill.

And that was only the beginning.

The pandemic swept the city. Its waves rose and fell. Its tides receded and returned. Its grip loosened and tightened. Its ambush killed some, crippled many, and confined everyone. The state, the region, and the municipality scrounged money to pay their citizens. San Taurino pleaded for Europe's aid. The Union refused to help a taurine city that defied its norms.

Once more, Willem stepped forward and helped the city.

During the lockdowns, whereas most employers sent their employees on government aid, which paid only a part of their wages, Willem paid full salary to his people. His philanthropy spread beyond his business's core. The arena's employees didn't work for him; they received his private aid. The bullfighting association got no aid from anyone; Willem paid its bills and kept it alive. Rafaela refused Willem's funds for her bull ranches, but she accepted his aid for her association.

Willem's protection of the bullfighting industry earned him more power and influence in taurine circles. He played vital role in their crucial decisions. The bull ranches that accepted his aid bred and raised his favorite breeds. He paid the matadors and forced his combat rules. Some veterans didn't trust his benevolence. They suspected he would swallow their tradition into his empire and earn more money.

Angel knew Willem's goal. The bullfighting magnate didn't just want money; he also wanted power. He was casting the pandemic's net to earn monopoly. And he was using its waves to spread his net wider. He wanted to own bull ranches. He wanted to buy cattle farms and convert them into bull ranches. He wanted to buy taurine clubs; own matadors and their agents; acquire more bullfighting bars, restaurants, nightclubs. He wanted to bundle them as a business unit and sell its shares. The pandemic's lever had switched him to a higher gear. But Willem didn't succeed. The cattle farmers refused his pricey offers. Paloma and Juan ignored his exorbitant bid and held onto their flamenco bar. They placed dignity above money.

During a brief respite, the city opened its arena and held a charity bullfight. In one single afternoon, Esteban killed twelve bulls in two hours, made a world record, and donated his fees to the city. The arena's attendance was poor. But this exceptional corrida, broadcasted only by Willem's channel, earned him tons of money and popularity around the globe.

Willem donated the entire amount to the city. He offered aid to activists resisting corrida's return; their dire needs forced them to accept his money. This exceptional corrida won Willem his opposition. Only Miguel refused his financial help and held out through the penury.

The pandemic's waves came and left. The starving region took risk and lifted restrictions. The government gave stimulus funds and restricted their use from bullfighting. The exclusion surged lobbying and lawsuits until the court declared it illegal and removed it. Pro- and anti-bullfighting groups clashed over the court's decision. Another lockdown separated them.

Throughout the pandemic, Willem's betting business earned him millions from the critical issues: the pandemic's variants and the lockdowns' durations; the city reopening its arena, and the nation its frontiers; the bullfighters' aid from the state, and the ranchers' from Europe; the court's decision on the stimulus checks' use for bullfights; the fate of Nuria's bill and the date for its debate...

He didn't pocket this profit; he donated it to the city. For the stimulus checks' use, when the court ruled in favor of bullfighting, he matched the amount and restricted his checks' use to bullfights. The veterans that suspected him earlier now saw him as their guardian angel. They lauded his defense, invited him to taurine circles, and nominated him for presidency.

These aficionados calmed when Willem's role in shipping the ambassador's son out of Spain started revealing. This kid, on his romp to a neighboring country during a lockdown, got picked up inebriated by their authorities. They discovered Judge Emilio's warrant and held him in detention. A legal battle ensued for the boy's extradition to Spain.

The scandal fired the ambassador from his post. He lost his immunity and couldn't leave the embassy. His government couldn't kick him out. They offered him a cell-size room in the attic, where he began his effective sentence. Lack of sufficient evidence kept Judge Emilio's net away from Willem. He ignored the fallen ambassador and his son. He grappled with the recurring variants of the pandemic and strived to save bullfighting from its tightening grip.

Then summer swelled the pandemic's next wave and drowned bullfight's fate.

37

The pandemic closed the legislature and opened urgent work for deputies. They toiled from home, rushed for new laws, and amended the old ones to cope with the crisis. The debate for her bill was postponed until next year. Pedro compensated her for the delay by allowing her a fourth witness. Nuria thanked him and decided to include both Julio's widow and Xavier.

The delay came with further benefits. Nuria found the time she needed to complete her economic analyses and build her arguments. She received no support from any experts, from academia or from think-tanks, but she received plenty from her colleagues. They buttressed her bill. Their help convinced her that the region would ban bullfighting.

She had other reasons for her conviction. The double death and the molestation from the previous spring's bull-run broke the city's triangle of power. Judge Emilio's wife joined the anti-bullfighting deputies. Soledad's shift rifted the pro-bullfighting camp and opened a gap large enough for Nuria to enter and change their game plan. What seemed remote earlier and impossible before the pandemic now looked close and possible.

The nine-month lockdown changed corrida's international landscape. Her legal pursuit failed in Asia, Europe, Middle East, North America, and the Pacific Rim. But Spain's former colonies in South and Central Americas took bold steps during the pandemic and aligned with her moves. Seventeen federal judges convened and suspended corrida in the country with the largest bullring. A month later, their legislators changed the laws and abolished bullfighting. After the lockdown, their pro-bullfighters protested. The government's three branches joined hands and maintained the abolition. Roads opened, but arenas stayed closed.

The three lockdowns broke some couples and built others.

During the first two, Nuria hosted Miguel on her parents' farm. Before the third, she moved into his apartment in the city and shifted her business address. The government lifted restrictions for the yearend feasts, and Miguel returned to her family for Christmas Eve. The sparkling winter brought the fourth lockdown and separated Julio's widow from her matador lover. She called Nuria and confirmed her decision to support the bill. Miguel declared Xavier as his tenant. The legislature accepted the homeless matador as her fourth witness.

The pandemic squeezed the necessities and split citizens. A small group saw this squeeze resulting from globalization that exported jobs and imported epidemics. They wanted Spain's commercial independence. They wanted production to return home. They wanted to remove restrictions that paralyzed Spain's economy and crippled its people's lives. They identified what was still Spanish and venerated those. One legacy they valued was bullfighting. They wanted to reopen Spain's arenas and restart bullfights.

The pandemic's recess opened San Taurino's arena. The journalist covering Esteban's charity bullfight claimed the successive lockdowns had moved Spain's youths toward a pro-bullfighting stance; their larger proportion among the viewers confirmed this shift. His claim ran against the trend. Nuria checked with the ministry, the statistical institute, and the social observatory. In absolute terms, all corridas still attracted poor attendance. Those attending at arenas were predominantly young; the pandemic forced the older to watch on television. She called the journalist and asked him to back his claim. He sent her a study done by a business consultancy. Nuria forwarded the report to Ishmael and asked him to check its facts.

Ishmael took his investigation far beyond what Nuria asked.

A clique of elite aficionados had paid this consulting firm to conduct this study, skew its findings, and propagate those to news media abroad. They wanted youths from other countries to attend Spain's bullfights. Ishmael dug out their official records and proved this fact.

Inducing youths to watch bullfights reopened Nuria's old scar. She took the firm's records to Soledad. Soledad passed those to her husband. They bled Judge Emilio's wound from his niece's violation. He summoned the journalist and the consulting firm. They testified against the elite aficionados. The court sanctioned the consultancy, fined the aficionados, and forced the journalist to retract his claim.

The same court then ruled in favor of using the stimulus checks for bullfights.

Europe responded by slashing aid.

The European parliament voted to stop paying farms that raised fighting bulls. The Euro deputies considered these bulls, raised on man-made pastures, as farm animals. By the council directives, these farmers must take all measures to ensure that these animals didn't suffer any unnecessary pain or injury. They saw bullfights violating Europe's common policy and these farmers defying their council's directives.

The Euro deputies' voice put bull ranchers in a dilemma.

On the one hand, if they claimed their bulls as savage, as *The Treaties* required them for fighting, they couldn't classify them as farm animals and ask for the Union's emergency aid. On the other hand, if they claimed their bulls as farm animals, Spain's bullfighting

361

laws and Europe's animal welfare rules wouldn't allow them to fight. Stuck in this mire, the ranchers weighed both sides and let Europe go. The pandemic made another practice more profitable. They slaughtered their bulls, booked them as loss, and asked the state to compensate them.

The state saw the truth and refused to pay.

These bulls' slaughter didn't all come from the pandemic stopping corridas. A large part came from *tienta*, the unique selection method used for this breed. Those animals that didn't meet its stringent criteria went to the abattoir. The pandemic didn't stop tienta. The ranchers counted these tientas' rejects with their unused bulls and sent their bills to the state.

Once more, Willem came forward and helped these ranchers.

He also donated large sums to the city and pushed them to resume corrida. Under his pressure, Mayor José agreed to reopen bullfights in March and doubled the amount pledged for April's feria. The cattle farms found themselves deprived of the municipality's aid.

San Taurino prepared its March corrida by removing restrictions. The shops, bars, hotels, and restaurants raised their shutters. The city hall reopened its door. The deputies returned to the legislature and held face-to-face meetings. The bullfighting association resumed its roles. The traffic revived the streets. The airport stayed closed. The seaport and the station opened. Ships and trains arrived and left. The stubborn snow refused to thaw, but fresh lives crawled underneath and lifted their heads. The sun warmed up and delivered its promise.

One morning, a caravan of trucks crossed the bridge over the Sangre de Toros River and entered San Taurino. They skirted the city's terrace, reached Plaza de Toreros, and stopped beside the square. Nuria was parking at her spot when the first truck opened its backdoor and released its cattle onto the square. Uproar started.

The other trucks repeated the procedure and raised the din. The cattle's cries filled the air. Honking cars jammed Avenida de Corrida and stalled its traffic. The passing citizens stopped in their tracks, watched, howled, and laughed. The organized cacophony drew out disoriented functionaries. They stood on their porticos and gaped at the growing chaos. The cattle farmers left their vehicles, marched to the square's fountain, and built a shoulder-to-shoulder rank.

Jorge stood at this rank's center. Nuria left her car and ran toward him.

"Father," she said. "What's this?"

"Do you care?"

"Of course!"

"You don't," Father said. "You care only about your bill."

"Did you organize this?"

"Someone had to."

"Why?"

"Our cattle can't starve."

"They don't."

"We pay tax to this city."

"The city knows."

"The mayor doesn't."

"We're working on your subsidies."

"You're working on your bill."

"Father," Nuria said. "Please!"

"Why did you let the mayor give all that money to bull ranches?"

"That doesn't depend on me."

"You make laws."

"Not those."

"See?"

"What?"

"Only *your* law matters to you."

"Father," Nuria said. "Laws take time."

"What do we feed our animals in the meantime?"

"The region is giving you money. The state is giving you money. The European Union is giving—"

"Stop!" Father said. "Someone will tell them what Rafaela did with Victor."

"You didn't sell him for corrida."

"But she used him."

"Do you have any control over her acts? Do you have any control over what anyone does with your cattle after you sell them?"

"Rafaela isn't anyone."

"So?"

"Someone will leak the news."

"Father," Nuria said. "We had this discussion before. Victor wasn't the *lidia* breed. You sold him to Rafaela for reproduction. She used him for corrida. You aren't responsible for her actions. If any problem comes from Europe or anywhere, we can deal with it."

"Who will defend me?"

"I will."

"You deserted our farm."

"Father," Nuria said. "Is that it?"

"You no longer come home."

"I'm busy!"

"With your bill."

"Father, please go back with your cattle."

"They didn't come here to go back."

364

"What do you want them to do?"

"Meet the mayor."

"The mayor won't come out."

"You bet he'll," Father said. "Look who's coming toward us."

"Father!"

"Leave us alone. Go back to your legislature."

"I stay with you."

"Your image will kill your bill."

Father broke from the rank, went around her, and shook Mayor José's hand.

38

The uproar came from the arena. It wasn't applause for a corrida. Ignaçio left his lunch on the table, hurried across his living room, and peered out from his sixteenth floor balcony.

The arena's arches blocked his view; its acoustics confirmed the clamor's origin. The demonstrators were no longer in the court; both sides were now inside the bullring. March's returning sun flashed arcs across his eyes and dug black holes in his vision. His face tingled. His ears hissed, his neck prickled. The church bells tolled on his flat's other side and wrung his chest. The height reeled his head and churned his stomach. He left the balcony, staggered back into the den, and stood before the television.

He didn't need to turn on the set; he knew what he would see.

After the fifteen-month wait, despite the persistent pandemic, the desperate region had decided to lift restrictions, hold the spring's first bullfight, and revive the economy. Pro- and anti-bullfighting groups—like him, tired of talking to their walls—had grabbed this chance to emerge, mix, and clash over this corrida. What now came from the arena sounded like a fight, but it didn't involve any bulls; it involved only humans. They fought harder than bulls.

His blood-pressure medicine made him drowsy. His eyes twitched, their lids drooped. He wouldn't sleep or sit like the ill; he would swim in the sea or run in the mountains. His lunch lost its appeal. He took the unfinished plate to the kitchen, brewed strong coffee, brought the cup to the living room, and turned on the television. The remote control trembled in his hand. His shaking fingers floundered on the keypad and found the bullfighting channel.

At the arena, only three of the thirty-six rows were filled. The travel restrictions revealed the reality of bullfights' attendance. The pandemic confined some native aficionados at home, but for most Spaniards, the arena's seats lay beyond their finance's reach; they could afford to see bullfights only on television. This afternoon, the few at the arena didn't seem thrilled with what they were getting for their deep-discounted tickets.

The protestors, chained by bicycle locks, formed a semi-circle on the ring's sand. Theresa, the dead *novillero*'s girlfriend, sat at one end; Xavier, the homeless matador, at the other. The arena's employees sprayed them with a hose. Thwarted aficionados punched and kicked them. The demonstrators didn't budge an inch or turn violent.

Ignaçio searched for Miguel and Nuria among these protesters; he didn't find them. They lived together now. Miguel's calls for the international boycott and the Union's exclusion of Spain wouldn't help Nuria's bill before the deputies. Last month, after Jorge released cattle on Plaza de Toreros, he didn't get in trouble; he got the aid he wanted. His act discredited Nuria and jeopardized her stance. Her bill wouldn't go far; she might as well abandon it.

She was stubborn not to see her bill as unfair. Like all animals bred for consumption, the *lidia* bulls were raised to die. While other animals lived in cramped places, like inmates on a death row, these bulls roamed free in vast open spaces and fed on fresh grass and herbs. They received more care than farm animals did and died a glorious death fighting humans. They could give twenty minutes' fight for a pain they didn't even feel from their adrenaline's peak.

Animals' destiny was to serve humans. Humans had ensured this. Animals existed to feed humans, give them company, entertain them, serve as their hunting targets. Miguel and Nuria could do whatever

367

they wanted; animals' plight wouldn't change. In one way or another, they would always end up as human feed. That was their fate. They might as well donate their lives putting up brave fights against humans. That was admirable and noble.

His intercom buzzed. Ignaçio tripped on the floor mat, regained his balance, and opened the building's door. The postman informed he was coming up to deliver a registered letter.

The letter came from his bank. It stated the facts cold and clear.

His mortgage was overdue by seven months. The pandemic's legal restrictions were now removed. The bank would start the procedure for his eviction unless he paid the outstanding capital and accrued interest by this month's end.

Ignaçio left the letter on the table and logged into his bank account.

The situation didn't shine for his car and consumer loans. The money left in his combined accounts wouldn't pay a tenth of those amounts.

His head fizzed, his face flushed. Veins throbbed on his temples; sweat dripped from his armpits. This bank's letter wasn't helping his blood pressure.

Applause surged from the arena, matched the noise on the television, and broke his line of thoughts. Guards dragged the chained protestors from the soaked ring toward the exit. Ignaçio muted the set and returned to his bank statements.

Since his agent vanished with his payments during the pandemic, not a single euro had come into his account. His professional insurance covered bullfighting injuries; bullrings' closure from fire, demonstration, and strike; disease, disability, and death; but not his agent's theft or nature's forces like this pandemic. The state didn't pay him. To qualify for its aid, he should have worked as a matador for a year, and the pandemic's breakout had let him work for only four months after his diploma. Being Spain's number three matador didn't help.

He didn't want to return to Willem. The bullfighting magnate had declined responsibility for his thieving agent and offered to help him by purchasing his farm at an elevated price. He didn't have money to hire a lawyer and pursue Willem's empire for his agent's delinquency. Despite this nonpayment, he couldn't break his five-year exclusive contract with Willem's agency without the court's intervention. His net worth didn't qualify him for the state's free legal counsel. Given how Nuria eyed him when their paths crossed, he wouldn't approach her or seek her help. He would wait, earn money, and pay a lawyer to straighten these matters.

Selling his farm lay far below dignity. He had purchased his penthouse flat, his sports car, and his nineteenth-century bullfighting paraphernalia on impulse. The pandemic had revealed his error and educated him for its repair. If necessary, he would dump this luxury on his bank and return to live in the trailer on his farm.

No, he couldn't go back to his trailer. The pandemic had given Jaime and Uncle Manu the time to convert his trailer into a dairy workshop for Paula, Ines, and Aunt Belen. They worked there now. As soon as the market reopened, they would sell their products. He couldn't claim his trailer and kick them out.

He couldn't go back to Nuria's parents. He couldn't ask them to return the money he gave them before leaving; they deserved that sum for raising him. He couldn't forsake his dignity, accept Willem's private aid for matadors, and swallow the man's preferred combat style.

These loans had squashed his bullfighting experience. He no longer performed corrida for arts; he slaughtered bulls in public to pay his debts. Money now told him how to do his work; he had abandoned choreography for butchery. He would find other ways to survive this crisis, reimburse his loans, and return to his fighting style. He wouldn't bend to Willem's rules.

He could; he had reasons to hope.

Bullfighting was reopening at home and abroad. Despite his setback, he still stood among Europe's top five matadors. Once his career resumed, he could borrow from banks using his new contracts; they would give him loans against future income. He could survive until then; these contracts shouldn't take long. After a fifteen-month slumber, the industry was bristling to resume business. Willem had pushed the city to restart corrida; he was now pulling strings to remove travel restrictions. This man always succeeded in his ardor. Bullfights would soon return at full speed and give matadors enough work.

The pandemic had uncovered the state's priority. The government that raised corrida to a national monument five years ago barely paid the toreros out of work during the pandemic. The government that wanted bullfighting to continue in Spain diverted emergency aid to the institutions it considered more vital. The government that claimed corrida as Spain's emblem excluded it from stimulus payments and reserved those for shops, restaurants, and bars.

A tradition that fails you in emergency doesn't furnish a reliable heritage.

His cell phone rang in the bedroom. Ignaçio left his bank statements, ran to his phone, and answered the call. He stood at the window and gazed at Iglesia Sacrata di Ser Vivo. Across the church's

370

square, Angel's shutters waited closed; his mentor wasn't calling from home.

"We need you," Angel said. "Are you in town?"

"Yes."

"Can you do a corrida?"

"Where?"

"In San Taurino."

"When?"

"Now."

"Pardon?"

"I'm serious."

Angel explained the situation. The bull had gored this afternoon's first matador. The other two matadors, thwarted by the arena's chaos, had abandoned the corrida. The viewers, furious with the event's turn, demanded their money.

"Will you finish this corrida?" Angel asked.

"For the six bulls?"

"You can."

"I'll call my toreros."

"Use the ones here."

Ignaçio reached the bustling arena. Pro- and anti-bullfighting groups crammed its court and hurled insults. They were too busy to notice him in his matador's suit. He navigated through the human maze, ignored the jostles and jabs, avoided the toreros' entrance, and reached the employees' gate. He didn't escape the eyes he wanted to avoid.

The raiders, kicked out of the arena, knew the replacement toreros would take this entry; they were waiting for him. Theresa, the

371

dead *novillero*'s girlfriend—her face covered in sand, her hair tangled in tendrils, her clothes soaked and dripping—separated from the ousted group and glared at him. She was shaking, but not from cold. She started going toward him. Xavier, the homeless matador, caught her by the hand and restrained her.

"You fool!" Theresa bristled at Ignaçio. "Where are you going?"

"To work."

"What work?"

"Matador's."

"You know what *matar* means?"

"I do."

"Good," Theresa said. "You're a killer. Your title has turned you into a murderer. You earn your living by killing innocent bulls. If I were you, I would rather hang myself than feed my mouth by your work. Shame on you!"

"That's enough."

"Now go and kill that suffering bull."

The bailiff received him at the entrance and escorted him into the trampled bullring. Fresh sand covered the wet patches underneath. Ignaçio saw the spot where the injury occurred. The gored matador's blood mixed with water and oozed through the repacked sand. The capes and the *banderilla*s lay around the spot. The matador's team had left their gears in the ring.

Willem wasn't in the arena. Angel stood under the president's box, his back against the ring's barrier, and calmed the agitated spectators. Ignaçio stopped. His mentor saw him, raised his arm, and waved for assurance. Ignaçio nodded. A sandman removed the capes and picks.

The bleeding bull sat against the barrier and heaved. Ignaçio saw the animal's agony in its eyes: it was choking with blood and laboring to breathe. The toreros, their arms folded, stood around the bull and waited for instruction. No fight was left in this animal. Adrenaline wasn't lessening its suffering. Tear trickled down the bull's muzzle and dripped onto the blood stain growing in the sand. One horse whined. Ignaçio asked both mounted *picador*s to leave.

He saw the matador's error. To sever the bull's aorta and evoke its immediate death, the curved sword's blade should enter the space between the fourth and sixth ribs—and at a right angle. The sword had missed this spot and delivered an oblique thrust. The blade had pierced the bull's lung, severed its trachea, and slashed its esophagus. Blood had filled the thorax. The suffocated bull was vomiting it from its mouth and nose. Such a respiratory failure also meant the blade had sheared the phrenic nerve. The bull's diaphragm was barely moving.

This wasn't a dignified way for this majestic animal to go. Ignaçio lifted his eyes, scanned the galleries, and soaked the surroundings. He could do little with this bull. He could only end its suffering, let it die, and spare it further indignity. He asked the *banderillero*s to leave.

Ignaçio took out his handkerchief and wiped the bull's tears. Spectators cooed and hooted. He ignored their insults, took the straight sword from the matador's assistant, and returned to the bull. His hand quaked, his fingers trembled. His eyelids fluttered. The bull multiplied. He waited until his hand steadied and his vision settled. He planted his feet and squared his hips. He held his breath and aimed the sword's blade between the bull's first and second cervical vertebrae. Shuffles stopped in the viewing galleries. Talks ceased.

The bull raised its head and opened its eyes wide. In their depth,

Ignaçio saw no fear. The animal didn't look at the sword. Its glistening eyes gazed at his, didn't bat their lids, and held an impenetrable calm and an imperturbable peace. This bull had trusted its end in his hands.

Ignaçio stepped forward, thrust the sword, and missed the vital spot.

The blade didn't sever the bull's spinal cord; it paralyzed the animal's neck. The bull hung its head, rested its chin on the sand, and pleaded him with its eyes. Ignaçio ran to the matador's assistant, returned with the *puntilla*, and plunged the knife behind the bull's head, between the skull's base and the first cervical vertebra. This time, he succeeded. The knife's blade hit the bull's medulla oblongata and severed the spinal cord from the brain.

Death didn't come immediately to this bull. Its breathing and heartbeat slowed. Ignaçio kneeled before the animal and placed his palm on its forehead. The bull's eyes opened wider, softened with gratitude, and then closed slowly. The animal still took fourteen minutes to die. Ignaçio ignored the viewers' jeers and stayed by the dead bull until the mules came.

He refused to fight the remaining five bulls. He told Angel not to pay him and walked out of the bullring. His mentor followed him, saw his condition, and didn't insist. They stopped, shook hands, and separated. Ignaçio climbed the staircase between the hooting galleries and left the arena by the employees' exit. The serene bull's departure remained in his head.

The sharp slap blinded him and stung his face. Theresa aimed for his other cheek. Xavier leaped, caught her hand, and pulled her back. Theresa lifted her fist and bared her teeth. Miguel rushed in and stood

374

between them.

"You coward," Theresa growled at Ignacio. "How you killed that bull!"

"I'm sorry," Ignacio said. "I couldn't do better."

"You're cruel."

"I tried my best."

"Your best is worse than clumsy," Theresa said. "Now get out of here before I break your neck and backbone, crush your fingers, and pluck your eyes."

Miguel pulled him away from her and led him through the bubbling crowd. Ignacio saw Nuria standing at the Roman statue's pedestal. Her cold stare told him what she was thinking of him. He lifted his eyes at the court's television and saw the two mules dragging the dead bull out of the ring. The sandmen brought their buckets and wheelbarrows. They replaced the sand and repacked it where the bull died. Ignacio thanked Miguel for his guard and returned straight to his apartment. He didn't dare turn on the television or go to the ring-side balcony.

He stood in his living room and took a stock of his place. His diploma and title, his awards and honors and trophies, his leather-bound set of *The Treaties*, his bullfighting gears, and his killing instruments—they kicked his ribs, tore his face, and gored his eyes. Ortega reached out from his portrait and slapped his cheeks. He had lost his poise and fallen far below his mark. He was killing bulls in disgrace. His performance this afternoon had revealed this truth.

His face stung. He went to the bathroom, peered into the mirror, and saw Theresa's finger marks on his cheek. Her words rang in his ears, echoed in his head, and burned his heart. He touched the dark pouches under his tired eyes and reckoned the glare Nuria flashed at him.

He closed his eyes and stood still. He saw where his suffering was coming from.

The truth was he loved these bulls. While fighting, he didn't stop loving them; he loved them more. He loved their beauty. He loved their spirit. He loved their poise, strength, force, and grace. He loved their dignified way out of life. He suffered their pain through the fights. He never inflicted more pain than necessary. He always strived for their quick, sharp death. Then he stayed in the ring and accompanied them till their end.

The truth was he hated killing these bulls.

At the same time, he loved the magnificence of their death. He loved their civility, their dignity, and their serenity when they went. The tragedy was as much for the bulls as for him. He admired their fight. He missed them after they died. He remembered them after they left.

He wished, someday, he too could leave life like them.

39

San Taurino planned its April feria. After the disaster two years ago, Rafaela didn't furnish her bulls for the fair's opening ceremony. Mayor José responded by doubling the number of bulls and purchasing them from a hundred-and-seventy-year-old bull ranch staggering from the pandemic's blow. The episodes had driven this family's ranch to the brink of bankruptcy. The ranchers rejoiced at the fortune of supplying their bulls for this city's symbolic feria.

Overseas travel restrictions remained, but, within Europe, the Union members reopened their borders. Willem's non-European aficionados flew into Europe and then traveled to San Taurino by the open routes. After a sixteen-month doze, the city's heart throbbed again to its taurine tourists' beats. The businesses rushed to recover their lost revenues.

On the feria's opening day, twelve bulls left the cramped port and ran up Avenida de Corrida toward the arena. A gang of insurgents intercepted their course. The thwarted bulls quit their designated route, entered Plaza de Toreros, and charged through the demonstrating groups. The forces of order couldn't stop these bulls, savage under their panic's spell.

Pandemonium broke out in the square.

Miguel stooped to help a fallen woman. Three men—wearing face masks, goggles, and helmets—caught him by the neck and arms, lifted him off, and carried him away. Nuria ran after them. Two adolescent boys and an adult woman blocked her path and then gave her the Roman salute. Nuria threw a punch at the woman. She deflected her blow, caught her by the wrist, and tugged her forward. Nuria fell. Her forehead hit the pavement.

They kicked her on the back and face. They pulled her hair, tore her clothes, and wrung her neck. They rolled her on the paving stones, dragged her to the fountain, and sank her head in the basin's water. Nuria threshed, thrashed, and flailed. She couldn't free herself.

All of a sudden, they let her go. Nuria sprang from the basin and fell on her back.

Rafaela leaped, turned in the air, and kicked both boys on the temple. They shrieked and recoiled. The adult woman cursed Rafaela and lunged for her neck. Rafaela caught her wrist, flung her over the shoulder, and crashed her on the pavement. The two boys lifted the fallen woman, carried her to their car, and drove away from the square.

Rafaela took off her jacket and covered Nuria.

The police never caught Miguel's attackers. They found Nuria's ravishers in a neighboring village: they belonged to the ranch the twelve bulls came from. Across Spain, four million citizens demonstrated and asked for their maximum punishment. The authorities listened.

The delinquent woman was a public-school teacher. The academy removed her from their official register. For aggravated assault and public disorder, the court condemned her to five years in prison and ordered her to pay one hundred and seventy-eight thousand euros in fine. Her both brothers received an eighteen-month sentence in a juvenile detention center.

Their names entered the troublemakers' database. Judge Emilio also prohibited them from entering the city during all taurine events.

Pedro took their sentences further.

He pulled his strings in taurine circles, removed the ranch from

378

the national roster, and cancelled their financial aid. Several taurine cities aligned with him and refused their bulls. Law couldn't close their ranch, but the financial drain set these ranchers up for ruin.

Meanwhile, Mayor José ignored these noises and continued his spring festival.

40

The plenary session opened at the regional assembly's debate hall. Pedro introduced Nuria's bill and passed the speaker to her. The testimonies from Theresa, Xavier, and Julio's widow didn't surprise the deputies. They listened with one ear and used the other to exchange with their colleagues. When Carlota took the stand, they set aside their distractions and focused their both ears on her.

"My fellow citizens," Carlota said. "This legislature has called me to testify on facts you already know. I shall not drain you with a long testimony. I shall refresh your memory on a few points and then trust you for the rest. If my words weigh on you, do stop me."

Carlota stood tall and continued:

"A corrida, as you've seen, lasts twenty minutes and comes in three stages, each called a *tercio*. The first of these is the tercio of lance.

"This lance's six-centimeter blade bears a two-and-a-half-centimeter pyramid tip, to dig into the flesh, and a cylindrical base, to prevent digging beyond eight and a half centimeters. The *picador*, the lancer on horseback, thrusts the blade into the bull's neck at this first tercio's start. The bull's head then stays low throughout the corrida. The animal appears to charge all the time, but it can't target the toreros' thoracic and abdominal viscera.

"These facts you already know. What you may not know or may not see during the corrida is the following.

"The mounted picador maneuvers this lance. Once the blade pierces the bull's neck, the picador twists and turns the lance's shaft. The blade penetrates deeper into the flesh than bullfight's rules permit, into the zone containing muscles, tendons, and ligaments for the neck's mobility. The blade can reach deeper than thirty centimeters; damage organs, vessels, and nerves for the animal's cardiac and respiratory functions; crack its cervical and thoracic vertebrae; break its ribs and fracture its shoulder blades.

"The bull loses as much as twelve liters of blood.

"During the second tercio, six *banderilla*s are thrust into the bull's flesh, close to the lance wound. Each banderilla, a collapsible baton covered by bright-colored frills, measures seventy centimeters and carries a double-harpooned steel end six centimeters long.

"After their batons collapse, these banderillas hang from the bull's flank. Each produces a circular wound about twelve centimeters in diameter. Every move hemorrhages more blood and aggravates the bull's pain. Endorphins liberated don't suffice to neutralize the animal's suffering. The bull weakens further before the matador enters the scene.

"For the third tercio, the matador uses the red cape and the *estoque*, the curved sword. The cape's final passes exhaust the bull. The matador prepares the animal for the final, *el momento de la verdad*, the moment of truth that establishes humans' supremacy over bulls. After these passes, the matador aims at killing the bull by the shortest route. This curved sword's eighty-centimeter blade, thrust into the bull's thorax, severs the vena cava and the posterior aorta, the two large blood vessels in the thoracic cage, and causes the animal's instantaneous death.

"The truth lies far from that moment. This severing rarely happens.

"Instead, what happens most frequently is the following. The curved sword severs crucial thoracic nerves on its path, disconnects vital organs from their nerve centers, disrupts critical body functions,

381

and disables the vasomotor system that ensures key activities in the thorax and the abdomen. The blade shears the lungs, the trachea, and the esophagus and provokes a deluge of internal hemorrhage. The blood floods the bull's thorax, chokes the animal, and emerges from its mouth and nose. You've seen this bleeding in arenas and on television.

"After this stroke, if the bull still refuses to fall, as it often happens, the matador uses the *descabello*, the straight sword with a stopper ten centimeters from its tip. The blade enters the space between the animals' first and second cervical vertebrae and severs its spinal cord. Its legs buckle. The bull falls but doesn't die. It only gets paralyzed. It still feels the pain.

"To end the bull's suffering, the matador then uses the *puntilla*, the knife bearing a ten-centimeter blade, prohibited today in Europe's abattoirs. This knife, repeatedly stabbed into the animal's neck, destroys its spinal bulb, which regulates its heartbeats and breathing. A slow, agonizing death follows. The high acidity of the bull's blood, found in post-mortem analysis, proves the animal's tormenting pain on a tortuous, torturous path before dying."

Carlota stopped and invited questions.

There were none. Not even a murmur. All mouths gaped at her, all eyes stared without blinking. From the back, a senior citizen broke the solemn silence by sniffling and blowing his nose. Carlota waved at this retired professor of veterinary medicine. Heads turned in his direction. The man lifted his hand, rose from his seat, and bowed to her.

Carlota gave the microphone to Nuria and descended from the podium.

Nuria held the microphone but couldn't recall her arguments.

Charo's speech, factual and neutral, had left her disarmed. Her own pitch now seemed redundant: irrelevant, impotent, and exaggerated out of proportion. She decided to trim her words and tone them down.

"My colleagues," Nuria said. "I'll skip the known. You know what the pandemic has already shown. You've seen what happens to a region that lives on tourism; in our case, taurine tourism. Let's examine a few points we take for granted and never stop to think."

Nuria set aside her notes and spoke:

"Like me, most of you own an animal or two. Like me, most of you will vote next week to extend the punishment for torturing these animals, from eighteen months to thirty-six.

"Why?

"Because you know these animals. Because you live with them and feel for them. Because you love them, and they love you. You feel close to them. They feel close to you. If I paid you a million euros to torture and kill them, in public or at home, you would refuse.

"Now place yourself inside a bullring. Someone gives you a sword and asks you to kill a bull. A bull you don't know. A bull you feel nothing for. A bull that's just another bull, with no feelings for you. Will you torture and kill that bull?

"I bet you won't.

"I've worked long enough with you to know this as a fact.

"Why?

"Violating a living creature in public violates our civic sense.

"Now, if you, yourself, won't perform this public violence, why allow others to do it? That is the point we each need to think this morning, irrespective of our bullfighting stance.

"As you know, the word "human" takes its root from an Indo-European origin. The word is composed of three parts: civility,

383

dignity, humility. These three qualities define a human. When we abolished execution of our enemies in public, we embraced all three.

"These bulls are our ancestors. Darwin has proved this fact. Embryology has confirmed his claim. We don't just descend from former life forms. We also pass through them before we're born as humans. You know these facts. I'm not telling you something new.

"Why subject our ancestors to a public torture and death we wouldn't inflict on our worst enemies today? That is another point we need to think this morning. We live in an epoch that recognizes animals as sentient beings. There's no reason to exclude the fighting bull.

"Don't get me wrong. I don't oppose slaughtering animals for food. Humans today, far from their vegetarian origin, have rights to kill other species for their meat; I accept that for truth. I advocate killing for food, not for pleasure. I advocate painless killing, not torture. I advocate slaughtering by the shortest route inside humane abattoirs, not in public venues.

"Imagine this other scenario. Instead of exporting bullfights to other countries, or selling our dignity for dollars at home, we raise these *lidia* bulls for their tasty meat and export it as our renewed brand. Would that change our country's image? Would that build a business less vulnerable to another pandemic? Would that lift our economy from tourism's quick sand and place it on a solid ground? The actors, employees, and entrepreneurs of bullfighting industry could be retrained to operate this new business. The ranchers could sell their rejected bulls at a higher price for meat and wouldn't need the state's compensation.

"Among you, many have helped me build this economic case.

"Now, we *all* need to think about it.

384

"Today, we see bullfighting as native to Spain. But we know bullfighting didn't originate in Spain. Romans brought it to the Iberian Peninsula when they colonized Europe. By holding onto their custom as our culture, we're perpetuating a tradition imposed on us from Rome two millennia ago. By holding onto their custom, we're setting aside our own traditions, those that originated in Spain, spread their roots, and grew as our culture.

"That is another point we need to reexamine this morning.

"The status quo's perpetuity doesn't confirm its validity. We can't evaluate the status quo while we're immersed in it. We need to rise above the status quo and examine it from the top. We have to forget our ranks and interests. We have to set aside our economic, political, social affiliations. We have to reexamine our situation today as humans, using the three qualities that define us. This morning, if we remove corrida from our region, we won't confirm these bulls' superiority; we'll confirm ours. Our decision will advance us as humans and set precedence."

Nuria thanked her colleagues and left the podium to Pedro.

Flurried exchanges followed among the deputies. Then a tense silence built up and filled the debate hall. Pedro took the microphone, broke the silence, and asked for votes. Murmur swept the hall and faded away. Some deputies stared at Nuria; others averted their eyes.

One by one, hands rose and cast their votes.

Nuria lost by a margin of three.

Nuria returned to her office and prepared to leave for the day. Mayor José's wife tapped the glass pane, entered the room, and stood with her back against the door.

"I couldn't vote for you," Margarita said. "But I wanted to thank

385

you."

"For what?"

"For educating me."

"Educating you!"

"On corrida's origin," Margarita said. "I didn't know. We keep repeating false beats until they ring true. I checked the facts after you spoke. Corrida didn't originate in Spain. We're holding onto corrida as our culture for money, but it's becoming a losing game for many."

"Not for Willem."

"I know," Margarita said. "He tells José what to do."

"Your husband can choose."

"Not yet."

"Thanks for coming."

"I came for something else."

"I've to leave."

"This concerns Miguel," Margarita said. "I thought you should know."

"I'm listening."

"Willem sees him as his worst enemy."

"That isn't new."

"The law against whistleblowers passed last week."

"The state has left it to the region's discretion."

"Willem is pushing our deputies to adopt it."

"How?"

"Don't ask."

"Why are you telling me this?"

"I want to protect Miguel."

"Why?"

"For you."

386

"Is this a warning?"

"No."

41

The region adopted the law against whistleblowers. Donors could no longer claim tax break for funds they donated to organizations that used illegal means to do their investigative work. Miguel's foundation survived because most of its donations came from regions and countries that didn't have such laws. Besides, many donors saw this law as unfair and increased their donations because they valued Miguel's work.

Spring departed early and left the city to summer. The warming air brought more tourists from cold European countries, not subjected to travel restrictions within the Union. The rising heat drove out the pandemic's remaining traces. Bullfights resumed in taurine cities and faced losses from partially filled arenas.

Willem came forward and made up for San Taurino's losses. The city rewarded him by announcing a *mano-a-mano* between Esteban and Ignaçio. The duel was scheduled for late summer. Willem started pulling his strings for lifting air-travel restrictions. Taurine diplomats cooperated with him. After watching bullfights on television for eighteen months, aficionados itched for the real stuff in arenas. They became desperate to see this duel between the world's number one matador and Europe's number three. Willem's betting business made a fortune.

The legislature closed for summer. One late afternoon in early August, after depositing the required legal notice at the city hall for conducting a demonstration against this mano-a-mano, Nuria came out with Miguel and stopped on the portico. Willem climbed the stairs, grinned at them, and extended his arm. She noticed the glint in his eyes and ignored him. Miguel didn't. He stepped forward and shook Willem's hand.

"I suppose you're lobbying for another international boycott," Willem said. "And pushing Europe further to exclude Spain from the Union."

"I can't," Miguel said. "Everyone is on vacation now."

"Good," Willem said. "I have something better for you."

"I love what I do."

"I doubt it, son," Willem said. "If you were happy with Spain, you wouldn't go around asking for these sanctions. This country raised you from the dirt and—"

"I do this to help the bulls."

"That I know."

"Stopping bullfights will help Spain."

"That I'm not sure."

"We've to go."

"Listen, son," Willem said. "What if you closed your foundation and worked for me? These bulls are raised to die anyway. Why not leave bullfighting in Spanish citizens' hands and—"

"I'm a Spanish citizen."

"By birth, not by blood."

"What difference does it make?"

"You're like me."

"I'm not."

"We both are Spain's naturalized citizens," Willem said. "We both are concerned about Spain's economy, heritage, and image. Unfortunately, we oppose each other and destroy our work. Instead, we could join our hands and—"

"I don't oppose you," Miguel said. "I oppose bullfighting."

"It's the same, son."

"You can live without bullfighting."

"My business can't."

"Then there's no deal."

"Look, Miguel," Willem said. "I'm trying to protect you."

"From what?"

"From the dirt you shoved under Europe's carpet before leaving Brussels."

Miguel's face darkened. Nuria pulled him by the arm, but Miguel held his ground. His jaw stiffened. His forehead creased. His eyes lowered, his lips puckered. Nuria dropped her hand from Miguel's arm and stared at Willem. He ignored her glare and beamed at Miguel.

"See, son?" Willem said. "You're like me."

"What do you want?" Miguel said.

"Ah, now you want to talk."

"I'll listen."

"Yes, son, listen to me," Willem said. "You live in a dump. You deserve better. You're good at what you do. Skills are skills; they can be used either way. You can switch side and do the same work. I'll pay you three hundred thousand euros per year. Seven million upfront, if you join me. Plus, a yearly bonus of—"

"You can't buy me out."

"I'm offering you a job."

"I won't work for you."

"That's a pity."

"Let it be."

"I wanted to help you."

"Please don't."

"You're arrogant," Willem said. "You descend from illegal

390

immigrants. Probably, as an illicit child too, the reason your parents left you in the dirt. Spain adopted you. Spain raised you with care, grew your talents, and bathed you in its culture. In return, what are you giving back to Spain? You're asking tourists not to come here. You're asking Europe to kick Spain out of the Union. You're asking the world to punish Spain. Those fit your origin. An ingrate of your order can only be born from prost—"

Willem recoiled and covered his nose.

Nuria checked the shoe in her hand and saw its sole cracked. She threw it to the ground and took off her other shoe.

Passersby stopped in their tracks and encouraged her for more beating.

She lunged for Willem's bleeding face. Miguel caught her arm, pulled her back, and held her in place. Willem uncovered his face, glared in cold furor, and marched down the staircase. Nuria struggled with Miguel and shouted at Willem. He didn't look back or utter a word.

Citizens gathered on the square and cooed at Willem.

He ignored them.

42

Late August, international authorities lifted their overseas travel restrictions.

Taurine tourists flooded into San Taurino for the city's three-week long feria, to end with the mano-a-mano between Esteban and Ignaçio. Anti-bullfighting demonstrators organized a city-wide blockade. They jammed roads, avenues, and thoroughfares. They closed highways, railways, waterways, airways, and bridges. They stopped people from reaching the arena. The city hung in limbo and complained to the authorities.

On the blockade's fourth day, a special force entered the city from its west. They cleared barricades along their way, approached the city center, and reached Plaza de Toreros, where Miguel was demonstrating with Nuria and his foundation. From the rank's front, four officers descended from a sedan, grabbed Miguel by the arms, and escorted him to their vehicle. They didn't touch anyone else.

The silent arrest left the demonstrators stunned.

When the sedan started rolling away with Miguel, Nuria emerged from her trance and realized what had just happened. Indignation rose among the demonstrators. They shouted at the officers and ran after their vehicle. The task force pushed them back to the square. Two female officers held Nuria in place.

After the sedan disappeared from her view, they let her go. Nuria took out her phone and sent an urgent message to Elena.

Within minutes, Elena called her back.

"Miguel is going for detention," Elena said. "They have a warrant for him."

"We declared this demonstration."

"That's not the cause."

"What is the cause?"

"I wish I knew."

"These officers belong to the secret service."

"They do."

"Are they taking Miguel to the city's jail?"

"No."

"Then where?"

"I don't know."

"Elena!"

"Hold on," Elena said. "I'm doing what I have to. We don't live in a country of rogues. These agents have a code to respect. If they don't, I'll go after them."

"What will they do to him?"

"You mean: with him?"

"Come on!"

"They're taking him to question."

"For what?"

"How do I know?"

"Where?"

"Does it matter?"

"What should I do now?"

"Get hold of that warrant."

"How?"

"You're his lawyer!"

The warrant told Nuria little more than she already knew.

After a full day's interrogation in a hotel room, Miguel was transferred to the state's anti-terrorist cell. Nuria was allowed to visit him there as his lawyer. He disclosed nothing, neither the reason for his arrest nor the details of his interrogation. His cold stance—solemn, solitary, and silent—told her to stay away from him if she wanted to help. She trusted his sense.

She stayed in Miguel's flat.

Her parents came to take her back to their farm. She declined.

The authorities revealed nothing and refused to release him on bail. Their attitude raised a national outcry and an international uproar. His supporters poured into streets and demanded his immediate release. They claimed his nonviolent methods couldn't border terrorism. Their protests swept cities, stopped their functions, and halted citizens' lives. They complained.

The complaints broke the government's silence.

A spokesperson emerged and declared Miguel's arrest didn't come from his acts against Spain's bullfights; it came from other activities of his foundation. He would stay in detention while the authorities carried out further investigation.

The ambiguous statement didn't calm his supporters. They raised more protests, organized more demonstrations, and paralyzed more cities.

Meanwhile, San Taurino ignored Miguel, opened its feria, and rescheduled its bullfights. One September afternoon, Ignaçio met Esteban in a duel over six bulls furnished by Rafaela. The mano-a-mano, fought before revered jurors from home and abroad, filled the city's arena and drew forty-six million views on television. The duel lasted three and a half hours and required four more bulls before the jury could reach their decision.

In the end, Ignaçio rose and displaced Esteban from the number one position.

43

The department of justice put Miguel's foundation on hold. The authorities froze its assets, forbade its activities, and stopped funds from entering and leaving its treasury. The service provider shut down its social media account. Agents raided and combed Miguel's flat. They seized his possessions under Nuria's eyes. They didn't give her further reasons for their acts. She refused to give them Miguel's keys. She ignored their threats and remained in his flat.

Little by little, the charges against Miguel entered his judicial dossier:

- allegations for financing the *correbus* three years ago on the city's terrace, an event that killed a *lidia* bull and several youths torturing this animal with flaming torches; allegations for organizing riots, arsons, and vandalism after this event that destroyed the city's properties and order, killed four citizens, and injured six officers

- allegations for thwarting a bull-run two years ago, an event that killed two women and violated Judge Emilio's niece

- allegations for orchestrating a chaos on Plaza de Toreros this year, an event that ravished Nuria while he escaped with minimal beating

- allegations for coercing regional deputies to vote in favor of Nuria's bill

- allegations for scheming an armed raid on the city during its upcoming second millennial anniversary; allegations for planning a terrorist assault during the night of San Silvestre on the city's arena, where a special corrida would commemorate its first historic bullfight

Nuria didn't believe any of these charges. She doubted anyone in the city did.

The disproportionate allegations inflamed Miguel's supporters, at home and abroad. A consortium of hackers formed around the globe. They vowed revenge and promised to break into the government's systems. Their concerted efforts soon became evident. They entered data centers, pulled out facts that proved these allegations as baseless, and published them on the social media. Judge Emilio dismissed terrorism charges against Miguel and moved him from the anti-terrorist cell to a normal prison. The transfer didn't calm his supporters' revolt.

Then a national newspaper hurled a fresh allegation against Miguel.

Some years ago, a pro-animal philanthropist legated his second home in Spain to Miguel's foundation. This property was valued at two and a half million euros. Miguel sold this house to a former colleague in Brussels for less than five hundred thousand euros, in exchange for a personal favor. The paper claimed romance between the two, a relation that started in Brussels and continued undercover in Spain. They published the villa's photos and its deal's records.

Once more, Miguel responded to this allegation by silence. The media interpreted his reticence as admission of guilt. Justice charged him with abusing social goods for personal benefits. His detention was prolonged. His foundation was left to dry on the judicial line.

Once more, his supporters poured out and protested. Once more, hackers promised their revenge and clogged the government's systems. Once more, the government ignored them, did their investigation, and held Miguel in detention. Once more, Nuria believed this new charge wouldn't stand before the court. But this time, it did. She confronted Miguel.

"Their claim is true," Miguel said. "I sold her the house."

"Who's this woman?"

"My former boss."

"You love her?"

"No."

"Then why?"

"You don't need to know."

"I'm your lawyer."

"Then behave like one."

"Pardon?"

"You live with me," Miguel said. "They could draw you in."

"Will you give me the details?"

"No."

"Why?"

"I don't trust your temper."

"Excuse me?"

"I don't want you to hurt my boss."

"So you do love her then!"

"You're again crossing the barrier of law."

"What do you expect me to do?" Nuria said. "Just sit aside and watch you rot in prison?"

"I expect you to behave like a lawyer," Miguel said. "I expect you to stay nonviolent."

"Why do you insist on nonviolence?"

"You know why."

"What are you saying?"

"Anger hurts the angry."

"Don't tell me!" Nuria said. "I'm suffering from what I did to Willem."

"Have you learned your lesson?"

"What do you think?"

"Promise?"

"Yes."

"I'll tell you then."

Miguel stated he had sold this house to his former boss under pressure.

During the ravage by a bovine virus, he inspected farms and ordered slaughters. One day, he witnessed how these animals were killed and dumped, as if they weren't living beings. He couldn't sleep. The farmers weren't compensated enough for their slaughtered animals. Many courted bankruptcy and asked for his pity. Some committed suicide. His conscience burned. The pangs pushed him to falsify tests results, spare these animals, and save their owners.

Then someone tipped his boss. The woman waited and gathered proofs.

When she confronted him, he told her the truth.

His falsification was a criminal act that could land him in prison and scandalize their department. By then, he had also discovered the collusion between their department and a pharmaceutical company. The department had authorized this company, in exchange for money, to test their trial vaccine on these farms' animals.

His boss forced him to resign. He accepted.

They agreed, as long as he didn't disclose their department's collusion, she wouldn't open her mouth about his crime. He returned to Spain, started his foundation, and claimed animals as nonhuman persons that deserved better treatment from humans.

All went well until his boss reached him for a personal favor. She had kept an eye on him and on his foundation. When this retired philanthropist's gift to the foundation became public, she wanted to buy this villa at a bargain price. By then, her department had purged their deeds with that pharmaceutical company, and she still held proofs of his wrongdoings.

At that time, his foundation was going strong. He didn't want judicial charges to disrupt its work. He agreed to this woman's demand. She promised him, if he complied, she would destroy her evidence. He had no choice but to believe her. He sold this villa to her at her offer price to protect his foundation. And he hid this sale from Nuria to keep her out of trouble.

"A human error needs another human to fix," Miguel said. "I fixed one by committing two more."

"I believe you," Nuria said. "Your acts weren't errors."

"They *are* in the eyes of law."

"We'll fix them."

"How?"

"Did you have any written exchanges with your boss?"

"No," Miguel said. "We did the deal over the phone."

"What's her name?"

"Why?"

"Miguel, I've learned my lesson."

"Will you remember it?"

"It's not hard to find her name."

"I'll give it to you."

"And leave the rest to me."

Nuria took the woman's name to Pedro. He pulled his strings in Brussels.

All efforts failed. The woman refused to collaborate.

Pedro counseled Nuria to leave the matter where it stood. From the law's viewpoint, this woman hadn't committed a crime by buying

400

the property from Miguel's foundation at a low price. Unless provoked by pressure, she wouldn't denounce Miguel in Brussels, because that would plunge her department into a serious scandal.

Nuria saw the logic behind Pedro's counsel.

Then she saw more.

Tax-exempt donations were a big catch for some organizations that ran with a nonprofit façade. The donors got their tax break. The nonprofits got their salaries paid. The donations were spent on a few symbolic cases with plenty of hypes, visibility, and communication. The real causes stayed unattended. Miguel's foundation wasn't one of those nonprofits. Whatever money his foundation received from donation served the cause it was devoted to.

This infraction was an exception to his norm: the only one.

Miguel didn't engage in other corruptions. He didn't hide his foundation's income and expenditure. He didn't draw any salary. He didn't spend his foundation's funds on luxury. He didn't even use his foundation's money to defend himself from the laws for his anti-corrida stance. He either used a public defender or paid the legal costs from his personal savings.

The justice overlooked his violations for corrida. This charge of using public goods for private cause was his first offense; it could be defended before the court. Miguel wasn't a perfect human; he was humane. His reasons for this corrupt transaction were credible and noble. A reasonable jury would understand his motives and soften his punishment.

His foundation was put on hold, but it still stood on solid ground for defending animals. The legal charges didn't turn away his donors and supporters. His troubles were temporary. Once he paid the fine and purged the punishment, his foundation would return to life and continue to grow. His comrades would nourish it while he served his time. He could guide them from prison. His foundation would perpetuate its mission. If she defended him with poise, patience, and perseverance, the Spanish court might even let him go.

On the contrary, if she pursued Miguel's boss in Brussels, she would drag him into the European court. Given his acts' timeframe, the statute of limitation still held for their laws. Her pursuit in Brussels would constitute a serious strategic error for Miguel's defense.

She thanked Pedro for his help and sent Ishmael a message.

The hackers broke into Brussels' systems. From the pharmaceutical's servers, they stole the trial vaccine's test files. They copied emails between this company and Miguel's boss and then published those on the social media. From the mobile network's archive, they recovered the woman's conversation with Miguel when she blackmailed him for favor. They also dug out her exchanges with Willem and revealed his hand behind these covert operations.

The woman resigned from her post. Miguel fell into a legal whirlpool.

A Europe-wide demonstration erupted in Miguel's favor. They claimed coherence in his acts, throughout his career, for defending animals. They traveled to Brussels and camped on the Union's stoop. They lobbied until the European court let him go. Spain's justice released Miguel on bail, maintained its charge against him, and kept him on probation.

Judge Emilio scheduled Miguel's trial for a date two and a half months later.

44

The revelations on Willem started with a leak from his days in commodity trading: his covert transactions that bypassed the trade embargo, supplied crude oil to South Africa, and kept its apartheid regime alive. The hackers retrieved these deals' details from his former company's digital archive and laid them bare across the internet.

They dug into his personal past.

From its dirt, they pulled out his pastime of shooting lions, raised in captivity and offered for thirty thousand dollars a piece, a pastime that grew into an obsession while his clandestine trades gathered speed. The obsession finally exploded into a political and economic scandal, a calumny that banned him from South Africa, despite his support for their incumbent regime. Willem moved his shooting feats to another country.

The hackers broke into that country's systems.

Unlike South Africa, this country saw its lions as a national symbol. Willem doubled his payment to poachers for his targets. An argument broke over a shooting arrangement. He shot the lion and the poacher and then claimed self-defense. After a six-day stint in a state prison, he bribed out using medical reasons and served home detention in a beachside resort. A week later, he paid ten millions to a trafficker, jumped bail, and fled that country. The hackers also published the fake passport Willem used during his shooting trips.

Then the world of commodity trading shifted. The power moved from trading houses to investment banks. Willem wasn't cut for this shift; he compensated for his loss by increasing his violence. After a few office incidents, his firm's partners retired him on a hefty package and sent him to a psychiatrist they trusted. The hackers entered this psychiatrist's computer, pulled out Willem's medical documents, and proved his taste for blood.

The early retirement channeled his adrenaline from trading to fighting animals. His blood-thirst grew with age. During this period, pro-animal groups rose around the globe and closed his avenues of violence. His psychiatrist advised him to watch bullfighting. Blood shed from torturing and killing bulls was legal in countries that hosted bullfights.

The trader in Willem saw in these fights more than blood; he saw money.

He reckoned he wasn't the only person addicted to blood for purging violence. He could trade these bulls' lives for money and get richer while satisfying his blood thirst. He decided to invest his retirement package into building a bullfighting business. The hackers pulled out the weighty check Willem wrote to this psychiatrist for his insightful guidance.

The following week, Willem arrived in Spain and incorporated his taurine enterprise in San Taurino. In due course, he paid his way through bureaucracy, anchored his bullfighting business, and obtained his Spanish citizenship. His past in commodity training was buried.

The revelations stunned San Taurino's citizens. Once they recovered, they remonstrated against hosting in their city a fugitive of justice who gave them jobs, fed them money, and told them what to do. They forgot their bullfighting stances and shouted alike in public places. Several countries closed Willem's taurine channel. For those who wouldn't, the hackers did. They jammed his tourist websites. They hijacked his betting business and reprogrammed it. They replaced the bets for corrida by bets for boxing, football, and wrestling matches.

Willem's cohorts revolted at these revelations. Some left him for ethical reasons. Others broke ties with him for their image. The hackers chased some more away. Only those with a genuine blood-thirst remained. Within two weeks of these leaks, Willem's business shrank to a tenth. But he continued unfazed.

The ousted ambassador, cloistered in the embassy, saw his opportunity to leave and return to his country. He told on Willem and negotiated a release. He left the embassy but didn't go far. Willem's thugs got him before he boarded the plane for his country. Judge Emilio seized Willem's three passports and forbade him from leaving Spain.

Four weeks later, thirteen judges convened in the capital. They revoked Willem's Spanish citizenship for hiding criminal convictions from his naturalization application.

None of this influenced Miguel's impending trial. Despite his supporters' cries, the justice held onto his line of guilt and kept him away from his suspended foundation. Twice per week, he was required to meet a probation officer and account for his activities. Nuria accompanied him for these visits. She couldn't reduce his legal burden, but she held onto her hope for him.

One morning, on their way back, they were approached by Alejandro.

The man now owned a company of cruelty-free food. He also invested in the enterprise of Margarita and Soledad that exported meat of *lidia* bulls killed by painless norms. Nuria knew the pandemic had changed him. He had given up his ambition in national politics and focused his attention solely on this region to revive its health. His smile and gesture seemed moderate. This time, she didn't turn her back on him. She stood in place and held Miguel by the arm.

"I won't pity you with clichés," Alejandro told Miguel. "But your uncertainty could also present you an opportunity."

"An opportunity for me?" Miguel said. "Or for my foundation?"

"For you."

"My foundation comes before me."

"Sometimes you take a small defeat now for a bigger victory later."

"That I agree."

"Good," Alejandro said. "I have work for you."

"I'm on the justice's peg."

"That's their problem," Alejandro said. "I know you're a good man. I don't care for the rest. The other businessman who offered you a job is going downhill. You're great at what you do. I'll appoint you chief-of-communication in my company and pay you whatever you ask for salary. You deserve to keep working."

"Thank you," Miguel said. "But I can't accept your offer."

"Why?"

"The foundation is my baby."

"Your baby is in the hands of justice."

"I put it in their hands; I need to take it out."

"I understand."

"I have someone else for you."

"For the same job?"

"That's for you to decide."

"Go ahead," Alejandro said. "Who's it?"

"Xavier."

"That homeless matador?"

"He has a home now."

"He can't do this job."

"But he can work for the vegan company you're launching."

"See, Miguel?" Alejandro said. "You haven't lost touch with reality."

"Will you hire him?"

"Of course!"

"Thank you."

"Didn't his girlfriend slap Ignaçio?"

"She did."

"What's her name?"

"Theresa."

"I'll hire her too."

"Ask her first."

45

The bull facing him was a *toro loco*. Two years ago, it killed a matador and received a pardon to reproduce. It knew corrida's rituals. It knew toreros' moves. It knew, after this *tercio*, either the matador or the bull would survive. It ignored distractions and saw its goal.

Ignaçio raised his eyes and scanned the arena's half-empty galleries. The spectators grew impatient. They didn't admire his cape passes or appreciate his dance. They wanted blood and they wanted it now. They wanted to finish this corrida and move onto the next.

This redoubtable bull wanted to kill. The bleeding animal ignored its pain from the lance wound and the six darts hanging from its back. He didn't have to shorten his passes and close their moves; the bull did those for them. The animal didn't let him exchange the fake sword for the real. Ignaçio signaled his toreros and received the galleries' hoots. Like his *quadrillo*, his viewers knew he was staging a miserable show. He heard bets running high against him.

The first warning call sounded.

Like him, the bull knew it had five more minutes; it knew who it had to kill to win. The animal ignored the other three toreros and fixed its eyes on him. His assistant brought him the curved sword. He swapped the aluminum for the steel. The animal knew this *estoque*. It knew where its death could come from. Its muscles tensed and its eyes moved to the curved blade.

The second warning call announced the two remaining minutes.

The bull charged. Ignaçio veered from the animal's path, turned on the spot, and held the cape higher. He didn't fool the bull. The animal braked, turned around, and charged with its head lowered. Viewers rose to their feet, applauded his maneuver, and encouraged for more.

Ignaçio knew the truth: he had just escaped the bull's horns.

The bull charged again. He withdrew the sword, turned against the charge's direction, and passed the cape over the animal's back. Applause exploded. He spun, stopped, and faced the bull. The animal turned, rushed, and hit the estoque's hilt. The sword left his grip, landed on the sand, and rolled to the ring's center.

Applause ceased. Movements stopped. Noises sank.

The toreros stood ready and waited for his order. Ignaçio kept his eyes on the bull and walked toward the sword. The final call broke the silence and ended the corrida. He stopped and watched the bull. The animal knew it had survived, not won the fight. It wanted more.

Ignaçio stood still and waited for the president's order. No one entered the ring.

The bull lifted its head and surveyed the toreros. It recoiled and hoofed the sand. Murmur rose from the galleries. Hurried footsteps descended a staircase behind him. The steps echoed from the arena's acoustics and fed the growing clamor. The bull ignored the chaos and fixed its eyes on him. Ignaçio braced for its charge. The bull lowered its head and aimed its horns.

The footsteps stopped on the stairs. A male voice shouted behind him.

The bull roared and galloped. Ignaçio swerved from the animal's path, turned around, and stood aside. The bull spun and leaped. A man jumped the ring's barrier, dashed to the center, and faced the charging animal. The bull rushed the trespasser and hit him on the chest.

The impact resounded through the arena. The horns pierced Miguel's chest.

Panic erupted. Confusion swept the ring. Terror filled the galleries. Uproar exploded the acoustics. The bull bellowed, lifted Miguel on its horns, and ran around the ring. Spectators cried out, covered their faces, and fled their seats. His toreros deserted the bullring.

Ignaçio retrieved the sword and slaughtered the crazy bull.

But he was too late for Miguel.

46

"Miguel was blacklisted from arenas," Elena said. "Did he tell you he was going to see Paula at the counter?"

"No," Nuria said. "He didn't tell me anything."

"Paula said he didn't phone her ahead."

"Why would he?"

"Did he know her schedule?"

"Is that difficult?"

"Do you believe the buzz about him?"

"Those are baseless rumors," Nuria said. "Miguel didn't go there to hurt Ignaçio; he despised violence. He didn't enter the ring to get himself killed; he wasn't a defeatist. His foundation is still in the hands of justice. He was fighting to free it. That was his priority."

"Then why did he do it?"

"You think I know?"

"Paula found him agitated," Elena said. "He was observing the bullring."

"He was worried about Ignaçio."

"He told you?"

"The video shows."

"Why would he care for Ignaçio?"

"Who knows?"

"Did Miguel do this for you?"

"Elena!"

"I'll kill Ignaçio."

"It wasn't Nacho's fault," Nuria said. "He did try to save Miguel."

"Are you defending Ignaçio?"

"No."

"You better not," Elena said. "I'll never pardon Ignaçio."

"Anger only hurts the angry."

"You speak like Miguel!"

"Don't provoke me."

"This wasn't the way for him to go."

"Probably it was," Nuria said. "From where and how he started, he had lived there lives. He had done enough to leave in peace."

"Come on!" Elena said. "You don't believe that, do you?"

"Do I have a choice?"

"Are you moving from his flat?"

"I have to."

"Have you found his folks?"

"He has no one."

"That's awful."

"It's real."

Nuria refused to enter the emotional morass. She did her work and dodged her feelings. Sorrow has its place in life. Fresh issues were cropping up and pressing her down; letting grief paralyze her spirit wouldn't solve them. Some see life as a race for longevity; others, as a race for their causes. Existence brings existential issues. She would face hers and Miguel's.

She could now. Miguel had taught her poise and patience. She could sift the false from the true; see the luminous beyond the nebulous; separate the positive from the negative. His death strained credibility but felt real. She had to rescue his mission. She had to perpetuate it. Those would revere this enigmatic man she had known, short enough to feel like a daydream.

She couldn't continue her reverie. She couldn't punish Ignaçio for Miguel's sacrifice. She couldn't sink deeper, wallow in sorrow, and postpone her actions. If she did, she would be the defeatist. She would rush her work and ensure Miguel's priorities. Those lay in her hands.

Justice dismissed Miguel's case and dissolved his foundation. They seized his flat and put it on sale. Nuria relocated to her parents' farm and called Xavier for Miguel's flat. To testify for her debate, Miguel had declared Xavier as his tenant; he owned the first right to buy Miguel's flat after his death. Xavier agreed to buy the flat and move in with Theresa before the year's end. They vowed to continue Miguel's mission using his nonviolent methods. Their ardor caught the youth's fervor and sheltered the animals that lost Miguel's defense.

Mid autumn saw Pedro elected at the national congress. Before leaving, he nominated Nuria to replace him at the regional legislature. The deputies listened to him and elected her their new president. Under her presidency, the first plenary session repealed the law against whistleblowers; the deputies, shamed by Willem's scandals, accepted illegal means of digging information as legal. They also elected the orchestrating hacker to Nuria's former seat.

These legislative shuffles pushed Nuria toward another avenue.

Since losing her debate at a close margin five months earlier, she had organized an inter-party coalition, drafted a new bill, and planned a fresh debate in autumn. Now her colleagues' collaborated effort to repeal the whistle-blowing law revealed their voting from an angle she had so far ignored: the citizens' collective wish, in their unified voice, decided their deputies' choice. To remove bullfighting from this region, she needed to explore its citizens' collective wish and expose it before their deputies. A bill born from inter-party collaboration wouldn't expose this wish; a bill birthed by a popular legislative initiative would.

Before this spring, two percent of San Taurino's citizens attended corrida, and eighty-seven percent opposed all public events involving bulls. The debate that killed her bill hadn't seen the citizens' collective stance, buried by their deputies' interests. The public initiative would extract this stance, shine and sharpen it, and lay it bare before her colleagues.

An organized society divides labor; money is the means to life. To preserve the lives of some, others sacrifice theirs. Bullfights' perpetuators didn't act from an evil nature. Some demanded blood and supplied money; others demanded money and supplied blood. Corrida stood at their nexus and met the two. There was no conspiracy against the fighting bulls. The citizens saw bullfighting this way before Willem's scandal. Their views had changed since.

The leaks had revealed Willem's true colors and tainted bullfighting. Today, ninety-eight percent citizens wanted bullfighting ousted from this region. She could ride this surge and end bullfights. Removing corrida from Spain needed the national deputies; her regional colleagues could set precedence. A systemic change starts in a limited space and enlarges its scopes. Her region could inspire the nation. Permanent removal required constitutional change. Her region could, by its administrative autonomy, ensure a de facto permanence.

Her bill's defeat wasn't a complete failure. The debate's tug-of-war, the deputies' long deliberation, and the votes' close margin— these had revealed how her colleagues' hearts analyzed versus how their heads voted. Their hands were tied by public causes that didn't fit their personal wishes. They voted because the electing citizens watched their debate.

The same public now watched them after Willem's scandal. They would watch more for a popular initiative than for an inter-party collaboration. Their collective wish would raise their deputies' stake in this new bill. The citizens would follow this debate closer and examine their deputies' acts. Other interests would fall aside. Her colleagues needed liberty. If she laid the citizens' choice bare before their deputies, they would vote freely for this fresh bill from their conscience. Bullfighting would quit this region and push others to do the same.

She couldn't repeat her errors. Deputies made laws, not ethics. She was fighting for bulls, as others fought for farm and company animals, for bees and trees, for air, water, and soil. Her cause wasn't better or worse than others'. For her, the fighting bull symbolized all animals sacrificed to entertain humans. To push her initiative, she should narrow its scope, limit her arguments to the act's legality, and place the law's validity within its legal framework. The initiative's question, short and sharp, must seek the citizens' view, a binary yes or no.

That wasn't an easy task. Her initiative's fate depended on its succinct formulation. For the polling phase, she wouldn't deal with deputies charged to raise law above ethics; she would deal with citizens raised to place ethics above law. Yet for the deputies to accept their citizens' choice and confirm it, her question had to align with the constitution and its laws.

She recoiled from all demonstrations and focused on her initiative.

Little by little, complex arguments simplified. Her clarified thoughts crystallized into three statements:

Public bloodshed, irrespective of the blood's origin and the reason for its shed, is violent.

A law endorsing public bloodshed encourages violence.

A legal system enacting and validating this law contradicts itself in its mission.

And a question:

Do you vote for public bloodshed?

Yes or no.

She avoided sensitive issues, such as corrida's art or culture, its origin, and its economic, political, therapeutic values. She focused solely on justice in modern society, the legality of bloodshed in full public view. The citizens and their deputies could forget bulls and vote on this legal issue. In practice, this initiative would help only the fighting bulls, because no other animals could be legally subjected to such a prolonged torture and hurtful killing in public. But that didn't matter. The justice for fighting bulls would also help other animals.

She met Ishmael and put out the word.

Among Miguel's supporters, the computer experts came forward. They programmed the system, roamed public places, and collected citizens' votes. Within a week, the mobile team obtained the initiative's required eight thousand signatures.

The legislature reimbursed them for the poll's cost.

The poll continued. Votes fed the system and buttressed citizens' wish. After forty-seven thousand signatures, Nuria stopped the poll and submitted its results to the regional congress. The steering committee validated the initiative and sent it for the deputies' vote. The assembly scheduled the debate for the year's end, three days before the San Silvestre bullfight.

On that day, if the deputies voted for their citizens' true wish, this symbolic corrida, set to celebrate bullfight's arrival in San Taurino from Rome two thousand years ago, wouldn't take place and slaughter another bull.

Or kill another human.

The debate's date would enter San Taurino's history.

47

The bugle blew for the *tercio de varas*. Ignaçio signaled his both lancers on horseback.

The pen's door opened. The bull charged out, ignored him and the cape, and galloped across the ring. Ignaçio turned on the spot, raised the cape higher, and ran after the bull. The animal showed no interest in fighting. It held its head high, kept its neck erect, and cantered along the ring's barrier. It stayed away from the center. It didn't slow or alter its gait.

The spectators applauded him for intimidating the bull. They condemned the animal as a *toro manso*. Ignaçio knew the truth. The bull's poise, pace, posture, and gait showed it wasn't a coward; it saw humans on two feet as fragile and confronting them as worthless. The brave bull saw no point in being cloistered in this place. It sought to leave the ring's confinement, return to its pasture's liberty, and find its peace. It didn't want to give into violence.

The lancer advanced his horse and stood in the bull's path.

The bull didn't charge; it went around. The lancer hitched his stirrup and hit the bull at the muzzle. The acoustics magnified the metal's clank. The blow cracked the bull's nasal bone. The shocked animal recoiled. Ignaçio shouted at his lancer and ordered him to respect rules.

The lancer shot a sharp glare at him. He raised the lance and plunged its tip into the bull's neck. The blade didn't enter the *morrillo*, the part of the bull's nape permitted by bullfighting laws; it pierced a forbidden zone. Ignaçio threw his cape and requested a break. The president ignored him and sustained the tercio.

The lancer withdrew the lance and raised it for another stroke. A second stroke would break bullfight's rules. Ignaçio leaped. Before the blade hit the bull, he caught the lance's shaft and wrenched it off the lancer's hands. The spectators rose and condemned Ignaçio.

"I warned you," Ignaçio told the lancer. "Play by the rules."

"This bull doesn't want to play," the lancer said. "I'm trying to help you."

"Don't."

"The president doesn't complain."

"You work for me."

"You didn't pay me for the last two corridas."

"I won't pay you for this one."

"You can't," the lancer said. "You have no money."

"Will you respect the rules?"

"No."

"Leave."

The lancer took his weapon and led his horse toward the exit. The bull blocked his path and swayed its horns. The lancer aimed the blade at the bull's head. Ignaçio rushed to him and stopped the blow. The viewers complained. Ignaçio guided the bull by the cape. The animal moved, let the lancer leave, and followed the cape. The spectators applauded his move.

The bugle blew for the *tercio de banderillas*.

The bleeding bull ignored the call. Ignaçio swayed the cape to lead the animal toward the ring's center. The bull stood in place, shook off the blood dripping from its coat, and refused to budge an inch. Ignaçio lowered his cape and signaled his three *banderilleros*.

The first picker dashed with two colored darts and planted them on the bull's mid-back. The animal didn't flinch. The other two pickers took their turns and plunged four more color-frilled darts on the bull's flanks. The animal resisted the pain, rejected their baits, and stood still. The bull's neck, hemorrhaging from the lance's wound, didn't lower its head.

The president waved the red handkerchief and ordered two black darts.

Ignaçio refused. He told his pickers to ignore the president's order; they listened to him. Murmur grew in the viewing galleries. The president waved the green handkerchief, stopped the fight, and ordered to remove the non-cooperating bull. The spectators stood and protested; they wanted this duel to continue. The president respected their wish. He put aside the green handkerchief and waved the white.

The bugle blew for the *tercio de muerte*.

Ignaçio exchanged the magenta cape for the red and the aluminum sword for the steel. His face tingled. His ears fizzed; his eyes saw two bulls. He noticed the cape's tremor; his sword-holding hand trembled. The ring's sand simmered. His eyes watered. His blood pressure was rising. He ignored his state, swayed the cape in wider arcs, and closed his passes on the bull.

The animal responded and closed its moves. The audience applauded his skills.

The bull lowered its head and prepared to charge. Ignaçio recoiled and aimed the sword's tip at the bull's cross. They each cried and rushed the other. Midway, the bull swerved, veered from his path, and escaped the sword. The missed thrust tumbled him and hurled him forward. The viewers hooted. Ignaçio released the cape, retained the sword, and rolled on the sand. The hoots ceased. He turned on his back and saw the bull standing over him.

The arena fell silent. Blood roared in his ears. Black dots blurred his vision.

The bull lowered its head and pressed its horns on his chest. The shearing pain stopped the echoes, cleared the black dots, and steadied the shifting lights. His vision sharpened. The dual images converged. The poised bull, determined to kill, applied its horns with precision.

Ignaçio released the sword's hilt. He recalled the dying bulls' dignity, how they always left without fear. His turn had now come. He closed his eyes and uttered his prayer. He waited for the bull's horns to smash his ribs, crush his lungs, and pierce his heart. Nothing happened. The horns only maintained their pressure.

Ignaçio opened his eyes and stared at the bull. The animal was gazing at him.

In the bull's eyes, he saw no anger, hatred, or violence; he saw an emotion he knew. But this bull was different. The animal withdrew its horns, lifted its head, and retreated. He wiped his face and watched the bull. The animal didn't change its expression or stance.

The bull had taken his prayer as pleading for life; it was letting him go.

Ignaçio rose from the sand and faced the bull.

The animal stood still.

His assistant brought him the cape and picked up the sword. Ignaçio threw them aside, shook his head, and marched to the ring's edge. He stood under the president and requested the bull's pardon. The president refused and waved the white handkerchief.

"Ask the audience," Ignaçio said. "They'll grace this bull."

"No," the president said. "You have three minutes left."

"I won't kill this bull."

"That's your choice."

"You're inhumane."

"I can bar you from bullrings."

"Please do."

"Do you want to fight this bull?"

"No."

"Then leave the ring."

Ignaçio left the arena by the door for the dead and took the quieter alleys toward his place.

Along the way, he didn't find peace. Aficionados watching the corrida on television hurled insults and threw objects at him from their windows. The corrida that killed Miguel had slipped him from first position to third; this one would slide him lower. His contracts would dry. His toreros would receive no payments. His *quadrillo* would leave him.

He reached the square of Iglesia Sacrata di Ser Vivo. Filthy water splashed his head and drenched his suit. He retreated from the sidewalk and saw the watering balcony. A fan of his revealed the empty bucket and gave him the Roman salute. Ignaçio understood this woman's frustration. He ignored his wounded pride, bowed to her, and moved on toward his place.

He reached his flat and turned on the television.

Esteban had killed the pardoning bull and was doing his *rueda de vuelta* around the ring. The spectators waved and applauded. The slaughtered bull lay at the ring's center, like a mass of abandoned muscles. Esteban finished his rounds of honor, took off his *montero*, and bowed low in front of the president's box. The president ignored his bow and looked past him.

The spectators asked for the bull's ears and tail as Esteban's award. The president refused. The audience contested the president's decision. The president held ground. Esteban replaced the broad-brimmed hat back on his head and strutted toward the exit. The viewers protested.

Esteban took a cleaver and returned to the ring. The viewers silenced. The president asked him to leave, ordered the bailiff to throw him out, but the heavy knife and its glistening blade deterred the bailiff. Esteban smirked at the president. In cold blood, he severed the bull's ears, tail, and hooves. He raised them above his head and hurled them at the galleries. The viewers roared. They rode each other and caught the trophies. A violent fight seized the galleries.

Ignaçio's stomach revolted. He flung the remote control and covered his face.

The blazing anger burned his heart. His chest swelled, his breathing stopped.

He turned off the set, went to the bathroom, and held his head under the running tap. The cold water didn't extinguish his flames. He removed his wet suit, turned on the shower, and stood under scalding water. The heat scorched his skin, burned his wounds, and soothed his heart. His lungs breathed. He left the shower, returned to the den, and sat still on the sofa.

His place didn't bring him peace. He spoke to his bullfighting gears; they didn't listen, they glared at him. More precious than money is company. He didn't have any. Other than his mentor, he had no friends. He couldn't tell Angel what he was feeling at this moment. He was responsible for his own acts; he would deal with their consequences. That sounded fair.

Man left the jungle but brought the wild with him. That was real.

Killing a bull that spares a human is more than inhumane: it's barbaric. It's violation of dignity—of the bull's and the human's. It's defiance of sanctity, sacrilege of the sacred. It's cowardice at its zenith, shame at its nadir. It's violation of valor by ignominy, massacre of the noble by the evil, defeat of the virtuous by the vicious. The act reverses progress, deteriorates humans, and hurls society from clarity into obscurity. It doesn't prove human superiority; it reveals human cupidity, inferiority, stupidity. It shows the human wild in society's jungle.

He was wrong to think the fighting bull didn't feel any pain: the bull's horns on his chest had showed him the truth. Adrenaline delays pain, but only for a few minutes. The pain then returns doubled. The endorphins liberated don't neutralize the pain. He was feeling it now.

The viewers' hoots had revealed other truths: how you hurt when they applaud your fall; how their insults inflame your injury; how you feel when you can't avoid a fight you didn't consent to, you were forced into, and you've to kill your adversary to defend yourself; how you regret when you pardon one human and then receive death for reward from another.

Corrida wasn't designed as an equal-to-equal fight between bulls and humans. If it were, they wouldn't bleed the bull before fighting. Those in the trade knew this shameful truth: if the bull weren't bled before fighting, the matador wouldn't survive even a minute. A matador claiming bravery for killing a weakened bull only exploited viewers' ignorance by trickery.

The duality was cruel for these bulls. Some humans raised them with careless compassion; others killed them with compassionless care. If you were a bull, how would you feel growing up on a ranch, seeing humans as your best friends, being raised by their meticulous care, and then meeting them at arenas as your worst foes, who tortured you alive and killed you with a methodic precision? Wouldn't your world flip horns over hooves? That was the reality.

The couple next door, reunited after months, cried from their pleasure's pain. Here, he was sitting on soft leather and wallowing in his pain's pleasure. An experience like today's encounter doesn't leave a breathing human living the same way. He couldn't sit like this.

He was still alive. He had to do something to change his way of living.

Life's length doesn't define its quality; the living experience does. Errors are life's liberty. What we do with our errors decides our identity. The wrong teach more than the right. Some take errors for waste and commit more; others learn, keep their lessons, and move on.

He would reduce, rearrange, and rewrite his life. He threw his blood-pressure medicines. Life lives a fine balance, but you can take risks. He would rather die from a failed heart or a ruptured artery than degenerate from swallowing pills. Fear of disease, disability, desolation, and death are your worst enemies. They should leave and let you live free.

He piled his collector's set of *The Treaties*. He took down his life-size portrait of Ortega. He gathered his lances, picks, swords, and suits from the nineteenth century. He added to that pile his trophies, rewards, and certificates of glory. He wanted to dump them but saw a better use. He carried them downstairs, loaded them in his car, and sold them to the souvenir shop.

His glory's dust buried a part of his debt; the rest he would see.

The purge freed his spirit and cleared its path. He made up his mind, returned to his flat, and called his mentor. Angel didn't answer. Ignaçio sent a text message, canceled his future fights, and waited for a reply; he didn't receive any. He switched off his cell phone, left it in

425

his flat, and went downstairs for a walk. His feet crossed the square of Iglesia Sacrata di Ser Vivo and stopped in front of Angel's closed shutters. His mentor was still at the arena.

He walked around the church and halted beside his sports car. On its windshield, the sun's departing rays illuminated a note in scarlet letters:

"Thank you!"

Ignaçio raised his eyes and scanned the surroundings. A woman, watching him from a top-floor apartment, ducked behind the window. Her vanished silhouette flashed his memory; he couldn't place her. He wiped the note, started his car, and drove away from the square.

In Plaza de Toreros, at the square's center glowing in the dusk, the television reported the scores of the day's bullfights. His fall from third position to seventh suited him. Beyond the city's terrace, against the sky's paling colors, the stoic fort rose from its confines and greeted the free clouds gliding above. The fluid fluffs embraced the fort's crest and bathed its façades in saffron. The orange trees, flanking the fort's alleys, caught the fading light and flashed their fruits; they hung like a flamenco dancer's jewels. Visitors soaked their beauty, revamped their steps, and climbed the slope with renewed energy. Ignaçio slowed his car and watched them.

Autumn was his favorite season to go to this fort's rooftop, peer through the telescopes on its battlement, and watch the flaming leaves on his farm shiver in the ocean's breeze. Since he joined corrida's trade four years ago, he hadn't returned to this fort, gone to the sea, or visited his farm. Bullfighting had taken his soul and altered its core. This was his time to change.

He turned left on Avenida de Corrida, drove along the city's terrace, and continued down the avenue toward the train station. At the fort's gate, his foot pressed the brake and stopped the car. He shifted his eyes from the inviting walkway, switched his foot to the gas pedal, and sped down the avenue. At the station's intersection, he slowed, merged into the port's traffic, and drove toward the city's exit. To change life, he would start by leaving San Taurino.

He didn't go far. Near Jaime's garage, his foot released the gas and pressed the brake.

This garage, now free from its mortgage, employed forty-seven young mechanics from their southern farmers' community. Willem's scandal had reduced his fleet's size but not affected these youths' employment. The garage got enough work from citizens, non-taurine tourists, and visiting businesspersons. Jaime had succeeded in his life's mission.

Alejandro's investments had revived this region after the pandemic. The trades of wine, olive, and orange, the enterprise of *lidia* bulls' meat run by Margarita and Soledad, the vegan company opened by Alejandro and managed by Xavier and Theresa were making news now, drawing youths, and bringing non-tourist visitors. The same pandemic that exposed the city's taurine frailty had excavated its other treasures and shined them for its citizens.

The pandemic had reunited families. Uncle Manu now made fewer trips for Willem and gave more time to his family's farm. Aunt Belen took more days off from serving tables for Willem and helped Paula and Ines at their dairy workshop in his trailer. Their new stall at the marketplace now received orders from the region and beyond. Jaime was working to extend their online presence abroad. Since joining this bullfighting trade, he had left sustainable farming in their hands, and they had sustained his projects as their mission on his farm.

Jaime emerged from his garage, his smock covered in soot. Ignaçio pulled over, cut the engine, and got out of his car.

"You should be in the hospital," Jaime said. "What's wrong with your car?"

"Everything," Ignaçio said. "Will you sell it for me?"

"Are you joking?"

"No."

"At what price?"

"Any."

"Wait, wait." Jaime raised his hands. "What's happening to you?"

"Nothing."

"You're just selling the car?"

"Yes."

"Why?"

"I don't need it."

"How'll you get around?"

"On foot."

"What a change!"

"Can you sell it?"

"Will you let me use your name?"

"Yes," Ignaçio said, "if it helps."

"I can get you a cheaper car."

"Not now."

"What else are you selling?"

"My flat."

"Your penthouse?"

"Yes."

"Do you have a buyer?"

"No."

"You want me to sell that too?"

"Can you?"

"I'll try," Jaime said. "Your fans bring me their vehicles."

"Use my name."

"Where will you live?"

"I don't know."

"We can clear your trailer."

"The dairy needs it."

"You want me to add a second trailer?"

"No," Ignaçio said. "I'll rent a place."

"In San Taurino?"

"Not sure."

"Man, you're leaving us!"

"Haven't I?"

"We don't see you that way."

"It's hard," Ignaçio said. "Don't make it harder."

"I'll sell your car and flat." Jaime pruned his lips. "You'll be free to go."

"How much will you charge?"

"Your return."

"Jaime!"

"We're waiting for you."

"Act fair."

"We'll wait more."

Ignaçio averted his eyes and turned his face aside. Jaime took the sports car's keys and drove the vehicle into his garage. He offered a lift. Ignaçio refused; he needed to walk. Jaime shrugged. Ignaçio tapped him on the shoulder, left his garage, and walked on the thoroughfare toward the station. Vehicles braked and honked behind him. He ignored them and continued.

Night descended its cover on the city. He didn't want to return to his lonesome flat or seek company elsewhere. Generous acts open old wounds. The bleeding hurts but purges impurity. You see yourself in your soul's mirror. Company dilutes these acts. These moments belong to you alone; you should be alone to feel their impact. The bull's pardon and Jaime's generosity had put him face-to-face with himself. He would revere those acts by embracing their power.

He stopped at the station and watched the travelers. The taurine season's approaching end and Willem's dying business had changed this city's tourists. Some carried photographer's equipment and painter's paraphernalia; others, flamenco guitars or hiking and climbing gears. They didn't pour out from the station and rush the city. They emerged in a steady stream and waited in queues for the public transport. Their profile and energy lifted San Taurino's face.

He recalled his flamenco tour in Japan six and a half years ago. He remembered his arrival from Madrid by train with the troupe. He reckoned Victor's birth and his mother's death. He replayed Victor's growth on Jorge's farm and his. Before leaving four years and two months ago, this bull had finished his work; his calves were now fulfilling his promise for him.

Ignaçio moved from the station and ambled toward the harbor. Since that scorched *lidia* bull jumped off the city's terrace and died on the port's promenade three and a half years ago, he hadn't returned to this quarter. Merchants that survived the pandemic failed after Willem's fall and closed their doors or shrunk their scopes. Most businesses now stood reduced.

The soft moon rose above the city's terrace. Its soothing glow shined the breakwater, the harbor's boats, and the port's paving stones. The still trees' shadows hid the closed shops' shutters. Under a desolate plane tree, the open bullfighting bar, its lights dimmed and its roll-shutter half-lowered, served the desperate, the disoriented, and the debauched. The pandemic and the scandal had left this destitute bar in the hands of the deprived and the depraved.

He heard the flamenco song but didn't recognize the voice. The singer sang in Spanish, in a voice that didn't belong to the Spanish. He listened to the live music and couldn't discern its instruments. The strums didn't come from a flamenco guitar; the percussion, not from a *cajon.* Yet they blended with the claps and counter-claps, the finger snaps and foot taps in a rhythm he needed now. This *palo* didn't lift his spirit; it challenged his soul and confronted him.

A troupe from abroad was performing at the *tablao.*

Ignaçio resisted; his feet moved.

He stood in the oak's shadow and watched the troupe perform on the flamenco bar's patio. Naomi danced to the samisen's strokes and the daiko's percussion. Paloma and Juan clapped to the Japanese troupe's rhythm. Both had aged more than the four years passed. But they had resisted the pandemic and Willem's pressure and held onto their bar.

His desertion hadn't killed this couple. His presence wasn't vital for them.

Naomi performed a *desplante*, bowed to the troupe, and descended from the patio. He turned to go. She ran to him, blocked his path, and lowered her hair. Her chest heaved. Her face sweated and her eyes beamed. Sweat trickled down her glistening cheeks, ran past her throbbing throat, and flowed into her flickering blouse. He waited. She didn't utter a word, move from her spot, or touch him. Her watering irises caught the moon and turned it into sparkling stars.

431

The troupe and the spectators came from the tablao and surrounded them.

Paloma and Juan stayed on their patio. They singled him out and stared at him.

He waited; the couple didn't move. Their eyes didn't leave him. Paloma's head and chin told him they wouldn't budge. They didn't ask him to come to their tablao or go away. Their stance showed him no animosity or sympathy. Their fixed regard held no pity for him.

Ignaçio separated the crowd, climbed onto the patio, and stood before the couple.

Juan's eyes lowered; Paloma's held his gaze. Her steadfast stare silenced his head's noise and recalled his days as a debut dancer, lacking skills, tact, and confidence. He found a word but lost it under his tongue. He averted his eyes; hers prevailed. His wringing hands stopped. His fidgeting feet steadied. Her presence stilled him. He could do no more than waiting.

Juan broke their impasse: he brought a pair of boots.

Ignaçio's face warmed. He took the boots and looked at Paloma. Her raised chin lowered; her head nodded. Juan cleared the patio. He sat on a chair and placed the guitar on his crossed knees. Ignaçio removed his shoes and wore the boots. Paloma moved and stood next to Juan. The Japanese stood behind the couple, flanked Naomi on both sides, and formed a half-circle.

Ignaçio waited for the palo; Paloma left it to him.

Ignaçio started a twelve-beat *taconéo*. Juan's guitar strokes matched the footwork. His tongue clicks halved the beats. The tempo quickened Ignaçio's feet. The Japanese clapped, counter-clapped, and snapped. The *compas* freed his hands, arms, and shoulders. They felt fluid. Ignaçio raised his speed, circled the patio, and added *braceos* and *floreos*.

Toma!

Que Toma. Que Toma.

Paloma's lips didn't move; her stance didn't shift.

Ignaçio bent his knees and descended into a *sentao*. He raised his torso, arched his chest, and did a series of back-bent passes. His chest released, his breathing eased. He stopped his feet and moved to *silencio*. He worked his arms, hands, and face. They mimicked his grief.

Toma!

Que Toma. Que Toma.

Paloma frowned. She opened a *seguiriya* in *voz rajá*.

> *Yesterday, your flame burned headlines*
> *Today, no one knows your renown*
> *Yesterday, you rushed to the summit*
> *Today, you wait in the oblivion*

The crude palo crushed his inertia and chucked his sorrow. The cruel voice, raw and rasp, shook his viscera, swept his fear, and freed his courage. He chased her words with his feet. He matched his hands and face to her lyrics. He flashed forward and backward. He spun, swung, swirled. He turned on the spot, rolled on his heels, then twirled and sprawled his arms.

He cried out and asked for more. Paloma didn't give in.

She descended from *cante grande* to *cante jondo*.

> *Winners lose, losers win*
> *Life treats the two as one*
> *The world takes your gains and losses*
> *And throws them when you're gone*

He stopped in front of her. He slapped his thighs, chest, and face. He stared into her eyes and demanded a faster palo.

Paloma ignored his demand and maintained her tempo.

Ignaçio slowed his *pasos*. He prolonged his moves, lengthened his passes, and hid his face. Paloma stopped the song and broke the palo. He felt her gaze, paused, and turned. She raised her eyebrows and tilted her head at the cajon. Naomi strode across the patio, straddled the wooden box, and filled the palo's pause with rapid-fire percussion.

Toma!

Que Toma. Que Toma.

The Japanese clapped, snapped, and tapped.

Paloma rose from *cante profundo* to *cante intermedio*.

Ignaçio's feet quickened.

He shortened his passes and sharpened his gestures. He defied her compas; his heart constricted. Spasms traveled down his throat and shook his chest. Her voice climbed higher. Her eyes hardened. Juan tuned his guitar and raised the palo. Ignaçio's temples throbbed. His heart pumped, his head reeled, his eyes blurred. He lowered the palo; Paloma raised it.

His heart thumped. His arms trembled, his legs quaked. He caught her compas but lost his breath. He covered his ears and cried for a break; she ignored his plea and climbed three more notches. His throat dried. His tongue stuck. Her words pierced his chest and wrung his heart.

Breaking barrier isn't a one-way street
You take the wrong path, you can return
Lower your pride and free your spirit
Your heart will rise and regain its motion

Ignaçio halted and hid his face.

His heart exploded.

He kneeled before Paloma and broke into a sob.

He reached Iglesia Sacrata di Ser Vivo on foot. The moon, sinking behind the fort, lengthened the shadows on the church's square. He lifted his eyes, scanned his moonlit flat, and watched the clouds' shifting shadows. The sun rose, dispersed the shades, and removed his remaining doubts. The moon sank lower and left the square. The sun climbed higher, bathed the paving stones, and painted them gold. The glow illuminated the church's door. Theresa descended the staircase, stopped in front of him, and stared into his eyes. Ignaçio froze in place.

Her stance tensed; her body stiffened. Her puckered lips quivered. Her red eyes glistened. Ignaçio recoiled and braced for another assault. Her face relaxed, her limbs loosened. Her lips smiled, her eyes beamed. Ignaçio stood still. Theresa stepped forward and closed their gap.

"I put that note on your car," Theresa said. "Thank you for sparing the bull."

"I didn't spare the bull," Ignaçio said. "The bull spared me."

"You asked for its pardon."

"The bull didn't get it."

"That doesn't depend on you," Theresa said. "Pardon me for the slap."

"I deserved it."

"Did this bull break you?"

"No."

"Good," Theresa said. "The bull that spared Xavier broke him."

"Xavier is a good man."

"He's genuine."

"I believe his pitch."

"We're moving into Miguel's flat."

"I know," Ignaçio said. "I'm happy for you."

"We don't loathe you."

"Thanks."

"Nuria doesn't hate you."

"I'll go now."

"She is worried about you."

"She isn't."

"Ignaçio!"

"I wish you a good day."

48

The city needed funds for its two-thousandth anniversary. Mayor José opened the treasury's coffer and found it empty. The post-pandemic low rates favored municipal-bond financing, but the city's penury scared the investment banks; they didn't risk their reputation by selling junk bonds to investors. After vigorous scouring, the mayor accepted Willem's donation.

The citizens revolted. Margarita separated from Mayor José and filed for divorce. Ishmael dug the deal and flashed its details. In exchange for Willem's money, the mayor had promised him presidency for the San Silvestre corrida.

At first, nobody believed Ishmael.

Directing a bullfight required a thorough knowledge of its rules. Citizens thought Ishmael was fooling himself. Willem came forward and confirmed the mayor's promise. The boasting fanned the fire started by his donation. Taurine elites denounced the mayor's act as a sacrilege to bullfighting. Animal-rights activists forgot their differences and hailed this year-end corrida as the port of Evil's entry. The city's united voice threatened the mayor's post. He swallowed his pride, called Angel, and begged him to persuade Rafaela to forget their friction, accept the corrida's presidency, and save the city from another crisis.

Rafaela accepted. She entered San Taurino's history as the first woman to preside over a bullfight.

For Angel, this historic presidency fit her unique trajectory. Born to a family of Galician cattle farmers, she never went to a taurine academy. She learned corrida's art by observing the pros and surprised the elites by quoting *The Treaties* verbatim. In due course, she enrolled at a university and left the same year. Her flaming blond hair, golden skin, and body streamlined like a lance had birthed this savage woman in her natural suit of light to fight bulls.

In that epoch, a corrida required the bull's fighter to be male. She was an exception.

By the time he met her, she had passed the region's *tientas*, spread her renown in taurine circles, and not entered a bullring; Pedro, the president of the region's bullfighting association then, hadn't allowed her. She didn't lose her steam. Three years later, when Angel offered to serve as her godfather for her accreditation in San Taurino, Pedro lowered his barrier, risked his image, and let her fight on horseback. The year after, she left the same arena's royal gate on four shoulders. The *salida à los hombros* recorded her carriers' names in the city's history.

In those days, she had proved her mark. Now, her presidency for the San Silvestre corrida, during the city's second millennial anniversary, sanctified its taurine legacy. Citizens rejoiced her decision and forgot Willem's donation. Mayor José kept his job and breathed in relief.

His peace didn't last long. The taurine legacy's sanctity was defiled when Esteban killed someone at a bullfighting bar. Shocked aficionados gaped at their televisions and watched the elite matador sever his adversary's brainstem with a *puntilla*. Judge Emilio held the bullfight dagger in full public view and sent Esteban to prison. The San Silvestre corrida, three weeks away, lost its designated matador. The key event of the city's anniversary hung in limbo.

Angel asked Ignaçio; he refused.

The sacrilege shunned other first-grade matadors: money couldn't lure them. The second-grade matadors didn't suit Rafaela's quest.

438

Taurine agencies opened their rosters and offered international stars. Rafaela refused them. For this symbolic corrida, she wanted a Spaniard. Elite aficionados buttressed her decision. The search for a substitute matador continued.

Rafaela's intent worried Angel. She saw a facet of hers he couldn't fathom. This woman knew no fear, but she respected God. For her, a debauched tradition became Devil's furnace. Bullfight's distortion by money troubled her. She saw bulls as God's children. She equaled them to humans. For her, a bull's death was a sacred tragedy—solid, solemn, and somber—a dignified exit for the animal to return and reunite with God. Money's dirt soiled this ritual's sanctity and fueled her desire to leave this world. Her continuing quest didn't reassure him.

Like him, she wasn't from this region. This city's millennial anniversary meant little to her. She didn't care where the mayor drew his lifeblood from and how he orchestrated this ceremony. Corrida's art was her religion. The San Silvestre bullfight would celebrate this art's sacred birth in Spain. This corrida was her baptismal offering to bullfight pilgrims. She didn't want its font to come from the demon's forge. Willem's money tainted this ceremony. She wanted a matador who valued this art for its sanctity and placed it above money's dirt.

A suitable matador didn't descend from Heaven.

While San Taurino's citizens babbled about their millennial festival and bubbled over its financing, the San Silvestre bullfight's fate stayed suspended. The pro- and anti-bullfighting groups quit fighting, returned home, and watched television. Willem silenced and waited.

Angel closed his office, went home, and didn't find peace.

439

His place smelled humid. Its stale paint peeled. His appliances refused to run; his unpaid bills had turned off electricity and gas. Hot threats served his cold meals on the bare table. His fifty-year mortgage, twenty-one of which already paid, would foreclose. The musty indoor air suffocated him. The mildew was conquering his place. He hadn't received his salary for nine months. He was hanging at his savings' end. Fines for skimming cash and laundering through Willem had emptied the association's treasury. The trickling donations after the bullfighting magnate's fall didn't cover the association's running costs. No relief appeared in sight.

Angel wrapped a rag around his torso, opened the church-side bay window, and stared at Iglesia Sacrata di Ser Vivo. December rushed in with cold breath and the church's warm light. Evening lowered its spell onto the square, soothed the church's glowing façade, and polished its frozen stairs in charming colors. This was time for change. Angel moved back, lit a candle, and sat at the table. His contemplation didn't work. He opened his diary and started writing.

A horse neighed in the square. Hooves trotted on its paving stones.

He knew this horse. He couldn't figure what the animal was doing here at this hour, in this part of the year. He closed his diary and locked it away. He returned to the window, leaned on its ledge, and peered into the square's glare. Rafaela, wearing her black *montero* and coarse-leather riding boots, descended from Zeus and led the horse toward the church's stairs.

She didn't look at him or his home. Gold hair flowed under her tall hat's wide brim, rolled on her scarlet waist-coat, and bounced at its hem. Her free hand carried an artist's satchel.

440

She stopped at the staircase and lowered her satchel. She straightened her skirt's folds, smoothed her pantyhose, and fastened her coat's buckles. She pulled down the horse's head, spoke into the animal's ear, and tied the reins to the railing. Zeus shook his mane, raised his head, and snorted. The nervous horse turned in place, rubbed his shoes on the paving stones, and released sparks. Rafaela ignored Zeus, lifted her satchel, and marched toward his home.

Angel opened the door. She entered, walked to the mantel, and placed her satchel.

She didn't sit on the molded sofa. She didn't take off her hat or boots. She paced the den, stopped before the extinguished hearth, and surveyed his home. A ring of finality marked her breath; a tone of fatality, her gaze. Her cold eyes stopped on him and scrutinized his rag. They warmed. Their corners glistened. She ignored his stare, bit her lip, and looked away.

Angel stood still and observed this woman he had known for three decades.

Seventeen years ago, her marriage to Pedro put her out of bullrings. She married him for the chance he gave her eight years earlier to fight bulls; he ended her bullfighting career and turned her into his social trophy. Politics took Pedro's priority over his wife. The man's high stress had never endowed their marriage with a child. At forty-five, she was at her peak.

Rafaela opened her satchel, took out a stack of banknotes, and placed it on his table.

"Wait," Angel said. "What's this for?"

"Stop."

"I don't need your money."

"You need your home."

441

"Rafaela." Angel touched her hand. "What's happening?"

"I'm leaving."

"For Madrid?"

"Yes."

"When?"

"After the San Silvestre corrida."

"We don't have a matador yet."

"I do," she said. "Count for a good match."

"Who's it?"

"Wait and see."

"Rafaela," Angel said. "Are you going crazy?"

"No."

"I'll never let you fight."

"You don't decide for me."

"But you accepted to preside over this bullfight!"

"You'll take my place."

"Will you use Zeus?"

"You'll see."

Angel recoiled and watched her. The flickering light shifted shadows across her face but didn't change her eyes.

He knew this woman. She wasn't lying.

Their relation started twenty-seven years ago, when she was eighteen. That was ten years before she married Pedro. Since then, time's erosion had sharpened her traits and strengthened his feelings. She was a steadfast woman a man could rely on. Her husband knew this side of hers; he was counting on her to join him in Madrid. Caught between her fidelity for both men, she was now forced to choose. She was making her choice by offering herself to her most dangerous bull, on a day the city's bullfighting history would

442

venerate her the most.

He wouldn't let her; she deserved to live.

If necessary, he would face that deadly bull and choose for her. He set the banknotes aside, pulled out the matadors' roster, and listed the pros and cons for each.

She spoke in his ear, raised his chin, and stared at his face.

He refused to meet her eyes.

She placed her index on his lips and then closed hers around his mouth.

49

His cell phone rang. Ignaçio checked the caller and answered.

"We did four Christmas without you," Paula said. "Will you come this year?"

"I don't know," Ignaçio said. "I'll call you."

"You should see Victor the Third."

"When was he born?"

"This April."

"Nuria gave him that name?"

"I did," Paula said. "I named his father Victor the Second."

"Do they look like Victor?"

"Only the calf."

"How is Santos?"

"The dog misses you."

"Paula," Ignaçio said. "Please."

"We set aside the money you sent."

"I didn't send any money."

"You did when you left four years ago."

"You didn't use that money?"

"No," Paula said. "You'll need it when you finish your veterinary school and buy Charo's clinic. She's getting old."

"You people are incredible."

"Jaime said he sold your car."

"He sold my flat too."

"Are you moving?"

"No," Ignaçio said. "The final signature's date isn't fixed yet."

"Where will you go?"

"I don't know."

"Nacho," Paula said. "Listen to me."

"I know what you'll say."

"No, you don't."

"Go ahead."

"Haven't you had enough?"

"Pardon?"

"In these four years since you left us," Paula said, "haven't you killed enough bulls? Haven't you hurt yourself enough? Haven't you hurt others enough? Those who raised you, those who loved you, those who stood by—"

"Stop!"

"That hurts, right?"

"You called me to say this?"

"I called you because you're still humane."

"You don't believe that."

"I do."

"What do you want?"

"Stop fighting bulls and return home."

"I don't belong there."

"Sure you do."

Paula continued:

"At times, against our will, we ride wild illusions and sail into destruction. There, moral storms rage our soul and punish our conscience. The menacing waves threaten our identity. We long for security, mourn for safety, yearn for warmth. That is humane. Believe me.

"We feel sick. We want to return home.

"Why?

"Because we know someone is waiting for us, someone who

loves us and cares for us, someone who understands us and will give us another chance. That is humane. Believe me.

"That someone is you and that home is your soul. You turned them away; they haven't left you. We're also there for you, waiting for your return. Why? Because we know you'll return, claim your place among us, and continue from where you left. That is humane. Believe me.

"We're doing what you trusted us to do. But we're not you. We can't do your work. Your work is waiting for you; your place, among us. You've to return and do it with us. You know this as much as we do. That is humane. Believe me."

Ignaçio covered his mouth, buried his face, and soaked her words.

The fall colors departed within a week. San Taurino hid its loss by wearing jewelry.

For its two-thousandth anniversary, the stunning city wore Roman glory bought with Willem's money. Ignaçio packed his overnight bag, loaded it in his new used car, and left after sunset. He needed peace for the night to decide his course.

He didn't go far.

On Avenida de Corrida, his steering wheel turned right; his car headed toward the bridge over the Sangre de Toros. He crossed the river and climbed the north hills. Since leaving for the taurine academy four years and three months ago, he hadn't taken this road once. The hills still welcomed him and gave him the same warmth. The winter's spell didn't deter them.

The hilltop road seemed wider; the valley's farms, larger under the generous moon. Those farmers who bought Victor's progeny had opened a cooperative, made Jorge its president, Uncle Manu its secretary, and Paula its treasurer. The seeds Victor planted before departing had borne fruit for this farmers' community. The bull had left, but its legacy endured.

He reached the mud trail that went into the farmer's valley. His foot left the gas pedal and pressed the brake. He slowed at the intersection and stopped at his farm; he didn't recognize it. Solid rails replaced the derelict gate's stakes. Tall winter-grass flanked the moonlit path to the trailer, hiding in the oaks' shadow. The sea breeze swayed their bare twigs and revealed the dairy workshop on the trailer's right. Christmas had closed the place, but the dairy's smell lingered in the air and told the workshop's story.

Ignaçio scaled the gate and jumped into his farm.

The sound stirred the shed's cattle. Cows emerged with their calves and watched him from distance. His presence frightened them. Lorenza came out last and stood at the herd's front; she didn't have a calf with her. He started going toward her. She turned back and returned to the shed. The lead cow didn't trust him. Others followed her. He left them alone, crossed the frosting pasture, and walked toward the pond.

He climbed the mound and stopped before the cottonwood tree.

The heron saw him and stood in its nest. The bird's eyes glowed in the moon. A second head rose from the nest and then a smaller one. He couldn't read their emotions in the dark. He left the heron's family in peace and walked toward the stone pile. Frost was growing on these stones. Their sheen refracted the moon's rolling beams.

He stood at the pile's foot. The wreath he left four years ago was still preserved inside a square shelter; someone had used a few stones and built this niche. The remaining stones hadn't moved. The rest of the pile hadn't changed. They still held his parents' promise.

The revived stones whispered to him. He could use these old stones, build a new home, and continue his parents' wish. After his flat's deal closed, he would have money to rebuild this home. While the home built, he could rent a cheap place in the city; his car's sale had left him enough equity. Renown breeds poison. But for these two sales, his name had helped. He climbed the stone pile and sat where Santos used to sit to watch his mock fights with Victor.

The moon's face bore a bull. Fluffs sailed, moved the animal's tail, and lifted its head. The bull shook its dewlap, swayed its horns, and walked in Victor's gait. The moon fell and sank behind the weeping willow. The bull's image shattered. The falling moon tangled in the branches, lost its light, and vanished. A single star rose and took the moon's place.

Night descended its blanket. The herons' eyes glowed brighter.

Since Paloma broke him four weeks ago, his bullfighting career had careened. His ardent ambition to turn corrida into choreography had dried. Bullfight's art didn't permit this shift; its business, even less. He preferred choreography to corrida. Dance suited him far better than duels. His progressive slip had revealed his makeup and shown his error. He would renounce his matador's title and return to flamenco. The four and a half years had rusted his dance. He would scrape that rust, recover his skills, and return to Paloma and Juan.

He would live on his farm and continue farming it.

His farm required another bull. Victor's grandson was growing on Jorge's farm.

While this calf grew into a bull, he would return to the veterinary school, finish his degree, and take over Charo's clinic. He descended from the stone pile, crossed the pasture's frosted grass, and marched through the woods toward Jorge's farm. He needed to see with his own eyes this calf Paula called Victor the Third.

He reached the woods' edge and scanned Jorge's farm.

The moon beamed at the pasture. The cattle stood on the shimmering grass. He saw Victor the Second stand among them and survey the herd: the surveying bull resembled Lorenza, not Victor. The bull saw him in the trees' shadows and approached him swaying its horns.

One cow separated from the herd. Victor the Third followed her. This young calf walked in its grandfather's gait and bore his silhouette and dewlap. Ignaçio leaned over the fence and peered at Victor the Third. The calf stopped in its tracks and returned his stare.

Ignaçio shivered. Victor the Third owned his grandfather's eyes.

The calf's mother called. His father groaned. The noise brought Santos out.

Ignaçio retreated. Santos saw him in the trees' shades and started howling. Ignaçio turned to leave. The dog entered the pasture and leaped through the cattle. Ignaçio noticed the dog's asymmetric gait. Santos dodged the bull's horns, rushed toward the fence, and stopped in his tracks. His barks changed into whimpers. Santos turned his ears forward, pointed his muzzle, and wagged his tail. Ignaçio came to the fence, passed his hand through the wires, and patted the dog on the head.

The dog's smell bothered Ignaçio. He turned Santos around, checked his drooping back, and felt his hips and thighs. The dog lowered his hindquarters and emitted a drawn-out howl. The palpation didn't reassure Ignaçio. He stepped back and scrutinized Santos: the dog had aged double the time eroded. He took out his cell phone and sent a message to Charo.

Across the pasture, lights came on in his old room. The sliding door opened. Nuria stepped onto the balcony, leaned over the railing, and peered into the moonlit pasture. Her eyes caught them at the farm's fence. She stood erect, folded her arms, and watched them. She didn't call the dog or raise alarm. Ignaçio sent back Santos, reentered the woods, and returned to his farm.

He sat in his car and started the engine. Victor the Third would do for his farm.

His cell phone rang. He hesitated to pick it up and then saw the caller. Last time he spoke with Charo was three and a half years ago, when the torched bull jumped off the city's terrace and died on the port's pavement. He wasn't expecting her to answer his message at midnight by a phone call. Old Santos must be ill and Paula must have skipped the news.

Ignaçio picked up his phone, answered the call, and stopped the engine.

"Humans don't change," Charo said. "Do they?"

"Have you?"

"No."

"I should have waited till the morning."

"Forget it," Charo said. "I'm happy to hear from you."

"Have you seen Santos recently?"

"No," Charo said. "But I'll now."

"What do you think of his symptoms?"

"You have retained your skills."

"Will you check him soon?"

"Tomorrow morning."

"Thanks."

"The dog went downhill after losing Victor," Charo said. "Like Lorenza, he's waiting for the bull's return."

"Why should they give up on Victor?"

"You don't know?"

"What?"

"Victor died in the South."

"Pardon?"

"They slaughtered him after a corrida."

"No way!" Ignaçio said. "How do you know?"

"They came to look for his mother."

"He killed a torero?"

"And blinded two more."

"He wasn't the *lidia* breed!"

"Rafaela makes her rules."

"Did she steal him?"

"She bought him from Jorge."

"Are you serious?"

"Yes."

Ignaçio ended the call. Charo's words still rang in his head.

He got out of the car, crossed the road, and stood on the sheer cliff's edge. Below, ruthless waves beat helpless rocks, frothed the sand, and roared like a bull. Four years and six months ago, Victor braved this relentless ocean and pulled him out of its merciless grip.

The ocean's breeze took his heat and froze his sweat. Ignaçio raised his eyes and scanned the sky. He found nothing to hold onto. Nothing anywhere stood still. The clouds sailed fast, rearranged the stars, and changed their lights. He turned and searched for the hills he knew. Fog fell on their ridges, rolled down their flanks, and hid their faces.

The night deepened.

No one emerged. No one cried. No one dared.

He returned to his farm's gate and peered through its rails. The stalks hid the cattle shed. He cupped his ears and listened for sounds. No one moved. This farm's lives had heard his conversation with Charo and abandoned their hope for Victor. He wanted to give Lorenza the news; the cow didn't trust him enough to believe it. Nobody would believe Victor's death.

He wanted his farm; his farm didn't want him. Like Lorenza, like the heron's family, like Victor's son and grandson, like other animals on both farms—all living creatures saw in him a bull killer and stayed away from him. Only Old Santos smelled the truth in him, trusted him, gave him warmth, and welcomed his return.

But the desolate dog was now sick.

Ignaçio reached Iglesia Sacrata di Ser Vivo and parked his car behind the church. He didn't go to his apartment: the flat didn't welcome him. He didn't belong to this place. He got out of his car, walked to the church's front, and saw a horse tethered to the stoop's railing.

He recognized this horse. The animal didn't belong to these surroundings.

He climbed the church's stairs and sat on the door's ledge.

Snow flakes glided across the patio, landed on his face, and searched for a foothold; they didn't find it. An off-season daffodil, off-track and lost, sat in an empty potter, turned toward him, and sought guidance; it didn't get any. The church's lights dimmed. A hawk swooped down and squealed for company; it found no one but him. The bird didn't want him.

The horse grew nervous. The animal ignored his presence, rubbed its shoes on the paving stones, and sent sparks flying like fireflies. Snow descended from heaven, extinguished their fire, and showed him the truth. His last tie on Earth had now broken; he was free to go.

Angel's door opened.

Rafaela emerged from his home and marched toward her horse. Glowing rivulets trickled down her flushing cheeks and dripped into her glistening throat's hollow. The horse raised its muzzle and neighed at her. She stopped beside the animal, placed her hand on its reins, and saw him sitting on the doorstep. She climbed the stairs and stood in front of him.

"Ignaçio," Rafaela said. "I have a request for you."

"I'll listen."

"I want you to fight on the San Silvestre night."

"I can't," Ignaçio said. "I don't have my *quadrillo*."

"I'll give you a team."

"I rank number ten now."

"You're still good."

"I'm turning in my title."

"Do after this one."

"Why?"

"You're the bull's best match."

Ignaçio scanned her from head to toe. She was the same woman who lifted Victor from his farm; the same woman who saved Nuria from the fascists' hands; the same woman who gave Victor a chance to fight and die in a bullring. Her blue eyes weren't iced tonight. Her wet corneas glowed. Her irises radiated warmth. Her dilated pupils moved.

"You bend corrida's rules," Ignaçio said. "I have a rule for you to bend."

"Shoot."

"Will you allow a corrida of a single *tercio*?"

"Yes."

"No *picadors*, no *banderilleros*?"

"Yes."

"Will you let the matador wear a grey suit instead of gold?"

"Yes."

"Fighting on foot, with only a sword?"

"Yes."

"We may have a deal."

"How much will you charge?"

"Nothing."

"Do you agree to fight?"

"I'll call you."

Rafaela turned back, strutted down the stairs, and released her horse. She vaulted over the animal's hips and sat on its unsaddled back. Her bare thighs squeezed the horse's flanks. The animal flinched. Its muscles twitched. The rebel horse shook its mane, raised its muzzle, and neighed at the pouring snow. She tugged the reins, turned the horse, and pressed its sweating flanks. The whinnying animal cantered away with her, scattering the square's growing snow.

Gleaming flakes fell from her black *montero* and slid down her scarlet waist-coat.

50

A sound Mors didn't know came from the ranch's far end. He turned with his brothers. This vehicle wasn't one that took bulls away from here and didn't bring them back. They relaxed. Those vehicles stopped coming when the leaves lost their colors and didn't start coming again until the trees put on new coats. For the colder days ahead, they could huddle and stay warm.

The vehicle rolled along the ranch's limit. It wasn't one that brought cows on heat for his brothers; they came when the air warmed and fresh buds peeked from the soil. It wasn't one that brought scared steers to this farm; they came when the sun traveled across the zenith and scorched the herbs, tress, and insects. This vehicle was drawn by a smaller one at the front. It resembled those houses-on-wheels that came when days grew hotter. Their biped occupants built fire after the sun went down. One such vehicle had burned his previous farm.

Mors separated from his brothers and marched toward the fence. The breeze brought dust raised by this vehicle. The dust carried a smell he knew. He stopped. Zeus always came with The Mistress of Bulls. He couldn't figure what the horse was doing here without her.

The house-on-wheels came closer. The Mistress of Bulls drove the smaller vehicle at the front. She was looking at him. Zeus must be inside the vehicle behind her. Mors turned his head and saw his brothers watching. Like him, they too were worrying about the horse.

Mors walked closer to the fence and roared for Zeus.

Zeus neighed. The horse sounded strange.

The house-on-wheels passed in front of Mors. Zeus thrust his head out and stared at him. The horse seemed troubled. Mors followed them along the fence. The tandem vehicle slowed and stopped at the ranch's gate. Zeus turned inside and whined. The horse was complaining.

The front vehicle's door opened. The Mistress of Bulls got out, went to the rear vehicle, and unlocked its door. Zeus started descending. She raised her hand and sent the horse back. She left the back door open. She pushed the gate, entered the ranch, and walked toward him. Her steps, free and fluid, swayed her hips. Mors perked his ears and observed his brothers. They, too, pointed their ears and watched her gait. She was different this morning.

The Mistress of Bulls stopped in front of him. She lowered his muzzle and spoke in his ear. Her words, few and firm, sounded sweeter and lasted longer. Mors raised his head and scanned her face. Her dilated pupils beamed. The skin between her eyes didn't crease. Mors understood. She wanted him closer. She was taking him from his brothers to keep him with Zeus. The horse loved his company. She loved him and Zeus. Having them together would make her happier. She was pleading him to leave his brothers and come with her and Zeus.

Mors fell into a dilemma. He turned toward his brothers; they didn't want him to go. He turned toward Zeus; the horse didn't want him to come. Mors sank deeper in his dilemma. He turned from his brothers to the horse. He stopped and watched her eyes. Her smile vanished.

Mors froze in place.

The horse neighed and reassured his brothers. They relaxed their ears and lowered their heads. Mors trusted his friends. He forgot his dilemma and followed The Mistress of Bulls.

They reached the vehicle.

She spoke again in his ear. This time, Mors noticed her changed smell and stared at Zeus. The horse nodded and then stepped aside. The metal room contained water, hay, and cereals. It had enough space for them. She was taking him someplace far, a place the horse knew.

Mors climbed in and stood beside Zeus.

The Mistress of Bulls closed their door and went toward the front. The engine started. The vehicle hummed and rolled. Mors poked his head out and found his brothers calm; they didn't worry about his return and follow the vehicle. The house-on-wheels turned around and moved away from the ranch. His brothers stood in place and watched him leave with Zeus.

Little by little, his brothers and their ranch disappeared. Mors withdrew his head from the door and surveyed the room.

The shining walls, spotless and intact, meant this vehicle wasn't often used. The metal's smell told him the vehicle was new. The fodder belonged to Zeus. The horse offered it to him. Mors left the cereal to him and chewed the straw. Its taste didn't belong to this region. It grew on a land he knew. She was taking him back to his old region. The horse must live there with her when she wasn't with her bulls.

The route confirmed their return. Along the way, they stopped at regular intervals. She opened their door, led them out, and let them walk. They never went far. They watched her clean their room, refill their water and fodder, and then consume her own food and drink. Her pregnancy didn't tire her. Unlike cows expecting calves, she retained her zeal and didn't sit down. After their short breaks, she reloaded them and continued their journey.

At sundown, she stopped by a lake and released them on the

meadow. She returned to the vehicle and raised its roof. While they chewed the withering herbs and drank the lake's water, she started a fire, cooked her food, and ate by the fireside watching them.

Mors came closer and observed her. She didn't look far or sigh as before.

The smoldering fire dimmed. She finished eating, took water from the lake, and splashed the fire. The embers sizzled and fumed. She waited until the fire died and then came to them and rubbed their muzzles. She returned to the vehicle and climbed into its raised top. She lay down and turned her head toward them. They stayed near her. She moved in her bed and spoke to herself. They listened to her words. Her breathing slowed. She fell asleep.

They too slept, but not for long. Creatures of different shapes, sizes, sorts crept toward her vehicle; they had to keep those intruders away. Zeus never sat down. After his futile attempts, Mors too forgot sleep and rose to his feet. Zeus was having trouble to dissuade a wildcat with pointed ears. The horse wasn't good with feline stalkers. Mors knew what to do with them. He approached the defying lynx; the delinquent wildcat growled and showed him its teeth.

Mors didn't waste his time or energy. His horns swept the lynx off its feet and flung it into the lake. The surprised animal screeched and landed in the water. The Mistress of Bulls lifted her head and watched the lynx swim out and dart into the woods. She waved at them, lowered her head, and returned to sleep. Zeus seemed surprised what a simple horn swipe could do.

The stealthy lynx didn't come out again. For the rest of the night, they heard only birds of prey and creatures they preyed on. Others slept in the woods' dew, in the water below the fog, and under the frost's blanket. The moon's glitter didn't bother their sleep or stir them.

The Mistress of Bulls woke before the sun rose. She rebuilt a fire, ate her food, and loaded them into her vehicle. They left the lakeside meadow, rolled through the woods, and merged into another road. More tandem vehicles traveled with them in both directions.

Mors recognized this two-way road. He recalled his cramped trip in a smaller vehicle with two scared steers that fought despite their fear. He remembered its filth and stench. He pushed those thoughts aside and reckoned his canine friend's bravery: how the valiant dog fought his ravishers, ran after their vehicle, jumped on its back door, and fell onto the road. He hoped the dog had survived that fall, returned to his old farm, and protected his cows. His canine friend deserved better. He hoped his biped playmate had retrieved and healed that brave dog.

When he left that farm, his entire herd was pregnant. Mors closed his eyes and imagined his herd, how it might have turned out after he left. He saw the cows give birth. Those calves grew under their mothers. Like him, they learned from their mistakes. Lorenza punished them if they defied the dog. The heron watched them from its nest in the cottonwood tree. His biped playmate stood under that tree—alone—holding their cape and sword. The mate looked ill.

Mors saw their last dance and game together. He saw the pond and its water. He saw the stones piled above that pond. But he didn't see the dog sitting on those stones. He called his canine friend and opened his eyes. The dance and the game vanished from his vision.

Zeus nudged him on the shoulder. Mors understood the horse and sighed. He abandoned the past, returned to the present, and watched the road from the vehicle's back.

But the receding road showed the past he was now leaving

459

behind.

The sun rose to its peak and started its descent. They stopped by an ocean; its sounds and smells he knew. A drive uphill brought them on a cliff-side road; he recognized the shore his biped mate took him to swim. His old farm wasn't far. The Mistress of Bulls was taking him back there. He glanced at Zeus; the horse gave no clue. Mors put his head out. He pricked up his ears, raised his muzzle, and cleared his nose. No sounds or smells came from that farm.

The vehicle passed by his old farm and didn't stop at its new gate. The farm didn't look the same. High grass stood behind its bolstered gate and hid the farm from his eyes. The tall tress rose above the grass, glowed in the waning sunlight, and showed their bare limbs. No life breathed on this farm. The trail, going from this farm to the other, lay quiet and empty.

Mors withdrew his head and lowered his eyes. The house-on-wheels descended along a hill's flank. He left the door and stood back. The vehicle crossed a river; he knew its odor. They entered and left a city; he knew its cries. They climbed another hill he didn't know, but Zeus did. The horse grew nervous. Mors moved forward and stood beside Zeus.

The vehicle passed a metal gate that closed after them. Tall hedges guarded the road's both sides; he couldn't see, smell, or hear what lay behind. The brushes continued until the road gave into a mowed pasture. A white house, higher and larger than the one that burned, sat on this land's end. The drowning sun's rays lighted this house's sloping roof, painted its red tiles in orange, and tinted the blue and yellow flowers on its walls in purple and violet.

A dog barked inside this house. The animal didn't come out and greet them.

The vehicle crossed the rolling pasture; continued among cedars and oaks, maples and beeches; turned around a pond that hosted rusting reeds, sleeping pads, and chirping birds; then backed up and stopped by a lush enclosure. This corral's grass knew how to resist the cold. Mors turned and stared at Zeus. The horse confirmed this place belonged to him.

The Mistress of Bulls came and opened the door for them.

51

Ignaçio buzzed the notary office's intercom. Their senior partner received him at the door, avoided his gaze, and led him to their office.

Ignaçio apologized for his persistence. He signed the power of attorney for his flat's sale, deposited his holographic will, and took a certified copy. He thanked the officer for receiving him during the Christmas break. The officer ignored his remark, opened the sale contract, and set a date in January for the final signature.

"I'll move out by then." Ignaçio said.

"Have you informed Nuria?"

"Why?"

"You gave her the power of attorney."

"Don't assume the worst," Ignaçio said. "All matadors do this."

"Of course," the officer said. "They always do this between Christmas and New Year. When they fight a twelve-hundred-and-seventy-six-kilo bull named 'The God of Death,' without the help of lancers and pickers, they do have reasons to hurry. I believe you."

"Have we finished?"

"Yes."

"How much do I owe you?"

"A short explanation."

"Pardon?"

"Why are you doing this?"

"It's my job."

"You want me to swallow that?"

"Please."

Ignaçio paid the notary officer, left their office, and drove from the city.

Past the veterinary school, he changed route and joined the traffic for Madrid. The villages along this highway provided shelter from the media flooding San Taurino's second millennial anniversary. He needed a hideout for the next three days. He wouldn't inform Nuria about the power of attorney; the notary had her number. Other priorities waited for him before the San Silvestre corrida. Only he could deal with them. Three days weren't enough.

At the next exit, traffic slowed and stopped. Ignaçio peered ahead and saw a crushed dog and another despairing beside it. This problem started after the pandemic ended. Before major holidays, it grew out of proportion. He pulled over, left his car, and ran for the two dogs.

The Retriever, on its feet and sniffing the fallen, saw him running. The dog lifted its snout and yowled. Its companion on the pavement didn't stir. Ignaçio reached the dogs, kneeled by the crushed one, and felt its pulse; he found none. He patted the living Retriever on the head, took out his cell phone, and called the emergency for animals.

"Sixteen today," the operator said. "We're expecting more."

"Can you get the surviving dog?"

"No."

"Why?"

"We have no place in the shelter."

"I can't leave this dog on the highway."

"Take it with you."

A hand tapped his shoulder. Ignaçio turned.

The patrol officer bowed to him and recited the known. During the lockdowns, to walk outside, citizens adopted dogs. Now they dumped their canine friends wherever they could. The state couldn't keep up with these abandoned dogs or their delinquent owners. The officer helped him load the surviving dog into his car, assured him serving animals suited him better than killing bulls, and then directed traffic until he left the shoulder and exited the highway.

The desolate Retriever continued to whimper. Ignaçio drove to a gas station, stopped the car, and checked the dog. He didn't find any injury on the animal. He went into the station's shop, bought dog food and water, and brought those to the car. The dog refused the food, drank the water, then lay on the backseat and buried its muzzle between its front paws.

Ignaçio withdrew his hand. He saw the dog's tremor and heard its shallow breathing. He couldn't take this mourning animal to the place he wanted to go. He could take this Retriever back to his flat—he had no idea what the dog would do after the San Silvestre corrida—but the traffic in the opposite direction had jammed the highway, and the impatient drivers' honks wouldn't help this dog's trauma.

The animal needed a break from its stress.

A walk would help.

He left the gas station and drove to the nearest beach. He parked the car on the cliff, found a trail going down, and descended with the dog onto the sand. The dog recovered its instincts, perked its ears and lifted its muzzle, and surveyed the spot with a revived spirit. The animal's tremor disappeared. Its breathing returned to normal. Its mournful whimper vanished.

The receded ocean had stretched the expanse of sand and slime. A descending fog hid the rumbling water. Cream foam slid under the fog's cover and rolled like tumbleweeds toward the shore. Sandpipers skittered after the foam rolls and stopped when they saw the dog. The Retriever ignored the birds, smelled the air, and listened to the ocean.

Ignaçio watched the dog's hesitant gait. The animal, about five years old, belonged to the breed that rescued people from snow, but its webbed feet also made it a great swimmer. He didn't see why this dog feared the withdrawn ocean that posed no danger to anyone.

This dog, shocked by its companion's death, was now acting over-cautious; it would need weeks to recover its balance. It had ignored the traffic and stayed by the fallen dog. The two must have descended from the same mother and been reared by the same owner—the host that released them on the national highway for their Christmas holiday.

This dog deserved a new home: a home away from crowded shelters; a home away from cruel death rows, where abandoned animals were put to sleep after a week or two at the most; a home away from human follies where doubling penalty for abandoning animals tripled their number. He couldn't keep this dog at his place; it would lose its home in three days. He could take it to Charo; she would find a responsible owner. Or he could give it to Uncle Manu and Aunt Belen; they would love to nurture a brave and beautiful dog like this one.

The Retriever stopped and sniffed the sand. Ignaçio left the dog and kept walking. The Retriever barked. Ignaçio turned and saw the dog watching him. He was setting up this animal for its second loss; in less than two hours, the Retriever had already attached itself to him.

His feet sank an inch then two.

He lowered his eyes and saw a pool growing around his soles. The water covered his shoes. The soles stuck in the muck. He lifted one foot; the other foot sank deeper. He was standing on quick sand. He stopped moving.

Unlike the legend, quick sand doesn't swallow you into its belly;

it holds you until water returns and drowns you. Most people panic, struggle hard, tear their tendons and ligaments; they can't leave. If he stayed calm and acted right, he would get out in time.

The approaching roar announced returning tides. He strained to see how far the ocean lay. The thickening fog hid the water from his view.

He kneeled on his left knee and slid his right foot out. He kneeled on the right and freed the left. His knees started sinking. The pool deepened around him. He couldn't crawl out on four without sinking his hands. Waves reached the pool, splashed him, wet his clothes. The fog thickened and descended on the shore. He couldn't see how far the quick sand extended. He could no longer stand, crawl, or creep without sinking. At this point, he could only spread his weight on a larger surface and hope to roll out of this mire before the waves caught him.

He lay down in the pool and rolled toward the shore.

The sand didn't get firmer. He stopped rolling and lifted his head. Freezing water dripped from his bangs, stung his eyes, and blurred his vision. He didn't see the shore; he saw fog. He turned his head and saw fog everywhere. His ears fizzed, his head reeled. He strained his ears and listened for the approaching water. The water approached him from all sides.

Someone tugged his collar. Ignacio turned his head and met the Retriever's muzzle. The dog slid backward and pulled him by the collar. He paddled with his hands and helped the dog pull him. The water's level fell. His hands scraped pebbles and felt firm ground. He drew his feet together, stood up on the packed sand, and then followed the Retriever along the shore.

He left the ocean; the ocean didn't leave him. Water covered the beach and hid its sand. The fog didn't let him see the cliffs. The Retriever cut through the veil and found the trail's mouth. He followed the dog up the trail. The fog's arm followed him up the slope.

They reached the cliff's top.

The Retriever stood beside him and watched the void below.

The ocean rumbled and roared under the fog's shroud. The sun defied the mist, rose above its cover, and sent its rays skimming, skipping, and skittering off the cliffs. Their soft warmth melted the frigid rocks' frost. The melt-water dripped in gold streams and fell into the abyss. The beacon rotated on the lighthouse and beckoned the souls lost in the sea's wilderness.

Ignaçio glanced at the Retriever. The dog smelled something he couldn't.

These animals that we see as lower than us stand higher in the evolution's hierarchy; we descend from them. Darwin proved this descent. Forget science. If we just trust our eyes and watch a human embryo grow in the womb, we'll see it pass through older life forms. We will see ourselves as fish, frogs, birds, and other mammals, before shaping into human beings.

These animals are our ancestors. They remain the starting point of our life's journey. We're birthed with their faculties. Our growth process and lifestyle then rob those faculties. Society excludes those faculties in calculating our intelligence. Perils reveal their value. We reexamine our ancestors, reevaluate their faculties, and raise them higher than us.

A storm-head was building above the ocean. Cloud masses stacked in rows and loomed over the darkening void. The stacks cracked. Three rays beamed through, sliced the mist's veil, and lighted the cliffs' pines. The clouds' top shaped into an anvil. A cold draft left its base, slid over the fog's shroud, and flattened the pines.

Ignaçio moved from the cliff and signaled the Retriever to follow.

The dog trailed him along the cliff-side road. The wind blew in the void and slapped the water at the cliffs' feet. The storm clouds separated and descended. The fog rose among them, wrapped the sun, and spun it like a colored globe. The wind swayed the cliff's grass, reeds, and brushes, swiped its pebbles, stones, and sand, and then swept them off into the abyss.

Ignaçio reached his car, opened the back door, and turned for the Retriever.

He didn't see the dog.

52

Dawn peeked into her home office and lighted its walls. Nuria lifted her head from the paper stacks, rubbed her burning eyes, and stepped onto the balcony.

The rising sun striated the sky's topaz-blue with violet and sprayed the fleeting fluffs with amber. The full moon resisted the sun, defended its place, and courted the cedars, cypresses, and junipers. Their foliage sifted the moonbeams and threw patterns on the withering pasture. The oaks, poplars, and beeches welcomed the sun and projected their skeletal shadows on the moon's artwork. Frozen dewdrops sparkled on the frost's silver mesh and shifted their colors.

The sun won the battle. The ground stayed darker than the sky. The orchids, belles de nuit, and jasmines stirred below the balcony, discarded their slumber, and dispatched their scents. A fox yowled, a hawk squealed. An owl hooted and replied both. Crickets screeched, cicadas rasped, frogs croaked. A motherless calf cried in the shed. Santos left his kennel and calmed the orphan. Nuria braced her arms, closed the sliding glass door, and returned to her desk.

Mother called her from the corridor. Nuria asked her to enter.

"Your lights stayed on last night," Mother said. "You didn't go to bed?"

"I will tonight."

"When does your session start?"

"At eight."

"Couldn't it wait till January?"

"Mother," Nuria said. "The San Silvestre corrida is in three days."

"Will this debate stop that corrida?"

"If the deputies vote for the law."

"Will they?"

"Yes."

"Ignaçio didn't return my call," Mother said. "Did you hear from him?"

"You think Nacho calls me?"

"He calls Charo."

"I know."

"Charo regrets telling him about Victor. She thinks the bull's death pushed him over the edge, and he accepted to fight at the San Silvestre corrida. Ignaçio loved Victor. We should have warned Charo and asked her to hold back the bull's death from him."

"What is Charo doing about Santos?"

"She'll remove the dog's tumor."

"When?"

"Tomorrow morning."

"Tell Nacho."

"Why?"

"He informed Charo about the tumor."

"That won't change his mind for the corrida."

"Mother, please!" Nuria said. "You can see I'm busy."

"Ignaçio is more important than your debate."

"If the law passes, he won't fight."

"I hope."

"Now let me do my work."

"I'll ask Charo to call Ignaçio after she operates on the dog."

"Make sure she does."

"She will," Mother said. "Now come down for breakfast."

"Promise me something."

"I won't call anyone else without telling you."

"Not even Rafaela?"

"Not even Angel."

"Thank you."

Nuria saw Mother's intent; she was dealing with this impasse in her own way.

Frustration has its source in expectation: what we expect from ourselves, what we expect from others, what we expect from the system. When interests clash, words become landmines; they explode. "Words" and "sword" carry the same letters. Yet words do more damage than a sword. Prosecution and defense use the same words and serve their causes. When trust aligns interests, silence speaks; words become redundant. Those who know this have an edge.

What she faced this morning was real. If she added the negative to it, she would become cynical. That would be her defeat. She needed to recognize human nature, acknowledge it, not complain or ruminate about it. She needed to use her knowledge of humans, her insights into their nature, to serve her objective for the bulls and remove corrida from her region. She saw Miguel do this before. Now she had to do the same, but without him. She could do this.

Nuria showered, dressed, and prayed. She packed her papers, took her satchel, and went downstairs. Father returned from the barn and switched on the television. The news channel replayed the opening ceremony of the city's second millennial anniversary.

A sixteenth-century caravel, flanked by a clipper and a frigate, sailed from the port. The mayor stood on the crow's nest, lectured diplomats from former Spanish colonies, and offered them conquistador vases. They refused. The camera shifted to the city.

A police van, patrolling the streets, hosted a rooftop banner:

Corrida is neither our tradition nor our culture.

Corrida came from Rome and seized San Taurino for dollars.

Oust corrida and save our honor.

Three firefighters held up a placard:

A nation's soul shows in its treatment of animals.

Civil guards wore a slogan on their uniform:

Humans have universal rights.

Why not animals?

The newscaster listed the threats the city had received for the San Silvestre corrida. The forces of order had refused to intervene. The mayor had declared emergency and asked for the military. Nuria pushed aside her breakfast and turned off the television. She sent a message to Ishmael, kissed her parents, and left with her car.

She stopped at the farm's gate and raised the barrier. The crabgrass patch, where Ignaçio stood and examined Santos the other night, lay flat. Nacho had grown into a man and stayed humane. Corrida balanced this choreographer, removed his frailty, vulnerability, melodrama. Experience took his innocence and forged a masculine presence. She preferred him this way. He was now closer to a bull than the boy she knew.

A beautiful bull. A humane animal. A handsome man.

She loosened her hair, reentered her car, and drove toward the city center.

This San Silvestre corrida wouldn't take place. The deputies would pass the law today. The initiative's poll had revealed the citizens' wish. They even wanted to abolish matadors' prizes. Her colleagues could now vote without fear. The enterprise of Margarita and Soledad showed exporting *lidia* bull's meat was more profitable

472

than importing taurine tourists. The region bristled for bringing production home than shipping bullfights. The country wanted Willem out. Judge Emilio kept him for his years in Spain's prison. By the day's end, corrida would leave San Taurino's arena. Ignaçio wouldn't fight this bull called Death's Advocate.

She reached Plaza de Toreros, parked her car, and marched into the legislature. She would stay calm and shorten her pitch for the deputies. She entered her office, shut the door, and sat with her eyes closed. Miguel rose, fought Ignaçio, and shamed her. She was far from perfect.

No living being is perfect.

A perfect vision is imperfect. A perfect quest is imperfect. A perfect act is imperfect.

Life needs flow, flow needs inequity, and inequity needs imperfection. Perfection levels inequity, stops flow, and kills life.

Progress doesn't seek perfection.

Progress moves life, changes humans' ways, and changes humans. What was valid in one epoch becomes invalid in another. What is valid now will become invalid someday. Humans err. Errors teach humans. The search for the absolute is absurd.

She prayed for Ignaçio, gathered her papers, and left for the debate.

The deputies filed into the debate hall and took their seats. Nuria rose, greeted them, thanked them for their diligence, patience, and support, and then started her pitch.

"A few months ago, we assembled here to vote on corrida's fate. Today, we forget corrida and vote on a legal issue: *bloodshed in full public view*. We ignore who this blood comes from and for what

473

reason. On this point, our citizens' collective stance lies in front of us.

"Do we retain public bloodshed as legal: *yes* or *no*?"

She closed her speech and opened the debate.

53

The house-on-wheels backed up and then stopped at the enclosure's gate.

Mors left the trough and searched for Zeus. The horse drank from the pond and worried the geese. The Mistress of Bulls descended from the vehicle's front. She wore a coat of the sun's color. She came to the vehicle's back and opened its door. Zeus stopped drinking and raised his head. She called them, came to their corral, and held its gate open.

Mors understood. He left the corral and climbed into the vehicle. He moved toward its front, made room for Zeus, and waited.

The horse didn't come.

There was no fodder or water in this vehicle. Its door panels didn't open at the top. Dusk peeked through its skylights and lighted its metal walls. The Mistress of Bulls reached Zeus and spoke in his ear. The horse shook his head and whinnied. She grabbed Zeus's muzzle, put on his bridle, and led him by the reins to the vehicle.

The horse climbed into the vehicle and stood at its back door. The Mistress of Bulls shut the door and walked to the vehicle's front.

The engine hummed. The vehicle jerked, jumped forward, and then rolled.

Mors stared at Zeus; the horse didn't meet his eyes. The vehicle lumbered uphill and sped downhill. It moved on smooth ground and bumped on coarse terrain. It cruised, slowed, and then stopped. A gate squeaked and opened. The vehicle rolled forward; the gate closed.

Since they came here, the sun had traveled the sky four times. They hadn't left this place or seen other bipeds, bulls, or horses.

Zeus's gestures didn't hint where The Mistress of Bulls was taking them now. The horse's forced poise didn't hide his anxiety. Mors moved forward, nudged Zeus, and tried to reassure him. The horse ignored and stood still.

The floor leaned forward. The vehicle slowed and rolled downhill. Bipeds cried, trumpets bellowed, and horns blew on both sides. Sharp rays entered the room and brightened its walls. Mors heard Zeus breathe and then saw the foam on the horse's coat. The closed air didn't heat them enough to sweat. Zeus didn't like what was happening around. The silent horse, refusing help, was boiling inside. Mors retained his poise and remained by his friend.

The sun deserted the skylights. The room darkened. More cries rose. The vehicle reached the slope's bottom, ran faster, and defied the noise.

The vehicle slowed. The cries grew louder and came closer. Lights flashed and flung their colors. Glowing disks skimmed the floor. Lightning hissed, cracked, and boomed. Explosions shook the vehicle. Bipeds shouted and thumped the walls. Zeus reared up, neighed, and struck back. The Mistress of Bulls spoke from the front. Her words didn't calm the horse.

The vehicle stopped. A gate creaked and scraped gravel. One biped spoke to The Mistress of Bulls. She gave him stern orders. The biped hurried and closed the gate. The noises muted and stopped. The vehicle rolled. Gravel crunched underneath. They turned right, turned left, and then halted. The Mistress of Bulls got out, came to the back, and opened the door.

Zeus refused to descend. She tugged his reins and took him to a corral.

Four bipeds came for Mors. He swayed his horns; they jumped

out. The Mistress of Bulls turned and shouted to them. She calmed Zeus, brushed him, and returned to the vehicle.

She climbed in and spoke to Mors. He descended and followed her.

They walked by the horse's corral, crossed the graveled yard, and reached a wooden door. Zeus whined and snorted. Mors turned. The horse shook his mane, reared up, and struck the corral's fence. The Mistress of Bulls ignored Zeus. Mors bellowed and reassured the horse.

The wooden door opened into a lighted pen. The Mistress of Bulls led him inside. The pen contained fodder and water. She rubbed his flanks and kissed his muzzle. Mors stood still and watched her face. Her cheeks rose, her eyes beamed, her crown's gems sparkled. She spoke in his ear, left the pen, and closed its door. Mors listened. He heard only the whinnying horse.

The pen's light went out.

54

Ignaçio muted the television and listened to Charo's message: "I removed Santos's tumor. The operation went well. The dog is doing fine." He replayed her video, watched Santos's posture and gestures and expressions, and knew the poised dog wasn't doing fine.

Animals know when their time ends. They become composed and calm, contained and content, detached and distant. They don't cling to life or rush to die. They discard their ties and live their lives. Old Santos knew his time had come to go. The dog's poise showed it.

The vet, too, must have seen this truth.

Charo took Santos from someone who buried his mother and siblings alive. The dog had seen humans' both sides. The dog had lived life's worst and best. What he was leaving behind wasn't new. His poised gait proved this. Santos had done his share of work on both farms. He could now leave the two behind and go in peace. He had no regrets. He didn't fear death.

There's equality at birth and death. Travel before birth and after death is the same for all living beings—all species, all races, all classes. It's on life's bridge that the journey differs. For some, it brings more pleasure than pressure, more compassion than compression, more humility than hostility; for others, the reverse. At the end, you leave both and return home.

You come naked, you go naked. You take only your souvenirs with you.

Ignaçio switched off the phone and put it aside. He prayed for the dog, left the table, and stood on his balcony. Fireworks hissed up, bloomed, and burst. Sparks spread, cracked, and descended. The bull must have reached the arena. Its acoustics, boosted for tonight, magnified the galleries' applause and drowned the court's cries. Ignaçio returned to the den and dressed in his somber suit. He avoided the mirror, packed his cape and sword, and waited for the call.

He checked his blood pressure: it was normal. He was ready to leave.

The intercom buzzed. The chauffeur announced the car was waiting at his building's door. Ignaçio lifted his bag, took the sealed envelope, and went downstairs. Security agents escorted him to a sedan; its windows were tinted to protect him tonight from the public. Ignaçio left his bag in the car's trunk, regarded Iglesia Sacrata di Ser Vivo, and marched across the church's square toward the mailbox. Citizens stopped to watch. The agents followed him close.

A Japanese woman halted and frowned. Ignaçio bowed to Naomi, reached the mailbox, and posted the envelope. Nuria should get these official documents before his flat's signature. He closed his eyes, prayed for her and her family, and then returned to the sedan.

The car moved. His flat disappeared.

The vehicle turned around the church, rolled by the paling Christmas crib on its patio, and left the square. The spruce, its light garlands and bobbles, the illuminated dwarfs and the animals retreated in the rearview mirror, shrank into pulsating dots, and then vanished.

The church left his view. Its square stayed behind. The sedan inched through the New Year Eve traffic and reached the jammed artery. His eyes, now freer and clearer, scanned quicker and ranged wider. On the side streets, he noticed jewels he had so far ignored. They boosted San Taurino's beauty and contrasted its patrolling military.

479

The heightened security didn't frighten this city. Her quarters, robed in glittering lights, paraded by and greeted him. White draped Plaza de Toreros. Blue covered the City Hall; red, the tribunal; yellow, the legislature. Avenida de Corrida wore twinkling garlands. Their lights' colors sharpened toward the arena. Beyond the city's terrace, the luminous fort raised torches on its four turrets. Their flames shot blazing arcs at the sky and shed burning droplets on the olives, oranges, and chestnuts. The purple sun sank into the ocean and turned the indigo sky violet.

The sedan skirted the arena's court and rolled toward the toreros' entry. The patrolling military cleared the vehicle's path and restrained the bristling protestors. Under the Roman soldier's statue, flanked by Theresa and Ishmael, Xavier raised the placard of Miguel.

Torture reverses progress.
I belong to no nation, no religion, no affiliation; I stand as a human
for our race.
Stop going to corrida.
Kill me and spare this bull.

Ignaçio shivered. He raised the window, closed his eyes, and prayed for Miguel.

Armed bailiffs received him at the toreros' gate. The floodlights didn't rush here and rob his final moments. Ignaçio lifted his bag, followed the bailiffs, and reached the dressing zone. From the stoop's crack, a winter marigold lifted its head and beamed at him. The flower knew the concrete would shorten its life; yet it greeted the passersby and smiled at them.

Ignaçio thanked the bailiffs, shook their hands, and entered a dressing room.

55

The debate stalled. Nuria lifted her eyes from the phone and surveyed the assembly hall. The deputies were frowning at their phones. Nobody listened to the speaker. Everybody watched the corrida's opening ceremony. The San Silvestre bullfight drew them more than this debate.

Like her, her colleagues were exhausted. The debate, supposed to finish in one day, had dragged for three, robbed their sleep, left them dazed. Hallucination reigned. Nobody spoke real, thought real, or acted real. She had lost track of the amendments submitted, withdrawn, redrafted, and resubmitted. These deputies had lost their heads. Like her, they now worried more for this corrida's fate than their debate on public bloodshed. The legislative initiative hung in limbo. At this stage, the deputies could vote either way; they wouldn't even know.

Nuria quit restoring order and returned to her phone.

Tourists filled the floodlit arena. Willem, despite his setbacks, had brought his clients, his cortege, and their cohorts. No Spanish elites, aficionados, or dignitaries sat on the galleries or in the royal seats. This corrida's national boycott had made international news. Willem stood at his usual place and leaned against the ring's barrier, facing Angel, Pedro, and Mayor José under the presidential box. Rafaela, wearing a suit of light and a diamond tiara, sat still in the president's seat. She ignored Willem's glare and watched the bullpen.

The spectators stirred and turned toward the gallery above the ticket booths.

A woman, dressed in a dove-white robe, descended the gallery's stairs, holding a banner above her head.

The camera shifted to the staircase and zoomed onto the descending woman's banner.

You come from civilized nations.
Don't promote in San Taurino what you won't permit in your city.
Corrida kills bulls and humans.
Please leave this arena and return home.

Nuria recognized her mother.

Mother ignored the spectators' protests, raised the banner higher, and entered the bullring by the matador's screen. No one stopped her. She held her head erect and carried the banner along the ring's barrier. The galleries silenced. Willem hollered at her; Rafaela shut him up.

Mother finished her tour and left the ring. The stunned arena sat silent and waited for the church's bell, the midnight toll that would start this corrida. Nuria turned off her phone and set it aside; she didn't want to see what would follow. She didn't want to hear more.

Rafaela, by wearing her matador's suit of light tonight, had once more violated bullfight's rules. And this wouldn't be her last violation. These taurine tourists would soon discover her power. This woman, reserved and resolved, loved to hold secrets and had steam for them. She took her privileges for granted. She forgot that life, too, could surprise her someday.

56

Bells peeled from Iglesia Sacrata di Ser Vivo. Drums rolled and trumpets blew; citizens cried and celebrated New Year. The tolls sharpened, quickened, and merged into a continuous ring. They congratulated the rejoicing city on completing its two thousand years. Ignaçio finished his prayer, lifted his cape and sword, and left the dressing room.

He walked into a silent arena. No one stirred on the filled galleries. The floodlights burned the virgin sand and watered his eyes. He ignored the relentless glare, marched around the ring, and stopped in front of the president's box. The arena held its breath and watched his moves.

This arena is more than a taurine showcase; more than a monument with its cloisters and columns, museums and shops, arches and floors, and vaults; more than an amphitheater with its galleries, stairs and seats, barrier and ring, and sand; more than an architectural feat with its inert bricks, cement, and iron. This arena has its vision. It's a creature of light that sees, whose dark depth human eyes can't fathom. This place hears. Its acoustics speaks. Its sand feels. Its barrier, rows, and doors understand. This creature soaks all that and acts by its own will. In its thrill and fear, in its daydream and nightmare, in its pleasure and pain, the arena's magnificent architecture fuses with its morbid work and becomes one. The fused shadow projects onto the viewer's soul and impresses upon it an indelible melancholy. This place transmutes you.

The arena serves as the Devil's accomplice: it violates civility, kills dignity, and devours humanity. The arena is a torture theater created by art and culture; killer machinery robed by architects,

483

masons, and blacksmiths; a living specter of unparallel beauty, lust, and thirst that draws its inexhaustible energy and vitality from all the blood it drinks.

He was standing on this arena's stage for the final time in his life, for his final act. Ignaçio removed his *montero*, bowed to Rafaela, and sought her permission to toast.

She granted.

He turned toward the pen and dedicated the corrida to the bull. He turned toward Rafaela and dedicated the bull to her. He turned toward Angel and dedicated himself to his mentor. The arena applauded his dedications. He placed the montero over his chest, recited his prayer, and then tossed the broad-brimmed hat toward the ring's center. The hat glided, turned upside down, and landed on its crown.

The galleries silenced. Sand shimmered around the still hat. The ring waited for its single *tercio*: the *suerte de muerte* that held the luck of today's death. The hat's landing position told him the opening move he should use. The sandman entered the ring, lifted the hat, and placed it behind the matador's screen. The spectators murmured and shifted in their seats.

Rafaela threw the pen's key. The bailiff caught the key and took it to the pen-keeper.

Ignaçio walked toward the pen, kneeled at the ring's edge, and faced the pen's gate. He placed his sword on the sand. He opened his jacket's buttons and bared his chest. He raised the cape above his head, spread his arms and stretched its tissue, and thrust his chest out.

The galleries exploded.

He waited *a porta gayola* for the bull.

Mors heard the sounds from his pen. He knew what he would face when they released him.

Unlike last time, The Mistress of Bulls hadn't left this game to others; she was at the arena to make sure the bipeds would play fair. Her few words—poised, patient, potent—had calmed Zeus. The horse no longer snorted, neighed, or hit his hooves on the corral's rails.

Mors waited.

The fanfare stopped. Bells tolled. Cries left the city, entered the arena, and filled his pen. The floor shook. The bucket rocked. The trough rang. Mors ignored the din and drank again from the bucket. The water still didn't quench his thirst. He stopped drinking.

A male biped spoke. The voice sounded familiar. Mors lifted his muzzle and pricked up his ears. His heart thumped. This game could differ from the last. The voice didn't stay. Mors walked to the pen's door and sniffed its crack. The still air didn't bring this biped's odor.

Cries rose and fell in the arena. Footsteps approached the pen and stopped behind its door. A key entered the lock and turned. The door opened. The light dazzled. The uproar deafened. Mors lifted his head, regained his full height, and charged out of the pen.

The blare stopped. The glare cleared. The odor sharpened.

Mors braked and arrested his charge. Sand left his hooves, hit the kneeling biped, and sprayed the raised cape.

He knew this biped.

The flying sand stung Ignaçio's face, covered his head, and drenched his suit. He rose to his feet, shook off the sand, and scanned the still bull. The watching animal, solemn and somber, didn't come from the *lidia* breed; it came from another breed not meant for bullrings.

Applause swept the galleries. The acoustics grew the praise, lauded the bull's beauty, and confirmed the matador's bravery: his position had frightened this notorious bull. The majestic bull ignored the noise, stood tall, and observed him. It didn't lower its head and charge.

Ignaçio turned toward Rafaela: she was frowning at her bull.

Under her box, flanked by Pedro and Mayor José, Angel sat clueless. Across the ring, Willem recoiled from the barrier—his jaws stiff, his fists clenched—and glowered at Rafaela. She ignored his glare and kept her eyes on her bull. The bull ignored her and watched him.

Ignaçio lowered the cape and lifted the sword. The bull didn't flinch or move; it kept its eyes on him. Ignaçio stepped closer and checked the *divisa* on the bull's coat. The emblem confirmed this non-conforming bull, at least three and a half meters from its hooves to horns, had indeed come from Rafaela's ranch and never fought another human on foot.

The bull, too, measured him from his head to feet. The animal's dark eyes, sober and serious, didn't move.

His approach alerted the bull. The animal tossed its head and swayed its horns. Its dewlap waved. The bull held his gaze, lowered its head, and stepped forward. Ignaçio moved the cape and stretched it to his side. The animal ignored the cape, kept its eyes on him, and maintained its gait. It didn't look at the sword or hasten its steps. The animal knew where it was going.

He knew these bulls. This battle would be short; the luck of death, quick.

Ignaçio swung the cape and shouted to the bull. The animal ignored his cry, kept its poise, and slowed its gait. The spectators applauded his courage. But he knew the truth. This bull's horns dwarfed his sword: the duel sided with the animal. This bull knew its arms' power; its eyes' sheen confirmed its knowledge. It didn't rush. It knew the matador couldn't escape.

Ignaçio raised the cape and rotated it above his head. He spun on the spot, kneeled on one knee, and lowered the cape. The bull didn't change its fixed aim or hurry its poised steps. The viewers lost patience and pushed for change. Rafaela spoke up and requested silence. The bull came closer. Ignaçio threw the cape, performed a *desplante*, and opened his jacket wider.

The bull stopped, lowered its head, and raised its muzzle.

Ignaçio saw the scar on the bull's nose.

Mors knew this biped male, but it wasn't the same. His former playmate had changed. The short hair replaced the long; the hard eyes, the soft; the large muscles, the lean; the pungent odor, the pleasant. His former friend now resembled a bull, a biped bull not to befriend with.

His sword was new. His coat was new. His hooves were new. In this new look, his former mate resembled not bulls but bipeds that tortured and killed bulls. These bipeds didn't deserve his trust; they deserved his horn thrust. They shouldn't persist; they should perish.

Yet Mors couldn't attack someone kneeling before him and begging for his mercy. Such cowardice didn't fit bulls. Like him, this new biped might have been forced into this ring to fight for life. The mate he knew didn't know fear. Mors felt sorry for this scared biped.

Mors turned his head and surveyed the ring. This game was different. There were no horses. No other bipeds in the ring. A lance, leaning against the barrier, revived his sufferings. Its blade was longer. The sword seemed a fair arm, but the biped could use this lance.

487

The Mistress of Bulls sat in a box above three male bipeds. Her gaze, steady and sharp, told him this game would be fair; this time, she sat above others to make sure. Mors hesitated. Fear defies power. This frightened biped might not obey her orders and use that lance.

He stepped toward the biped and then halted. He couldn't charge someone who didn't hurt him. He stared at The Mistress of Bulls and sought her guidance. Her face hardened, her eyes sharpened. The galleries' bipeds stood and shouted. She gave orders and restored silence. The ring's biped listened to her and revered her order. In the end, they might have a fair game.

The biped rose, swayed the cape, and shouted at him. Mors approached the biped but couldn't lower his horns. He raised his head, kept his gait, and avoided his mistress's eyes. He still couldn't charge. He stopped, turned toward her, and pleaded; she didn't relent. He turned toward the biped and urged him to charge. The biped refused and deepened his dilemma.

He couldn't obey her order and charge his former mate. He owed loyalty to both; to please one, he couldn't hurt the other.

The Mistress of Bulls had saved him in one battle and restored him to health. His former mate had saved his life many times and provided care whenever he needed. This new biped wasn't his former mate; yet he couldn't overlook his old mate's acts, attack this new being, and please The Mistress of Bulls. Such infidelity didn't fit the brave bulls.

Mors slowed.

He, alone, didn't disobey her; Zeus, too, defied her at times. The horse knew when to disregard its owner and exercise its will. If Zeus were in this ring now and received her order to attack Mors, the horse would ignore her. If Mors now forgot his old mate's kindness and attacked this new biped, Zeus would condemn his betrayal and retract their friendship.

Mors slowed further and altered his strategy.

The biped changed position. It revolved the cape, turned on its heels, and challenged him. Mors didn't change his gait. The biped grew edgy. It sprang to its feet, leaped in the air, and performed a melodrama. The acts didn't fit it. The drama failed. Mors stayed out. The biped kneeled again, spread its coat, and thrust its chest. More now knew what to do. He stopped in front of the biped, lowered his head, and raised his muzzle. He trusted the biped's sense.

The biped froze. Its rolling eyes scanned his muzzle's tip. Its lips trembled. Its nostrils flared, its pupils dilated, its throat swallowed. Mors stood still and watched the biped.

This new biped wasn't cruel. It was humane; it could become his new mate.

Ignaçio rose to his feet and watched the bull's nose. The animal didn't react or move.

The scar on this bull's muzzle wasn't an illusion: it came from Jaime's harvester four years and nine months ago. The time passed had grown the muzzle but preserved the scar's form. This bull wasn't Mors; it was Victor.

Ignaçio retreated and scanned this twelve-hundred-and-seventy-six kilo bull. This animal wasn't a mirage; it was real. Its legs had doubled; its muscles, tripled. Its horns and hooves had grown and matched its weight. The dewlap had firmed and extended its folds. Experience had sharpened the bull's eyes but preserved its soul. This bull had recognized him right from the beginning. Its somber regard he took for cold aggression expressed the bull's sorrow.

This bull, not six-year old but six-year-and-eight-month old, was *his* Victor.

But this wasn't the old Victor that lifted both farms before leaving; this was a new Victor that survived another corrida and had returned for the San Silvestre. The past bull still lived in its present. Ignaçio turned and watched Rafaela. This corrida's proceedings didn't shock her. His neck pricked, his ears burned. This woman who saved Nuria had pitched him against his bull. Ignaçio rubbed his face and shook his head. She had set herself up for a big surprise.

Ignaçio ignored Rafaela's order and placed himself in Victor's perspective. The bull had recognized him, but it didn't trust him enough to come near. He understood. This bull wasn't the only animal to mistrust him; others also saw in him their killer. The Retriever had left him. Lorenza didn't trust him. He was a matador who lived by his title. The same held true for this bull: its new name made it the god of death. Your title decides your fate. While the old Victor slept inside Mors, this retrained bull saw the outside world from a killer's eyes. The animal, caught in its dilemma, didn't trust its new instincts; it stayed away to avoid killing him.

The reason for this bull's sorrow lay deeper. The animal wanted to approach. At the same time, the change it saw on its former mate raised its guard and held it back; it didn't want this change to provoke its acts. Four and a half years is a long time to grow. Close friends separate and go apart. Old actions mean new intentions and evoke different reactions. Like him, this bull too was giving new meanings to their old looks, gestures, and moves.

Yet change is life. You embrace life by adopting its changes.

He couldn't shift this bull back to the god of life it was once. But he could still give this animal a glimpse of its soul and show what it could become. The past isn't there to hold onto; it's there to draw lessons from and shape the future. They wanted each other but didn't dare. He would retrieve a memorable souvenir from their common past, bring it to the present, and adapt it to suit this moment. The doubts would leave. The trust would return. The bull would recover its bearings and do its part for their reconciliation. He still trusted this noble bull.

Abrupt moves don't build trust. To reassure this hesitating bull, he had to steady himself. Holding this morbid cape and this killer sword wouldn't help him regain his poise. He threw both to the ground. The bull flinched and tossed its head. He turned up his palms and showed his empty hands. The animal calmed but kept Mors's eyes. There was more work to do.

The spectators shuffled and shouted. The acoustics magnified their words and the noise. The rising agitation wouldn't help this situation. The moment had come to break this bull's resistance, to win or lose its confidence. He reckoned how Paloma broke him six weeks ago and restored him. If he wanted to break Mors and release Victor, this was his time to act.

Like Paloma, he would keep his act short, sharp, and loaded.

He stood erect. He raised his head, tucked his chin, and met the bull's gaze.

The animal mirrored his stance.

"Victor!" he hollered. "Let's dance."

The old order, from this new mate, stunned Victor. He resisted the call. His resistance didn't suit his hooves; they moved. He stopped. He stood still and watched this new mate. The sharp words boomed the arena, reflected from its bounds, and rang in his ears. The

491

galleries' bipeds shouted. Their cries grew louder, crushed his mate's order, and rattled his brain.

The cries died. The order lived. His mate's words shook his memory and woke souvenirs he had swept aside. They froze him, overpowered him, and started a change. Mors resisted it and failed. He accepted the change. The sonorous words also showed him something else.

His former playmate was now a different sort of biped.

He could take this new mate to his brothers and show them with pride: they would admire this biped bull. He should take this new mate to Zeus and reassure him that they would do all right in this ring. Zeus loved bulls; he would want to meet this new breed. Victor turned his head and watched The Mistress of Bulls; Mors raised its head within him.

He didn't want Mors, but Mors wanted him.

The new bull in him fought the old Mors. Victor stood aside and watched the two bulls clash. The fight grew violent, but it shed no blood. Mors broke and shattered. The two bulls merged into one. The forged bull took Victor's name. Mors faded away and left the ring.

The Mistress of Bulls called Mors; Victor ignored her call.

His new mate called him by his old name. Victor dropped his guard and went forward.

His new mate leaped, turned in the air, and did old passes. Victor reared up, mimicked the passes, and then added new moves. His mate took his moves and stretched them. Victor stood still and admired the stretches. His mate sprang, keeled head-over-heels, and vaulted over his horns. Victor turned around. He leaped over his mate and soared in the air. The mate turned and gaped at him. Victor flipped head-over-hooves, landed on four legs, and stood erect.

The galleries fell silent.

Victor stayed in place and waited for his mate's applause; he didn't get any.

His new feat had shocked his old mate.

57

Angel heard Rafaela fidget in the president's box. She called Mors; the bull didn't respond. She ordered Ignaçio; he ignored her. She had compressed this corrida into a single *tercio*, used a non-*lidia* bull, and allowed the matador to fight in a grey suit without lancers and pickers. She didn't fool the two fighters. They knew each other. They defied her rules and refused to fight. She who surprised others was surprised by both. She should have known.

He was wrong. She wasn't surprised; she was acting by her plan.

The thwarted *rejoneadora* had anticipated this corrida's turns. She would now remove Ignaçio, ride her horse, and finish this fight. That's why she wore her gold suit. That's why the lance stood against the ring's rails. That's why Zeus waited in the corral. This symbolic corrida would serve her choice. Tonight, her both men were present in this ring. Instead of choosing one and hurting the other, she would sacrifice herself before them.

This woman loved to hold secrets. He understood why she had hidden this bull from him. Mors was Death's forerunner. She knew that her seventeen-year absence from bullrings had rusted her fighting skills. She would leave her life's dilemma today from her bull's horns.

He wouldn't let her. She had taken him for another pawn on her chessboard and ignored his independent will.

This time, he would surprise her.

58

Ignaçio froze in place and watched this new Victor. He couldn't believe what his eyes had just witnessed from this bull. In his twenty-seven-year life on Earth, he had seen animals perform miracles but never of this order. His stark invitation had broken Victor's barrier. The bull, too, knew this fact and saw his own feat as natural. His head-over-hooves had silenced the viewers and stopped the dance. The bull had taken that silence for applause; he now wanted more.

Ignaçio started a *buleriá*. Victor bellowed and matched his moves. The acoustics stretched the deafening roar, shook the arena's structure, and charged its confined air.

The spectators rose and protested. They had come to see corrida, not choreography; they wanted blood. Willem yelled: he wanted his clients' wish fulfilled. Rafaela rose and tried to restore order; nobody listened to her. The chaos grew out of control. Angel entered the ring and picked up the sword. Ignaçio stopped dancing and signaled Victor to move back.

"Leave," Angel said. "Right now."

"I'm the matador."

"You're not."

"You'll fight this bull?"

"Yes."

"Angel," Ignaçio said. "You haven't fought a bull in twenty-three years."

"Get out."

"Victor will kill you in less than a minute."

"I'll kill him before."

"No, you won't."

495

Angel went past him. Ignaçio turned and grabbed his mentor's sword-holding arm. Angel wrenched off his wrist and punched him on the chest. The blow stunned Ignaçio and hurled him onto the sand. The spectators applauded. Willem entered the ring and urged them to fight. Rafaela ordered Angel and Willem to leave; they ignored her.

Angel pointed the sword and ran toward Victor. The bull lowered his head and pointed his horns at Angel. Ignaçio rose to his feet, raced across the ring, and leaped between his mentor and Victor. Angel swung the sword and warned him. Ignaçio ignored the warning and shoved his mentor back. Angel thrust the sword at him. Ignaçio stepped aside and escaped the thrust. The returning blade caught his suit, tore its fabric, and slashed his elbow.

Blood squirted from the cut. The shearing pain ruined Ignaçio's poise and drained his patience. He lowered his head and charged like a bull. He hit Angel on the chest and flung him to the ground. Angel retained his grip on the sword's hilt. Ignaçio jumped on his mentor, held him down, and pinned his sword-holding hand.

Angel released the sword and thrashed Ignaçio with his fists. The spectators exploded. They were getting more for their money. The fight grew. Both fighters ignored Rafaela's orders and fought under thundering applause. The battle raged. The sand churned and flew from the ring. Angel had strength; Ignaçio, agility. In the end, agility vanquished strength. Ignaçio won. He rose from the sand, lifted the sword, and threw it over the ring's barrier.

He turned his back to Angel and walked toward Victor.

Victor charged at him.

When two equal bulls clash, other bulls stay out. Victor respected this rule, stepped aside, and watched the two equal bipeds fight.

He marveled at this new bull in his old playmate. He would have loved to continue their dance, but he accepted this interruption. He was learning fresh tricks from this new mate; he could use them later in their games. The other biped was larger and stronger, but his mate had speed and skills. He wasn't surprised to see his mate gain the upper hand and win the battle.

His mate rose from the sand and pardoned the fallen opponent, a mistake he would never make. You spare a vanquished enemy; it returns and gets you. Past encounters had taught him this lesson and gifted him this wisdom. His mate, lacking experience, had trusted this enemy. The mate then turned his back to his adversary and committed an error larger than pardoning.

The pardoned rose and glowered at the pardoner. The trusting mate couldn't see this. The vanquished grabbed the lance, rushed the vanquisher from behind, and committed treachery. Such cowardice didn't fit the bull's code. This vanquished enemy needed to vanish.

Victor lowered his horns and charged at the coward.

Ignaçio faced the charging bull.

Victor leaped past him, slammed into Angel, and crushed him against the wooden barrier. The lance flew from his mentor's hands and plunged into Willem's chest. The impact cracked his breastbone, hurled him backward, and flung him onto the sand. Rafaela jumped from her box and vaulted over the ring's barrier. She ran to Willem, wrenched the lance off his chest, and charged at Victor. Ignaçio leaped between them, spread his arms, and blocked her path.

"You can't," Ignaçio said. "The president doesn't fight the bull."

"I know the rules."

"Then pardon this bull."

497

"He slaughtered two humans."

"They broke rules."

"I'll kill this bull."

"Only the matador kills the bull."

Ignaçio quoted the rules. In the arena, a bull has its rights. By ignoring her orders and by entering the ring, both Angel and Willem broke bullfight's rules and gave Victor the right to kill. She couldn't punish the bull for using its rights. She had her right not to pardon Victor. She could restore the ring's order and resume the corrida. He and Victor would obey her.

"No," Rafaela said. "This corrida is finished."

"Will you spare Victor?"

"Take him "

"Pardon?"

"He's your prize."

"I'll buy him."

"Remove your Victor from my sight."

She threw the lance and ran to Angel. She kneeled at his side and bent over him.

59

Ignaçio returned to the dressing room. He took out his cell phone and called Nuria's parents.

They didn't answer.

He looked up Jaime and Uncle Manu. He noticed the time after midnight and set aside his phone. They shouldn't leave their beds at this hour to solve this new problem; he would solve it. Society imposes its notions on you. They breed illusions and dig pits for your elimination. You break those illusions and discover life's truths. Only your own actions accomplish both. The acts hurt but they illuminate. Failure teaches more than success. He wasn't going back.

His phone rang. He checked the caller and picked up his phone.

"You called for Victor?" Paula said. "Jorge left with his van."

"Who told you?"

"Santos."

"Pardon?"

"The dog was watching the corrida with us."

"No way!" Ignaçio said. "Santos recognized Victor on television?"

"Faster than you did in the ring."

"Tell Nuria."

"I did."

"Put Victor on my farm."

"Look after your arm."

Paula hung up. Ignaçio stood on the spot and watched his phone's screen.

His arm wound stung. The falling adrenaline clotted the blood and revived the pain. He couldn't go to the hospital now and have the wound stitched. Jorge, alone, could never load this new bull into his van. He found a first-aid kit. He disinfected the wound and wrapped it. He ignored the pain, left the dressing room, and returned to the arena.

The nebula had dispersed from the ring. Willem lay on blood-soaked sand; the patch had stopped growing. Rafaela held Angel and spoke in his ear. The spectators left their seats and ran from the galleries. Pedro and Mayor José stood with the bullring's employees.

Rafaela lifted her head and called him; Ignaçio went.

Angel, still alive, struggled to breathe. The gored mentor strained his lips, apologized, and regretted their scuffle. Blood spurted from his mouth and nose, dripped down his cheeks and throat, and drenched Rafaela's arms. Angel still didn't writhe in pain or fall into agony's grip. Twenty-four years ago, this elite matador was hit by another bull and left the arenas. Today, he saw his gore as his exit of honor. Ignaçio kneeled beside Angel. He reassured his mentor he would survive this injury too and return to arenas. His words didn't sound right.

The paramedics came with the police. Ignaçio stood up and moved aside. The rescue team lifted Angel onto their stretcher and carried him away from the ring. Rafaela watched Angel leave. Tears welled in her eyes and rolled down her cheeks. She didn't utter a word.

The paramedics returned for him; Ignaçio refused to go.

Rafaela rose to her feet. The police asked her to come with them. She didn't resist. Pedro stepped forward and defended his wife. Rafaela stopped him. She told her husband she might have killed Willem by pulling the lance off his chest; the police had their rights to take her for justice. She apologized for ruining his image and offered

500

her wrists to the police. Silent Pedro squeezed his lips, lowered his eyes, and turned his face aside.

The officers didn't cuff Rafaela. They escorted her out of the ring.

Pedro and Mayor José followed.

60

The ambulance rolled. The forward move propelled Angel backward in time.

He saw Rafaela enter his home and offer him money. He saw her leave his home and lure Ignaçio to the San Silvestre bullfight. He saw her risk her life for Nuria and save her from the racketeers. He saw her resist Willem, refuse his baits, and defend the taurine tradition.

He saw her guide him when he lost his bearings. He saw her become their association's president yet respect his decisions. He saw her marry yet keep their love alive. He saw her rise as a matador. He saw her accreditation ceremony and her tears of gratitude for his sponsoring. He saw her push Pedro to recruit him after that accident threw him off bullrings.

He saw her sitting at the front row on the day of that crippling accident. He saw her jump the barrier and rush into the ring when that other bull broke his back from behind. He saw her standing behind those ranches' fences where he went for his off-season trainings.

He saw the first time his path crossed hers. She was barely…

He couldn't remember. He couldn't go back further. His memory was failing.

He returned to the present. His present didn't please him. He looked into the future. His future looked bleak. He had lived his life; he should now leave.

Despite her blues and cravings, Rafaela was a majestic woman: magnanimous at her heart; magnificent in her head; memorable in her reliable, resilient, robust being. And rewarding. He was a difficult man to deal with. She had tolerance, patience, and forbearance for him. If he had to start again and choose a woman, he would go for her and want her the same way.

He was leaving.

What remained of him in her would continue their legacy.

61

The pen-keeper called him: Jorge had arrived with his van.

Ignaçio took the key, unlocked the pen, and opened the door. Victor refused to come out. The bull stood at the back and stared at him. Victor's gaze, dark and steady, told him the bull had taken this lockup as punishment and reverted to Mors. Events have their own will. They never follow your plan. He couldn't force this bull now to go with Jorge.

A horse neighed. Victor perked his ears, struck his hooves, and roared.

Ignaçio understood. He moved from the door and waited outside. The horse and the bull called each other. After a few rounds, Victor emerged from the pen, marched on the gravel, and reached the corral. An Egyptian stallion met the bull at the corral's fence.

Ignaçio recognized Zeus: the horse was the bull's new friend.

He saw his error. Goring Angel might have revived Victor's killer instincts, but the bull hadn't regressed to Mors. The bull had retained his regained identity, remained Victor, and wanted to say goodbye to this horse. Zeus, too, was bidding farewell to his friend. Like him, the horse also knew that Victor suited this bull better than Mors.

Ignaçio left the two animals alone. Victor finished with Zeus, walked to Jorge's van, and climbed in. Ignaçio followed. Jorge pulled him back, pointed to his bleeding arm, and urged him to go the hospital. Ignaçio heard Jorge's words and saw the bull needed to be alone. He waited until the van left, went to the dressing zone, and fetched his bag.

He stopped on the stairs. The marigold, peeking from the crack, didn't smile. He saw he was still wearing his somber suit and holding his cape and sword. He returned to the cabin, threw his bullfighting gears, and changed into plain clothes. They suited him better.

His heart lightened. His head cleared. He left the cabin and thanked the flower.

The hour passed four in the morning. If he hurried now, he could shower, get his wound stitched, and reach his farm before dawn. Victor would need his help to regain footing among this new herd: neither the bull nor the cows were the same. He also needed time alone before he could help this bull. The hospital, at this hour, might give him solitude and silence.

He left the arena and rushed for home.

He didn't go far. Theresa blocked his path. Xavier and their supporters stood behind her. She stepped forward and crouched before him.

"Ignaçio," Theresa said. "Get on my shoulders."

"Pardon?"

"Xavier, help him."

"Wait, wait." Ignaçio recoiled. "What are you doing?"

"I slapped you before," Theresa said. "I'll carry you now."

"Carry me?"

"Yes!"

"Where?"

"You'll see."

"For what?"

"Be patient."

The supporters lifted him, sat him on her shoulders, and held him in place.

They left.

62

Victor stood still inside the moving van. Until now, the turbulent rapid-fire events hadn't left room for anything but instincts. The van's movement, slow and steady, recalled those events, rearranged them, and renewed his perspective. Victor closed his eyes and reviewed them.

He didn't understand The Mistress of Bulls. He didn't see the reason for her rage. He had angered her by not obeying her orders, but that alone didn't justify her grabbing the lance and charging at him. She never went that far. She should have seen the biped he gored had broken more rules than he did. She should have seen this biped was going to kill his new mate. She should have seen his mate had released him from a role that didn't suit him.

Something must have pushed her that far. The Mistress of Bulls never behaved that way.

He reckoned how she bent over the gored biped, held him in her hands, and shed tears. This biped male must have impregnated her. Her rage for hurting her male didn't differ from Lorenza's when his ravishers hurt him. He didn't know the relation between The Mistress of Bulls and the gored biped; unlike Lorenza, she didn't stay by her male. If he had known their relation, he would have never killed her male. He would have only stopped that biped. Before attacking her male, he hadn't seen any of this; he could still trust his fidelity and fairness.

His guilt lifted. His heart lightened. He saw himself in a brighter light. He wasn't a killer by nature; he killed for valid reasons. The light dispersed his haze. His vision sharpened. His eyes saw clearer. He recoiled farther in time and watched the fight's sequence.

The Mistress of Bulls had pitched him against his mate. The mandate was clear for both. But one couldn't hurt the other. She should have seen their dilemma and relieved them from their impasse. She didn't; his mate did. If his mate hadn't switched their fight to dance, they could have killed each other. Only after her male fell, she saw her error, stopped the fight, and offered him to his mate. That act of hers was noble. But it was too late.

He preferred his mate to her. He preferred dancing to fighting. He was moving from Zeus, but the horse preferred this move. Before they parted, the horse confirmed the change suited him better, accepted their separation, and regained his poise. Zeus would now look after The Mistress of Bulls and defend her in need. He could count on the horse to do this job well. He missed Zeus. Yet he looked forward to a new life: a life without fighting bipeds. He wished Zeus well. He hoped the horse would make new friends and find peace without him.

The thoughts relieved Victor. He moved inside the van and sniffed its walls.

They smelled new; he didn't know this vehicle.

But the older biped driving this van wasn't new. Victor now knew where he was going. The vehicle slowed, turned, and stopped. The driver descended from the front, came to the back, and opened the door. Victor smelled the ocean and his old farm. He climbed down, turned around the vehicle, and went toward the farm's gate. The new gate smelled strange.

He stood back and watched this new farm. The walkway was new; the entry, paved. Tall reeds lined both sides. The metal house at the far end had changed. A dome sat next to it and emitted the odor of milk. The cows and calves smelled different. He raised his head,

507

stretched his neck, and tried to see the pasture. The reeds' stalks and their thick brushes didn't let him.

Like him, this farm had grown and changed beyond recognition. He wasn't sure this place wanted a bull like him. His new mate could have helped. Victor turned toward the driver. His former master had changed through the time passed. This new biped might help him now.

The driver opened the farm's gate. Victor went in and waited for him. The biped didn't follow. He closed the gate, climbed into the vehicle, and drove toward the other farm. The van disappeared from his eyes and ears. Victor waited. The biped didn't return to help him.

Victor missed Zeus and his brothers. He missed their ranch. He forced his hooves; they moved. He left the paved path, passed the reed stalks, and stood at the frosted pasture's edge. The herd wasn't on the grass. He noticed the new shed at the far end. The herd's smell came from there. His moves brought the cattle out. Lorenza wasn't among them.

He raised his head and scanned the new farm; he didn't see her anywhere. He lowered his muzzle, cleared his nostrils, and sniffed the air; her smell didn't come. His cow was no more on this farm. The place felt deserted; its spirit, desolate. He didn't want to live on this farm.

The heron squawked. Victor turned and saw the bird in its nest. The heron wasn't alone. Another adult and two cheeks flanked the bird. Victor left the pasture and climbed the mound above the pond. He stopped in front of the stone pile and checked the place his canine friend used to sit. The place hadn't been sat on since he left. The dog hadn't survived the fall.

Victor lowered his head and ears. He turned around and saw the two adult birds rise to their feet and watch him from their nest. They didn't trust his change. He left them alone and went downhill. Wings flapped and followed. Victor lifted his head and saw the heron chicks leave the nest. They crossed the pond, flew toward him, and sat on his back. Victor turned his head and checked their parents. Both adults watched their cheeks and then sat down.

Victor stood still and observed the two cheeks on his back.

They trusted him.

Zeus, too, would love this place by the pond. The horse, too, would love to have these two chicks on his back. Victor raised his muzzle and roared for the horse. Another bull roared on the other farm; it wasn't the bull he knew. A calf bleated on that farm and got in trouble. The calf's mother bellowed and defended it from her bull. This cow wasn't Lorenza's mother, the cow that gave him milk after his mother died and protected him from her bull.

That farm, too, had changed.

A dog barked on the other farm; it wasn't the same dog.

Victor panicked and pricked up his ears.

The dog barked again. This time, Victor recognized his canine friend. Like his call, the dog's bark had changed. His friend had recognized his call and was now coming to this farm. Victor descended from the mound and ran toward the dog's barks. The heron chicks flew off his back. Victor slowed and listened to the approaching dog's sounds. He didn't need to run so fast; his friend wasn't hurrying for him. The dog might not want him to stay on this farm.

Victor smelled an odor he knew and stopped in his tracks.

Lorenza was staring at him.

The cow had aged more than the time passed. Victor strained his neck and peered at her. He couldn't see her eyes; he couldn't feel her emotions. The sinking moon lengthened the shadows and hid her muzzle. He stepped closer; Lorenza swayed her horns. Victor halted and watched the cow. Other cows and calves surrounded Lorenza. She had no calf next to her.

The dog slipped under the farm's fence and limped toward him. The years had removed the glow from the dog's coat and dimmed its eyes. Victor didn't like the dog's new smell. He saw the white wrap on his canine friend's hips and noticed the fur withering around that zone.

The dog had aged more than Lorenza. But this dwindling state hadn't ruined his loyal friend's trust. The tired dog's warm gaze confirmed what Victor needed to know: this farm still belonged to him. His new friend was welcoming him here to redeem his old role.

Victor raised his head higher and roared louder. The other farm's bull roared. This time, Lorenza bellowed and silenced that bull. Victor approached the cow. The moving shadows shifted from her muzzle. He stepped closer and peered into her eyes. They filled with tear.

Victor reached Lorenza, stopped in front of her, and lowered his muzzle.

She lifted hers and touched his.

63

The uproar woke Nuria and broke her nightmare: Ignaçio and Victor vanished. She saw she wasn't sleeping on her bed; her cheek was resting on the debate hall's desk. She stayed low, tried to make some sense out of this nonsense she had dreamed, and failed. She gave up.

Compassion isn't life's law; aggression is. Life exists by eliminating others.

She lifted her head and surveyed the hall. The deputies, disengaged from their debate and engaged in the corrida, had forgotten her and lost themselves in their phones. Vapor rose from their gaping mouths, covered their faces, and hung above them. The digits of the hazed wall-clock flashed and moved from five thirty-five to five thirty-six in the morning.

Her colleagues' adrenaline peaked. Their staccato speech matched their wild gestures. The fragments like "double death" confirmed her nightmare. The bull and the matador must have killed each other. She didn't want to see Ignaçio lying dead from this Mors's horns.

Another outcry rose. This one didn't come from her colleagues; it came from outside. She turned on her phone and heard her mother's message. She didn't trust her ears. She went to Ishmael's website, opened the corrida's video, and watched it; she didn't believe her eyes. She replayed the clips, checked the double death, and saw Rafaela leaving with the police.

She set her phone aside, buried her face, and burst into tears.

Only the insecure seek perfect order. They don't know how to handle disorder. They don't trust themselves in the face of disorder. They trust no one. Life ignores their fear. Life breaks their order and sets hers. They accept the change, see its benefits, and forget the old order.

The cries outside grew louder and came closer. She looked up and saw the deputies leave. They didn't wait for her.

She suspended the debate and followed her colleagues.

64

Theresa carried him on her shoulders and left the arena's court. Her rank followed.

Ignaçio tried a few times to descend; her followers held him in place. He gave up.

From Avenida de Corrida, she didn't turn south toward his flat; she continued west down the avenue. A cloth ball flew at him from an apartment building. Ignaçio caught the red ball, saw the bra, and looked up. A woman smiled and ducked behind a twinkling window. Raw cheers descended from that building and drowned Theresa's raucous laughter. Her rank raised their arms, joined the rejoicing crowd, and asked the thrower to reappear. The woman didn't.

The avenue ahead glittered. The rank grew and advanced. Theresa didn't relent.

The throng reached Plaza de Toreros. The square's mob saw them advance and exploded in applause. Ignaçio urged Theresa to let him down; she didn't hear his words. Xavier moved ahead and cleared the path. Theresa passed through the gap, brought Ignaçio to the legislature building, and lowered him before its staircase. Her rank remained close behind them.

Ignaçio looked up the stairs: Nuria was standing at the top.

Theresa retreated with Xavier. Their supporters recoiled and stood in a semicircle. From the crowd's back, a solemn voice sang a *fandango*.

> *When ways don't meet and wishes don't mirror*
> *Remember contrast sparks life and complements love*
> *Rivers run separate courses and meet the same water*
> *When they resist opposing terrains and don't dry up*

Palms clapped, fingers snapped. Nuria descended the stairs. The *palo* grew somber; the claps and snaps, slower.

Solitude renews love
Silence heals hurts
Ignore your love's strife
And watch how life trusts

Nuria reached the bottom and stood on the last step. Her swollen lips stretched across her mouth. The cascading curls framed her haggard face, hardened its features, and sharpened her eyes. The portico's light shined her cheeks and darkened her irises.

Love again, with a stronger heart
Traverse Earth and reach the universe
Dance together and flare in the dark
Let your firm steps speak your verse

The song stopped. The beats silenced. Ignaçio watched Nuria but didn't dare. His heart thudded, his breath quickened. His sinews stretched, his muscles pumped. His eyes focused, his ears sharpened. His wound lost its pain. His head cleared. His arm regained its strength.

He stepped back from the staircase. He placed one foot behind the other, squared his hips, and held his neck erect. He lifted his bleeding arm and folded it across his chest. He raised the other arm above his head, tucked his chin, and met Nuria's eyes with a steadfast gaze.

She descended from the last stair. She faced him and mirrored his stance.

65

Willem's legatees sued San Taurino. Their lawyers bankrupted the city before Judge Emilio could apply bullfight's rules and prove Willem's fault.

The justice then pursued Willem's empire for money laundering, tax evasion, and illegal building permits. The battle dragged until Willem's successors gave up and sold his defunct business. Alejandro bought its ruins, furnished money and brains, revived the dead enterprise, and oriented it toward cultural tourism. He sought Nuria to lead it; she accepted his offer.

Corrida died in San Taurino. The region's legislators buried it.

The bankrupt city fired Mayor José. Its arena, a national monument, couldn't be sold. The interim mayor sought ways to reuse it and make money. Alejandro took it on a thousand-year lease and hired a Spanish architect to remodel it into an international convention center.

The works started. The citizens elected Alejandro as their new mayor. He hired the ousted mayor and employed him to manage the convention center's works. The old mayor embraced this new role with a frenzied vigor and set out to prove his valor. He employed former taurine workers, now without jobs, to remodel the arena and regained the city's sympathy.

Nuria didn't leave Rafaela in jail. The unintended manslaughter had earned her a three-year sentence. Nuria evoked Rafaela's pregnancy, removed her from prison, and placed her under house arrest. Rafaela moved into Angel's home and gave birth to Carlos.

Pedro divorced Rafaela but didn't desert her. He gave her his pastures and negotiated her semi-liberty for social service. With

Ignaçio and Charo, she engaged in restoring her fighting bulls, retraining them for reproduction, and employed former bullfighters in this work.

Her reproductive bulls traveled beyond Spain and spread their names. Other bull ranchers found this new business profitable and followed her. The *lidia* breed's bulls and cows earned their renown for meat and milk. The trade grew and rebuilt Spain's brand.

The new brand needed protection. With Nuria and Charo, Rafaela rewrote the old treaties for this new lidia breed. *The New Treaties* revised old norms and redacted new ones for these bulls and cows. Ranchers adopted these norms. Farmers of sustainable agriculture joined this endeavor. The enterprise led by Margarita and Soledad ratified their initiative, sold their meat and dairy, and added a business unit that exported their olives, oranges, and wines. This new business, led by Theresa and Xavier, employed the region's youths.

Production returned home. The economy stood on a solid ground.

The taurine academy reincarnated for choreography. Ignaçio renounced his matador's title and taught flamenco at this new academy with Paloma and Juan. He returned to the veterinary school, finished his degree, and took over the clinic from Charo.

His teaching and tours renewed San Taurino's image. The symbolic city honored him by making the lidia bull its symbol. Avenida de Corrida changed to Avenida de Toros de Lidia; Plaza de Toreros, to Plaza de Toros. The region's flag bore the remodeled bull's insignia.

Ignaçio rebuilt his farm. Victor revived his herd's quality. Ignaçio took Zeus from Rafaela and placed the horse on his farm. Like Rafaela, her son was a born rider. Starting with Santos, Carlos soon turned the bull and the horse into his devoted carriers. By the age of two, the boy was riding all three. Ignaçio cleared the mound above the pond and built a new home with the old stones. Nuria left her parents and moved in with him.

Ignaçio heard the car and went out. Carlota entered his farm and stopped in front of his home. Victor roared from the pasture's far end and came toward her vehicle. The bull knew.

Ignaçio asked Nuria to go and rest in their bedroom; she refused. Rafaela and Carlos led her out by the arms. They descended to the place by the pond where Nuria's parents waited. Ignaçio went to Charo and took her satchel.

"Nuria's showing," Charo said. "When is she expecting?"

"In six weeks."

"Is she taking a break from work?"

"Soon."

"And you?"

"No."

"Ignaçio," Charo said. "Keep your mind off Santos."

"I'm trying."

"Where's the dog?"

"In my office."

Santos saw her satchel and lifted his head: he was waiting. The inevitable didn't kill the dog's spirit or dim his eyes. Santos knew what he was leaving behind. The dog had seen the old stones and the new house built from them. For him, the promise was fulfilled; he didn't need to see more. He knew his tumor was incurable. He knew he had done his years on both farms; he had no regrets to go. Ignaçio filled Santos's bowl with water and held it before his muzzle. The dog drank from his hands and watched his watering eyes. Ignaçio bit his lip.

The dog finished drinking, shifted his regard, and surveyed the room. He lowered his head, rested his muzzle, and closed his eyes. Ignaçio kneeled beside Santos, lifted the dog in his arms, and held the serene animal against his chest. The dog's heartbeats soothed him.

Charo injected the morphine into Santos's hip. The dog sighed in relief and descended into sleep. Ignaçio lowered his face, held back his tear, and spoke into Santos's ear. The dog didn't fear death. The next shot slowed Santos's lungs and then stopped his heart.

The dog's limbs stirred. His skin twitched, his muzzle quivered. His eyes reopened. Life returned to them and then faded away. Their beams remained. Ignaçio closed the dog's eyelids and grabbed the departing animal tighter against his chest. He couldn't keep the dog. Old Santos crossed Life's divide and left him in this new house to continue its promise.

Victor roared outside. The horse neighed, the heron squawked. The cows bellowed, the calves bleated. Ignaçio ignored his streaming tears, brought Santos outdoors, and carried him toward the pond. The animals stopped in their tracks and watched their friend leaving.

The wind moaned, the ocean groaned. Trees swayed, leaves rattled. Flowers turned and sprayed their scents. A nightingale hid in the weeping willow and opened the funeral hymn. The orchestra grew. Bees hummed, birds chirped. Crickets creaked, cicadas rasped. Frogs croaked, hawks squealed. Beams pierced spring's foliage and honored the dog's coat.

Ignaçio reached the grave, kneeled at its edge, and lowered Santos into the pit.

Sobs rose. Petals burst, rained in, and covered the valiant dog. Rafaela sniffled; Carlos stood stunned. Paula uttered a prayer. Jorge wiped his eyes and picked up the shovel. Ignaçio covered his face, turned away from the trench, and ran into Victor's muzzle.

The bull was crying.

Ignaçio took out his handkerchief and reached for Victor's eyes. The bull raised his head and roared away from the grave. Carlos ran after Victor. The bull ignored the boy and went on roaring. Lorenza and Zeus followed Victor. They couldn't stop the mourning bull.

Victor kept running and crying. He circled the farm and lamented his loss.

Rafaela left her son with Nuria, separated from the group, and marched toward Victor.

Until now, she had never talked to this bull, touched his coat, or looked at him. Victor turned toward her, lowered his head, and pointed his horns. Ignaçio ran after her. She turned, raised her hands, and pushed him back. Nuria restrained him by the arm and placed her other hand on Carlos's head. Ignaçio watched the boy. Carlos didn't worry about his mother.

Rafaela proceeded toward Victor. He flapped his dewlap, tossed his head, and fidgeted on the spot. She maintained her gait. The bull watched her steps, took his stance, and stood tall. She reached him and stood in front of him. He became still. She raised her chin and spoke to him. He lifted his muzzle, sniffed the air, and turned toward Lorenza and Zeus.

Both animals called out and reassured Victor. They told the lost bull what to do.

Victor listened to them. He lowered his head and held out his muzzle.

Rafaela reached up and wiped his tears.

The new convention center opened in spring. International animal-rights groups awarded the former taurine city their autumn summit. Summer brought new clients to the hotel, shops, and restaurants on the remodeled arena's three floors. The city's businesses rushed and hired more working hands.

In fall, The San Taurino Summit saw one hundred and seventy-six nations meet and sign *The Universal Declaration of Animal Rights*. To mark this historic convention's conclusion, the restructured arena rewarded the consortium members by hosting a *farruca* performance.

The redesigned bullring had preserved its wooden barrier. A raised platform replaced the golden sand. Ignaçio climbed onto the new podium, walked along its old fence, and listened to the new galleries' hum. His solos from the old arena returned and compressed his chest.

The hall's breath quieted for the farruca show. Ignaçio leaned on the barrier's rails and saw the spectators watching him. Their tense gaze and pose didn't ease his breathing.

His son's laughter broke the silence.

The boy sat up on Nuria's lap and flashed a toothless grin. The toddler's warmth melted his father's inertia. Paloma, Juan, and Rafaela applauded. Life thrives in flux. The search for the fixed is pointless. Ignaçio returned to the ring's center and took his stance.

Paloma started a *soleá* in *canto profundo*.

The revamped acoustics deepened her voice, prolonged her words, and rolled her notes through the floors. Ignaçio drew his feet, raised his arms, and opened up with *braceos* and *floreos*. His handwork moved the southern farmers. They clapped, snapped, and tapped. Juan beat the *cajon*. The wooden box's strokes shook the

520

podium and revived the hall's air.

Paloma rose to *cante intermedio*.

Ignaçio switched to footwork. The spectators rose and shouted. Ignaçio arched his back and stretched his moves. Paloma rose to *buleriá*. More hands clapped, more fingers snapped, more feet tapped. Juan left the *cajon* and strung the guitar. Ignaçio shortened his passes and quickened his turns. He waved his shoulders and played his face. Paloma rose to *alegría*. Ignaçio leaped, vaulted, and flipped head-over-heels.

The hall boomed.

Paloma called for *salida*. Ignaçio performed a *desplante*, bowed to her, and returned to the podium's center.

Paloma stopped. The hall continued her *palo*.

Ignaçio lifted one leg, folded it, and pressed its foot against the other knee. The hall silenced. He spread his arms and started his spin. Applause swept the galleries. The claps and snaps returned. The acoustics fused the beats and fanned his spin. The barriers vanished. The figures merged into a mass and left the hall. Their claps and snaps stayed. Ignaçio folded his arms, flung his hands to the chest, and sped up his spin. Cheers swelled and fueled his turns.

The arena expanded.

The galleries exploded. The walls crashed. The arches fell.

The hall disappeared. The azure sky roared into the arena, filled its expanse, and removed its rubbles.

The horizon rolled out.

A vertiginous space opened up and stretched before him.

San Taurino is fictional; its resonance, real.

Printed in Great Britain
by Amazon